the
twins

SASKIA SARGINSON

piatkus

PIATKUS

First published in Great Britain as a paperback original in 2013 by Piatkus

Copyright © 2013 by Saskia Sarginson

The moral right of the author has been asserted.

A CIP catalogue record for this book
is available from the British Library.

ISBN 978-0-7499-5869-5

Typeset in Goudy by M Rules
Printed and bound in Great Britain by
Clays Ltd, St Ives plc

Papers used by Piatkus are from well-managed forests
and other responsible sources.

MIX
Paper from
responsible sources
FSC
www.fsc.org   FSC® C104740

Piatkus
An imprint of
Little, Brown Book Group
100 Victoria Embankment
London EC4Y 0DY

An Hachette UK Company
www.hachette.co.uk

www.piatkus.co.uk

In memory of my mother
Jill Sarginson

1

We weren't always twins. We used to be just one person.

The story of our conception was the ordinary kind they tell you about in biology lessons. You know how it goes: an athletic sperm hits the egg target and new life forms.

So there we were, a single ho-hum baby in the making. Then comes the extraordinary part, because that one egg split, tearing in half, and we became *two* babies. Two halves of a whole. That's why it's weird but true – we were one person first, even if only for a millisecond.

Mummy always said that having twins was the last thing she'd expected, except she knew there had to be a good reason why she couldn't fit through doors at four months, let alone do her jeans up. Mummy was beautiful. Everyone said so. She looked like an ice queen from the pages of a fairy tale. A queen who wore flip-flops and Indian skirts with tassels dangling down, and whose fingers were stained nicotine yellow. She wouldn't tell us who our father was. Not that it really mattered. We just pretended it did, because it felt exciting to try and guess who he might be, as if we could invent the story of our own birth.

There's a Greek myth that says if a woman sleeps with a god and a mortal on the same day she'll have two babies: one child from each father. Even our mother wouldn't do anything as slutty as that. But when we climbed the branches of the lilac tree to sit on the roof of the shed, sharing an apple and discussing possible paternal options, the idea of being fathered by a god was satisfying.

The obvious choice was a rock god. Our mother played The Doors obsessively. She looked at Jim Morrison's picture on the album cover and sighed. The only thing we knew about our father was that our mother met him at a festival in California. Bingo. It had to be Morrison. We didn't want our dad to be one of the creeps and weirdos we lived with at the commune in Wales. Lanky Luke or smelly Eric. Mummy didn't love any of them. We wrote Mr Morrison a letter once, secretly, signing it from Viola and Isolte Love. We never got a reply.

On 3 July 1971 Jim Morrison was found dead in his bath in Paris. Cause of death: heart failure brought on by heavy drinking. He'd planned to stop being a rock god and become a poet. He'd been waiting for his contract to run out. The day the news broke we came home from school to find our mother playing 'Hello, I Love You' over and over and weeping into her glass of red wine. We cried too, up in our bedroom, howling into our pillows. At first it was a kind of show; but then fake turned to real. You know how sometimes when you laugh really hard you can trip some emotional switch and start crying instead? This was a bit like that. Except pretend crying tripped the real thing, and suddenly we were drowning in tears, taking shuddering gasps, snot smearing our cheeks. We had no idea what we were crying about. Later, when Mummy was sober and we were all hiccuping

2

and squinting through swollen eyes, she told us that Jim Morrison definitely wasn't our dad. 'You nitwits,' she said wistfully, 'where on earth did you get that idea?'

We tried a few more times to discover who our father was. But Mummy got irritated. Shrugging and rolling a cigarette slowly, she'd blow smoke spirals and look disappointed by our dull questions. 'I've started a new dynasty,' she explained. 'I want you to build your own future. You don't need a past.' We knew that she thought our desire for a father was petty and bourgeois. All the worst things in the world were petty and bourgeois.

It was the spring of 1972, and Mummy said that, what with the miners' strike and the three-day weeks, the country was going to hell. Ted Heath was a Tory fool. We had to be prepared for the worst. We needed to be self-sufficient. She dug up the weedy flowers and planted vegetables and bought two nanny goats: Tess and Bathsheba. One brown and the other black; they both had switchy tails and cloven feet like the devil. We wanted to love them, but they just chewed all day, grinding their long teeth. Even when we squatted to scratch their ears, they kept on chewing, marble eyes looking through us. The goats broke free of their tethers and trampled the vegetable patch, pulling up plants by the roots. Every morning, Mummy spent grim hours trying to replant limp broccoli and carrots before she sat with her head in a goat's flank, fingers working, swearing at their fidgeting, to emerge with thin milk as rancid as old cheese or stewed socks.

She had a book showing which wild foods were safe to eat and when and how to pick and cook them. That book was consulted constantly, pondered over, worn and stained from being taken along on walks and splattered from being propped next to the

3

stove. Foraging became a new religion. Plucking berries and mushrooms and apples from the hedgerows – now, Mummy said, that was free-spirited *and* free. Two things she approved of.

We got scratched from pushing through brambles to get at the crab apples, our mother barefoot beside us. 'Higher, Viola. That's it.' Tossing her hair impatiently. 'Get the ones on the next branch up, Issy.' She made jelly and wine from those: tangy-tasting and pink as a tongue. Once we got terrible stomach cramps from some speckled mushrooms she'd put in a stew. But we got to like brain fungus fried in butter with salt and pepper and a little curry powder; a crinkly, rubbery, pale fungus that grew at the foot of pine trees – we tore up handfuls whenever we found it. And puffballs, picked when they were fat and white, rolling in the dewy grass on autumn mornings like misplaced snowballs. We had them sliced in batter for breakfast with crispy bacon.

*

Have you ever felt real hunger pangs? Not just a growl, the casual complaining of your stomach missing a meal, the inconvenient rumble and gurgle when lunch is late. I mean the deep birthing pain of true emptiness. The hollow ache of nothing. Fat is a human fault because it's only humans who are stupid with greed. Birds are light as a handful of leaves. I want the lightness of wings to enter me. I've learned to eat like a bird, not a human. In this place they try and trick me into eating, they play mind games, stick tubes down my throat.

Of course, it hurts to starve. But you can use those pangs like a knife to slice out the bad things inside you. Eventually you'll come to crave that feeling. Because hunger is a friend. With it you can get down to your bones quicker than you'd think. I feel them under my fingers, nudging up close below my skin, closer every day: smooth and flawless and hard. That's what everyone says about bones, don't they? That they're pure. Clean. I trace the lines of mine and they make a shape: the scaffold of myself.

It's all we are in the end anyway. Sometimes not even that. Sometimes there aren't even bones to show for a life – just molecules shifting in the air – and a few memories locked up in your head, yellowed as old photographs.

I'm tired now. I'd like to go back to sleep. I'm rambling. I know I am. Issy wouldn't like it. She told me to shut up when we had to sit in that little room with a man and a woman asking us the same questions over and over.

What did we do? What did we see? What time and when and where?

They thought we were wicked, you see. They thought we'd done something unforgivable. I cried and shifted on the hard chair, feeling a shameful warmth seep through my knickers. Wet dripped over plastic until there was a puddle on the floor, and a policeman came with a bucket and cloth. I closed my eyes, trying not to inhale the sharp stink of urine. My bare legs stung.

Those days were filled with listless waiting, people whispering about us behind their hands. We were trapped in that bleak room, while they stared at us and tapped their pencils and made notes. I noticed them looking at the scar on my face and I pulled my hair across, trying to hide it, scared that they would recognise the mark of Satan.

But I wasn't alone – my sister was next to me, like she always was, stronger, bolder. Her eyes were dry and there was no wet patch under her chair.

'Don't say anything, Viola,' Issy said. 'You don't have to say anything. They can't make you.'

And she holds my hand tight, her curled fingers squeezing hard, steely as a trap.

2

1987. Bill Withers is playing loud on the stereo, and rolling sound fills the depths of the photographic studio with an atmosphere, creates a mood to work to. Except work has stopped for a moment because Ben is fussing with the lights, directing his assistant to rearrange the roll of paper that's serving as a backdrop. Away from the bright glare of the lights and the pale sweep of paper, the echoing room, once a warehouse, is a hollow cavern.

Through a side door there is a narrow space that passes as a hair and make-up room; there's hardly room for three people to move about, and the air is thick with stale cigarette smoke. The table below the mirror is covered with a mess of eye shadow palettes, crumpled tissues, empty takeaway cartons, overflowing ashtrays, coffee cups, lip brushes and eyelash curlers.

Isolte stands watching Julio, the make-up artist, as he bends over the model. Isolte frowns into the mirror, watching the reflection of the model's face. The three of them, crammed together, are framed by a square of naked bulbs. Julio finishes drawing a gold line with a flourish and looks up at Isolte enquiringly, one eyebrow arched.

7

'Well?' he says. 'Do you want more of a theatrical effect, Isolte, darling? Or is this enough?'

Isolte squints at the girl's face, considering. The model, impassive, blinks heavy orange lashes. She's got a towel wrapped around her to protect the sheath of silk underneath. Standing above her, Isolte notices a fine down, like baby hair, growing all over her back: a pale fur glistening along the ridge of her spine. Wasn't it Marilyn Monroe who was supposed to have been covered in hair? It accounted for her luminous appearance in photographs. But this girl has the extra hair of the malnourished. Isolte knows it well.

She shrugs. 'It looks great. But let's get a Polaroid done. Then we can see.' On set, the model positions herself in front of the lights, legs apart, hips thrust forward. She glares into the camera, a questioning sneer on her lips. Ben's assistant has switched on the wind machine and fine strands of coloured silk blow up around her like torn butterfly wings.

Ben is already bending over the tripod, one hand poised on the camera. He is absorbed, all his energy channelled into this moment. His jeans are creased around his hips, his dark hair flopping forward. It's the last shot of the day. Everyone is tired.

'That's beautiful.' He clicks, and clicks again. 'Lick your lips. Look at me, sweetheart. Right. Gorgeous.'

Ben is a chameleon. His working talk is fluid, changes from girl to girl, shoot to shoot. Isolte has seen him play the roguish male, but he'll camp it up or turn gentle and sweet to get the best out of a model.

'How do you make a duck into a soul singer?' he's asking and the model shrugs.

'Put it in the oven until it's Bill Withers.'

The girl throws back her head and laughs. Ben snaps. Isolte has heard the joke before. She stands with arms folded, imagining the picture on the page, the caption already running through her head. It's a good shot. The model is almost transparent; the angles of her face work the shadows, pull the light on to the right planes so that she looks like an exquisite alien. Maybe it will make the cover.

It is spring outside. A rainy London day. But here she is in a windowless room creating pictures to be looked at in July. Isolte likes the way that working three months ahead pulls her through the year as if clock time has shifted into sixth gear. 'I think we've got it.' Ben straightens up, claps the room briefly, holding his hands high. 'Well done, people. It's a wrap.' It is a corny thing to do. He gets away with it because, from his scruffy dark hair to his Converse All Stars in faded red, he inhabits the kind of shrugged-on style that marks him out as cool; the sort of person who slips across invisible social barriers, who knows how to be in the world. It helps that he has a sensuous face with sculptured bones; swooping eyebrows that give him, depending on his mood, the look of Groucho Marx or Byron; lips that take the natural line of a pout. Isolte notices that Ruby, the hair stylist, blushes as she turns away to collect her sprays and brushes.

The wind machine and the burning lights have been turned off. The model, rubbing her eyes, reaches for the towel. The studio is nearly empty, dim and forlorn without music. Julio has gone already, lugging his make-up box, and Ruby is packing up in the back room. The model shrugs bony shoulders into an old tweed overcoat and lights a cigarette; she's checking her Filofax as she waves goodbye. Ben shouts over at his assistant: 'Take the cameras down to my car, will you? And stand guard till I get there.'

9

'Fancy a drink?' He turns to Isolte, smiling. 'Orange juice, of course.'

She scrunches up her face at him. 'Can't.'

'Shame.' He's suddenly close, and she feels his hand on her thigh, fingers rubbing across her tights. His mouth is next to her ear, hot breath and muffled words. Deep inside she feels the flip of desire, her breath coming faster. She swallows, leans into him for a moment and then, 'No chance, pervert,' she whispers, slipping from his grasp.

'You can't blame me for trying.' He grins at her. 'I've been dying to get my hands on you all day.'

'I'd never have guessed it ... Anyway, I've got to go.' Isolte shoves him away, smiling despite herself. 'I told you already. I'm seeing Viola.'

Changing her mind, she steps closer and kisses him. She's wanted to do that all day too – although she doesn't want him to know, she's always found it safer to be the one who holds back in a relationship, the one who doesn't love as much. His lips are soft, slightly dry; there is the clash of teeth against teeth. She inhales deeply, breathing in the day's sweat, the hint of steel and plastic on his fingers. Moving across the room, she straightens her clothes, glancing in the mirror as if to check for evidence of the kiss.

'Women.' Ben shakes his head, licking his lips thoughtfully. 'Are you all this mad?' He shrugs on his leather jacket.

'Well, you're the expert,' Isolte says. 'You tell me.'

He grabs her by the waist, pulls her close. 'You think the worst of me, don't you, my doubting Doris?'

She struggles, breaking away with a breathless laugh. 'Don't call me that.'

'What?' He raises his eyebrows. 'Doubting?'

'No. Doris, you idiot.' She shakes her head. 'Now let me get on.' She throws her bag over her shoulder. 'I've got places to go. People to see.'

Her minicab is waiting downstairs.

'Does that mean you're coming over tonight?' he calls after her.

Isolte softens. 'Yes. I'll see you later.' She ignores the lift, takes the stairs, her feet clattering on the concrete.

'Give my love to Viola.' His voice reaches her as a wavering echo inside the hollow acoustics of the stairwell.

Taxis are Isolte's indulgence. Usually she can write them off for work. But if she must, she'll pay black cab rip-off fares to avoid the squalor of the tube, or the pushing and shoving to get on a bus at rush hour.

Isolte leans back, watching the darkening streets. The traffic is at an impatient crawl. London is thick with people on their way back from work or out for the evening. Speeding commuters spill into the road as they push past tourists gathering on corners with upturned faces and cameras. It's stopped raining but viscous puddles are slick with oil, all the pavements alight with wet reflections.

Her driver crouches over the wheel. Ornaments swing from the rearview mirror: a plain cross, a photo of a dark-eyed child, a plastic Mickey Mouse. Sometimes his eyes slide across the mirror, watching her. She wraps her coat tighter, gazing out of the window. The radio splutters and crackles.

Horns blare and someone shouts angrily. There is a drunk pitching and weaving among the cars, his hands out as if he is blind. A cyclist has to swerve to miss him; and the man on the bike turns, his mouth a circle of outrage. Isolte shrinks into her seat as the drunk staggers past the cab. But she can't help glancing into his face, seeing his blank gaze swim towards her and away. He has the blunted features of the homeless. Out of the corner of her eye, she catches a sudden swing of movement, hears the thump of bony fingers against glass. His fist hitting her window. Isolte jumps, biting the inside of her lip. The driver turns and swears, changing gear, moving away.

Isolte puts up a finger cautiously; she can taste blood. The drunk's lost expression has got stuck inside her head, the staring face a blurred caricature of itself. She doesn't drink. She's never had the desire to drown herself in that kind of oblivion. There are no gaps in her memory. She likes the feeling of control she has when other people are loosening up, their words running too freely. She's been at parties where people she hardly knows have confided secrets, whispered their sexual preferences, confessed to infidelities. That kind of vulnerability scares her. Why would anyone do it to themselves?

'She's been sleeping a lot today,' the nurse warns Isolte. She shakes her head, gesturing towards the corner bed where there is a small mound. A sleeping form. The shape so narrow it's more like a ridge thrown up by a plough.

When Viola was first admitted to hospital, Isolte thought she would be cured. Nine years on, Viola has seen several therapists, and spent a month in a psychiatric ward; she has got a little better and then worse again. This is the third time she's been hospitalised. Viola's disappearing act has been going on for a long time.

Isolte moves forward cautiously. The elderly patient in the bed opposite Viola is lying on top of her covers, propped up against pillows and knitting laboriously, loops of purple wool trailing from the bed. She glances up at Isolte and smiles. Isolte smiles back, noticing with a small shock of embarrassment that the woman, who's sitting with bent legs, has no underwear on. Why hasn't one of the nurses told her? Why haven't they simply tucked the covers around her? Isolte turns away quickly and pulls up a chair at her sister's bedside.

Viola is on her back, neat and straight, her eyes closed, the sheet folded across her chest. She makes no sign that she's aware of Isolte's presence.

'Viola, it's me. I said I'd come after work. Remember?' There is no reaction. Isolte sits forward and watches her sister's face. Viola has a thin yellow tube threading from her right nostril across her cheek and behind her ear. The tube is stuck down with several tabs of clear tape that pucker the skin beneath. Liquid calories are sent creeping through the tube straight into Viola's stomach.

Viola stirs abruptly, moving her head to the side with a ducking motion as if she can feel something brushing across her face, the slap of a branch perhaps, or an insect bumping against her. Isolte bends closer, whispering, 'Viola, can you hear me?' But Viola remains locked in her dreams. Her hands lie on the sheet, curled into fists. Her wrists, sticking out of her blue pyjama cuffs, are painful nubs of bone. Isolte reaches out as if to touch them, fingers hovering. Instead, she folds her hands in her lap.

It's another world in the hospital. A different kind of time exists here, slow hours drag inside a weatherless zone. Viola's ward is on the fourth floor in the old Victorian section. It has high ceilings and windows placed at a level that makes it impossible to see out without standing on a chair. The walls are a sickly institutional green; the colour reminds Isolte of her primary school. She can't think of anything worse than being stuck here for weeks. No wonder Viola sleeps all the time.

There is a restless shifting from the beds: coughing and throat clearing and twisting of covers. A cleaner is mopping the floor half-heartedly, pushing the mop in slow semi-circles in front of him. Isolte can see scummy water collecting inside spidery fronds of cloth. She resigns herself to doing nothing. Instead she sits back in the chair and studies her sister's face. She feels strangely furtive. Looking at Viola used to be like looking in a mirror that offered all angles. Observing her didn't count as spying, because it was only as if she was criticising or admiring her own features. (Aha, she would think, so *that's* what my nose looks like from the side when I laugh.)

Viola continues to face the ceiling with blind eyes. Her nose and cheekbones protrude in sharp ridges, shadows darkening the hollows. Under her slack lips the outline of her teeth is visible. Isolte can see a skull through her sister's face; the planes and curves, the gaping eye sockets; the shape swimming into focus like a developing photograph. Isolte blinks and looks away. She can't get used to seeing her sister like this. It's becoming a struggle to remember Viola with her childish, rounded cheeks and broad smile, but Isolte knows exactly when the change began: it started when they lived with Aunt Hettie in London, after their life in the forest had ended.

*

The front door opens, letting in the sudden roar of traffic on the Fulham Road. It slams closed. The noises of the street are muffled. One of the dogs gives a welcoming bark; Hettie glances at her watch, frowning. 'Where on earth has she been?'

Hettie and Isolte look up from their supper as Viola sidles into the kitchen, hands in pockets, a tatty bag trailing from her shoulder; the spaniels already sniffing blindly at her feet, panting with pleasure, tails wagging, and her reaching to touch their silky ears.

Isolte remembers the smell of burnt lamb fat, the kitchen cosy and warm, curtains drawn against an autumn evening. And Viola: gaunt and defensive, waiting silently in the doorway, as if she couldn't bring herself to enter the room. The alarm bells should have been ringing. Isolte should have known then that she must do something to help her sister.

Viola stands before her aunt and sister with her long hair shaved close as a convict's, a crop of dark bristles revealing the pallor of her scalp. She runs a hand over her head warily, as if surprised to find the grate of stubble under her fingertips.

Hettie makes an odd sound in her throat, coughing quickly to stifle a gasp.

Viola gives them a defiant glare and shrugs. 'It's my hair.' Her nose ring glints. It's a recent addition and the skin around the silver flames red and sore.

'Not now it isn't,' Isolte can't resist pointing out.

And under her show of humour, Isolte felt a prickle of anxiety. She saw how her sister's collarbone stood out like a yoke; the hands poking out of her drooping cuffs, thin as birds' claws; nails chewed to the quick. It was four years since they'd left Suffolk, and it was obvious that Viola hadn't adjusted to living in the city, hadn't even made friends at their new school.

But mixed in with the anxiety was irritation. Isolte couldn't help it; sometimes she thought Viola was being deliberately difficult. She drifted about the house like a ghost, uncommunicative and distant. She left her curtains closed all day and her bed went unmade despite Hettie's complaints, joss sticks filling her darkened room with a sickly smell. She locked her door, staying there for hours. And she almost never sat down to eat with her aunt and sister any more, finding endless excuses to avoid it.

'Like some supper, then?' Isolte rises purposefully to go to the oven, as if the energy in her movement could force Viola to accept.

'We've saved you mashed potato and a chop, dear,' Hettie adds. 'Kept it from the jaws of the hounds.'

The spaniels shift hopefully in their beds by the radiator, looking at Hettie with their tongues hanging out.

Viola shakes her head. 'I've eaten.'

'There's ice-cream ...' Isolte tries to keep her voice bright and enticing, tries to mask the distaste she feels at the sight of her sister's shaven scalp.

But Viola is already halfway out of the door.

Isolte recalls looking at Hettie as they listened to Viola's footsteps on the stairs. They were united in their frustration. But not really understanding the extent of the problem – not yet. Viola was concealing the extremity of her weight loss from them under baggy clothes. Isolte never saw her sister naked.

There is the click of the bedroom door closing; Hettie wincing. 'Here it comes ...'

A few minutes later, music hammered through the ceiling.

Viola was up there alone, her thin fingers pulling singles out of covers: the Sex Pistols, The Clash, the Ramones.

Isolte couldn't work out why her sister liked that noise.

'I don't think she does, really,' Hettie said. 'I think she's just making a point. Isn't that what young people like to do nowadays?'

But Isolte no longer understood what Viola was trying to say.

*

In her hospital bed, Viola hasn't stirred again and there is no sign that she will. Isolte stands up, slipping her coat on. The woman opposite is alert to Isolte's departure; she stops knitting, beckoning urgently. Isolte walks over with a polite smile.

The woman's face contorts and twitches in excitement or pain. She pushes away a tangle of purple and clutches at Isolte's sleeve with her gnarled fingers. 'Would you be so kind,' she gasps, as Isolte bends to her level, 'only I'm expecting my son, you see, and his children. If you see them, could you be sure to tell them where I am?'

The woman's voice is surprising; her accent makes Isolte think of shooting parties and the tearoom at Fortnum & Mason. Isolte hears breath rattling inside a chest.

Isolte nods, swallowing. She pulls her sleeve from the woman's grip. 'Yes. Of course I will.'

She walks quickly between the beds, head down, shoving her hands into her pockets, guilty and glad for her freedom.

She is overcome by a need for Ben, for the healthy bounce of his step and his male nonchalance. Ben fills a room with his needs and his opinions and his jokes. Sometimes that irritates her, but at other times it is the most comforting thing she can think of. They've been together for over a year now, and she keeps spare

17

underwear, make-up and a wash bag at his flat. There's no need to go home, she'll go straight to his place. She presses the button next to the lift eagerly. She feels as though she's running away.

Isolte plans to distract Ben from his phone and the TV, dissuade him from dragging her out to bars to meet friends keen to down vodka martinis in his company. They can stay in, just the two of them, shut out the rest of the world, phone for a takeaway from the local Indian. That's another reassuring trait of Ben's – his thoughtless, uncomplicated relationship with food. Later, in his king-size bed, she'll feel safe inside his embrace. She loves it when Ben hugs her so tightly her breath is squeezed out of her lungs. She can already taste the chilli flaming between their lips.

3

Mummy was sleeping on her side with one long foot dangling out of the covers. Her hair stuck out of the gap between sheet and pillow like a nest of spiders. We left her drooling. The morning was waiting for us, full of wood pigeons calling. We didn't bother with breakfast, cramming biscuits in our pockets for later, shutting the kitchen door quietly.

The pine trees went on for miles, dissected by sandy tracks. There was nobody to see us on our bikes. The men from the Forestry Commission moved around in vans. We heard them coming long before they saw us. And it was too early in the season for the caravan site to fill up. At the first warning of other people we threw our bikes under bushes and dived into the undergrowth. Inside the forest, we became pliable as sapling branches, melting into shadows like Red Indians, stepping without sound. We rubbed crumbling earth on our cheeks and separated husks of pine cones, spreading the sharp green smell over our fingertips.

They thought we were strange, other people. They stared. They asked stupid questions like, 'Who's the clever one?' or

'Which is the quiet one?' When I was alone, classmates whispered behind their hands, 'Which one is it?' But what can you expect from creatures who are only half of themselves? Issy said they were jealous and I knew she was right. They must have felt the lack, the loss of the one who wasn't there.

It didn't matter what we put on; nobody could tell us apart – even though I'd always been the bigger baby, and then the plumper child. 'Cuddly,' Mummy called me. Sometimes, if Isolte and I stood together, someone would point at me as if discovering something extraordinary, exclaiming, 'Aha! You're the bigger twin!'

Bigger. I hated the word.

'Clever, aren't they?' Issy whispered loudly. Saddos, she called them. Halflings.

That day we were both in jeans, and under my anorak I wore my yellow T-shirt with a picture of a jar full of cars on the front. The brightly coloured cars were lined up neatly, bumper to bumper, in horizontal lines behind the glass. Underneath, it said *Traffic Jam.* I loved that top. Mummy bought it for me when she went to Pilton festival. She'd got a blue one for Issy with a thick rainbow arched across it. Mummy never made us wear the same things; we swapped some stuff and kept favourite clothes separate. Issy eyed my T-shirt, chewing the corner of her lip. She knew I wouldn't share it.

We were going up the track towards the lake. On either side of us the flanks of trees rose tall and straight, brambles tangled at their roots and bracken sprouted like glossy umbrellas. Deeper in, the shadows thickened. Nothing grew in the darkness. Dead branches rotted over a layer of fallen needles, and slippery fungus, pale as parchment, clung to the carcasses of trees.

As the track turned uphill, it got harder to ride, not because of the slope but because the sand got deeper, soft like sugar. My legs were tired. I stood up on the pedals, making an extra effort. But as I strained, the wheels turned awkwardly and stuck fast in a ridge of sand.

Issy had already abandoned her bike, leaving it in the middle of the path with the wheels spinning. She was crouched by the verge, poking at something she'd seen in the long grass. 'Look,' she pulled the green to one side, 'look, Viola, a rabbit. It's sick.'

The rabbit trembled under our gaze, ears flattened across its thin spine. The fur was dull and dry. Its nose twitched, scenting past the mask of resin on our fingertips; smelling the danger of our human skin. It couldn't see us. Its face was swollen. Big balls of pus were seeping and bubbling where the eyes should have been. Fat flies clustered on the sticky fur.

I put out my hand and touched the rabbit's back. It was sharp, like touching a blade. The creature flinched and huddled into the grass. 'What shall we do?' My voice wavered. Lapped up against the knowledge that she would know. She always knew.

'We'll have to take it to the vet's.' She was pale under her tan, her lips thin with determination.

We pulled up handfuls of cow parsley and twisted shoots of bracken, splintering and tearing away the fat stems, laying them like palm fronds in the bottom of my bicycle basket. The rabbit stiffened as I picked it up. I felt the pulse of its heart quicken, and a whisper skipped lightly across my hand. I frowned at the plague of black dots that had appeared on my skin, puzzled for a moment, and then, 'Fleas!' I yelped, smacking the backs of my hands on my jeans.

In the basket, the rabbit made no difference to the pull on the handlebars as I pushed my bike through deep sand. Flies followed in a lazy, persistent cloud. My lips were dry. I brushed a fly away from them. It would be a long ride into town. And we'd have to go on the main road past the base, through the village. It was a school day. We'd be seen.

*

I can hear other sounds, above the green wind and the swish of our bike wheels: voices intruding from another world, brisk feet walking on a shining floor and the gasp and pump of an oxygen machine.

I won't go back. I refuse to leave this moment. If I don't open my eyes I'll be safe.

'Viola?'

Someone is calling my name.

'Can you hear me?'

There's an irritated intake of breath. A shadow moving away.

My hands close into fists, as if I'm gripping handlebars tight. I want to be there again between the trees, with the morning sun warm on my back. I don't want to surface inside my other body, inside the hard edges and sucked-out cavities of myself. In the forest it is 1972 and we're twelve years old. I frown and lick salt off my lips. My forehead is damp with sweat. I'm going back to my lost sister, back to a day when I had a dying rabbit in my bicycle basket and believed I could make it live.

*

We cycled on through the trees, our wheels moving more easily as we turned on to the stony track that led out of the forest. I sang to the rabbit, leaning over my handlebars, a low crooning tune. Issy took the lead, blonde hair whipping behind her. The set of her shoulders was determined. I knew exactly how her face would look, the slight downturn of her mouth, eyes squinting into the sun, the splatter of freckles bleached by the light. Those markings painted our skin like a camouflage. In shadowed places you couldn't begin to count them. We each had a unique freckling. It was funny, but nobody used that difference to tell us apart. 'Freckles are freckles to them,' Issy said.

It was just before we got to the edge of the forest that the stone ricocheted off Issy's front wheel. A sharp ping, like a gunshot. It had come from the bushes to our left, a mean-spirited missile flying straight. She grabbed the brakes, coming to a sudden halt. I swerved round her, flailing to keep upright. The basket tipped, and I watched the slow slide of the rabbit falling sideways: the crumple of fur and skin. It stayed, head flattened against the wicker side.

There was laughter from behind a tree. The undergrowth rustled. Issy was there in a moment, pulling the branches to one side.

'Idiot!' Her fists curled tight. A boy stepped out from behind a tree, taller than us, about the same age I guessed, maybe a little older. He had red hair. Deep red, like rust on old metal or a horse chestnut leaf in autumn. He held his slingshot above Issy's head. 'What you gonna do about it?' His triumphant smile showed a chipped front tooth.

She jumped up, snatching at the sling, thin arms waving wildly. She'll go for his eyes in a minute, I thought. He tossed the weapon behind him with a flick of his wrist. There was another boy. Another laugh. The other boy stepped into the light, the slingshot dangling from his fingers.

Issy went strangely silent, walking backwards, moving into the road to stand with me. We stared at the boys. There was respect in our looking. We'd never come face to face with other identical twins before. These two were as alike as we were – exactly the same as each other, except for the chipped tooth. And the second boy had a black eye. It was a real shiner, just turning from inky blue to a dirty green.

Issy recovered first. 'We've got a sick rabbit,' she said, gesturing at the basket.

'Show us then.' The first boy sauntered over.

I put my hand out protectively. But he was quiet and gentle as he bent over the rabbit, wrinkling his forehead, hands deep in his pockets.

'It's got myxy.' He frowned, shuffling his feet, shaking his head, indicating that his brother join him. 'See.' He nodded at the basket.

The other one rubbed the back of his neck and grunted. I caught the smell of him, raw and earthy. His shirt was ripped and there was a long, peeling scab running up his arm.

Issy and I looked at each other. I could see that she wanted to ask them what they meant. Her pride prevented her. She frowned at me. I frowned back. I didn't want to do the talking. That was her job. She gave her head a small shake.

My heart was pattering in my chest as if I was about to run a race. I swallowed. 'What is it?' I asked quickly. 'What's myxy?'

'Rabbit disease. They're pests, see. Farmers hate 'em. So they give it to 'em.' The first boy spoke. 'It's a bleedin' bad way to go.'

'No cure then?' Issy put her chin up.

The boy shook his head.

'What's your name?' Issy swallowed. She was trying to take it in. Trying to work out what to do.

'Michael,' he said.

'John,' the other one said. The one with the eye.

'I'm Viola,' I offered, feeling brave, 'and that's Isolte.'

'Funny names,' Michael shrugged.

We didn't think they were funny. They were just our names. Mummy said that Viola and Isolte were names of characters in plays. She chose them for us because they were beautiful and belonged to strong women who'd both known true love. I opened my mouth and closed it again. I was doubtful that these boys would be interested in this information. They might even laugh.

Issy was already explaining that, actually, people usually called her Issy, but Michael wasn't listening. He was frowning as if in concentration. He gestured to the slingshot in his brother's fist. 'We could finish it off.'

It took a moment for me to understand that he meant the rabbit. I felt the air leave my body. I slumped forward, my fingers moving towards the basket.

John and Michael looked at each other. 'Fairest thing,' John said.

I touched the rabbit's ears. They were silk, ribbons of silk, specked brown and silver. Then I looked at the tight stretch of the eyelids, stuck down over swollen mounds of pus. I bit my lip, glanced up at Isolte. She nodded.

'Will it be quick?' I asked.

Michael was kicking at the stones on the track, as if he was searching for something. He picked up a flinty rock and weighed it in his cupped palm. 'Best do it by hand,' he said to his brother. He rubbed a grubby finger over the flint, feeling the edges.

We put the rabbit down on the verge gently. Its long

protesting nails, like splayed hooks, dragged trailing bits of grass and bracken from the basket. It stayed where we'd put it, sides pulsing in and out. I let out a sob and clamped my hand over my mouth. Issy kept her gaze fixed on the rabbit, but I shut my eyes as one of the boys, I can't remember which, brought the rock down hard. I felt the movement, the deft speed of it.

There was a soft thump. A muted noise, not the firm thwack of ball against racket, not metallic like a stone against a road. Something smaller and quieter. A caving in of thin bone and flesh. I was afraid that the rabbit would scream. But it made no noise.

'It's done.'

I sniffed and swallowed, scrubbing at my face with the back of my hand, wiping away the wet.

Afterwards Isolte said, 'They're all right, aren't they? Those boys.'

1974

John,

I keep writing these letters and then tearing them up. I'll probably do the same with this one. I'm not even sure what I want to say. Except I miss you. I miss you so much. It's been two years, one month and three days of not seeing you. I don't belong here. Never will. I long for the forest – the smell of pine and mist on the ground – the herds of deer grazing. Do you remember that adder that went across the path under our feet – I don't think I've ever jumped so high! You put your hand on my chest, feeling my heart to tease me. But I think you were scared too. Only you would never admit it, would you? You always thought you had to be brave. I think of you all the time, John; and I go over everything, driving myself mad with the 'what if's'. Can you sense me at your shoulder; feel me missing you, wanting you? I'm sorry for everything, for the way things ended. I wish I could go back in time and make it right. But we all do, don't we?

Viola

4

Ben is on the phone. He makes a pleased-to-see-her face, but doesn't stop talking. Isolte shrugs off her coat and reaches around his waist for a hug, smelling traces of his peppery aftershave and the oil in his jumper. He pulls her to him absently, nodding and saying, 'Sure. Yes, fine. Yeah,' into the receiver. She feels the vibration of his voice through his ribcage. She can't hear who's on the end of the line. She lets go of him and wanders next door.

The television is on in the living room. Sound turned up loud. There is a picture of a ferry on its side, wallowing in grey water. Isolte reads the caption: *Herald of Free Enterprise salvage operation.* The newsreader looks up under a peroxide helmet and tells Isolte that of the 539 on board, 193 people perished in total.

'Shit.' Isolte turns it off.

She's familiar with the North Sea. An expanse of muscular waves thickened with grit. She's swallowed mouthfuls of its brown water, felt its insistent currents tugging at her legs, persuading her away from the beach. It would have been freezing. How long could they have survived in the water – seconds, minutes? Sucked down by the sinking ship. The cold and the currents would have got them. Children too, probably. Babies in their pushchairs. The weight of all that water. They wouldn't have had a chance. She doesn't want to think about it.

She goes over to the record player and starts to flip through Ben's albums. She can hear his voice in the other room: his telephone voice. It's rude not to finish the call and come and say hello to her properly. Indignation makes her throat tight, almost tearful. She feels an airy fizzing in her fingers and toes; little bubbles of frustration snapping in her blood.

She slips Bowie's *Let's Dance* out of its cover and puts it on the turntable. It would serve him right if she went home. And then he's behind her, burying his scratchy chin in her neck, biting at her earlobes.

'Sorry, sweetheart. Business. You know how it is.' He breathes in heavily. 'God, you smell good.'

Sweetheart. His name for everyone. Not just her. He says it with an urban growl, a slight South London twang. Ben went to public school and his parents live in a six-bedroom house in Kent. But you'd never know. He's invented a new persona: a streetwise swagger, battered leather jacket, lazy vowels and the careless way he moves – bouncing on his toes, long loose strides, more of a prowl than a walk. She wonders how long it took him to perfect. She thinks about the little boy in the stripy blazer and the grey shorts. The one she's seen in photographs looking out at the world with a grin; the one who wore a straw boater in the summer and played cricket for his house team. Did he know then that he wanted to shrug off all that privileged history and reinvent himself?

Her back is still pressed into his chest; she resists him, her mouth tight. She can feel the muscles in his arms flexing; his biceps harden and tense. Ben works out every morning. He keeps silver dumb-bells under his bed. Straight after their first night together, he'd flung himself out of bed to perform his fitness routine. Isolte, sprawled naked and lazy in the crumpled sheets, had watched him in amazement. She'd buried her face in the pillow it made her laugh so much – the vanity of it. But now she admires his discipline; she likes the clenched power she feels inside him.

As if he can sense her resistance weakening, he curls tighter, his hands wrapping around her breasts, finding her nipples. Her stomach does a little somersault. She forgives Ben. He can't help himself; he wants to please everyone. It's his failing and his saving. She reaches up and tangles her fingers in the curls at the nape of his neck, searching for his mouth. He slides her closer, obliges her with opened lips and probing tongue. And then the phone rings. She feels him tense, the muscles in his shoulders bunching under her touch. He can never resist. He follows the pull of it.

'Sorry.' He breaks away.

'Ben.' She holds handfuls of his jumper. 'Not now.'

But he's already cradling the mouthpiece and talking quickly, the cable curling in his other hand.

'Sure.' He nods. 'No problem, mate. Be good to see you.'

He gives her his best confused look, rumpling his hair with his long hand, shrugging. 'It's Stevie. He's in the area.' Appealing to reason with raised eyebrows. 'You know I'm getting in with that crowd. *Harpers* is a good gig. He'll only stay for a moment.'

People are always in the area. Bloomsbury is just round the corner from the British Museum, only a short walk from Oxford Street, an easy stroll from all the darkrooms and magazine houses in Soho. There is always someone calling, someone ringing the doorbell. It makes Isolte want to run away. She can't bear the exposure – the feeling of being hunted.

Stevie, art director of *Harpers & Queen*, is sallow and thin with a dominating nose. He reminds Isolte of Venetian princes in Renaissance portraits. He sweeps in, flicking a trailing black shawl over his shoulder, taking his trilby off with a flourish.

'My dears, what a filthy evening.' He unbuttons his coat slowly, revealing a fuchsia shirt. 'Why do we put up with it? Why don't we all just emigrate?'

Stevie has come, not just for a drink, but to take a look at the transparencies from the shoot he and Ben worked on earlier in the week. He reaches for the shiny stack of plastic sheets with eager, manicured hands. Soon both men are bent over the light box in the kitchen, taking it in turns to peer through a magnifying glass.

'This is cover material,' Ben is saying eagerly. 'Take a look. Do you want to chalk it up?'

Isolte leans against the doorframe watching them. She's made herself a sandwich and she eats it standing up, slivers of ham and cheese between her teeth. Her plan for an Indian takeaway is ruined. This evening is not working out as she'd hoped. She feels strangely numb. It's too late to go home. The thought of calling a cab, letting herself into an empty flat, gives her a defeated, hollow feeling. She shivers, pulling her cardigan tighter around her. When will Stevie leave? How many drinks will it take?

'So, Isolte, dear-heart,' Stevie straightens, and looks at her over his shoulder, 'guess who I saw in Groucho's?'

She can't be bothered with this game. She shrugs.

'Your new editor.' He watches her carefully.

'Really?' Isolte keeps her voice level, lets a hint of boredom creep in.

'She's quite a little firecracker, isn't she? Not afraid she's going to shake things up?'

Isolte sighs. 'Really, Stevie, you are such a troublemaker. Why would I worry? She's already said she loves the fashion pages.'

Ben grins at her. 'Isolte will have her eating out of her hand in no time.'

He picks up the bottle of wine from the table, sees that it's empty and gives a start of surprise. 'Another?' He's already reaching into the cupboard to pull out a burgundy.

Isolte looks out of the window; through the glassy reflections of the kitchen she sees the lights of the city blinking. Feels the faint rumble of a tube train passing deep underground. Hears a high-pitched shriek from the street. She can't tell if the shriek is one of pleasure or fear. Stevie is talking about an underwear advert. 'I don't know why they gave the campaign to Josh Anderson. Your book's never looked better.'

Ben leans forward, nodding, his lips wine-stained. 'I'm thinking of changing my agent. Amanda's made too many mistakes. She's lost her hold in New York.'

Isolte's back is aching. She's been standing up all day. She swallows her last mouthful and puts the plate on the granite counter. The men don't notice when she slips away. Locked inside the humming space of Ben's white-tiled bathroom, she takes off her make-up, dragging pads of cotton wool across her skin, smearing away streaks of black and red.

Isolte shivers in Ben's king-size bed. She's put on one of Ben's T-shirts but it hasn't helped. She lies in one place to avoid the icy sheet. She can hear Ben's voice, the tumbling slur of his words and then Stevie's short, hard laugh. She hugs herself, trying to get warm, trying not to be self-pitying. She's past the point of anger.

There is the clink of glass against glass. Ben won't be coming to bed for hours.

She thinks about Viola, lying alone in her hospital bed. What will she hear? Isolte imagines the squeaky footsteps of nurses, the movement of equipment, phlegmy coughing, retching, and whimpering patients. Noises that go on all night. It would drive her mad. But she doesn't know how much Viola takes in. Like a diver, Viola is swimming away from the surface, kicking and paddling into some clouded, dreaming place. Of course, Isolte knows what Viola is doing. She is escaping from their past, hiding from guilt, from the memories.

Viola is fading away, little by little. She will have succeeded when she's disappeared completely. 'Stay with me,' Isolte whispers into the darkness. I can't do this on my own. Viola, don't go. I need you. You know I do. Isolte clenches her fingers into fists, nails digging into her palms. If only it was as simple as holding on physically. If only she could restrain Viola with touch, haul her back into a safe place.

She turns over in bed, pressing her face into the pillow, trying to muffle the sounds from the kitchen: the clinking of glass, indistinct snatches of conversation and irritating bursts of laughter. Without wanting to, she sees her mother's hand curled round a glass of wine: more glasses drunk alone at the kitchen table at night when they were in bed. Dark bottles lined up in the morning, green-lipped and empty. 'Come and give me a hug,' Rose had called, still in bed although it was nearly lunchtime. Her eyes pink-rimmed. Isolte always hung back, letting Viola be the first to clamber into the crumpled sheets and taste their mother's foul breath.

It wasn't always like that. When they'd first moved to the

33

forest, Rose wasn't drinking, and more often than not she got out of bed before them, going downstairs to make porridge. 'This is our fresh start, my angels,' she sang out. 'Isn't it exciting! Just the three of us. No Welsh drizzle and selfish men.' Humming, she'd take the washing out into the garden; her fingers steady as she pegged socks and vests on the line, the flapping washing a tangible promise that everything could be rinsed clean.

One school morning, when the air was dense with gathering energy, Rose stood barefoot, pegging out clothes. A sudden shadow snuffed out the sun, and the sky cracked open with a sound like an axe splitting a tree. The downpour was fierce. Rose dropped the washing, calling them into the rain. 'Look!' She stretched out her arms and tipped her head back. 'Come and feel. It's lovely! Such lovely, wet rain!' They raced each other round the sodden lawn, still in their socks and no shoes. Hair plastered to their skin, water flooding mouths and eyes. Rose grabbed their hands and danced with them, singing and skipping. Their legs were splashed with mud, their hearts a wild thundering. And they laughed; they couldn't stop. It made their faces hurt and their chests ache.

In the kitchen, their mother pulled them to her in a damp huddle, clothes dripping on to the linoleum, and whispered, 'My darling girls. We're going to be all right, aren't we?' Isolte felt the chilled skin of her mother on one side, shoulder blades curved like a flightless bird's, and on the other, Viola, as insubstantial as Isolte's own reflection. In that moment she was afraid that their circle of three was too fragile. The dark mouth of the forest and the wet tongue of the rain would swallow them up. It made her shiver.

Rose chased away the thundery dark. There was a pile of shillings waiting to go into the meter. Even though it was morning, she put on the kitchen lights and the electric fire to dry their clothes, three bars glowing orange. The smell of damp, hot cotton filled the air. The radio was playing 'Here Comes The Sun', and their mother turned it up loud and sang along, standing at the stove making hot chocolate. Isolte got out the tin of golden syrup for their porridge and dipped her finger in, sucking globs of it, letting strands of sticky sweetness loop across her chin. Viola sat on the floor peeling off her muddy socks. The rain falling outside, steaming up the kitchen windows, the cat weaving herself around their mother's legs asking for milk.

My darling girls.

5

Luke and Abby arrived from Wales in a purple VW camper van decorated with stars, moons and flowers. The paint was cracked and peeling around the petals and there were dribbles running down from the points of the stars. They parked the van in the drive next to Mummy's Vespa with the egg-shaped sidecar.

Abby tumbled out of the van straight into Mummy's arms. They stood on the sandy path with their arms wrapped around each other, while Luke, a bony man with hair in a bowl cut, yawned, scratched his stomach and stretched, showing dark patches under the arms of his shirt. Luke didn't seem to mind that Mummy and Abby were making a spectacle of themselves. He smiled at us vaguely and cracked his long fingers, one by one.

'Oh, it's so lovely to see you. I've missed you!' Mummy sighed.

Mummy had told us only the other day that one of the reasons we'd left the commune was that none of that lot had any manners or true generosity of spirit. Yet here she was inviting them to stay, behaving as if they were long-lost relatives. These two came with the smells of the commune wafting behind them.

Our noses recognised the mouldy damp, overcooked rice, patchouli and sandalwood – that clinging smell, how it got into all our things, even our hair. We liked living without other people's rules, constant rows, rotting clothes and muddy shoes, without having to share everything. We liked not having to call Mummy 'Rose'. Most of all we liked having her all to ourselves.

'Sleep in the house,' Mummy told them, 'we've got a spare room.' (She'd spent all morning cleaning it, hair in a scarf, dusting, even pushing the ancient vacuum around, risking electrocuting herself with the dodgy switch. She'd put a new bulb into the lamp with the hessian shade and hung a rag rug over the damp patch on the wall.) But Luke and Abby had said they didn't want to put anyone to any trouble and had gone out to the van later that night and shut themselves in.

The next morning the windows of the van were foggy with condensation. The couple emerged barefoot and fusty. Abby and Mummy sat at the kitchen table sipping tea and talking in low voices. They ignored us. 'Gossip,' Luke nodded over at the women, 'so tasty.' He winked. 'Watch how those two love to swallow it.' And he grinned, not moving from his position on a stool by the wood burner, a guitar on his lap and his fingers clasped round a cup of coffee. He put a rolled-up cigarette between his lips and inhaled deeply, eyes slow as a cat's. His feet were up on a chair and I saw that the soles were grey, toenails thick and yellow, curling at the edges. I looked away quickly.

Abby flicked her hennaed plait over her shoulder. It hung like a skimpy tail down her spine. I longed to give it a sharp tug.

'Shut up, Luke, we're just catching up. It's been ages.' Abby made a sort of pouting baby face at him. 'Just because you're an emotional fuckwit and can't reveal your inner self.' She fluttered her hands, putting them over her mouth as she laughed. She had a high-pitched squeaky giggle. She giggled a lot.

'Sounds like she needs oiling,' Issy whispered to me, pushing her chair back and scowling.

The women were slicing mushrooms and aubergines to make lasagne.

'You really love it here, don't you?' Abby rolled up her sleeves to expose plump arms and a small butterfly tattoo on her wrist.

'God, it feels so free. Sort of liberated, you know?' Mummy breathed out loudly, waving her arms. 'The deer come into the garden. I'm growing my own vegetables. I make my own decisions. There's no crappy politics to deal with.' She put her hand on her stomach and patted. 'I know deep down, in my guts, that it was the right thing to do.'

Mummy glanced over as if she'd only just noticed us. 'Oh, there you are. Have some breakfast. There's muesli in the jar,' she said vaguely. Luke tipped his head back and began blowing smoke rings. We watched, reluctantly impressed by the hovering discs melting one into the other.

Abby put down her knife and bent over Luke, pinching his cigarette between her mushroom-speckled fingers. 'Give us a drag, babe.'

Taking the rollie from Luke's lips, she kissed him before she put it in her mouth. Their lips made a smacking sound. I saw her tongue, the end of the cigarette brown and soggy with his spit. Then Mummy took it and put it in her mouth. It was as if she was sharing their saliva, their kisses. It put me off my cereal. The thought of their tongues was even more disgusting than the little white maggots that we sometimes found at the bottom of the jar.

Mummy blew a smoke ring as well. Luke looked up at her,

smoke still drifting from the sides of his mouth. His thin fingers began to pluck the strings of the guitar. 'Oh, baby, baby, it's a wild world.' His wailing voice rose and faltered like a bird. Isolte kicked me under the table, her head jerking towards the door. Outside we breathed in fresh air and snorted with laughter. Issy raised her head, wolf-howling, the words of the song a long, drawn-out screeching, 'Baby, oooowwwww, it's a hoowwl wild world!'

'Shhh.' I pushed her, looking behind me.

We opened the door to the camper van; it had a bench running down one side, a small table and a sink hardly bigger than one belonging to a doll. There were some crumpled clothes on the floor. An Afghan coat sprawled, exposing its insides: an underbelly of discoloured fur, spiky with grime. We sniffed. The air was stale and musty, sweetened with the horrible stink of sandalwood. Crumbling tentacles of mould crept around the plastic window frames. Above our heads was a platform with a mattress; we could just see a rolled-up sleeping bag. 'That's where they have sex,' Isolte said.

'They're too old to have sex.' I pulled her sleeve. 'Come on. Let's go, *babe*.'

It didn't take us long to cycle to the barns at the edge of the marsh. We could hear the clash of wood against wood as we freewheeled into the farmyard. The boys were slashing at each other with long sticks. They were aiming as if they had swords, stabbing and flailing. The sticks hissed through the air. Whack! Wood made contact with John's arm. He yelped and brought his weapon down hard on Michael's shoulder.

Issy and I abandoned our bikes and sat on the low wall of the farmyard to watch. The boys made no sign of acknowledgement and carried on with the sword fight. It must have been going on for some time. Their faces were red and damp, strands of hair sticking to their skin. They lunged at each other, feet sliding and shuffling backwards and forwards across the black dirt and bits of straw. Watching them, I could see now that Michael was a little taller and heavier. A different kind of energy crackled around him, turning his hair into a wild halo. He fought with aggression, his blows carrying more weight. But John had nimble feet. He ducked and danced like a boxer.

The day was cloudless blue, sharpened by a salted wind coming from the sea. We shivered, shrugging into our anoraks, hands deep in pockets, and waited. There was a smell of dung coming from a manure heap. A faint cloud of steam drifted above it. I noticed that John still had the grey shadow of his bruised eye and that his laces had come undone. I watched anxiously as they flopped around his feet, knowing that eventually he would stand on them and go flying.

A tractor pulled into the yard, its great wheels festooned with clumps of mud. The man in the cab opened the door and leaned out. 'Clear off, you lot!'

John and Michael stopped, sticks at their sides, panting. They looked up at the man and Michael tilted his chin and stabbed his middle finger up. 'You gonna make us?'

We slid off the wall and ran, following the boys as they dodged up the track towards the river. I trailed behind, scrambling under a barbed-wire fence and sprinting through a field of cows. My lungs heaved; the field sloped steeply. I seemed to be losing control of my feet, tripping over tufts of thick grass, once hitting a cowpat dead centre with a splat. I didn't dare glance over my shoulder. I was sure the farmer was following us. The fear of it forced hysterical laughter into my mouth.

As we ran through the field, the cows shifted uneasily, broad heads low, eyes rolling. One of them blundered towards me, snorting through flared nostrils. It was big enough to block out the light: a wall of muscle and bone and hair. I glanced helplessly at the others who'd reached the safety of the gate. I was trapped, panting. The cow regarded me impassively. She took a step closer, lowering her weighty head, and I saw the slimy wet of her grey nose, the stubs of horns protruding between her ears. I took a step backwards. She snorted, swinging her horns at me. I squeezed my eyes shut, flailing my arms.

'Get lost!' I roared. 'Go away!' I opened my eyes to see her stained backside swaying as she stumbled uphill.

Issy stood with the boys on the other side of the gate, elbows on the top bar. They were slumped against each other, laughing. It was me, I realised: I was the joke. I walked over to them, my cheeks on fire. I glanced at Issy quickly. But she was flicking her hair, an animated smile transforming her face as she looked up at John. And I felt a different kind of panic: the ground falling away beneath my feet.

We sat on top of the hill, looking down to the river. The land here rolled and dipped in an uneven, tussocky surface, speckled with coltsfoot and sow thistle. There were graves below us. Ancient graves belonging to people who'd lived here thousands of years ago. The whole hill was a burial ground. Pots and bits of bone, arrowheads and even brooches made of bronze and shaped like shields had been dug up and displayed in a museum in town. Mummy had told us that the hill was a magic place, full of the spirits of the dead. I wondered if there was a body below me at that moment, some child perhaps, curled in her ceremonial grave, and if she minded me sitting on her.

'I knew a man crushed by a herd of cows,' John said conversationally, as we all gazed across the long sweep of river to the distant glint of the sea on the other side. 'Couldn't recognise him. His face was a pile of mush.'

I didn't want to do anything else that would single me out. So although I was interested in this story, I said nothing. But Michael pushed his brother roughly at the shoulder. 'Bollocks! Who's that then?'

Michael turned to us, his hands spread. 'Such a liar!'

'Am not!' John hooked his arm around his brother's neck and the two of them wrestled each other into the long grass; Michael had got on top and was pushing John's face down. 'Liar! Liar!' Then a twist of torso and a grunt, and John was writhing out from under Michael, his fist finding Michael's ear. Thin arms and legs pummelled and jerked. Isolte and I looked at each other, eyebrows raised.

'Our goat has had a baby,' Isolte announced loudly, standing over them. The boys stopped rolling and sat up, grass seeds in their hair.

'A kid, you mean.' John rubbed his nose. 'Boy or girl?'

'It's a boy,' I said.

Michael got to his feet, drawing his finger across his throat. 'He's for the pot then.'

'Don't be silly,' Issy said coldly.

'Careful Black Shuck don't get him.' John shook his head.

'Who?'

'Ghost dog,' Michael explained. 'Bigger 'n a wolf. Kills yer with a look.'

Mummy had shut Tess in the shed with the kid. He was fragile and white with long knotted legs. He'd licked my fingers with
his raspy tongue. We'd looked in on them that morning, scattering fresh straw; the baby had been on his front knees, suckling
with serious intent from Tess, who, for once, seemed happy to
stand and wait.

There would be no ghost dogs creeping in to eat our goats.
We'd bolted the shed door when we left. I was sure of it.

'I'm hungry.' Michael turned away, brushing grass from his
knees.

It was lunchtime. I knew that the lasagne would be cooked,
cheesy and hot, the pasta slices peeling and crispy at the edges.
Mummy would have placed it on the woven mat on the table.
Maybe there would be a green salad to go with it and big chunks
of brown bread and butter. My stomach rumbled. I stared down
into the pattern of light and shade moving across the marshes,
watching seabirds gathering on the molten water. There was a
ferry crossing over to the other bank. The man at the oars rowed
slowly, the blades making no splashes.

We collected our bikes from the bank of nettles behind the
farm where we'd left them.

'Come back to ours,' the boys said. 'Ma will cook us something.'

We weren't going to refuse such an offer, lasagne or no lasagne.

They lived on the edge of a field in a semi-detached house sitting
with a row of others along a narrow, muddy road. The identical
cottages were red brick under slate roofs; each had a single green
door and three windows. There was uniformity in the white-
painted windows with net curtains; the front gardens tablecloth

squares of lawn dotted with gnomes, pebble paths flanked by flowerbeds. Some of the gardens had vegetable patches sprouting lush thickets of green and curling tendrils. Bits of silver foil fluttered to keep the birds away. There were boxes placed at garden gates filled with produce: bunches of carrots and bags of potatoes, the prices chalked on squares of cardboard – 3p a bunch – with faith jars set out to collect the money.

John and Michael's cottage was the odd one out. Paint was peeling from window frames, slivers and flakes hanging like oversized dandruff. The whole place was almost hidden by a large, tumbledown shed erected in the front yard and a jumble of car parts, an old motorbike, piles of tyres and a decaying tractor sitting in the dirt. Beside the scabby front door, a kennel was piled high with rusting petrol cans.

We followed the boys inside, breathing in a smell of frying. A teenage girl with a cloud of frizzy white hair was slumped on a sofa watching a large television. Gum snapped between her teeth, pink bubbles rising on her tongue like boils.

I stared at the flickering screen, watching a muscular half-naked man in a loincloth. The man scooped a chimpanzee on to his broad shoulder and clasped a vine in his hand. A horde of chanting natives gathered behind him. We didn't have a television. Mummy didn't believe in them.

'Ma's in the kitchen,' said the blonde girl, without taking her eyes from the screen. 'You're for it.'

'That's Judy. She's a cow,' Michael said loudly. Judy continued chewing, her gaze unwavering from the film. She must have been about fourteen or fifteen. But we knew at once that the age gap between us was stretched and elongated by a glamorous wealth of teenage knowledge and secrets that we could only guess at.

The inside of their house was really no smaller than ours, but it felt tighter, busy with ornaments and crammed with furniture. I wanted to examine the china cats and cherubic children carrying baskets of fruit. My fingers itched for them. We could hear a woman's voice calling from the next room. An orange carpet blazed on the floor, crackling under our feet as the boys pushed us ahead of them.

A short, plump woman was standing at a cooker; behind her a pan of oil boiled and spat. She dipped a metal ladle into the pan and brought out a heap of shining chips. In her other hand she held a cigarette. She turned when she heard us, her mouth open as if to say something. Seeing us, she just stood there, the ladle of chips in one hand and her cigarette in the other, her mouth hanging open.

'Who's this, then?' she asked eventually.

John poked me in the small of the back. 'Issy and Viola. They want some lunch.'

She made us chip sandwiches on sliced white bread with margarine and ketchup. We ate sitting at the Formica table, swinging our legs, cups of hot, sweet tea at our elbows. The twins' mum kept asking us questions. She didn't seem to mind us replying with our mouths full. She called us both 'love'. The boys ignored her, eating quickly, using both hands to stuff the bread into their mouths. We could hear the television in the other room, the echoing call of Tarzan and the roar of a lion. The sandwich was deliciously oily. I wondered if we would be allowed to go and sit with the blonde sister and watch television afterwards. I took a sip of tea, my fingers leaving greasy prints on the handle.

'They never brought girls home before,' the boys' mum said to us, 'never mind twins. I hope they're treating you right.' She turned her attention to her sons, rubbing her chin, fingers heavy with gold rings. 'You mind yer manners, or else.'

John took a slurp of tea and kicked me hard under the table. 'Uh-huh.' He pushed his plate away. A streak of tomato red glistened there. Putting his finger into it, he swirled it around, placed it in his mouth and winked at me.

6

Isolte half wakes, drowsily aware of the bed shifting under Ben's weight; she sighs, readjusting her position against the tilt of the mattress. He mutters, and his arm slides across her waist, inert and heavy. He's asleep immediately, his feet cold against hers.

Her heart is thumping fast. Outside, trees rustle and shift in the darkness. She doesn't know where she is. Isolte stares up at the invisible ceiling, listening. Something woke her. Noises downstairs. She gets out of bed. Disorientated, Isolte stumbles across the darkened room and slips the catch.

She pushes a door open and steps into their old kitchen in the forest.

Her mother is blundering around the room with erratic movements, flailing past the table, hip bumping a chair. She is drunk. Isolte can see urgency written in her face; her stuttering limbs are fuelled with intention. Rose leans down unsteadily and pulls a bottle of vodka out of the kitchen cabinet from behind unused dusters and a tangle of broken Christmas-tree lights. She goes to the foot of the stairs and pauses for a moment, muttering. Isolte can't hear the words, but she knows where her mother is going.

Isolte goes to the door and stands there, feet firmly planted, arms out straight to brace herself in the doorframe. 'Go back,' she tells her. 'Go back to bed.'

Of course, her mother can't hear. She comes close, close enough for Isolte to see her blind eyes, her wet cheeks and gaping mouth. 'I'm so tired,' she whispers. Her breath is fetid, as if there is rot inside her. Her hair falls across her forehead, long and lank. She pushes the door, her hand passing through Isolte's skin and ribs, fingers moving through lungs and the bones of her spine.

Outside, in the moonlight, the trees are beaten about by an easterly wind. It hisses inside long grass, rushing across the sodden surface of the lawn. Rose staggers to the Vespa, the bottle dangling from her fingers. She attempts to start the scooter but can't fit the key in the ignition. Metal slides across metal, scratching and scraping. Isolte reaches forward to grasp her mother's hand, to take the key from her. Her fingers close on empty air.

The Vespa whines into life. Her mother grips the handles and releases the clutch. The scooter moves forward in bunny hops, lurching along the puddled track. And then she is firing the engine, moving recklessly away at full speed. Isolte is running behind, running as hard as she can, until she can't feel the wet sand beneath her feet. Leaning forward with arms outstretched, she exists inside the slipstream of the scooter, watching her mother's hair scatter behind her, sparks of red and gold in the darkness.

The machine wobbles dangerously around potholes, screams around corners, skidding as it hits slick tarmac. Isolte is everywhere. She swirls around her mother, sees the stretch of her gaping mouth, the shine of her glazed eyes; she swoops above the

Vespa, staring down at the dark road and pale yellow glow of the headlight. The light sweeps in and out of trees, catching the flutter of tiny insect wings. And then they are moving along the main road, through the village and out the other side. Over the bridge, taking the narrow road alongside the marshes. There are no horses in the fields. Isolte can hear the sea.

At the beach road, her mother pulls up near the coastguard's cottage. She unscrews the top on the bottle of vodka, tips her head and drinks as if it's milk. Now she's lurching over the shingle and her feet, crunching across stones, suddenly twist beneath her. Rose falls to her knees and laughs, throwing her head back, exposing her white throat. 'Your fault!' she shouts. 'Your fault.'

'I know.' Isolte puts her hands over her ears; whispers it again. 'I know.'

Rose lifts the bottle to her lips, swallows, and throws it away, hurling it into the darkness. Isolte hears the thud as it lands, the rattle of dislodged stones. And then her mother is weeping, crawling across the pebbles, her hair tangling and dragging, her skirt catching under her. She sobs so that her chest heaves and her shoulders shake. She staggers to her feet.

It happens in slow motion, as it always does: her mother walking into the rush of foamy waves, her toes disappearing into the first bubbles of white. Her nightdress puffs at the surface and then deflates, sinking into the waves. She doesn't pause or wince at the cold.

And this is when Isolte follows, stumbling into the water, hands outstretched to pull her back, trying to catch hold of her arm. Each time she attempts to grip flesh and bone, her hand slides through a buzz of electrified air. Her fingers hum and fall away empty. She feels the bite of ice around her legs. Her skin recoils. She gasps, bracing herself against the push of the waves, balancing on slippery stones. 'Stop!' she shouts. 'Stop. Mummy, I'm sorry. Don't go! Don't go . . .'

The whistle of waves and wind swallows her words. Her mother is already submerged in inky water. Her hair floats in a lighter fan around her. Her face is a pale blur. Isolte can't see her eyes, can't see her expression. And there is nothing but the night and the dark sea.

'Issy . . . darling . . . it's all right . . .'

And she is awake, flailing inside Ben's arms, her cheeks wet. She buries her face in the curve of his shoulder. His arms are around her, tight. She stops struggling, breathes in and out, tasting Ben's fusty breath, the blue detergent smell of the sheets.

'You're safe.' His mouth moves against her neck. 'You're with me.'

The darkness of the room recedes as her eyes grow accustomed to it, and she makes out the shapes of Ben's bedroom: the glint of the mirror on the wall, the angle of a lamp, the faint glow of a streetlight through the closed blind. And Ben, raising himself on to his elbows, his hair sticking up, the bulk of his shoulders a weight above her.

'What's the matter, Issy?' he says softly, his voice rough with sleep and wine. 'This isn't about me coming to bed late, is it?'

She mutters, shaking her head.

'A bad dream?' He strokes her hair clumsily, fingers catching in the tangles. 'You've had them before. Do you want to tell me?'

She swallows, licking dry lips. She feels exhausted. She

50

remembers now. Stevie was here. Ben climbing in beside her much later, his hot hand on her hip.

'I'm sorry about last night,' he says sheepishly into the silence. 'I drank too much. Too excited about the pictures. I think I'm going to get a cover out of them . . . but I shouldn't have stayed up with him. It was going to be our evening. Sorry.'

'It's a recurring dream . . . about my mother,' she says suddenly. 'I can't get rid of it.'

Ben is quiet; she can feel him waiting. She puts her head on his chest, his skin warm, slightly sticky, and hears the thump of his heart under her ear, a liquid gurgle inside his stomach. Perhaps it is the comfort of the darkness, or exhaustion, or even the sly sense of safety that has crept up on her over the last few weeks, but Isolte begins to talk.

'She killed herself.' She keeps her eyes closed as she speaks, her ear against the curve of his ribs. 'She drowned herself off a beach. Late at night. She was drunk, but it wasn't an accident. They found rocks in her pockets.'

She hears his heartbeat accelerate into a dull thundering. 'God.' Shock makes his voice falter. 'When?'

'We were twelve.'

There is the wet click of Ben's swallowing, the opening and closing of his throat. 'Darling, I'm so sorry.' He strokes her back. Long steady strokes. 'No wonder you cry in your sleep.'

She shivers.

Isolte takes a deep breath. 'Things . . . well, things had got very bad at home.'

A door slides shut inside her. Her fingers curl into balls and she rolls away from Ben. 'It was a long time ago,' she says with finality, thumping the pillow and settling into it. 'Sorry I woke you. Guess we'd better get some sleep.' She yawns. 'Early start tomorrow.'

'OK.' Ben pulls her closer, buries his nose in the back of her neck. He yawns as well, a rush of exhaled sound. 'Have it your own way.' He smacks his lips together, reaches out to take a gulp of water from a bottle on the floor. 'I'm not going to pry. But I'm here, and I care; you know that, don't you, Isolte? I'm here if you want to talk to me.'

Isolte threads another piece of paper into the typewriter. She frowns, and her fingers hit the keys, rat-a-tat-tat. *This summer is about colour. Hot pinks and sunny orange. Don't be afraid to mix them. Clashing is the new matching.* She sighs and unscrews a bottle of Tipp-Ex, painting over the last sentence. The letters are still visible, grey shadows under blobby white. She picks up her take-away coffee and sips. It's tepid and bitter. She should have asked for sugar.

She leans back in her chair, stretching. She's been at her desk since she got in this morning. She needs to finish this copy by lunchtime. She swivels and looks around her. The fashion department is at the centre of the open-plan office. From her vantage point she watches the girls on the subs' desk scrutinising copy for widows and typos. The art department, positioned at the end of the office, is where page layouts are created and mocked up. Jason, the art director, is there now, perched on a stool.

Isolte's assistant, Lucy, appears at the door of the fashion cupboard; a silver evening dress slithers over one arm. 'Is Chanel sending someone to pick this up?' she calls.

Isolte nods. 'This afternoon.'

Isolte can just see the profile of the new editor: Sam Fowler, fresh-faced as a twenty-year-old, black hair close-cropped. She is smoking and talking on the phone. She exhales a long plume of smoke and laughs, swinging her chair round, flashing a sudden slash of red lipstick and white teeth.

Isolte starts, colour rushing to her cheeks. She feels as though she's been caught out. She drops her head quickly, her fingers hitting the keys. *Let your palette be a riot of colour.* Oh God. What's the matter with her? She's never going to get this done on time. She picks up a pen and begins to tap it against her front teeth. Her attention strays to the pinboard by her desk. There are cards for models, photographers and make-up artists; some Polaroid out-takes from recent shoots. In the middle is a picture of a big golden horse standing in a field of yellow grass. She'd come across it in a magazine months ago and, on impulse, torn it out and pinned it to her wall. She leans forward and takes it down, staring at it as if it might give her inspiration.

'What kind of creature do you call that?' Lucy is looking over her shoulder.

'Suffolk Punch.' Isolte rubs a finger over the image. 'Beautiful, isn't he? There aren't many left now.'

'I'm scared of horses,' Lucy admits, 'prefer them at a distance.'

*

It was summer when they came across the stallion. The fibre of trees popping and cracking. The air full of gold, and smells of moss and bark. They had been bunking off, of course. A hot Friday morning, the four of them aimless in the forest, beginning to feel hungry. And there he was.

He'd been grazing in a clearing. He wasn't wearing a head

collar. When he heard them he put up his head and stared. There was a thin blaze of white between his eyes. He twitched his sandy tail to get at the flies that buzzed around his warm skin.

'Here, boy,' John called in a low sigh.

Michael whispered, moving forward with his hands held open, clicking his tongue, 'Let's take him back.'

John was treacle-slow inside a shaft of light, stepping soundlessly.

The horse shivered violently, kicking up a back hoof under his belly and stamping it down, his tail thrashing back and forth. Viola braced herself, swallowing.

'It's just a fly bothering him,' John muttered. Reaching the animal's side, he slipped his hand up to touch its neck. 'Quick,' he said over his shoulder, 'Issy, give us yer belt.'

John put his mouth close to the horse's muzzle, blowing softly into flared nostrils. The horse's ears pricked forward. He stood still as Michael threaded the belt around his neck and buckled it. He had to use the very last hole.

'Want to get up?' Michael jerked his head a fraction.

'Without a bridle or anything?' Isolte looked at the dinner-plate hooves and then up at the horse's naked back. His withers stood higher than the top of her head.

'We'll hold him. He won't hurt you.' John laid his cheek against the horse's neck.

Isolte's mouth was dry. She put a hand on the stallion, feeling the pulse inside his living flank, the depths of his heart. And it seemed that she heard the voice of the horse, the slow rhythm of him. She put a foot into Michael's cupped palm, his fingers grazing her ankle. He pushed up underneath and she made a grab for the coarse mane, clutching handfuls. Sliding one leg over, she was able to straddle his back. Michael gave her an approving nod and there was sudden heat in her cheeks; she raised her chin to hide it. Viola clambered up behind. She pressed close against Isolte's back, hands around her waist.

John and Michael walked either side of the stallion, one hand each on the belt. He seemed happy to go with them, taking long, unhurried strides. Viola and Isolte swayed together, rolling with the measured gait. Viola's voice, singing an old nursery rhyme, was muffled against Isolte's shoulder.

Isolte wasn't scared. She wanted to hold the moment: the smell of horse and his warmth on her skin; Viola's breathing weight; the boys' slide and scuff as they walked; steady hoof fall. It was all connected. Nothing mattered outside it. She wanted to travel like this for ever. But even as she touched the beautiful belonging of the moment, she was losing it.

They left the forest and reached open fields, scrubby grass and sheep grazing. On the tarmac the horse's unshod hooves hardly made a sound. There were seagulls wheeling and a salt bite in her mouth. From her elevated position, Isolte could see over the sea wall, watch the white tops of rolling breakers. A lone car came up behind, a blue Cortina, changing gears with a metallic grating. It gave them a wide berth, accelerating off into the distance. The horse twitched one ear, and kept walking.

Because they were bunking, they didn't dare go to the farm, couldn't risk having to explain to adults. They stopped at the first field with Punches. Viola and Isolte half fell, half slid from his back, landing with a jolt. The boys closed the gate behind the horse, fastened the latch. The other horses turned towards him, whickering. He walked lazily into the long grass, as if wading out to sea, his tail trailing over pale fronds.

Afterwards Isolte could smell him on her hands. Sweat and dirt stuck to her skin where she had stroked his coat. She rubbed it off in tiny black balls, like disintegrating rubber between her fingers.

*

'Have you got the copy ready?'

Isolte jumps. Sam is looking down at her, eyes narrowed, a burning cigarette between her fingers.

'Nearly there,' Isolte lies. 'I'll put it on your desk.'

'By the way,' Sam says casually, engulfed in a cloud of her own cigarette smoke, 'someone said your sister was anorexic. You know we're running a feature on it. Can I tell our writer to get in touch with you? She may want some quotes.'

Isolte stops breathing. Smoke fills her lungs. She feels as though she is suffocating. She wants to say, 'Do you know what you've just asked me? Do you understand that my sister is killing herself?' She rubs her nose.

Over at the art desk, Isolte can see Jason, the art director, looking through the shoot she and Ben had done the other day. Dresses waft and float in brilliant colours. The blonde girl turns and bends, all angles and bones against the paper backdrop.

'All right,' Isolte says. 'I suppose so.'

The picture of the horse lies on top of her copy. She picks it up and pins it back on to the noticeboard, sits down and threads another piece of paper into the typewriter. Types three lines and stops, staring into space. She can't take the call. Won't talk to the writer. She should have said no.

Isolte knows how the feature on anorexia will look. There'll be real-life pictures of girls: shocking black and white images with loud red writing over the top. There will be ribs, hipbones protruding and skull faces grimacing for the camera.

Years ago people read about Isolte and Viola and Rose in newspaper articles. Their story was discussed over breakfast; blame was apportioned, sides taken. Isolte wonders how many people ate their fish and chips out of their story, polished their shoes on the back of it.

The story ran for weeks. At first it had been on all the front pages, but gradually it became stale and slipped further back. It had been on the evening news too; but the TV channels soon dropped it to move on to recent crimes and fresh disasters. It had gone altogether by the time news broke that there were survivors from the Chilean air crash, and their exhausted, emaciated faces stared out of the front pages.

Rose slept the days away, like a sick person, her mouth sagging open. By the bed an empty bottle and a packet of sleeping pills. Isolte had begun to count them, hiding the extra packets. Viola was listless, pinched around the mouth, eyes staring at nothing. She'd already begun to push her food around her plate, not eating much. But Isolte carried on: getting up in the morning, breathing in and out, making meals, eating meals, feeding the cat. She still had ambitions and plans. She hadn't wanted to look for oblivion at the bottom of a bottle or stop living. Did that make her a bad person? Did that make her heartless?

She rips the sheet from the typewriter with a satisfying zipping noise and crumples it into a ball, flinging it towards the bin. It misses, rolling on to the green carpet tiles.

'Hey,' Jason bends and picks it up, 'you won't make the Olympic team.'

Isolte inclines her head, forcing a smile. 'No.'

'Just had a look at the pictures.' Jason lingers by her desk. 'They're good.'

He tips his head in Sam's direction. 'Don't mind her. She's just trying to make her mark.'

Isolte grimaces. 'Somehow I get the feeling she doesn't like me.'

Winding in another sheet of paper, she calls Ben at the number he left for emergencies. She just wants his voice for a few moments. It will hold her steady. She thinks of how he was last night. She had surfaced from the nightmare into his arms, salt water still in her mouth, her mother slipping through her fingers. The dream had raised the grief inside her, dragging unwanted feelings to the surface like rotting things released in a flood. She's never told anyone about her mother before. It had felt extraordinary to speak the words aloud. She wants that sense of closeness, of trust again. She needs it now.

The number rings. She remembers that he's doing an advertising campaign on location. He's out of town, at some stately home. Someone else answers and there is a long pause while Isolte listens to an empty crackling, before Ben's voice comes on the line. She can hear noise in the background. It's not a good time.

'What, Issy? Sorry.' A muffled thump, as if he's dropped something. 'Didn't catch that? What did you want?'

A girl is asking a question. Isolte can't make out the words, just the tone of voice. He must have turned away from the mouthpiece or put his hand over it. She can hardly hear his reply. And then he comes back, sounding breathless. 'Look, if it isn't important then I'm going to go, OK? I don't want to piss the client off.'

She puts the phone down. Drops her head into her hands. She doesn't know what she wanted to ask or tell him. It was only a feeling of need. Even if she could have put it into words he wouldn't have been able to hear. Not when he's working. But her nightmare has stirred up echoes from the past, and Viola's skeletal face hovers over the page, making Isolte's fingers skitter over the typewriter keys, thoughts about fabric colours dissolving, as she hears, from long ago, the sound of rainwater dripping into a bucket.

*

Water dribbles through the ceiling in their bedroom. It seeps around the light fixing, spreading like a shadow, and drips into a bowl that Isolte put under it. It smells of moss and wet wood.

It's been raining for days. Sudden squalls splatter loudly against the windows. The lane outside the garden runs like a river, pebbles carried off in the flood and the sand darkened and sopping. There are puddles everywhere. Nobody comes.

Their mother is in bed, her face turned to the wall.

Isolte has opened a can of baked beans and she scrapes them into a bowl and puts a spoon in the cold mush. She has cut her finger on the edge of the tin. She sucks the stinging split, her tongue rubbing at the blood.

'Mummy?' Isolte hovers, proffering the bowl. 'Here. For you.'

The mound of bedclothes doesn't move. Rose's hair, spread over the pillow, is lank and tangled. Some days she sits up with wild eyes and holds her arms open to them, calling, 'Come and give me a hug,' clasping them tight. 'My darling girls.' It feels different from her lovely warm bear hugs; it feels like being strangled. She pats their faces with fluttery fingers, telling them over and over, 'I know you didn't mean it. I know you didn't.' Other days, like today, she looks through them as if they're not there.

The girls had forgotten about the goats. Poor Tess and Bathsheba. Isolte is horrified by her lapse of memory; but it's so hard to think of everything. The goats must be starving, she worries, tethered to the same patch of worn-down lawn. She hurries out to them, bread in her pocket, calling. But they have gone. They might have slipped their collars, she thinks; but there are no collars or ropes lying in the sodden grass. There are just the metal spikes stuck into wet ground, pulled over at an angle, and piles of droppings.

When she wanders into the trees, calling for them, she hears the rustle of rabbits scurrying under bracken, and a flutter of wings. No bleating goats appear out of the shadows. And suddenly she knows that the forest itself is watching; that something bad is out there waiting. The darkness shifts, uncoiling, and it reaches long arms to her. Frightened, she turns and races back to the house, heart thundering, slipping and sliding, brambles catching at her clothes. She slows down as she enters the garden, tries to calm her laboured breathing. She doesn't want to scare Viola. It's bad enough that she has to tell her about the goats.

'Perhaps the poacher stole them?' Viola's bottom lip trembles. Neither of them wants to say the words Black Shuck.

8

The woman in the bed opposite is humming loudly. Her fingers push and tap at the plastic needles in her hands. She's still knitting the purple thing. It's a monster of dropped stitches: a bulky woollen snake, shapeless and pointless. I turn my eyes away quickly as she glances up.

If I lie with my eyes half shut like a crocodile, I see her whispering and gesticulating to the shadows by her bed. She has long conversations with imaginary friends. At least she has her skinny legs under the covers today, her greying pubes put away, the dark, hanging folds of her labia covered. Some dignity has been restored.

I let my head fall back into the pillow. The anticipation of oblivion is good. Because there's always the chance that John will be there again, waiting for me at the edge of the forest on his bike, grinning at me, with sunlight on his hair and his skin smelling of moss. I teeter on the brink of losing the present. The lights above my closed lids blur and flicker.

*

We were halfway up the sandy track leading towards the cottage when we saw the stranger, bald-headed with hefty shoulders, coming out of our drive. He got into a white van parked at the side of the lane and drove past slowly, avoiding the potholes. We stared in through the window. His face was like a potato, with thin lips set in a line. He didn't glance in our direction.

We ran the rest of the way, socks falling round our ankles, our school bags bumping on our backs. A quick glance reassured us that Tess and Bathsheba were safely tethered at the top of the garden; they had their heads down, grazing on the long grass.

We turned towards the shed where the kid was kept. It was our habit to visit him as soon as we got in from school, letting him suck at our fingers. He liked it when we scratched his ears and kissed him. Abby stood at the kitchen door, wiping her hands on a tea towel.

'Hey, girls!' she shouted. As we turned she added softly, enticingly, 'Come over here, come in. I've made cake for you.' She was leaning against the doorframe, smiling and beckoning. Her plait coiled on her shoulder like a snake. She reminded me of the Child Catcher in *Chitty Chitty Bang Bang*.

Issy got to the door handle of the shed first. She turned and pushed. We caught our breath in surprise: our mother was just inside. She looked pale. She put her arm out, barring our way, and smiled weakly. 'You can't come in,' she said. 'I have something to tell you.'

Issy let out a small moan, as if she'd seen something terrible. I tried to see too, but Mummy shoo-shooed us, making us go ahead of her into the kitchen where Abby was waiting with the cake. Abby took a knife and stuck it into the sponge, cutting slices. 'How about a glass of milk with this?' she asked. Mummy stood with her back to us and fumbled with the cork on a bottle of wine. She poured herself a glass and took a big gulp.

'He didn't suffer,' she said, turning round. 'Mr Gibb is a butcher. He knows what he's doing. And I was there. I didn't leave him ...'

'No!' Issy shouted. 'Murderer!' She raised her arms as if to hit Mummy, but dropped her face into her hands. 'I hate you,' she whispered fiercely, 'I hate you. I hate you. And I'll never forgive you.'

Issy turned to me, eyes shiny with tears and fury, appealing mutely, reaching for my hand. I couldn't move. I shook my head and looked at the floor. I thought of my fingers in his pink mouth, the rub of his tongue.

'Look,' Mummy's voice trembled, 'I tried to explain. But you didn't want to listen.' She held out her hand to me. 'Viola, you know we're self-sufficient, don't you? You understand?'

I stared at the floor. Numb.

'Oh, for heaven's sake!' she said wearily. 'This isn't a bloody joke. We're not playing at it, you know.'

Abby shifted in the corner of the room, watching us, the tea towel still clasped in her hands. Slices of cake untouched on the plate. She bit her lip, agonising perhaps over who she should be hugging or patting. Luke, lying sprawled on the sofa, seemed unconcerned by the drama. 'Yeah,' he intoned lazily, 'it's a hard lesson,' he twitched his toes earnestly, 'but it's the natural cycle of things. And nature is cruel, man. Life is cruel.'

We stared at him. 'We don't like you,' Issy said.

Abby let out a mew of distress and put her hands over her mouth, checked cloth falling to the floor.

We never ate her cake, even though it was chocolate sponge.

In the shed we found dark splatters on the concrete floor. In the corner there was a bucket containing his feet and ears. His hooves were pale as babies' nails. His ears, tiny and perfectly shaped, fringed with soft white hair. The blood was dried and crusted, brown around the severed edges.

Mummy cooked him the next day. It was to be Abby and Luke's goodbye supper before they went back to Wales. The thing was, she had warned us. Thinking back to when we'd discussed names for the kid – Snowy, we'd suggested, or Silver Shadow – I remembered Mummy shaking her head, telling us, 'Call him Sunday Lunch.' We didn't think she meant it. But Michael had been right all along.

We didn't cry. It was too awful for crying. Heaviness entered us. A kind of bleak despair. The daffodils were out, colour returning in yellow and lucent greens. But behind the lovely surface was something dark and evil. We felt wounded by it. Wrapped in coats and scarves, we went out of the garden, over the track, and lay in the long bracken on the outskirts of the trees. We didn't have the energy to go any further; but we couldn't stay in the house. Under us insects moved, following invisible tracks, carrying bits of leaf and bark.

Poking my head above the bracken, I could see that the kitchen windows were steamy with cooking. Mummy was in there making a stew out of the kid with apricots and almonds, her hair screwed into an untidy knot. I imagined loose strands sticking to her neck and the flush of her cheeks as she chopped and stirred. A sweet, meaty smell made its way out of the cottage. We were cold and hungry lying in our lair. Luke was playing the guitar and someone had lit candles so that gold lights flickered against the windows. We shivered inside our coats, our stomachs rumbling. We hadn't eaten anything all day. Behind us the forest gathered blue shadows, netting the night inside branches and trunks. We moved closer together. The earth was damp. I felt the dampness seeping through my clothes.

'At least Black Shuck didn't get him,' I said, squashing a hand over my belly, to flatten the hunger.

'But if he had,' Issy replied, 'Mummy wouldn't be a murderer.'

Now we thought of Black Shuck, we sensed the movement of paws in the fallen pine needles. The soft panting of his breath. I imagined him a cross between an Alsatian and a panther. Lean-limbed, muscles moving beneath a jet-black coat. His eyes would be like sulphur, a hissing acid yellow. Ghost eyes.

Dusk closed in on us, cold and clammy against our skin. The edges of things blurred and wavered. Trees and sky and grass took on a milky glow and lost their definition. Even Issy, inches from my face, began to smudge and fade. Nothingness claimed us. I had the sense that the world had lapsed, become slack and fallen away. I imagined that the friendly trees had slipped their roots from the earth and gone slithering across the moss, trailing their branches, the bracken rustling below. I heard the whisper of wild creatures scurrying away. I knew Isolte was aware of it too: the lack of everything. We became silent. I felt my sister take my hand and I held on to the warmth of her skin, the shape the bones made under her flesh. Fingers I knew as well as my own. The fact of her sustained me. I squinted and saw the shapes of trunks, the outline of bracken fronds, Isolte's silhouette. The world flowing back to us.

Mummy came out into the night, calling loudly as she stumbled around the garden. She was drunk. 'Girls, come inside! Enough now! Come in!' Abby and Luke joined in. 'Isolte! Viola!' Our names echoed around the forest, flew up towards the sky. We heard them catch in twigs and fall against the compost of the forest floor, muffled and dead as shot birds.

'Look, for God's sake – I've had enough!' Mummy's voice had become a thin wail. 'Do you think I liked eating the wretched animal? But it had to be done.'

We heard Abby, soothing and maternal. 'OK, Rose, honey, let's leave them be. We'll never find them. They could be anywhere. They'll come in when they're ready.'

Standing up inside the bracken, cloaked in darkness, we looked at the huddled figure of our mother being led into the cottage by Abby. The women's shapes, joined by shadows, looked like a monstrous beast. I heard our mother's angry, slurred protests. Behind us the forest pressed at our backs.

I swallowed. 'Come on,' I said quietly.

Issy shook her head. 'I'm not going in.' She sat down again. 'She killed him. She ate him.'

'Please,' I begged. The lit kitchen windows pulsed with the ordinary security of the human world. I looked longingly, feeling the urge to run across the damp grass towards them. 'Please, Issy.'

Her face had receded into a bluish blob looming through the dark. For a horrible moment I wondered if the anonymous thing was her. Perhaps it was a ghost. Perhaps Issy – the real Issy – had been taken by Black Shuck. He could have pulled her legs from under her, loped off, dragging her behind. Then she spoke. 'Go on,' she said. 'Go on then, run inside to Mummy. Be a traitor.'

The Issy-ness of these words filled me with relief. Behind it other feelings tangled and snagged: anger at Issy's selfishness, sorrow for our mother. I opened my mouth to argue, but the words died on my tongue. Issy was right. Even if she was wrong, it didn't matter. I sighed heavily and turned my back on the cottage. Clenching cold fingers, I shoved them into my pockets and sank to the ground. I sat with my knees up, resting my forehead, making myself small. She settled closer to me. We didn't talk. After a few minutes I let myself relax into the curve of her shoulder, a patch of warmth blooming at the join between our bodies.

9

Isolte met Ben at a supper party in Notting Hill. A mutual friend, Alice, seated them together. There had been candlelight, a lot of alcohol and cocaine. Sade on the record player. The ten party guests played games between courses. The name-guessing game had them all scribbling on bits of paper – names of historical and fictional characters or celebrities – folding them and putting them into a hat. The game involved choosing a name from the hat and sticking it on your forehead. You had to ask questions of the others in order to guess who you were in as short a time as possible.

'Am I dead?' asked the man sitting on Isolte's right. Isolte looked at the name stuck on his forehead. It said 'God'.

'Not really,' she said.

'Yes or no answers only,' Alice shouted.

'Am I female?' Isolte asked the room. The scrap of white paper Sellotaped to her forehead tickled her eyebrows.

'Without doubt,' Ben told her gravely.

The game ended in an argument about whether 'God' could be included as a character. 'Come on,' Alice argued, 'he's fictional, isn't he?'

Isolte had failed to guess that she was the Lady of Shalott. Ben had taken only five goes to guess that he was Barry White.

'You've played this before,' she accused him.

He nodded. 'And don't tell anyone,' he leaned in close, 'but I've been Barry White before too. You, on the other hand, had a hard one. I'll tell you another secret. The Lady of Shalott was my contribution.' She stared at him, distracted by the slight droop to his bottom lip, the robust shine on his skin. 'I hoped you'd pick it,' he was saying. 'You remind me of that painting – you know the one I mean . . . '

'The Waterhouse one?'

He nodded. He'd taken a strand of her hair and wound it round his finger.

'But I'm not a redhead and I like looking out of windows,' she protested, watching her hair make gold stripes across his skin. 'And I don't believe in knights in shining armour.'

'Just details.' He'd waved away her protests, holding on to her hair with casual possessiveness, so that she was caught with their faces almost touching.

'You'd be Lancelot, I suppose?'

He grinned. 'You said it.'

They monopolised each other after that. Ignoring the other guests, much to Alice's irritation. They started to tell each other what they considered to be essential in a lover.

'Bravery. Sensuality,' Ben listed. 'A sense of humour.'

'Kindness. Honesty,' Isolte said. 'Faithfulness. Definitely faithfulness.'

Ben peeled away the leaves of his artichoke, putting the succulent nub of flesh into his mouth; he'd been confident about it, sexy without being obvious. Certain foods – figs, oysters, artichokes – could be eaten the wrong way. Something that should be sensual and earthy could become obvious and vulgar – or worse, just inept and messy.

'So you don't hold to the principle that what you don't know can't hurt you?' He smiled at her, hard to read.

She'd shaken her head. 'No, of course not! Cheating is the beginning of the end, whether the other person knows or not.'

'I wouldn't be unfaithful to you,' he'd said, licking his fingers slowly. 'I wouldn't need to.'

In between courses, drunk on anticipation, she'd been piling plates in the kitchen when Alice appeared at her shoulder. 'Be careful,' Alice told her, reaching for a jug of cream on the table. 'He fucks all his models, of course. Photographers are such pricks.'

Isolte went home with him. She wanted to sleep with him and taste his artichoke breath.

She's wondered several times since they started to see each other if Ben has stayed true to his word, or if Alice had been telling the truth.

In the late 60s and early 70s, it had been considered normal to share partners at the commune. The disapproving locals suspected as much. The Welsh villagers regarded the commune as a den of iniquity: a place of bed-swapping and free sex. There were frequent meetings at the Methodist chapel to discuss what could be done about it. And there was truth in the rumours. Some of the children born there had no idea who their biological father was. According to the commune rules, it didn't matter. It was one big family. That was one of the reasons why Rose had left – what started as a way of simplifying life, another kind of sharing, had made everything more complicated in the end. But the habits of

71

the commune must have lingered, because Isolte remembers that on the night they'd stayed late in the forest, in protest over the kid, they'd fallen over Luke's sandals as they crept back to their bedroom. The sandals had been abandoned outside Rose's door.

Raised voices woke them the next morning. They'd stumbled over to the window and looked down on Luke limping over the stony drive. His hair flopped into his face as he made his way towards the camper van. There was something about his long, ungainly limbs that reminded Isolte of a broken puppet. Funny, but it was him she'd felt sorry for, not dishevelled and tear-stained Abby, waiting for him outside the van with her hands on her hips. Abby pushed him away, pointing towards the house with a jabbing finger. The girls ducked, dropping out of sight below the windowsill. After a slamming of doors and the stutter of an engine, the van started. They remained squatting on the floor as they listened to it drive away, gears grinding, bumping over the ruts.

Rose stayed in bed that morning with the covers over her face. 'Well, suppose I've burnt that bridge now,' she said when she emerged. They'd smiled, not understanding. Isolte and Viola were glad that there'd be no more Welsh visitors. Much later, Isolte found Luke's tobacco tin under their mother's bed while playing hide-and-seek. It was lying in the dust behind the chamber pot. She popped open the lid and fingered spidery threads of tobacco, pulling them out and sniffing with her lip curled, before stuffing them carefully inside the crack between carpet and floorboards.

Isolte doubts that Ben's parents, Anita and George Hadley, were ever involved in any bed-hopping. There had been no communes for them, no barefoot afternoons lost to dope and Janis Joplin and casual sex in the Kent fields. Ben's mother, Anita, is big-boned and handsome. She dresses in sensible, smart clothes that she shops for three times a year in Harvey Nichols. George wears a pinstripe suit and gets the train into the City every morning, the *Financial Times* tucked under his arm. They are the most ardent representatives of what her mother would have called the Establishment. She's even heard them talk of socialism as a 'creeping cancer'. It's odd to be in their company, especially if she allows herself to see them through Rose's eyes: then it's like being in the enemy camp, wearing only the thinnest disguise. A sensation of disbelief and disgusted fascination comes over her.

In the presence of Ben's parents, Isolte feels flimsy and incomplete. She knows that she teeters on the brink of being exposed as a fraud. Ben's family tree hangs on the dining-room wall, framed, and etched in gold and red. This is a family that can trace its roots back to the sixteenth century. Who does she have? Hettie, who would have to be fetched from Ireland, dog hairs removed before she was presentable. And Viola.

It had been all very well for their mother to talk about freedom and explain about starting their own dynasties – but she hadn't appreciated how inconvenient it would be not having a father to wheel out on social occasions. Being fatherless renders her a source of speculation among people like Ben's parents. It also means that a whole chunk of potential family is missing. But she doesn't want to think about that, about how different it could have been.

June 1987, and the Hadleys are holding a cocktail party to celebrate Thatcher's re-election. 'Just what this country needs,' George says to a nodding circle of guests. 'She'll get it back on its feet, face up to the unions, teach all those welfare leeches that the world doesn't owe them a living.'

Standing with a glass of orange juice in her hand, heels sinking into the deep-pile carpet, Isolte remembers when Thatcher banned school milk. It was their last year at the commune and a whole group of them had gone to demonstrate outside the village primary-school gates, shouting, 'Maggie Thatcher, milk snatcher.' It was the first time the locals and the hippies had been in agreement over anything. *Bloody Education Secretary, who does she think she is? Taking milk out of our kids' mouths!* Rose linked arms with a thin woman with a pinched face and tan stockings round her ankles. 'She spoke to me,' Rose boasted afterwards. 'I couldn't understand everything she said, of course. But it was the feeling that counted. The solidarity of mothers and workers.'

Isolte is always wary of answering probing questions, especially those that come her way at Hadley occasions. She's good at changing the subject. Or lying. So when Anita turns to her and asks abruptly, 'And what is it exactly that your father does, Isolte? I don't believe you've ever told us?' there is no pause. 'My parents both died in a car crash.' Isolte looks at Anita, watches for the slight flush of embarrassment on her cheeks, the nervous swallow. This is a reply that seals off any further discussion. Ben raises his eyebrows but says nothing, spooning trifle into his mouth.

Later, in the car on the way home, he says, 'I know you don't want to have to explain to people what really happened to your mother. It's private. But just for the record, it doesn't make any difference to me what you tell my parents. I don't need their approval to know how I feel about you.'

He turns and glances at her over his Ray-Bans. 'You shouldn't be ashamed of your past, you know. Being illegitimate – all that crap. It doesn't matter any more. You were a love child. So what? It's not a big deal.'

'Listen to you!' Isolte retorts. 'Pretty good at hiding your home counties accent when it suits you, aren't you?'

'That's different,' he shrugs, changing gear, as they slow at a junction, 'my accent's good for business. All those prim fashion editors love a bit of rough.'

'Right.' Isolte looks out of the car window, watching scratchy red-brick streets and mean roundabouts replace the hills of Kent.

'And look at the road, idiot. Not me,' she adds, without conviction. Because in her head she hears Alice's voice asking loudly – and what else do those editors love him for? What else does he do to please them? He was *joking*, she wants to tell the voice. He's being ironic. I know him best. But she feels hollow inside, and there's a slippage of something, and Alice's voice won't shut up.

She slumps lower in the seat, trying not to listen, knowing that the loss of trust is where love trips and falters: the beginning of the end.

*

'You're one of those girls, aren't you?'

Peter is sprawled across her bed, rumpling the antique silk bedspread she found in Portobello Market last weekend. Isolte feels a pinch of irritation. She's regretting her impulse of two weeks ago when she invited him back for coffee. He was one of those shiny advertising types, with creased trouser fronts and the ubiquitous fast car. She thought it would last a couple of dates at the most; but he's called her every day, and he persists in asking questions, making guesses about her personality, trying to work out how she 'ticks'. It makes her shudder, all that forced intimacy; right now, all she wants is to enjoy the luxury of her new flat on her own.

'What do you mean?' She leans against the doorframe, unwilling to get back into bed with him. She'd like him to go.

'You know, the enigmatic type.' He smirks, pleased with his analysis. She stares at his chest, which is strangely smooth and hairless. 'You like to have them on their toes, running around you. But you don't let anyone in, do you?'

She swallows, looks away. It takes more than a barrage of prying questions to earn trust, she thinks. But she doesn't say it, because his words have made her blood leap in her veins, and she's afraid of what her voice will betray.

She gives herself a moment. 'It's a little too late for a therapy session.' Her tone is level and cool as she pulls her dressing gown across her shoulders. 'Actually, talking of late, I have to do some work. An article for tomorrow.' She glances pointedly at the typewriter sitting on a small desk before the window.

'Right.' He stands up slowly, stretching. 'Sure you do, princess. I'll get out of your hair.'

She waits behind the front door, listening to Peter's footsteps on the stairs. She presses her palms against her eyes, hard, bringing sparks of red and green jumping behind her lids. Emptiness washes through her; she is overwhelmed by how lonely she feels. But it's better to be lonely like this, she tells herself – the pure kind, like being on a beach at dusk, seagulls crying above – than the messy loneliness of being inside a dishonest relationship.

She won't see Peter again. The only person she wants to be with now is Viola. But Viola is in her squat in Brixton, in that awful seedy damp room. Isolte has only visited once, and then she'd been introduced to a tall, skinny man wearing a minidress and an earnest boy with a mop of filthy hair who tried to engage her in conversation about the evils of capitalism and hunting.

Isolte asked Viola to move in with her as soon as the contract had been signed on the bright and airy third-floor flat. Her new place is in a Victorian house in Battersea, close to the park, and overlooking a garden square. How could Viola not prefer it to the dingy squat with graffitied walls? 'I've been promoted to fashion editor. I'm earning proper money now,' she'd explained, trying to erase the pride in her voice. When Viola demurred she added quickly, 'You can pay me a bit of rent if it makes you feel better.'

Viola had shaken her head. Her hair, grown back years ago into a shaggy bob, had swung across her face in points. 'I like the squat,' she'd said obstinately. 'Everyone is really friendly. I feel at home there. They're all misfits, I suppose. Like me.'

'You're not a misfit.' Isolte had bitten her lip in angry frustration. Her sister was still playing the victim. It was almost as if Viola delighted in being a failure. They weren't teenagers any more. They were twenty-four years old. That was when you were supposed to be shaping your life, thinking about the future. And here was Viola with her finger on a self-destruct button. Her punk phase might be over, but her anorexia was another kind of statement: a deadly one. At her thinnest it was uncomfortable to look at her – frightening even. She'd dropped out of college and was eking out a living as an artist's model and working for a homeless charity. Whenever Isolte suggested that Viola try going back to studying or think about a real career, she looked blank, as if the suggestion was impossible to understand, let alone act on.

10

Every Thursday evening Mummy went to a woodwork class at the local tech. She would dash about getting ready to leave as we ate our tea. This particular Thursday evening, we were having a picnic on a blanket in the living room: hard-boiled eggs, cheese and toast with Marmite scraped on top. We watched her lean into the mirror on the wall and smudge dark gloss on to her lips, scooping blobs of Frosted Cherry from a pot.

She pulled on a crash helmet. It squashed her face, changing her. A different Mummy looked out through the visor. No longer our pretty mother with Nordic colouring and slender bones. This was a woman with hamster cheeks and mean eyes. This was a woman who'd murdered a baby goat and kept the dried skin on her bedroom floor as a rug.

'Right, I'm off.' She stood in the doorway in her dungarees and blue cheesecloth shirt. 'Don't do anything silly while I'm gone. And do your homework.'

Why did she bother to say that? She never checked to see if we had any, or looked at anything we did. It made her feel better, I think. It was like a lucky sentence. A charm to make things all right. I understood. Isolte and I had lots of secret sayings – words with magic in them. We invented spells. Issy even made up foreign sounds that she said had real meanings. These strange words had powers – could ward off evil. We spoke them aloud to bring us our hearts' desire. Isolte and I wanted to be:

1. invisible as the wind
2. able to fly
3. fast and stealthy as a puma.

That was the list we came up with, sitting on the bedroom floor. We spent ages writing ideas down and crossing them out. We didn't want to be too greedy. I see us there crouched over the scrap of paper, Issy sucking the end of her pen, making our list.

The April evening was gathering a chill, a slight mist rising from the grass. Mummy's Vespa disappeared up the track, straining over potholes, accelerating up the hill. I looked at my sister. The sun would set at about half past seven. We needed to get ready.

The dressing-up box was stuffed with damp clothes. Our fingers searched through Mummy's stale cast-offs: long, flowery maxiskirts, crocheted waistcoats and lace blouses. I slipped off my shirt and vest. Isolte squinted at the bee-sting swellings on my ribcage. We were slow developers. We wanted a bra more than anything. Girls at school had them. When we'd asked Mummy about bras, she'd laughed, cupping her hands over her breasts and giving them a careless squeeze. 'You are funny! Don't you know that women don't have to wear those things any more?'

We pressed our lips together, not wanting to hurt her feelings, but we wished that she would wear one. Her breasts were embarrassing. We were mortified by her nipples poking through her shirts.

I struggled into a long white nightdress. There were several transparent layers, making it soft and floaty. It had a rip in one of the panels and there was an indecipherable dribble on the front. I breathed in the musty smell. I wanted to make the fabric swish and move. Isolte kept catching her foot in the hem of her trailing skirt. She wore a small homemade tutu upside down on her head, which stuck out like a crown made of pointy orange netting.

We walked barefoot to the perimeter of the garden where lawn became wild grasses and brambles. Beyond was a dense wall of pine trunks stretching for miles. The evening was full of wings. Flitting bats, almost invisible, darted above our heads. The swallows were back, skimming the lawn, accurate as fighter pilots. We stood to attention, watching the sun slip behind trees, shadows running like ink across the garden. Tulips shone in the gloom, the daffodils already browning at the edges. Against a thicket of pine trees our silver birch stood like an imperious pale finger. For a moment I was a creature crouched among trees, looking in at the garden. I heard the murmur of the earth turning under my feet, the strata of before and after shifting slowly. And I saw us with our human skin and thin limbs. I could hear the faint pulse of our twin hearts. I blinked, not wanting to understand how the forest dwarfed us.

Issy began the ceremony – raising her arms, stretching up to the sky. We started to moan and sway on our heels, swinging our heads, letting our hair sweep the ground and tangle in our faces. *Forgive Mummy*, I prayed silently. *Keep Tess and Bathsheba safe from Black Shuck*. The tattered tutu came loose, waistband slipping over Issy's eyes. She tore it off impatiently. It lay in the grass like a monstrous butterfly. *And let us have oranges to eat*, I added. *So we don't get scurvy*. Mummy said that we had to make cuts. First there had been no hot chocolate or biscuits. Now there were no oranges.

Isolte began to sing strange guttural words. She called up sounds from inside her. She said the words came from somewhere else – that they were beyond her control. We thought it might be an old language, Welsh perhaps. We saw Druids once. When we lived in the commune in Wales, Mummy took us to Stonehenge. We walked inside the circle of stones. There was a man with antlers on his head. Honour the sun, they said, there is a god in him. I remembered the shout they made, the cry sent up into the sky, as the sun went down.

When Mummy got home she was smiling. 'I'm making a letter-box,' she said, putting her helmet on the chest of drawers. 'I'll put it at the end of the drive when it's finished. You girls can check it every day for letters. That'll be fun, won't it?'

She seemed to have forgotten that we hardly ever got letters. And the ones we did get ended up in the bin unopened. But we nodded, pleased to be included in her plans, caught up in her mood of enthusiasm. She'd hit her thumb with a hammer and it was turning a beautiful plum colour. She sucked it cheerfully. 'I'm getting better at carpentry. Frank says I'm going to be more than competent.' She paused for dramatic effect. 'I'm going to see if I can mend the shed door tomorrow. Frank's lent me some of his own equipment. Look.' She opened her bag so that we could admire the tools she'd crammed inside. I touched the edge of a dull grey thing that Mummy said was a lathe.

It got late, Issy and I sitting at the kitchen table, drawing and listening to the radio. Mummy mixing up pancakes, whisking eggs, milk and flour together absent-mindedly, turning up the sound on the radio when a good song came on. Music made her dance around the table, dipping and swaying, her arms spread wide. Issy and I grimaced at each other when she shook her hips and bottom like a tribal woman. We distrusted her oozing sexuality. She was our mother and we wanted her virginal and chaste.

Dollops of batter hit the hot pan. She let us flip them. 'Use both hands,' she instructed, as we took it in turns, biting our lips in concentration, going cross-eyed watching the airborne tumble of pancake. There was the rich smell of burning butter, the hiss of fat, and the kitchen thick with smoke and music.

At the table she went through her ritual of making a cigarette, rolling it in a fragile slip of paper. I loved to watch her quick fingers, the flick of her tongue licking the edge, the way her eyes narrowed as the match flared. She leaned back in her chair and inhaled. She let us sprinkle huge spoonfuls of sugar over the pancakes. She even gave us the last half-lemon; she'd been saving it in the fridge for so long it was hard as a bone. She smoked and hummed and watched us eat, laughing when we picked up our plates to lick them clean. 'Anyone would think I starved you.'

We staggered up the narrow stairs to bed, stomachs full. Mummy followed, collapsing on our bed with a heavy sigh. She sprawled between us, idly stroking our hair, her fingers loose and dreamy against our heads. 'I think,' she said, biting the end of her thumb carefully, 'that I shall lose this nail. But I'll get a new one. Soft and smooth as a boiled egg.'

'Mummy,' Issy said suddenly, clasping her round her neck, 'I like it better when it's just us. Can it always be like this?'

'Absolutely,' Mummy agreed, yawning. 'Just us three.'

The cat leapt up, bringing the scent of the outside with her: lilac, grass and mouse blood. She twitched her tail, working her claws against the blanket, purring in an ecstasy of approval. We rolled close; Issy's breath was sugar sweet. We'd forgotten to brush our teeth, and our feet, under the covers, were covered in grass stains. Mummy leaned over us, hugging us tight.

'Goodnight, my funny-face girls.' She brushed her lips over mine.

She tasted of Old Holborn and Frosted Cherry. When she kissed Issy, she pretended to give her a proper film star kiss, gluing her lips on tightly, twisting her head from side to side, making 'mmmmm' noises. Issy almost choked she was laughing so much, writhing under the covers.

'Me too,' I begged, impatient for my turn.

*

I can't remember when anyone last kissed me. I can't imagine anyone kissing me again. Except him. Sometimes I let myself imagine that old dream. I run my finger over my lips. They are dry, chapped. The action of my fingers has roused a discovery, though – the felt sensation of skin on skin flickers through my body. The connection between nerve endings is still there. The pleasure of the senses makes a queasy tugging in my groin. I trace the shape of my mouth over and over, the breath on my fingers warm and damp, lingering over the feeling, eyes closed to con-centrate, shutting out the ward.

When I open them the old woman from the bed opposite is standing over me. I stare up at her, stupid with shock, my body recoiling, clenching tight.

She's taller than I'd realised. Big-boned, straight-backed in her nightie. She's dragging a drip behind her. The needle sticks out of her ropy arm. 'I'm Justine Mortimer.'

I blink. 'Viola.'

She repeats my name, rolling the sound around her mouth thoughtfully.

She has an impossible voice, the kind that is preserved in aspic in the bowels of the BBC. She suddenly shuts her eyes and sways towards the metal stand holding her drip. I hold my breath, thinking that she's going to fall and the stand will come crashing down too, the bag splitting and spilling its contents all over the floor. But she recovers.

'Forgive me. I'm still a little weak.' She shakes her head. 'I'm waiting for my son to visit me. He's bringing his children with him ... five grandchildren.'

She's grey-skinned, shaky on her feet. I wish she would go back to bed. She coughs, a deep rattle of a cough. She puts a hand out and holds my bedside table to steady herself. 'The oldest is thirteen, Pandora, such a clever girl ... and the youngest just a baby.' She smiles. 'A round-faced boy who reminds me of Alec, my late husband.' She rubs her nose, her face breaking and crinkling. 'Do you know, I've forgotten the little one's name ... ' Her face contorts and she coughs again. 'I'm a stupid old woman.'

I look around anxiously. Where are the nurses when you need them?

She shuffles away, muttering, traversing the gap between our beds slowly, the wheels of the drip squeaking and rolling behind her. 'I'll remember it,' she promises grimly. 'Harry? No.' She's tapping her head.

Her bare feet are blue-veined, misshapen by bunions. The staff won't be pleased. They insist on patients wearing slippers. A nurse is already holding her arm, remonstrating gently with her, pointing at her feet. The nurse turns to look at me. She frowns, as if it's my fault.

Justine, tucked back into bed, calls to me brightly, 'I have photographs. Lots of them. I'll show you later.'

*

'Goodness me, I haven't looked at this photo for a long time,' Hettie says. 'Of course, people often didn't realise that we were sisters. Your mother was ten years younger than me. I must be about fourteen here.'

The same age as me, I think. She holds the framed photograph that I've found on the oak dresser ('Seventeenth century,' Hettie told us. 'Don't put cups on it.'). Hettie turns the picture towards the light and examines the image of herself pinned in time; her teenage face slightly blurred by her turning or speaking as the shutter was pressed. A young, blonde child stands in front of her much older, darker sister. Both are dressed in formal coats and berets. The girls hold monkeys. One of the creatures squats on Rose's arm, long tail swinging down, and she's laughing into the camera, delighted. The monkey looks at her quizzically, mouth open, as if it's about to ask a question.

'We must have been at a fair. I don't remember.' Hettie takes her glasses off and gives the photo back to me. 'We didn't spend much time together. I was at boarding school while she was little, and when she was packed off to school I'd already made the ghastly mistake of getting married.'

I make myself comfortable in the hollows and dips of the old sofa. Even at midday the room is gloomy with shadows, weighed down with heavy antiques and thickly woven tapestries; the grandfather clock in the corner ticks as loudly as a metronome.

It is a place that invites confidences. One of the spaniels jumps up and curls itself against my leg. Hettie is in a talking mood. All I have to do is open an inviting silence.

'Mother died while Rose was still at school.' Hettie sits on the arm of the sofa, pushes at the sleeves of her bobbled cardigan with stubby fingers. 'After that, Rose ran away a couple of times. Always brought back in disgrace for Daddy's interminable lectures.'

'So she was a bit of a rebel then?' I ask, fiddling with a strand of my blue hair.

'Well, she certainly didn't like institutions or rules.' Hettie smiles to herself as if remembering a private joke. Looks at me, and nods. 'She wasn't exactly academic, dear Rose. But she had plenty of ideas about how the world should work and what was wrong with it.' Hettie crosses her legs, adjusting her skirt. 'After she left school she started seeing this writer chap – I forget his name. Very Beat Generation with his dark-rimmed glasses and narrow trousers. Daddy took an instant dislike.' She clears her throat. 'Rose went off to America with him. Sent me postcards. Told me she was going to be an actress. I thought I'd see her up in lights.' Hettie shakes her head. 'She was so pretty.'

'But then what happened?'

The dog sits up and scratches earnestly, ears back and eyes closed.

'I hope that creature doesn't have fleas ...' Hettie gives her large bosoms an absent-minded pat and leans forward to inspect the dog's ears.

'Hettie?' Isolte calls in her London voice. 'I did tell you, didn't I? I'm going to a party tonight. That OK with you?'

She comes clattering down the stairs in red platform shoes,

bringing all her demands and bright plans for the evening; she stands at the other side of the room, dressed in a glittery skirt that swishes around her knees, and the distance between us is so much greater than a stretch of worn carpet. Her happiness makes me feel ashamed. Why can't I follow her example? Why can't I 'make the most of it', as she puts it?

Holding the heavy frame, I stare at the child in the photo: my mother, preserved in black and white. She stares back. She is radiant, her nose wrinkling above that wide smile. Issy seems to look out at me through my mother's features, sharing the joke. But I am not there. I can't find a reflection of myself in my mother, or my sister any more. Not even in my aunt. I hunch up on the sofa, lost in shadows, my stomach clenched, cold and empty. I don't know who I am.

11

'Can you spare a moment?'

Sam calls Isolte, beckoning from the other side of the room, cigarette in hand. She leads the way to the meeting room – the one place that's separated from the rest of the open-plan office – and Isolte follows, feeling irritated, thinking of the list of things she has to get through.

Sam has chosen a chair that's larger and higher than the low, squashy one she's left for Isolte to occupy. Isolte tries to sink into it gracefully, but her knees are up by her chin and she has no idea how she's going to get out again. Sam crosses her legs and clasps her hands together as if about to pray. Her fingernails, Isolte notices, are short and masculine, her fingers weighed down with chunky silver rings. The cigarette burns in the ashtray, smoke rising in an acrid curl.

'As you know,' she tells Isolte, 'I have a new vision for the magazine and change is essential. I've been trusted with the job of taking this magazine on to the next level.' She frowns. 'We've really got to get it noticed, push up the readership, pull in new advertisers. It's a big task and, quite frankly, sacrifices will have to be made.' She leans back and sighs. 'What I'm saying is, it's time for you to move on, Isolte. You should take a holiday, move into the next phase of your career.'

The next phase of her career? It takes a few moments for her to work it out. 'You're firing me?'

'No,' Sam gives her a pasted-on grin, 'of course not. We're offering you redundancy. There'll be a payment. Think of it as a chance for better things.'

Isolte looks at the cup of coffee in front of her. The liquid is gathering a skin on top, puckered and pale as scum.

'What if I don't want to take that chance?'

'I think you'll find that option isn't available.'

How clever Sam is at saying something with words that mean nothing. Isolte is almost impressed. She stands up and finds that she is defenceless. Words rise from somewhere inside her numb brain, forming sentences of protest and self-pity. Isolte opens and closes her mouth soundlessly. It can't be right, she thinks. They can't make her redundant if they're going to replace her. Can they? She swallows and stands up straighter, scrabbles around for some dignity. 'I'll have to speak to my solicitor, of course.'

'Of course,' Sam agrees sweetly.

Isolte wonders if she's in shock. She feels as though she's floating. The magazine has been more than her place of work – it's been her identity, her home. She's been here for five years. Her fingers move automatically, flying over her desk, gathering a green bottle of scent labelled Poison, her leather Filofax and her work address book. She picks up an inscrutable marble sphinx small enough to sit on her palm, brought back from a shoot in Egypt. What else really belongs to her? What else does she want? She looks at the pictures and cards pinned to the noticeboard – all those hopeful models and jaunty advertising strategies – and takes down the photograph of the horse, slipping it into her bag.

Lucy is sitting at her desk. She is crying.

'It'll be OK,' Isolte says brightly. 'It'll all be all right, Lucy. I'll be fine. And you've still got your job. Sam won't get rid of you.'

She pulls on her jacket, slings her bag over her shoulder, looks round just one more time and walks out, head held high. There is a quiet, shocked whispering coming from the subs' desk. Isolte feels the news travelling through the room behind her like a bush fire: the bright consuming flames of gossip.

She'd been so naive. She hadn't suspected a thing. Stevie had hinted at something like this. But still she hadn't suspected. Not when Sam called her into the meeting room, or when she offered her a coffee, not even when she began her little speech. So much for loyalty, Isolte thinks. She had been only a little cog after all.

The daylight of the street is shockingly bright. She takes big gulps of dirty air. She is disorientated. Looking right and left, she has no idea which direction to take. A siren starts up in the fire station opposite. A big red truck cruises out of the double doors and on to the street, heading for Piccadilly Circus with lights blazing and the siren shrieking.

There's a homeless girl huddled on cardboard against the wall of a theatre; she gazes at the firetruck listlessly. Isolte walks over to her and riffles through her purse for change. The girl looks up hopefully and Isolte stares into her face: she guesses that the girl's in her teens; she has bruises under her eyes and puffy skin, her matted hair sticks to her small skull like clumps of weed. Isolte's fingers fumble inside her purse; she ignores the coins, digs out a five-pound note.

The girl looks surprised. She folds the note inside her hand, conceals it within her old coat with furtive speed. 'Fanks,' she murmurs. Her eyes are the palest blue, Isolte notices, like fragments of ice.

They don't have strict visiting hours at the hospital. The nurse at the front desk tells her that she can go through. There is a smell of overcooked vegetables. Viola is propped up on her pillows with a book in her hands that she's not reading. When she sees Isolte she raises her eyebrows. 'This is a surprise,' she says. 'Why aren't you at work?'

'Long story. I'll tell you later.' Isolte sits next to the bed and nods at the tray with a glass on the side table. 'Have you had lunch?'

'I've had some of my drink,' Viola's voice becomes guarded, 'the stuff that goes down my tube. They wanted me to try taking it by mouth.'

'Was it OK?' Isolte crosses her legs, sits back in the chair. Mustn't talk about food any more. She always says the wrong thing.

'Issy, this is a concoction of fat and liquid with some vitamins mixed in.' Viola gives a shadow of a smile. 'What do you think?'

'Point taken.' She reaches across. 'I'm parched. Can I steal some of your water?'

Viola's gaze is unwavering. 'What's wrong?'

Isolte takes a long sip of tepid water and frowns. 'What do you mean?'

'Come on,' Viola moves painfully on the bed, shifting to one side, 'something is going on.'

'I've been sacked.' It's a relief to say it. 'Well, they're calling it redundancy. But they'll replace me with another version of myself. Someone younger, more to the new editor's liking. She'll already have someone picked out.'

'Can they do that?'

'Seems they have.'

'What will you do?'

'I don't know,' Isolte shrugs, 'I really have no idea. Get another job, I suppose.'

'Why don't you go away – do something different? You haven't been happy for ages.'

Isolte is startled. She opens her mouth to protest. Up until today, she's had a great job; she owns her own flat and has a handsome, successful boyfriend. Why wouldn't she be happy?

'But I am, I have been—' she begins to argue.

Viola shakes her head dismissively. 'Not properly happy. You know you haven't. Neither of us has, have we? Not for a long time.'

Isolte sets her mouth in a stubborn line. But Viola's words have burrowed through the surface of things, stirring up an old darkness. Isolte looks at the floor and frowns. 'Well, I don't know . . .' she says, 'perhaps not.'

Viola makes an effort to sit up straighter, and Isolte leans across to help, holding her frail shoulders, plumping the pillow behind her.

'I think in a way it's positive – this, this redundancy. That job wasn't good for you. It made you, I don't know, hard or something.' Viola looks at her earnestly. 'Think of this as an opportunity.'

'Funny,' Isolte says bleakly. 'That was what my editor – ex-editor – said.'

'I just mean maybe you can be yourself again, Issy.'

A small plump nurse arrives at the bedside and looks inside the cup on the tray. Seeing that some of the liquid has gone, she says briskly, 'Good girl,' and takes Viola's wrist in her doughy hand. 'Time for you to have a rest. I'm just going to take your pulse and blood pressure. Maybe your sister can come back later?'

The nurse, placid and smooth-faced as a doll, gives Isolte a pointed stare. Viola does look tired. Her eyes ringed with purple, lips bloodless and cracked. The tube is still in place, like a transparent vein weaving across the outside of her skin.

From the street there is the yelp of an ambulance siren, muffled by the closed window. Isolte remembers the homeless girl slumped on her cardboard. She has a need to hold Viola – to hug her tightly and press her own face against the face of her twin, to spread her warmth into the cold blue lake of Viola's body. She touches the back of Viola's hand. The skin is thin as paper. The knuckles pressing through are too big. She stands up. 'See you tomorrow.'

Viola nods, her head heavy on the stalk of her neck. She lies back, exhausted. The nurse is already holding Viola's arm, wrapping it in black, her fingers busy with a small pump.

At the flat she wanders around empty rooms, switching on all the lights. She's hardly ever at home – not on her own, never during the day. When she first moved, she was excited, spending every weekend at markets and rooting through thrift shops to find interesting bits of furniture and pictures. She spends most of her time at Ben's now. Her place smells unlived-in. An open book pressed face down on the sofa has been in the same position for days. It reminds her of a dead bird, the pages splayed out like limp wings.

The cactus plant is rotting; brown-fleshed, it leans to one side drunkenly. Isolte shivers. She wonders if she's catching flu. The muscles in her shoulders ache.

She has a hot shower, using generous handfuls of body wash, filling the space with steam and Moroccan Rose. She stays under the jet of water until it begins to go cold. She scrubs every inch of her skin and washes her hair. Wrapped in a towel, she phones Ben and asks him to come over to her place on his way back from work. She makes herself some pasta and forces herself to eat a little.

The thought of explaining it again to Ben makes her feel exhausted. She doesn't want to think about the redundancy. She doesn't want to think about anything. What Viola said in the hospital has stayed with her. She never considered whether she was happy or not. It had been enough that her days were full. She felt the comfort of belonging to a particular world and the relief of being good at her job. She tried to be busy, to be necessary. But she didn't have the ache of ambition in her. Otherwise she would have jumped ship before, taken a step up into a more prestigious magazine. This job suited her perfectly. Had shaped her life. Now she has no idea what to do. A void is opening – and she's stepping into it: a calendar of empty days.

She can't tell Ben. Not just yet. She feels the failure of it dismantling her, exposing her. The job had been an identity. And that identity had been a shield. She's not sure who she is without it. She feels humiliation smeared across her like something embarrassing. She doesn't want him to see her like that.

She needs Ben to make her forget. Sex is something that demands complete focus. She is always hungry for him. He's completely different from the kind of men she normally finds attractive. The maleness of him is irresistible – there's something almost vulgar about his broad hands with rope-like veins over the back of them. The thickness of his skin makes her want to bite it. One day, she thinks, perhaps it will burn out, this desire they have for each other, and then she'll be released. She'll be safe from needing him.

Isolte opens the door to him. He puts his bags on the floor, shrugs off his leather jacket. His chin is scratchy with stubble; his eyes close as he leans in for a kiss. She knocks her foot against the bags in her hurry. A camera edge bruises her shin, as she stumbles awkwardly into his arms.

12

The boys were at a different school from us. They were in the second year at the comprehensive in town: a sprawl of concrete blocks and Portakabins arranged beside a windswept playing field. All of it fenced around with wire. Luckily for us they were experts at bunking off, so we saw them nearly every day. Sometimes they turned up at our back door with black eyes or split lips. We never mentioned their injuries – the damage was a part of them, like their red hair. The bruises their father inflicted on them blended with their own, the boys' hot-headed scrapping disguising his abuse from anyone who might have cared. Our hair-pulling and squabbling seemed tame in comparison – the worst we'd done to each other had been accidental; Issy caught my eyeball with her fingernail, and a flame seared across the wet flesh.

The doctor said I had a scratched cornea. He gave me an eye patch to wear. It made me look rakish and dangerous, like a pirate. I had constant sight of the glowing ridge of my nose, and the world seemed lop-sided. My eye healed quickly so I didn't have to wear the patch for more than a couple of days. I was loath to give it up, even though I'd been teased for it at school. The class joker, Henry Green, his face split by a leering grin, had stuck out his foot to trip me up: 'Not much of a treasure chest on you, is there?'

Mummy's experiment in home-schooling while we lived in Wales meant us lagging behind in all things academic. The result was that we were put down a year and had to go to the village primary, a squat Victorian building next to the church. The day after the patch came off, we were back at school chanting times tables and writing out pointless spelling lists. Girls in white socks with their hair in bunches ignored us. 'Hoist the Jolly Roger!' the boys sniggered, saluting both of us, not knowing which one had worn the patch.

We played on our own at break, escaping through the hedge into the out-of-bounds churchyard, loitering among the listing, mottled gravestones marooned in the long grass. 'Twinnies,' they called us. 'Dirty hippies.' 'Home-schooled.' 'Mental.' We were sick of being outsiders, the others whispering about us behind their hands, scrutinising our straggly hair and weird shoes, our homemade dresses. Mummy never got seams straight. She favoured the easiest patterns – no gathers, no sleeves, no collars – making everything out of utilitarian cotton gingham or, worse, she cut down her own clothes and then we got stuck with printed velvet and embroidered cheesecloth. Mummy liked us in navy knee socks, and best with bare legs. All the other girls had full gathered skirts with ribbons tied in bows at their waists. They wore ankle socks with lace trimming.

John and Michael must have had a sudden passion for school, or else they were ill, because we hadn't seen them for a whole week. They hadn't even come over in the evenings. They'd missed seeing the eye patch – I was disappointed. I'd hoped to impress them with my jaunty Blackbeard look and the state of my gory iris. We were hungry for their company, Issy and I. We had a plan for a den in the forest, a longing to trespass on the Malletts' farm. We decided not to go home when school ended but walk to their house instead.

'Maybe we'll have chip sandwiches again?' Issy wondered hopefully.

It was a long walk along a narrow, winding road. Thick mud lay crusted on the outer rim of the tarmac. On either side of us the grass verges rose at steep angles, sloping up to meet scrubby hawthorn hedges. It was like being enclosed in a maze. Nettles sprouted tall, tangling with cow parsley, throwing thin green stalks towards the sky. Every time a tractor or a car came past we had to scramble on to the verge, hopping and teetering to avoid the vicious nettles. We passed a couple of dead rabbits – heads crushed flat as cardboard cutouts. A rook lay torn to shreds at the crossroads, black wing feathers scattered in the dust, the fragile bones tossed like skittles in the dirt. I bent down and put one in my pocket. A slender fluted thing, smooth against my thumb. Farm dogs barked at us as we passed gates. When we saw the familiar row of cottages we stepped up our pace, thinking of cups of sweet tea and the flicker and blare of the television.

But at the drunken gate fallen off its hinges, we slowed down, dragging our feet, suddenly aware of our lack of invitation. The cottage looked deserted. Smeary windows held the smudged reflection of clouds and sky.

'Let's go round the back,' Issy suggested, thinking, as I was, of the boys' plump, smiling mother. We imagined that she would always be in her kitchen. She'd welcomed us warmly, told us to call her Linda.

The kitchen door stood open, but as we put our heads round, we saw that the room was empty. No Linda with her chipped nail varnish, breathing out cigarette smoke. No Judy snapping gum between her teeth. We entered cautiously. The small room was cluttered. Fishing rods against the walls, boots piled up on the mat. It smelt faintly of hot oil and burnt toast, as if someone had only just finished a meal. We lingered nervously by the table. Doubt twisted in my stomach, and when Issy made a grab for my arm, I let out a tight yelp. 'Don't move,' she hissed. She inclined her head. 'Look!'

I glanced down and stiffened. A long creature with a pointed face had slunk into the room, nose quivering, tail flicking from side to side. When it heard or smelt us it reared up on its back legs and squatted there, glittering red eyes regarding us intently. It opened its mouth, showing a row of sharp little teeth.

'What is it?' Issy whispered.

'Don't know. Keep still.' I'd noticed the creature's curved claws.

There was the sound of footsteps, a shout from somewhere above us and the thunder of feet on the stairs. John crashed into the room. The creature fled, scrabbling across the kitchen floor, a streak of muscle rippling under white fur.

'Shut the door!' John yelled.

But it was too late. The animal had shot across the yard and under the fence, swallowed by the long grass behind.

'Shit!' John smacked his forehead, and slammed his other hand down hard on the table. 'Shit! Shit!'

'What was it?'

'Dad's ferret. I left the latch off,' he frowned, 'they're gone. All of 'em. Bollocking hell.'

A teenager with a face full of acne wandered in. He was

wearing blue overalls tucked into enormous wellingtons. It was Ed, the twins' older brother.

'What yer shou'in about, boi?'

'Ferrets're gone.'

Ed winced and shook his head. 'Better clear off – he'll be back soon.'

'Where's your mum?' Isolte asked nobody in particular, gripping the back of a chair.

'Cleaning job,' Ed answered shortly. He was at the sink, turning the tap on with his elbow, sticking his hands under the gush of water.

Michael came into the room. He went straight up to his twin and clipped him around the ear. 'Dozy dollup!' He stared furiously. 'Now we'll have t' leg it. He's gonna kill us this time.'

John hardly flinched, although I saw his ear smart purple. 'What about them?' He jerked his head at us.

'They can ride behind.' Michael pulled at my sleeve. 'You comin'?'

They took their bikes, sprawled in the dust in the garden, leading them on to the side of the road as if they were horses. Two beaten-up choppers. We perched on the bike seats. They stood up in front. I was on John's chopper. The bike swung from side to side as he pressed his weight down on each pedal in turn. I didn't like to put my arms around his waist. But if I took my hands away I wobbled and the bike lurched, making John swear, his knuckles blanching on the handlebars. So I kept my fingers there against the curve of his ribs, feeling his boy-heat through the worn-smooth acrylic sweater, the twist of his back muscles jumping beneath my touch.

We went quickly past the farm, past the church with our

school behind, and the turning into the village. After bumping along the sea wall we came to a Martello tower, a huge circular fortress of sombre stone, built as a lookout post in the Napoleonic wars. It stood, empty and abandoned, a hulking silhouette against the flat landscape.

The boys dragged the bikes under bushes, concealing them inside the scratchy depths, throwing grass and burdock leaves over the spokes.

'We're going to let yer in on our secret,' John told me, his forehead glistening. 'Swear on yer life you'll never tell.'

I looked into his hot face. His eyes were a startling blue. I nodded. The tang of him was in my nostrils: salty, yeasty, and strangely pleasant.

The tower seemed impenetrable. There were no doors. The glassless windows were high up in the blank stone face. Rooks flapped in and out, wings spread dark against the sky. In the side facing away from the sea, about ten foot above ground level, with no apparent way to reach it, was a battered wooden door. Issy and I stood below in the thistles, perplexed, shading our eyes as we watched the birds flying off. Behind us was a stream cut deep into the ground, and we could smell the reedy, black water drifting past. Michael placed his hands against the wall, leaning his cheek against the rough surface as if he was listening to something. He closed his eyes and his fingers felt above his head for handholds in the crumbling mortar. Then with a low grunt, he heaved himself away from the ground. He moved slowly, inching from one shallow toehold and fingerhold to another. I watched anxiously. It seemed impossible that he could scale the wall. But soon he was pushing the door open and wriggling on to the stone lintel. I looked up to see his hand opening like a star, and a snake came slithering towards us. A rope dangled by my nose, frayed ends swinging.

John gave me a small push. 'Go on then.'

My knees sagged. But the others were watching. I had no choice, or I'd always be teased about it. Then John was behind me, stooping to make his linked hands a step. I felt his arm on my leg, steadying me as I hauled myself up, hand over hand on the rope, feet scrabbling against the stone, palms on fire. And I was kneeling in the grit of the opening, smelling something acrid over the stink of damp. The rope was tied to a rusty metal plank set at the foot of the door. Michael gave my shoulder a brisk pat, while he reached past me to catch my sister's hand in his.

We'd come in on the second level, clambering into the echoing, vaulted space that used to be the soldiers' quarters. The air was a slow mass, thickened with dust motes that shimmered inside shafts of light coming from the windows. My limbs twitched with tired muscles. I followed the others, not wanting to be left behind, edging carefully over rotten floorboards, jagged gaps revealing a long drop into blackness. The floor was covered with scattergun splotches of white, green and grey. Seagull shit. Rook shit. This was what I'd smelt; the whole place reeked of it. Hundreds of small feathers glowed at our feet. Issy had begun to sing tunelessly, so I knew that she was scared too. We followed Michael and John up the narrow stone staircase set against the curved wall, stepping over a straggly nest with three blue eggs in it.

Salty wind blew in our faces as we stepped on to the roof. We opened our mouths to the relief of it. The stone floor, cracked around sprouting weeds, had a high surrounding wall. The boys beckoned and we climbed up. The ground fell away far below, and we could see for miles across the fields and marshes to the church tower behind trees. I could see someone walking along the edge of the trees, a stick figure cut out of black.

'Wow!' Issy forgot to be cool; she was grinning and staring at the view, two dots of red flaming on her cheeks.

Three white swans stood in the middle of the field, one of them spreading its wings. On the other side was the sea wall, with the beach stretching down to the sea: a brown weight of water, darkening under cloud shadows. The waves shone where they caught the gleam of the dying sun. My stomach turned at the steepness of the drop, but I felt a longing to stretch out and embrace the vaulted sweep of sky.

'This is our place,' John said, leaning over at a dangerous angle. 'No one ever comes. Nobody can get us here. We fixed the rope up. It's the only way in.'

'They had the cannons here,' Michael patted the solid wall, 'when it was a fortress. Two of them.'

He put a pretend gun to his face, and closing one eye as if taking aim, he made shooting noises. 'Take that, bastard Froggies.'

There was one ship on the horizon, small as a Dinky car inside the curl of my fist. Gulls wheeled and dived over our heads. John brought up armfuls of driftwood from their supply below and Michael squatted to strike a match. The wood was dry and it caught immediately. We sat around blue flames, looking into the disintegrating branches, watching them turn from molten gold to ash white. Sometimes an ember would leap out and land on our feet. But the fire was greedy, and there wasn't any more wood. It died, falling in on itself, blackened skeleton twigs curling and col-lapsing. I shivered, realising how cold it had got. Issy bit her lip, looking regretfully into the grey sky. 'Suppose we'd better go.'

Michael and John let us down by the rope. When we stood at

the foot of the tower staring up we could see only parts of their faces, distant and disembodied, suddenly impossible to tell which one was which.

It took hours to walk home. Issy got a blister. She sat on the ground and rolled down her sock to reveal a raw, weeping patch on her heel. We tried padding out her shoe with dock leaves and she hobbled beside me, her face grim. It grew darker, until we were fumbling through moonlight, so that we stumbled over pot-holes and caught our feet on stones. When we got to the road we had to throw ourselves on to the verge to avoid oncoming cars, no longer caring about nettle stings, squinting against the glare of headlights. Once we heard some loud male voices jeering at us as their car accelerated away.

When we reached the forest track we cheered up, thinking of our supper. 'Do you think they stay there often?' Isolte mused. 'I mean, they don't have anything to sleep in or eat or anything.'

I thought of the twins, huddled shivering in the dark, the flap of rook and seagull wings around them. I imagined the wash of the sea and sigh of the wind. They must have been very scared of going home. But I don't remember talking about it. It seemed disloyal somehow, to admit that the boys were frightened.

It was a relief to see our cottage. Lights on in the window. It looked tiny, like an illustration from a fairy tale. Shadowy trees almost engulfed it. Our mother was waiting. We knew at once that she'd been drinking. She staggered getting up, her hand slipping off the edge of the table. We stood open-mouthed as she swung her arm back and struck. It was me she slapped. I felt the imprint of each finger. A roaring went off in my head, my ear ringing. I let out a noise halfway between a gasp and a grunt, and Issy took hold of my arm.

'Where the hell have you been?' Mummy's voice sounded strangled. Her breath stank. 'Have you any idea—'

She let out a sob and turned away, trying to light a cigarette, but her hand was shaking too much. She dropped the match and pressed her hand over her mouth as if she was going to be sick. Unwashed, ratty hair fell forward across her eyes. She shook her head from side to side. She kept shaking it.

'Sorry. We got lost,' Issy whispered, slipping her hand down to find mine. 'Sorry.'

Fingers squeezing fingers.

We went to bed without any supper. The kitchen door shut with a bang behind us.

Issy looked at me. 'You've got marks on you.' She came close, touching me cautiously. I smelt her – briny air, bonfire smoke and faint traces of the dank tower – could see the freckles on her skin, the individual speckles of brown. 'Does it hurt?'

I shook my head.

I didn't want to think about it. Mummy had never hit us before. I wanted to pretend it hadn't happened. But I kept seeing her face. It was as if she'd unravelled before us, losing herself in messy threads, becoming naked and strange. I thought about the boys instead.

We'd only seen their father a couple of times. He was a long-distance lorry driver. Linda urged us home when she heard the lorry. She'd suddenly cock her head, listening, eyes glassy and small. 'Best go now, girls,' she'd say, pushing us towards the door. We'd break into a run as we heard the hiss of brakes behind us, feeling the heavy grumble of wheels under our feet. We were allowed to be there when he was at home if he'd gone to bed; then we all had to be quiet. Even the TV was turned down. But

105

once I'd walked into the living room and he'd been sprawled on the sofa, a beer in his hand. I'd jerked to a halt, holding my breath. He was a giant of a man, with red cheeks and a startling red beard. He'd looked at me sideways as if I was a spider crawling out of a crack. 'What you lookin' at?' he'd snarled, his fingers curling into a blunt fist.

I touched my cheek tentatively. I thought of the boys' bruises. I shared this with them. Not Issy. Only me. The marks on my skin distinguished me. I felt as if I'd stumbled into a secret club: an honourable place full of dignified, silent sufferance. I thought about Jane Eyre the child, and the young Heathcliff, both beaten and abused.

'I suppose they'll still get a thrashing.' I pulled my nightdress over my head. 'I mean, they'll have to go home in the morning.'

Issy shrugged. 'Maybe their dad is off in the lorry tomorrow.'

My right cheek and ear continued to sting. I felt as if Mummy's fingers remained there, touching me. She would be sorry now. I imagined her apologetic, begging my forgiveness. I lay awake beside my sister listening to the quiet stirring of Issy's breath, the catch of saliva in her throat, the exhalations of her dreams. Sometimes I wondered if we inhabited the same ones. It seemed impossible that we should wander separate worlds while we lay next to each other. I thought we must meet up somewhere in between – in sleep space; I pictured us flying towards our dream landscapes, waving at each other. But we lay on opposite sides of wakefulness that night and loneliness hollowed me out. I thought of prodding her awake. I put my hand on her arm, feeling it thin and finely fleshed. I didn't shake her. I knew she'd be annoyed.

I headed for the light of the kitchen, the winding stairs creaking, armed with the old excuse of wanting a drink of water. My hands were raw from the rope. I held them away from the brush of my nightdress. I was ready to retreat if Mummy looked like she wanted to give me another slap. My bare feet made no sound as I padded cautiously into the room.

She was hunched over the table, empty glass by her hand. She'd piled up coppers and silver coins in three small stacks. There was an open exercise book and an abandoned pencil. I saw angry scrawls across the page. Had she been doing maths exercises? She was crying quietly. When she saw me she sat up quickly, wiping at her eyes, and reached out to pull me close. Her face next to mine was a crumpled, blotched mask. I suffered her embrace, locked stiffly in her arms, wine breath in my hair.

'I'm sorry, Viola. I'm sorry.' She hugged me even tighter, her voice trembling, her chest shuddering. 'I don't know what to do, you see.'

And suddenly I was crying too, my arms tight around her neck, squashing my cheek against her nose, her mouth against my ear.

*

There are muffled sobs coming through brick and plaster, through the floral paper on my bedroom wall. My sister, who has slept with me since I can remember, limbs entwined with mine, is crying in her own bed on the other side of a wall.

'Here you are, girls.' Hettie had thrown open two doors. 'You can decide between you who gets what room.'

I'll always remember the look on Issy's face. My mouth had fallen open. We'd never been parted; never had separate beds, let alone rooms. But how could we tell her that? Hettie was the only safe thing in the world, the only link left to Mummy. We wanted to please her.

My feet steal on to the carpet. The curtains are slightly open and a strange orange light seeps in. In London the night sky is never properly dark; it is stained by streetlamps. You can't see the stars.

'Issy?' I whisper, tiptoeing into the gloom of her room. We find each other in the darkness, under cool sheets that smell like lavender and old ladies. She rubs at her wet face.

'I keep thinking I'll wake up and be in the cottage,' and her voice breaks, 'I keep thinking that Mummy is downstairs.'

We curl up together, hip against hip in the hollow of the bed. Outside there are strange noises: cars changing gear, a sudden blast of voices, the gabble of strangers and their slurred laughter. I hear a bottle smash and my heart kicks in my chest. The city never sleeps; even if I wake in the early morning hours, I can still hear the distant hum and mutter of machines and voices and sirens.

We are going to start at a new school in a couple of weeks. We will go into a class with other thirteen-year-olds, and not be kept down a year any more. We'll have to wear a uniform and travel there by red double-decker bus. I feel sick at the thought of it. Hettie says that it will be good for us to make new friends. Michael and John are the only friends I've ever had; the only friends I want. But Issy won't talk about them, she grimaces when I mention their names. At night, alone in my bedroom, I compose different versions of what I could say to John in a letter. But nothing seems right. Nothing seems possible.

Issy has fallen asleep, her breathing full of uneasy sighs and mutters. I press my nose into the looping strands of her hair, thinking that I can still smell the sea and pine mixed in with her own particular scent.

London stinks of bodies and petrol fumes, chemicals and rot.

When Hettie took us to Harrods to get shoes, I thought my lungs would burst. It's hard to breathe the gritty air. My neck is grimy every night and my hair feels dirty. I've noticed wild things; but they have to be secret and cunning. Foxes slip through the shadows of parked cars at night, rats scuttle between bins. Weeds cling to railings and poke through the pavements near Hettie's house. People stared when I knelt to feel the small, brave leaves.

Issy liked Harrods, she wanted to visit all the departments and ride up and down in the lift with the elevator boy wearing his green uniform. 'When I'm older I'll buy everything here,' she said, taking in the sweep of gleaming counters and laden shelves with shining eyes.

Tomorrow we'll have breakfast in Hettie's basement kitchen. Instead of porridge and golden syrup and Mummy singing to the radio, there will be cornflakes with white sugar and triangles of toast. Hettie sits at the head of the table drinking tea out of a cup with a saucer and offers us marmalade scooped into a silver pot. She has a special knife for butter. She looks over her glasses and talks to us in the voice that adults use when they're not used to talking to children. Hettie is trying so hard to be nice that sometimes it makes my tears start up, hot and blurry, and my throat tightens. She doesn't look anything like Mummy; she's short and square and much older. But yesterday I noticed that her eyes were the exact pale blue of Mummy's, and when she smiles, she has the same dimples.

13

The party is in a photographer's studio, in an old warehouse in Islington. Guests are carted up to the top floor in an ancient goods lift. The metal door shuts behind them with a crash. Isolte puts her hand up, tangling fingers through her hair. She had a perm a couple of months ago, and she still can't get used to not brushing it. As they are taken slowly, falteringly, upwards, they can hear music and raucous voices getting closer. The lift jolts and lurches to a stop. Ben heaves the door open.

The couple that came up in the lift with them are Japanese, silent and smiling in flowing Comme des Garçons robes. They follow behind.

Standing on the brink of the party, Isolte feels slightly sick. She has no idea if anybody knows about her leaving the magazine. Stupidly, she still hasn't told Ben. It's been two days now. A kind of obstinate refusal fills her every time she opens her mouth. She's hanging on to who she was. But she's not that girl any more, that busy fashion editor wearing the right clothes with a diary full of appointments. She's frightened that Ben won't want the new, nothing person she's become.

The place is packed. Ben struggles ahead, intent on finding drinks. Isolte follows in his path. There are shouts of greeting and pats on his shoulder as he passes. With an abrupt slither her feet go from under her, sliding through a puddle of liquid. She flails for a moment, gasping, thinking she's going down, but there's a steadying hand on her elbow. It remains, grasping her firmly, holding her up. Boy George smiles down from his great height, spiky bleached quiff quivering under a red baseball cap.

'Oops-a-daisy,' he says. She glances at the mass of badges clustering over the lapels of his jacket. A jumble of letters and colours. She nods her thanks, her hand pulling at her top, smoothing it down.

'Darlings!' Their host, Jonathan, wears a yellow shirt and a distracted smile. He gestures towards a table loaded with alcohol. 'Help yourself. Supposed to be some people doing the pouring, but fuck me if I know where they are.'

Ben is already engrossed in a conversation with a tall black girl with a shaved head. He leans forward with a laugh and puts his hand on her arm, next to three bands of silver enclosing her biceps. Isolte admires the sheen on the girl's skin, finds herself waiting to see how long Ben's fingers remain there. With a sigh, she forces herself to turn away. She lets the party suck her in. Bodies part for her as she wanders through the crowd. The music is so loud it's impossible to be heard without shouting. Some people are attempting to dance – the limited space forcing a contorted bobbing and jigging. A girl with her face powdered white lurches into her, spilling some of her drink over Isolte's sleeve. The girl hardly bothers to apologise. A huge crucifix swings around her neck. She is wearing a black T-shirt. White lettering across her generous chest shouts *Vote Get It Straight by 88.*

Frowning, Isolte makes her way over to the wall, hoping to hide. She dabs at her sleeve, bending awkwardly so that she can use the hem of her skirt, transferring a certain amount of damp and the smell of lager from one fabric to the other. One of the bookers at Models One stumbles past. She stops when she sees Isolte. 'Hey, babe, how's it going?'

'Fine.' Isolte is guarded.

'Did you see the news today? Princess Di visiting AIDS patients? That woman is a saint. Amazing. She was touching this one guy, holding his hand. The poor bloke was crying.'

'Oh, I missed it,' Isolte says. 'She is incredible, isn't she? Best thing to happen to the royal family.'

'There's Lola. I must say hello. Nice chatting to you, Isolte. By the way,' she shouts back over her shoulder, 'sorry to hear about the job.'

'What about it?' Isolte bluffs.

The girl grimaces. 'Like that, is it?' She puts her finger to her lips. 'Won't tell a soul. Promise.'

So the whole world knows. She has to find Ben. He'll never forgive her. She pushes her way back through the wall of bodies. This time they don't give way. There's laughter, shouts of hilarity, eyes sliding towards her and away. Panic kicks inside her chest. The noise and energy of the party gathers into a coloured cloud roiling at the edge of her vision. She sees Ben; he's still with the black girl. She's a model. Isolte can't remember her name. 'Hooverville' by The Christians is playing. Isolte is shoved hard in the ribs; she winces, straining to keep her sights on Ben. He's wiping his nostrils surreptitiously with the back of his index finger. And she knows by the way he dips his head in that animated, conspiratorial manner that he'll be impossible to talk to now.

Panic takes over. She feels as if a fever has her. Sweat prickles. She closes her eyes, opens them again. Stevie is looking across the tops of heads at her, craning to see above the crowd. He's wearing a red hat. His eyes narrow and he says something to someone out of the corner of his mouth. He laughs, showing his teeth, nostrils flaring violently. Isolte turns round. Taking deep breaths, she makes her way to the door. The Japanese couple are there, heads inclined towards each other, engrossed in earnest conversation. They nod at her gravely. She brushes past them into the corridor, making for the lift.

Out in the drizzle of the night, she remembers that she'll have to walk for ages before she has a hope of hailing a cab. The high street is a good ten minutes away. Stevie knows about her. She saw it in his face. He's going to tell Ben. There's nothing she can do about it. She walks on, heels clicking on the wet pavements, the impractical shoes already rubbing her ankles.

She doesn't belong any more. Not to the party, or the magazine, or the fashion world. Even before she was sacked, she'd been slipping away from the bright sanctuary of that life. If she's honest, it's something that's been happening for weeks – the recurring nightmare has given her a vertiginous sense that something is breaking beneath her. She's lost focus at work. She keeps remembering things, things that she's managed to block out for years.

Isolte pulls her coat around her. She can smell summer in the air, the familiar raw, green under-scent of cut grass and pollen. The leaves are out on the trees. There are tulips clustered in brilliant circles under the trees in the park. But the chill of the evening presses at her, sliding under her skin, making her shiver. Cars roar past, sending waves of dirty spray over the pavement.

She crosses a railway bridge, hearing the rush of a train beneath her feet, and notices a group of teenage boys leaning against the wall at the corner of the street. Her heart accelerates. She swallows, clasping her bag tighter to her side. She can feel them staring. One of the boys calls out and the others laugh. She feels ashamed of being afraid of a few spotty youths. But she listens for their sudden footsteps behind her, anticipating the pull on her bag. Are they following? She can hardly hear anything for the blood roaring like an ocean in her head.

Turning the corner, she sees the lights of the high street and relaxes her grip on her bag, slows her pace. Her chest is tight. It feels bruised, as if she's fallen down a flight of stairs. Ignoring the blister on her heel, she continues past shops and cafés, scanning the traffic for a taxi. When she sees a black cab with a yellow light she steps into the road, raising her arm as if she knew who she was and where she was going.

At home, she opens the kitchen cupboards, looking through them, scrabbling past packets and tins, until she finds what she's searching for. A bottle of red wine, left by Ben.

Ben. Her job is gone. She's losing her sister. Everything is falling away. So much has gone already. Will she lose him as well?

She fumbles in the drawer for the opener. It's a modern, plastic invention with some kind of complicated lever system. Isolte tries to work it, fails, and clasps the bottle between her knees, using brute strength to pull the cork free. She pours herself a generous glass and walks into the bedroom, the bottle dangling from her fingers, kicking off her heels, shrugging off her clothes, flinging her necklace on the floor, bangles clattering at her feet.

In bed, she tucks the covers around her and takes a big gulp of red liquid. It's slightly sour in her mouth, potent. She smells it, earthy and vital, the scent of fruit in it. It reminds her of their mother. She won't think of Rose. She won't think of anything or anyone.

She can hear her phone ringing. It stops. Starts again. There is the distant click of the answer machine. She can hear the tone of her own recorded voice, cheerful and tinny: *It's Issy. Sorry I can't get to the phone right now. You know what to do.* Someone talks urgently. She can hear her name repeated several times. It's Ben. He is angry. She takes another sip of wine, licking her lips, and another. She begins to feel the edges of things blurring, the softening of the world. The room mellows and expands like an overripe peach. It has the effect of cushioning her. She likes the effect. She finds that the glass is empty and reaches for the bottle. She wakes to find Ben shaking her.

'Isolte! What the hell do you think you're doing?' Her head rattles, snapping back and forth on her neck. Her brain is a pea bouncing from surface to surface, bruised and dented. It hurts. Damn. She'd forgotten he had a key.

'Stop!' she manages to say, flailing her arms at him. 'Leave me.'

'Not a chance,' he growls, 'not till I've got some answers out of you.'

She whimpers. She only wants to sink back into the lovely pit of oblivion. He can't possibly expect her to talk.

'Go 'way,' she manages to say, trying to push her head back under the covers.

'Why didn't you tell me, Isolte? I had to learn from Stevie of all people!'

There is cold liquid sliding down her throat. She chokes. Swallows. Water. A lot of it spills down her front, icy and uncomfortable, seeping through the sheets under her.

'God, you're pissed! A whole bottle! Jesus. Drink up. You need it.'

More water filling her mouth. It's hard to swallow. A river of water flooding into her throat. She panics. Her tongue doesn't work. Her teeth feel like cheese in her gums.

After that she is sick. She remembers Ben's arms around her. The floor rearing up to meet her. The lights in the bathroom impossibly bright. She can hear Ben's words. 'Trust me . . . job . . . Stevie . . . worried . . . got into you.'

Nothing joins up. Nothing makes sense. She is longing to lie down and close her eyes. And then she is lying down, clinging to the mattress, the smell of vomit in her hair, the room spinning like a ride at the fair. She can hear fairground music. The electrifying thunder of the rides.

*

She sits between Michael and Viola; John is on the other side of Viola; they are all screaming in unison, hands gripping the bar; the car lurches and turns and turns. Her hair whips across her face, stinging her skin. The neck-cracking movement forces her over to the left. Viola slides into her with a yelp of pleasure-fear. She feels the weight of her twin crushing her. She sees John's arm around Viola, his fingers gripping her sister's shoulder tight; John nuzzles into Viola's ear, saying something. Viola laughs.

Lights flash. Yellow. Green. Red.

14

Today the art lady comes. She has a trolley full of equipment – pens and paper and sticks of glue and pots of glitter. I like the art trolley because it reminds me of primary school. It seems impossible now that there could have been such a safe and innocent place.

Some patients are making marbled paper, pouring inks into oiled water: spirals of yellows, reds and blues unravelling into a colour-clouded liquid. They hobble around the trolley in their dressing gowns and slippers, peering into the water, dipping paper into trays and pulling it out, sodden with inky swirls. I gaze at them enviously. There's a little girl there; she bobs and ducks under elbows and arms, eager to see. She isn't a patient. She is too young for this ward, too plump and healthy. Who does she belong to? Her brown hair falls across her face as she examines the shining paper, her surprised fingers opening like starfish. The art lady ignores the child, patting a patient on the back, exclaiming over the loveliness of the newly coloured paper. They are laying the sheets out to dry now, placing them carefully on the floor at the foot of beds.

I would like to make marbled paper. But I'm not strong enough. I can't get out of bed. My body is too heavy: a sack of shingle. I am weighted by the pull of gravity, by the flaps and folds of flesh on my bones. I can feel my cells swelling, spreading, filling up the space under my skin with fat.

They want me to put on twenty-eight pounds. That's what he said. Mr Groff leaned back in his important chair, a small, earnest man, wearing a white coat open over his shirt, playing with the end of his tie. 'We're aiming for a gain of twenty-eight pounds. Then we'll be able to discharge you.' Looking over my shoulder, he'd nodded encouragingly, as if I should be glad about it.

He's crazy. That's two stone. Two boulders strapped to my skeleton, hobbling me, crushing me. They've added more calories to the drink. I know they have, and it makes me sick to think of that yellowy fluid, sneaky with fat, sliding into my stomach. I've thought about cutting the feeding tube. But if I do that they'll send me to the psychiatric ward. I don't want to go there again.

I will never be free.

*

Judy was stick-thin.

'Can't get any curves in the right places,' she'd complain, looking down at her chest and pouting, pushing folded tissues into her bra. Her hair and skin glowed bloodless white. She was nasal, slightly asthmatic, impossibly glamorous. The first time she'd acknowledged us, we were crowded next to her and her mum on the sofa, the boys on the floor, watching *The Generation Game*.

'Cuddly toy, game of Kerplunk!' we'd yelled, and Judy had turned and offered us each a piece of bubble gum. I felt honoured, as if some foreign princess had presented me with a token from her country. We were at the twins' house so much, she even began to ask our advice: 'Does this look all right?' she'd say, striking poses before us in some new outfit, basking in our admiration. 'Does my bum look big?' Frowning, turning to show us her behind. 'No,' we'd reply truthfully, looking at her bony bottom, flattened by skin-tight denim.

As the only girl, she had the privilege of a bedroom to herself. A bed covered in a pink bedspread and heaped with fluffy toys took up most of the space. The dusty dressing table was crammed with make-up, bottles of nail polish and clumps of tangled necklaces and bracelets.

'Come over here,' she commanded, pushing an avalanche of teddies on to the floor. She lay on the bed, sucking her belly in, grimacing and holding her breath, so Issy could hook a wire clothes hanger into the zip of Judy's jeans. Issy pulled hard. I knelt, holding the straining halves together. There was a glimpse of white lace, the fuzz of hair sticking through. I'd looked away quickly. The zip bit and slid into place.

But it was still a surprise when she invited us, ordered us really, to accompany her to the disco. 'My mate Alison has let me down. Cow. I can't go on my own, can I?' She frowned into the mirror in her bedroom. 'You're old enough. I'll put some slap on yer. Make yer look the part.'

We looked at each other doubtfully. 'Will the boys come?' I asked.

'Bleedin' hope not! What d'you want them fer?' She stared at me. 'They'd be an embarrassment.'

'We can't. Mum doesn't know,' I said. Remembering the feel of her hand against my face. Remembering her tears. Lately, she'd been muddled and snappy. She'd begun making rag dolls. Her plan was to sell them at the weekly market outside the town hall.

'This is going to pay for those new shoes,' she'd said, brandishing a lop-sided, floppy thing with glazed button eyes. She kept raiding the dressing-up box and all our ceremonial clothes had holes cut out of them.

Judy wasn't going to let anything interfere with her plan. She marched us down to the red phone box on the corner. We squeezed in together. It stank of stale piss. One of the panes of glass was missing. Judy took the receiver down and handed it to me. It sat greasy and heavy in my palm.

Mummy answered after a long time. Hearing my hesitant attempts at persuasion, 'A disco, it won't be late ... Yes, we'll be with their older sister,' Judy rolled her eyes and took the phone from me. 'Don't worry, Mrs Love,' she told our mother in soothing tones, 'I'll make sure they get home safe.' She winked at us as she replaced the receiver.

'You could be quite pretty,' she said, squinting at Isolte first and then me, her head on one side as if she were calculating the value of recently discovered works of art. 'You just need to make a bit of effort. Define yer eyes. Give yer face some colour, y'know?' We were like rabbits caught in the headlights of her attention. We had to submit. We thought the boys might rescue us, but they shrugged and ignored us.

Shut in Judy's stuffy room, it took hours to get ready. The boys disappeared off on their bikes with their fishing rods, tackle boxes bouncing on their backs. We watched them go from the window. They turned at the road and stuck their tongues out. Judy had put a single on the record player; the needle dropped and David Cassidy's soft voice crooned and sighed, asking us if it could be for ever. Judy licked her finger and rubbed pink glitter over our cheeks. She painted my nails in sparkly blue polish and Isolte's in green. I sat like a doll, letting Judy paint and prod. The stink of the polish pressed on my lungs like poison. Half of me craved this initiation into female secrets, half of me flew over the fields looking for the boys. Searching for them among dank grasses and wild fennel, listening for the stealthy rub of their fingers fixing worms on to hooks.

While we blew on sticky nails, Judy stood in front of her untidy wardrobe, hands on hips, considering – and then she began to throw items of clothing at us: a yellow tank top and hot pants for Issy and a purple flowery minidress for me. 'Lucky we're the same size.' She watched us zip ourselves up and nodded in approval.

I helped Judy wash her hair, pouring jugs of water over her soapy head as she knelt at the kitchen sink. I looked down at water spiralling across the tendons of her thin neck, thinking her as beautiful and vulnerable as a queen on a chopping block. And I was her chosen one: the last person to touch her before she died. It took hours with a hairdryer and brush to coax her pale frizz into straight bangs, and then a can of hairspray to sculpt her fringe into splayed wings. We coughed, trying not to inhale. 'Farrah Fawcett,' Judy explained, wheezing, moving her head carefully, admiring her reflection. 'My favourite angel.'

We looked at each other. We only knew the angel Gabriel, and his hair didn't look anything like Judy's. Our feet were a size bigger, so, like the ugly sisters, we didn't fit into any of Judy's shoes. We had to keep our old plimsolls on, which spoiled the look a bit. 'At least we can walk,' Issy hissed as we followed Judy down the stairs, noticing her ankles wobble precariously over her five-inch platforms, under the flare of Oxford bags.

I'd been hoping that the boys would be in the kitchen, back for supper, a bucket of roach at their feet, fish scales winking on their skin, hair musty with river water. I thought they'd be impressed by our transformation – even if they didn't show it. In the mirror, I looked prettier, freckles powdered out, lips and cheeks plump and slick with shine. I wanted to see the surprise on their faces, perhaps even admiration. But the boys were nowhere to be seen. Linda was there, cleaning a pair of boots on newspaper spread over the kitchen table. 'Very nice.' She nodded when she saw us. 'You behave, Judy, and make sure the twins get back home all right. Get one of yer friends to give 'em a lift.'

The disco was in the village hall. We walked along the lane through the dusk, birds singing and clouds of midges around our heads. All the country smells were erased by Judy's perfume. We breathed it in like a promise, the intoxicating aroma of Rive Gauche.

Loud music swallowed us. Shadowy teenagers hung around in groups at the side of the hall. Isolte and I followed in Judy's wake, meek as handmaidens, not looking left or right. Judy made a big show of talking to us, shouting above the music, delving into her handbag to find some money. She got us all shandies. Then she left us and wandered off across the floor.

We didn't know the etiquette of discos. We recognised some kids from the village. They drew together and gave us hostile stares as we walked past. Judy didn't come back. We sipped at our drinks slowly, licking the last drops from the plastic beakers. But when we finished them we had nothing more to occupy us. So we sat, awkward and uncertain, on the wooden chairs that lined the hall and watched. The music thundered. 'Bennie and the Jets.' There was dancing, girls and boys forming separate groups, eyeing each other and talking behind their hands. Judy was in the centre of a gaggle of older girls jigging around their handbags. She was circling her hips slowly, her body careless and loose, but her eyes were alert, fixed on a tall boy lounging at the bar. She seemed to have forgotten us. At half past ten the music changed, and couples swayed, slumped against each other, feet hardly moving. Judy was hanging on to the tall boy, who stared over her head, his mouth chewing gum. Meaty hands cupped her buttocks.

'I want to go,' I shouted over Roberta Flack's voice. I was nauseous, sickened by shandy and betrayal. I gazed furiously over at Judy. She was sitting on the tall boy's lap. 'She *said* she'd make sure we got home all right.'

With the courage of the humiliated, I marched across the floor, stepping around swaying couples, the soft glitter of the disco ball scattering petals across my arms and hands. Judy and the boy were glued at the lips. I coughed loudly. They remained stuck to each other, eyes closed. I waited. Tongues poked and entwined, lips explored. Eventually, the boy opened one eye. 'Yeah?' he snarled.

Judy blinked at me, pulling at her dishevelled clothes, covering up her pale stomach. She had a nasty-looking bruise on her neck. She whispered something in his ear and he laughed, squeezing her closer, his thick fingers creeping under her halter-neck. I turned away in disgust.

Outside, a group of boys stood around under a spluttering light, clasping beer bottles, moths fluttering around their heads. 'Oy, twinny, I haven't had me oats tonight,' one of them called. 'Fancy goin' behind the hut with me?' There was sniggering and shoving. 'Bit scrawny, in't she?'

I let out a gasp and clutched at Issy's hand. She held on tight. We walked quickly along the dark lane, eyes stretched wide into the black. The music followed, trailing away. We glanced behind us nervously. Issy's yellow top glowed. I heard footsteps, heavy breathing. 'Run!' I yelled, taking off into the pitchy air. But it was Michael's voice calling us.

The boys caught up, their legs and arms making bright angles. 'You stayed fer *ages*,' Michael said. We could just make him out: a grey shape under the stars, moving closer. 'Bet you was smooching with William Gibbons. Bet yer snogged Robert Bore.'

I heard Issy slap his arm. Sharp, not playful.

I was glad of the darkness. I felt embarrassed by my glossy purple eyes and short skirt. The word 'snogged' hung in the air.

'It was boring,' I said.

My sense of smell, sharpened by blindness, had picked out John. He was standing close, my fingers within touching distance of him. I sniffed at furred warmth, the tang of living wood and crushed greens. He smelt of the forest; and the smell seemed to curl around me, stroking me with feathery fingers. The idea of snogging made me nervy and dry-mouthed. I let out a choking giggle, quickly smothered, and hoped no one heard.

'Your sister's a liar!' Issy's voice flared. 'She made us go and then she ignored us.' I could hear fury crowding her throat, constricting her voice.

'Don't know why yer went anyway,' John said calmly. 'She only wanted to get off with Kevin Kerry.'

A single headlight came searching out of the darkness and we heard the familiar put-put sound of the Vespa. Our mother appeared like a knight on a shining steed. Anxiety uncoiled, my shoulders slumped with relief. I didn't even care if she was angry.

'I was expecting you ages ago,' she said.

She glared at the boys, caught blinking in the sudden beam. 'I told that girl ten o'clock.' She revved the engine. 'Jump on.' She peered closer at us. 'What on earth are you wearing? You look like prostitutes.'

The boys stood scuffing their feet, eyes cast down. 'Goodbye,' we called into the silence.

I sat on the back, hugging my mother, my cheek pressed against her spine. The disco music still thundered inside my skull. The scooter juddered around corners, bouncing over mud. Rabbits ran in front, eyes like luminous dials in the dark. Yawning, I remembered the curious suction of Judy's mouth on the boy's, the twist and slobber of their lips working against each other.

*

The art lady has gone, taking her trolley with her. The patients have disappeared back to their beds. The marbled paper remains on the floor to dry. It's already lost its sheen, the colours dulling and darkening into muddier shades. I feel sad for the loss of the wet brilliance. I look for the child; but she has gone too.

Across from me, Justine is a motionless huddle under her covers. She's begun to sleep for much of the day. There is no more knitting. She lies against her pillow, her eyes closed. Her cheeks fall inwards, cadaverous around her thin mouth. I can see the shine of scalp through tufts of thin, tea-stained hair. A passing nurse stops to pick up the chart at the bottom of her bed. She frowns over it for a moment before putting it back.

I wish Isolte would come. I want to talk to her. There is so much to say. I can't find an order for my words. I don't know how to begin. I struggle to make sentences in my therapy sessions too. Even one-word answers defeat me.

'Now, Viola,' Dr Feaver said, leaning closer, 'what do you think the difference between having a feeding tube and eating by mouth is?'

'You have to chew and swallow when it goes into your mouth,' I said eventually.

'Yes.' She was patient. 'But how does that make you *feel*?' She looked over her glasses hopefully. 'That's the difference, isn't it? How does it make you feel, Viola?'

'Tired,' I answered. And I knew it was the wrong answer.

Dr Feaver sighed and wrote something in her notes.

It's like that with Isolte too. If I could find the right words, the significant sounds, they might allow a slackening in the mesh of time, let me reach through to release something, to mend what has been broken.

> *All my desire has stripped me bare,*
> *all my lies eaten by the hungry air.*
> *I move through friendly trees,*
> *wanting stillness to cover me.*

It made me feel better to scribble words down. Sometimes I could make a pattern with them that answered a yearning inside. They didn't rhyme or scan or any of the things they were supposed to. I didn't show them to anyone. I didn't call them poems. They felt almost like prayers to me, or confessions, as I sat hunched over a notebook in my room at Hettie's, a bitten pen in my hand.

Speaking never came easily to me. I stuttered and blushed and lost the thread of what I'd wanted to say. It was Issy who was the communicator. She wasn't afraid to tell people what she thought or who she was. She could be funny or angry or sweet – but she didn't keep it inside. She let it out.

Since leaving the forest, she uses words meekly. She seems

afraid of their power. There are no more spells. Language has become something that helps her fit in. At the new school, she picked up the way the other girls spoke, adopting their little mannerisms and school slang. Now she's made a career out of writing about fashion in a magazine, describing skirt lengths and seasonal colours. When she speaks, she avoids metaphors, won't prod at what lies beneath. I was relying on her to be the one to talk about what happened. She has the ability to explain difficulties, open things up. She's always been the one to take charge. It was she who decided on our rituals, she who spoke the ancient language. When Mummy left us, she knew what to do, who to speak to. But now, when I need her to, she won't or can't speak for both of us. She is holding her tongue.

*

Issy chewed her lip, gesturing at the bed. 'It's still made up. I don't think Mummy slept here last night.' The cat was on her back, stretching luxuriously, her mouth opening in an unconcerned yawn. There was a sour, puffy smell. Clothes abandoned in desolate heaps on the dirty floor. We checked under Mummy's bed, and looked behind the sofa in the living room.

Traipsing across the wet lawn to the shed, Issy pulled open the door. Mummy wasn't there either. We'd left a trail of footprints behind us. She would have left prints too. In the privy, spiders scuttled into the cracks between the tarred planks. I breathed in the chemical stink.

Mist rose from the ground. It coiled around our ankles. The forest was dripping. It had been raining for days. We pushed through fat clumps of bright green bracken, peering into the gloom under the tall trees. My legs were soaking; the jeans clinging to my skin, cold and heavy. We shouted her name and a pheasant flew up with a flurry of brown feathers, its loud squawks echoing inside the stillness, stirring other birds into flight. Wings clapped above our heads.

I tugged at Issy's sleeve, noticing that the Vespa had gone. I felt sick. 'She's left us,' I whispered.

As soon as she got the phone call, Aunt Hettie came from London in a Mini with two spaniels in the back. Isolte had found her number in Mummy's diary. Isolte tried to be grown-up. 'Mummy's not here,' she'd said loudly into the black mouthpiece. 'Can you come?' She was trying to be sensible, but her voice came out wrong, as if she was being strangled.

It was Hettie who called the police. She phoned them from London before she drove down. When she arrived, late that night, fumbling through the darkness into the cottage, with the dogs at her feet, I broke down in tears, hugging her comfortable shape, burying my face in the folds of her coat. I thought she would bring Mummy back to us. Hettie made no such promises; she was brisk and calm, sending us to bed with hot-water bottles and glasses of milk. Underneath, she must have been sick with anxiety. But she didn't let us guess it.

Someone had already spotted the Vespa parked at the beach. After Hettie's call to the police, the coastguard was alerted. A body had been washed up further along the coastline. A day after Mummy went missing, the police came calling.

'She's dead, darling.' Hettie's face was pushed close to mine. Her soft, powdery skin became wet as her eyes crinkled and brimmed. 'I'll have to go and see her, to ... identify her. But it's her, I'm certain. I'm so very sorry.'

I felt something tighten around my heart. I couldn't talk. I stretched out a hand to Issy and she took it silently. I hung on to the living warmth of my sister's fingers. The policemen at the front door, in dark clothes with silver buttons, were talking in low, serious voices. Issy had pulled me aside and we crouched behind the kitchen door. 'They've come to take us away,' she muttered fearfully.

'Don't be frightened.' Hettie was beckoning us from our hiding place. 'They're not going to take you anywhere. You're coming home with me,' she added, crushing us abruptly to her chest, so that we were caught against the stiffened mountains of her breasts, while the hard bones of a strange undergarment dug into our cheeks.

Two weeks later, we were crammed into the Mini on the back seat, the sharp-clawed dogs stepping over our legs. The cat, shut in a cardboad box, made a low moaning in her throat. The car was full of our suitcases and dog breath.

We'd left the cottage locked and empty. We knew we'd never see it again.

It was raining hard. There was the swish of windscreen wipers and hiss of tyres on the shiny road. Hettie crouched over the wheel. Oncoming lights lit up her head in a halo of light. Her hair was rough and short – not like Mummy's silky plaits. My fingers longed for my mother's pale hair to twist and stroke.

I thought of John. I didn't know if I would see him again. My chest hurt as if there was a weight on it, crushing me. I pressed my face into the muscled neck and floppy ears of a dog, making him wet with my tears.

It was inky outside. Headlights flared and dazzled, making me squint. Issy and I sat close; her breathing left her and entered me.

I let my head flop sideways on to her shoulder, and she shifted a little to accommodate my weight. I needed to touch her, to reassure myself of our sameness.

I didn't know what kind of life we were going to. I'd only seen the British Museum and Liverpool Street, anonymous roads and glittering shops. I remembered black taxis and red buses. I hadn't liked London when Mummy took us; walls cut out the light and pavements hurt my feet.

The forest was already far behind. As Hettie drove us on through the night, I felt everything we'd ever known falling away and disappearing, like parcels tumbling out of the back of a truck and smashing against a dark road.

15

'I told yer,' Michael explained wearily, 'if yer see Black Shuck you have to say his name. Say it loud, see, and it'll protect you. Everyone knows that.'

Issy looked at me, and I knew she was wondering if it was a trap, if they were poking fun at us. The boys were so earthy, so bound into the everyday and the physical exactness of the world; it was hard to believe that they had their own magic. Their wit came sharpened with irony, always calculated to pull the rug from beneath our feet, to throw us into confusion.

'What do you mean,' she said cautiously, 'say his name?'

'Names are like, I don't know' – Michael scratched his head – 'they've got powers.'

Issy pushed the toe of her shoe into the grass. Her shoulders hunched stubbornly, not looking at him. She was silent.

'Well, you wouldn't understand.' Michael sighed, skimming a stone along the road. 'You don't belong round here anyway.' His eyes were sly, looking at Issy without seeming to.

The stone took three wide hops across the track, smaller pebbles flying, an almost indiscernible miniature dust storm rising behind it.

'We do,' I stressed loudly, 'we live here.'

'Ma says yer only belong in the village if yer grandad's grandad's grandad was born here.' John picked up a stone, lined it up, arm drawn back, squinting down the track.

'Well our mum says you belong where your heart is,' Issy retorted.

John let fly with his stone. It hit a rut and fell with a clatter just a few feet away. Michael laughed.

'Anyhow,' he said, 'you comin', or what?'

Issy pursed her lips as if about to whistle, scratched her head, shrugged, and glanced at me. 'All right.'

The oak woods were hundreds of years old – the oldest in England. They were privately owned. Several signs attached to the drooping barbed-wire fence reminded people to *Keep Out*. The trees slumbered on, putting out tangled roots into the decaying ground. Branches that cracked and fell in storms stayed sprawled like forlorn monsters, bellies down, gathering a thick pelt of brambles and bracken around them. A heavy canopy of branches and leaves made the interior dim and tenebrous.

The oak woods lay about half a mile outside the forest. We took our bikes, leaving them in a ditch because there was only one path through the woods, and it was blocked off at several points by fallen trees. We followed the boys, climbing over tree limbs and ducking beneath swags of low-slung greenery. Twisted branches clawed the air, strips of tattered bark hanging loose, as if the trees had been flayed.

I had the uneasy sense that we were being watched. A prickling crept along my spine. I was sure Issy felt it too. I smelt fear fizzing on her skin. 'Black Shuck,' I murmured to myself, over and over, practising the roll of syllables, trying not to trip over the name, holding it in my mouth ready to spit it out loud. The boys had picked up branches, testing them for rot before grasping them firmly. They stabbed at the ground with their weapons as they walked, sometimes thrashing the bracken around them with vicious swipes.

Nothing snarled at us from the undergrowth. No splayed claws came springing for us with hot breath flaming. We didn't see a squirrel or an adder either. Not even a rabbit. There was just the occasional bird, a whisper of wings in branches. A quick fluttering behind us. Perhaps the boys had scared everything else away. The woods seemed deserted. We walked until the narrow path ran out and we were striding away from the trees down a sandy track leading over open, scrubby moor. The spring sun was hot on our backs. There were patches of violet blazing inside green, the heather coming out. We heard a car engine in the distance. We couldn't see anything, but it was approaching steadily, would appear at any moment round the bend in the track.

'Gamekeeper,' Michael said. 'Go back.'

We turned and ran for the cover of trees, John shouting behind us. Our feet laboured inside folds of sand and by the time we got into the gloom of the oaks, we were breathing hard.

We slumped on to damp moss, thirsty and dispirited, feeling irritated by the way the tightly coiled day had come undone, had fallen apart into nothing. Our sullen mood made us separate from each other. Michael was scraping away moss with a stick, jabbing into the earth pointlessly. I licked salt from my lips, pushed a wisp of hair from my eyes. I wanted to go home. Mummy had been sewing her rag dolls with passionate stabs of the needle, surrounded by mounds of fabric. 'Don't be long,' she'd said, orange cotton dangling from her hair. 'You can help with the faces.'

'We've got to go,' I said to Issy, my eyebrows raised.

'Yeah,' she agreed, 'Mummy will be wondering.'

John made a noise, an exhalation of breath, a snorting half-laugh.

Issy glared at him. 'What?'

'Your *mummy* don't know what time of day it is,' Michael said.

'What's that supposed to mean?' Issy flicked her fringe back, chin raised.

'Everyone knows it,' Michael said. 'She's doolally, your ma. Hippy-dippy.'

'Piss off!'

Michael and John moved closer to each other. 'What's yer problem?' one of them said. 'It's true, in' it?'

Issy scrambled to her feet, putting out her hand imperiously. 'Viola!' she ordered.

My heart was thundering. The world had flipped upside down. The air was full of spite, balled up and murderous inside the branches and leaves. I couldn't breathe. I stood up shakily and took Isolte's hand. Her fingers were sweaty.

'Don't follow us,' she said.

'Fuck off!' Michael's voice was hot and angry.

We walked quickly, branches snapping across our faces, arms up to ward off scratches. The dark greens of the woods confused us. The single path seemed to split and become two. Issy set off along the wider path, but it narrowed quickly, running out into a wasteland of bracken and brambles. 'Fuck off!' she muttered. Brambles tore at us, ripping our skin and clothes. I stopped to untangle myself, unhooking the small thorns from my jeans. 'We have to go back. This is wrong.'

I thought of John, his mouth slack, shoulder-to-shoulder with his brother, looking at me with his eyes unhappy and full of a question. I didn't know what it was. 'Issy,' I said, sucking a ripped finger. 'Look! We can't get through. We've got to turn back.'

Isolte shook her head. She couldn't acknowledge that we were lost. Her chest heaved. She bit her lip.

A fly bumped against my cheek and I brushed it away. Another skimmed past. And another. I watched its uncertain, airy path, looping up and dropping inside a hollow tree. I took a step closer. I could hear a persistent dark rumbling, like the cluster of buzzing bodies. I followed the noise, climbing up, using rough bark as handholds, to peer inside the rotten opening.

A face looked at me. I floundered backwards, fingers gripping crumbling wood to save myself from falling. The face had a long snout curved over a stiffened snarl. There was the point of tooth, a grey tongue, milky eyes staring. A dog. A black dog, its hair matted with congealed blood. At the neck I saw the white of bone stub severed short. It was like something on a butcher's block. The decapitated head lay among bloody, rotten leaves. It looked almost peaceful, while the flies moved quickly, busy at the gaping wound, wings and legs rubbing together.

I half fell, half scrambled down. Leaning against the tree, I covered my face, smelling death on my fingers.

'Call the boys,' I whispered, feeling suddenly sick. 'Call them quickly. Black Shuck's dead.'

16

Isolte gets the cheque out of the envelope again. She reads the figure in the box, although she already knows the number by heart. She smoothes her fingers back and forth across the paper. She's had the cheque for a couple of days. Today she will put it in her account. It will mean that she's accepted their terms. She'd checked with a solicitor, just to make sure they'd come up with the right sum, and he said, 'It's a good pay-off. It's not worth fighting this one.'

Ben had whistled low, appreciatively. 'Take the money and run, Issy. We can have an amazing holiday in the Seychelles or something. Fuck 'em. You're worth twenty Sam Fowlers.'

The money means that she doesn't have to look for another job straight away. She's got enough to pay off her debts and live for ages, months and months, she thinks vaguely, if she's careful. But she doesn't feel like being careful. There's an unfocused energy building inside her like steam in a kettle. It's not a holiday she wants. She doesn't know what it is.

She wonders for a moment if she should let Hettie know about the redundancy. But Hettie has always been unclear about what

Isolte does for a living. The magazine world is meaningless to her. Since she moved to Ireland, Hettie is caught up in her daily battle against animal cruelty and with the collection of stray dogs and cats that share her cottage. Isolte realises she could go and visit her aunt – get a flight to Cork and spend a long weekend – but although she loves Hettie very much, she's not sure she's in the mood for incontinent creatures and the bowls of food left out all day, and the hairs and dirt that accumulate on every surface, including pillows and bed sheets.

It's not the first time that Isolte has neglected to let Hettie know what's happening. She'd wanted to write and tell her that Viola was back in hospital, but Viola had been furious at the suggestion. 'Don't you think she's done enough for us already?' she'd said. 'You know what happened last time she rushed back. She had to try and find people to look after all the animals. And when she got here she couldn't do anything for me, so it was a complete waste of her time. There's no point in telling her – please don't.'

Isolte has an entire day with no agenda, except seeing Viola. How can she fill the hours? At the magazine there were always urgent editorial meetings, while models, clutching their books, queued for her in reception. She imagines her replacement – a faceless, nameless, genderless being – putting outfits together in Isolte's fashion cupboard, riffling through the rails with Lucy. A reel goes spooling through her head, like a film in overdrive, of a stranger's fingers pulling out hats, tossing aside dresses, flinging scarves like bright streamers at a party.

Opening her own wardrobe, she touches wool and leather, picks up a handful of black pleated silk skirt and lets it fall. There is no need to dress up any more. She can wear what she wants. Nobody is watching her or judging her. She settles on jeans and an old shirt of Ben's. Does she need a jacket? She peers out, checking the weather. Trees and buildings stand out against a cloudless sky, dark edges sharpened. She can hear exuberant bird-song even through her closed window.

Squinting into the dazzle of the morning, she has a sudden memory of those rituals that she and Viola devised to worship the sun. Some notion they'd got when their mother had taken them to a Druid ceremony long ago. Isolte had made up her own language, garbling pretend words. Viola had thought she'd accessed some ancient tongue. She always meant to tell Viola that she just made it up, but she never did. Then they stopped believing.

On the mat in the communal hall there's a couple of letters addressed to her. A gas bill and a handwritten envelope in writing she doesn't recognise. Inside she finds a letter from the Suffolk Punch Stud. She reads and rereads it, following the sentences with her fingertip and frowning. Surprise parts her lips, and she shakes her head into the empty hall. They are inviting her to visit the new stables, to see a foal just born to one of the mares. She understands that she has herself, unwittingly, caused this disconcerting invitation to arrive. Months ago Isolte heard that the Suffolk Punches needed financial rescue, remembered those huge, honey-coloured horses kept down on the marshes near the sea. A fashion show and a sale of the contents of the fashion and beauty cupboards had been all that was needed to collect a generous contribution. She'd been glad at the time to offer some help. She liked knowing that the horses were still there, wading through long grass, standing patiently at the gate, ears pricked, as if listening to the waves.

But she hadn't had to do anything difficult. It hadn't involved going there. She hadn't had to leave London. She puts the letter in her bag. She must remember to send a polite declining note.

She decides that if she's going to be financially responsible, there can be no more cabs until she gets a new job. She'll take the bus to see Viola. She remembers Ben laughing at her: 'Call yourself a Londoner! Not only is there a number 87 that'll take you practically to the front entrance of the hospital,' he'd rolled his eyes, 'but the stop is at the end of your street.'

So she waits at the bus stop, with a young mother and her grizzling baby and an elderly man who picks his nose while staring into the middle distance. Isolte puts her dark glasses on. She couldn't explain to Ben, but since coming to London she had promised herself that she would never be poor, never be dependent on anyone else for anything. She doesn't want ever to be like Rose.

The bus shelter has been smashed. Broken glass crunches under her shoes. Through the jagged opening she watches rooks stalking across the grass in the square opposite – a whole mob of them. A brief image flashes behind her eyes of dark birds winging out of a window in the Martello tower. She frowns, blinking it away. A rook sits on the railings and regards her with bold appraisal, opening its scavenger's beak as if about to tell her something. There's a nursery rhyme about birds like these in a pie. No. That's wrong. It was four and twenty blackbirds. Rooks are too ominous and cruel. They're better suited to the darker tones of a fairy tale – to the company of wolves and witches.

Entering Viola's ward, she can't help glancing at the old lady in the bed opposite, grateful that she seems to be asleep. Her relief turns to fear when she sees Viola. She lies on her pillow, eyes closed, wired up to a heart monitor. And there is a new drip in her arm. As Isolte approaches, Viola coughs, a hollow, hacking sound.

'What's all this?' Isolte clears her throat, gesturing towards the drip and blinking machine. 'Is your heart playing tricks again?'

Viola shakes her head. 'My blood pressure is down. They're just keeping an eye on it.'

'That cough sounds nasty.' I must stay calm, she thinks. But already fear is forcing air from her lungs, setting her own heart racing.

'Just a cough,' Viola wheezes gently, 'I've got some kind of stupid chest infection.'

Isolte feels brutally whole, defiantly human. Her sister is hardly made of flesh. She is shadow, air and spirit. Her blue-tinged skin is a web that holds the shrinking bones together. Viola suffers like some ancient saint.

'No!' Isolte says loudly. She didn't mean to.

Viola looks up, puzzled.

'I don't like this,' Isolte gestures again, her hands falling limply by her side. 'God! Viola!' Her voice cracks. 'Why are you doing this? Why?'

Viola goes blank. It's as if a film of ice forms across her features, sheeting her. She turns away from Isolte. 'Don't.' The word is a whisper, followed by more coughing. Isolte watches the spasm rattling Viola's bones, the shudder of her ribs and shoulders. It seems she will come apart. She begins to gasp and wheeze.

A nurse appears at the bedside. She takes Viola's wrist in her hand, checking her pulse, glancing at the monitor. She looks at Isolte. 'Maybe come back later.' She nods, not unkindly. 'I think your sister could do with a rest. We'll get some oxygen into her.'

Isolte wanders the corridors of the hospital. She finds the café on the ground floor and orders a drink. She sits at a green plastic table on a green plastic chair and sips an insipid coffee. The life of the hospital bustles around her. There are patients in their dressing gowns buying sweets and magazines from the shop across the corridor. People sit on the shiny plastic chairs, hunched over their food, staring into space. A male nurse at the next table leans on his elbow, listlessly flicking an empty sugar packet. He looks exhausted.

Isolte turns the paper cup; it makes damp circles on the table. She shouldn't have lost her temper. It never does any good. She was frightened, seeing Viola wired up to machines. She is scared that her sister has no resistance to fight an infection. Starvation has depleted all her reserves. In the end, it is something like this that will kill her. And there is nothing that Isolte can do.

Her reckless mood has gone. Her throat aches. She hardly ever cries. Her grief is dry, gritty, inflaming her throat. She feels her vocal cords contract. She feels bruised. She looks in her bag, hoping to find a mint to chew on, and discovers the photograph of the horse. She'd forgotten it was there. Will Viola remember that morning? she wonders. Will she remember finding the lost horse with the boys?

Back in the ward, Viola turns her head and gives Isolte a smile. Her skin stretches painfully at the corners of her cracked lips. Viola forgives easily. It has always been one of her virtues. Isolte sits carefully by the bed. She gets the picture of the horse out and places it in Viola's hands.

'Look,' she says, 'remember?'

She doesn't know what response she expects Viola to make. The picture of the horse feels like a peace offering.

'Oh, yes. You raised money, didn't you?' Viola glances at the horse. 'That was good.' Her eyes are dull. She lets the picture fall, as if her fingers don't have enough strength to hold it.

'Uh-huh.' Isolte takes a deep breath. 'I had a letter from the stud today. They've invited me to go and visit them.'

'Go to Suffolk?' Viola murmurs, picking up the picture again and looking at it. 'Go back?' There is alertness in her, a spark of interest.

'Yes.'

'And?'

'I don't know.' Isolte wishes Viola would look at her. 'It's a mad idea, really. I don't want to go. It's ... been too long. Anyway, it's too far for one day.'

Viola turns her head painfully. She speaks, struggling with the urgency of her words. 'Go. You should go.'

'But ...' Isolte frowns, surprised and doubtful. 'I don't know ... I mean, how would I get there? I don't drive.'

'It's a couple of hours. Take the train.' Impatience tightens Viola's voice.

Isolte clears her throat, looks at the backs of her hands. Her body is rigid with resistance.

'Please.' Viola moves her fingers towards Isolte. 'I think about it all the time. I dream. I daydream. Going over and over it.' She grasps Isolte's wrist with surprising force.

Isolte wants to tell Viola that going back is impossible. Nothing remains the same. Everything is altered. No actions can be undone. No words unspoken. There is only movement and change, and hope that time will carry you far enough away from the horror for it to pale and blur.

'We can't change anything,' Isolte says quietly. She keeps still under Viola's skeleton fingers.

'I know. I know. But ...' Viola shakes her head, moves her hands away, '... I want to know what happened to the boys. You must want to as well. We deserted them, Iss. You know we did. We've gone on pretending none of it happened. Never talking about it. And I'm sick of it.' She coughs again, a deep racking cough. 'I'm sick of everything. I'm sick of me.'

'All right,' Isolte snatches a glance at the heart monitor, 'if you want me to go. If it's that important to you. But you've got to promise me that you'll try, Viola. Try and eat. Try and get better.'

Viola looks at her and nods.

'I'll phone you every day.' Isolte bites her lip. 'I won't go for long. A weekend. I'll ask around. See if I can track them down.'

'Go for as long as it takes.' Viola closes her eyes. 'Don't worry about me. I'm not going anywhere.' She looks at Isolte suddenly, attempts to raise her head, forcing herself on to her elbows. 'I have a feeling that they need to be found, Issy. I keep dreaming about them.'

She's still clutching the photograph of the horse.

The full realisation of what she's let herself in for makes Isolte stop on the street outside the hospital, unable to move. Traffic grinds past. Schoolchildren shout at each other from across the road. Fear gathers inside her, tangled and tight as a knot. There's no getting out of it. She has to go. She has made a promise. She's let Viola down in the past. If she can do this perhaps it will make up for other things. Perhaps it will help to make things right between them at last.

*

Isolte stands inside a group of girls gathered around a noticeboard. She's searching for her name on a list. She bites her lip in excitement when she realises that it's at the top of the end-of-term exam results. She stares at the words. *Isolte Love*. 87%. *English Literature*.

'Well done,' someone says to her.

'You've come first by five marks.' Helen puts her hand on Isolte's elbow. 'Wow. Amazing.'

Isolte feels pleasure infusing her cheeks.

Girls' voices echo around her. Feet clatter down the corridors. Whispers brush the magnolia-painted walls, sweep up among the vaulted rafters of the hall. The science labs smell of chemicals and hissing Bunsen burners. On Tuesdays they play hockey in Aertex shirts and navy skirts on the windy playing field. Isolte has found that she is skilful with a hockey stick, guiding a ball through clods of mud and other girls' goosepimpled legs.

'Can you come?' Helen waits expectantly.

Fourteenth Birthday Party, the paper says in swirly letters. There are stars and balloons. Isolte looks up. 'Yeah, love to.'

Weirdo. Dirty hippy.

She and Viola, skulking among the gravestones, waiting for the school bell: the home-schooled loners, waiting to be released back into the forest. Waiting to lose themselves among trees.

'Cool.' Helen smiles.

Isolte can feel sweat prickling her underarms. She clamps her arms against her side. It's hard work being popular. It takes effort to put on an act. Viola won't help. She has made herself as ugly as possible and she refuses to even try and fit in. Isolte pushes her hair behind her ear casually, uses the right kind of voice. 'So, what are you going to wear?'

But Helen is frowning slightly, shifting uncomfortably. Viola has appeared soundlessly from the mouth of an empty classroom;

she hovers next to them, glancing up from under a fall of newly dyed black hair. She sniffs, looks at Isolte. 'Are you going to catch the bus?'

'Viola.' Helen clears her throat, says loudly as if Viola is deaf or stupid, 'Do you want to come to my party?'

Viola's eyes widen. She looks at Isolte, chews her lip and glances down at her scuffed non-regulation shoes.

'No,' says Isolte quickly. 'Viola doesn't really like parties. You wouldn't enjoy it, would you, Viola?'

17

I am poised for flight, my body held at an angle by the wind. The air is thin and fierce, salty with brine. I lick my lips. If I were to lean forward just a fraction more, tilt myself further out, then a gust would take my body in its arms and cast me up into the wide basin of sky. But I am rooted to stone.

I kept the wing bone of a bird in my pocket. Felt it smooth against my thumb. How light it was, pale as the moon, slippery in my hand. Close up, the texture was laced with holes like a fossil.

Beside the sea, startled rooks flew out of a tower window. Black shadows scattering. They returned when we were gone, coming from sun-steeped heights, gliding back to reclaim their home on outstretched wings.

One day I will step into space. I'll feel the air catch my hollow bones, rippling across tight-stretched skin. And I will be gone, just a shadow running across reeds, a cast-off shape on the shingle.

Green walls close in. The fluorescent light slaps down hard, hurting my eyes. By my bed the monitor winks red, proof that my heart still works.

Nurses move among the beds, bending and straightening, chatting to each other. 'Did you see *Dallas* last night?'

'Do you think JR did it?'

A laugh. 'Yeah, Sue Ellen is on his case.'

'Has Mrs Scott had her meds?'

'Half an hour ago, but she needs her bloods done.'

Their words jumble, becoming a blur of noise moving further away. On the other side of the room an orderly draws the curtain around a bed with sharp tugs. There is a retching sob from behind the fabric, a splatter as vomit hits a pan. I put my hands over my ears.

Where is Issy now? Is she on the train yet? I hear a train, the rattle of speed and whoosh of wheels on tracks. We made that same journey when Mummy took us to London to see Tutankhamun's tomb at the British Museum. Isolte will get the train from Liverpool Street to Ipswich, just as we did then, our minds full of gold sphinxes and a dead boy, with his heart in a box beside him.

On her journey, Isolte will see muted greens and violets, the surprise of mallow against stone and dun. Gorse flashes bright inside dark prickles. The sky opens wide – as if peeled back by distance and flat horizons. Wild garlic and fennel sprout inside hedge grass. The sea grinds over shingle; lapwings swoop and call.

She'll go to their cottage first. I place her in the lane outside the boys' house. She looks at the peeling windows, the heap of tyres and sagging motorbike. A tractor crawls past; there is mud under her shoes. She sneezes. Fear makes her nose tingle. In my mind, I focus hard to release some inner part of me and send it to stand beside her. I tangle my fingers with her fingers, breathing words of comfort and encouragement. She's watching Michael or

147

John come out of the front door. It's John. Of course it is. He'll be taller and wider than when I last saw him. He's shading his eyes, disbelief on his face. But then he smiles and with his smile my pain falls away, the clawing in my gut stops, the nightmares fade.

I rub my eyes with a bit of the sheet. Fool. Nothing will put an end to it. My chest hurts as if something crouches over me, flattening my lungs. I cough and cough. Please let her find them.

The little girl is back in the ward. She is a distraction. Just watching her makes me feel better. I've been too long among all these sick bodies. She darts about between the beds, brown hair flying, dodging patients and nurses. Her quick feet don't make a sound on the floor. I am surprised someone doesn't tell her to stop running. The nurses are too busy to bother with her; she skips lightly behind their backs. They couldn't catch her if they tried.

The child pauses by Justine's bed and leans against the end of it. She must be one of the grandchildren that Justine is always talking about. The child spreads her hands over the covers. Her body is relaxed; all the supple grace of the young is in her flexed spine and rolling foot. Her fingers move over the hospital blanket, pressing invisible keys, as if she's playing the piano.

*

'We're going to have a picnic this weekend.' Mummy smiled. 'There's someone I want you to meet.'

She was back from her final woodwork class. In her arms was the letterbox, the thing she had been labouring over for the whole term. It was a plain box with a hinged lid. There was a simple catch on the front. And she had painted our surname on it in uncertain letters: *LOVE*.

'I've invited Frank, my teacher, to meet us at the beach. I said we'd bring lunch.' She paused to put the letterbox on the kitchen table. 'He has a daughter. A few years younger than you, I think.'

We lifted the lid on the box and looked inside. It was empty. I ran my hand along the rough sides, testing the raw grain. A sharp pain jabbed. Darkness wedged deep under my skin. I whimpered, sucking at the splinter.

Mummy stood over the letterbox. 'It looks OK, doesn't it?' she said, blowing a strand of hair out of her eyes. Turning from us and stretching up to open the cupboard, she frowned. 'Blast. No bread. I'll have to do a shop. We should make a cake. But do we have any self-raising left?' And then, rounding on me, 'Oh, do stop making a fuss, Viola! It'll come out when it's ready. Why aren't you in bed? It's school tomorrow.'

Lying in bed, I thought about the dog's head. It seemed like the worst kind of omen. What sort of message could it possibly bring? Issy didn't know. 'I don't understand,' was all she said, after she'd peered into the tree. And she sneezed. The boys spent ages examining the head. It wasn't Black Shuck, they said, he could never be caught. It was a sacrifice left by witches. An ordinary dog, then, some stray or perhaps a gypsy cur, caught and smuggled into the woods at night. I imagined the moment they cut its throat. The neck forced back, a blade slicing into the vein. A sudden jerk and blood spray on holly leaves, the trusting dog's eyes turning dull and empty.

'But why?'

'Old customs.' Michael shrugged. 'I dunno – people come from miles to do their rituals and stuff.' He looked perplexed. 'The woods are magic.'

He was speaking to me. He and Isolte were still avoiding direct communication. She was crouched by the foot of the tree, examining the remains of a small fire we hadn't spotted before. A circle of cold ashes. She poked at it with a twig, refusing to look up. I knew she was angry with me for calling them.

I'd been glad though, seeing John crashing through the brambles towards us, stick in hand.

'Are there many witches?' I'd asked, looking around at the dense thickets of holly bushes and tangled trees.

'Lots,' John said. 'You know the big house where Ma works? She says there's special "witch marks" carved in the ceilings. From the olden days. And there's witches alive now. We've got a horseshoe on our door to stop them. Old man Brabben has a bottle dug under his floor with bits of human hair and a dead chicken.'

Issy and I had always believed in witches. But ours came from the pages of books. They were line-drawn, inked-in creatures belonging to another world. We sensed them in darkness, in the moments between waking and sleeping. But the witches that the boys talked about were almost as normal as farmers or milkmen. They could be someone we knew. These witches breathed the same air as us. They came creeping through the woods, slaughtering dogs and lighting fires among the roots of holly trees.

'The head is a sign,' Issy said, rubbing dirt off on her jeans.

We began to make a plan to spy on them. We would rescue the next sacrifice. We'd take it home and it could be our pet, its furred neck safe under our kind hands.

'It's horrible,' Issy said. 'Cruel.' And we nodded in agreement.

'We'll come back when there's a full moon,' said Michael.

The plan drew Issy and Michael together, covered up the hurt, like kicking ash over dying embers.

Mummy took a brush to our hair on Saturday. Tangles jagged as they caught on bristles, and we resisted with jerking heads. But she was determined. She even managed to rub a flannel over our faces. Standing next to the Vespa, we tossed a coin for our positions, flicking a ten pence piece high into the morning air. 'Heads!' I yelled. Isolte won. She got the pillion spot behind Mummy.

Crammed into the egg-shaped sidecar, wedged between the thin fibreglass sides, I had to keep my knees drawn up to make room for the picnic basket, a fusty-smelling rug and the swimming towels piled at my feet. Mummy drove fast; the wind whistled around the canvas roof, and I was jolted over every bump. The egg sat so low that lorry wheels turned at head height, hedges blocked my view and stringy branches slapped across the windscreen.

We got to the meeting place early – the coastguard's cottage at the end of the beach road – and hauled the basket and rug across sinking mounds of shingle towards the sea. It was the beginning of summer. There were clumps of sea kale, pale green and rubbery. A cool breeze sliced across waves and banks of pebbles, ruffling the white petals of the mayweed, raising goosebumps on our bare arms.

The sea was surly, waves snapping at the shore. Clouds gathered across the horizon, fat and dark with the threat of rain. It wasn't the best day for a picnic. Mummy remained cheerful, taking containers of food out of the basket, laying out the rug and securing the edges with heavy stones. We took lids off tins and inhaled aromas of breaded ham and cheese and musty tomatoes. It looked like she'd spent the week's allowance. Our mouths watered.

'Look,' Isolte nodded towards the coastguard's cottage, 'is that them?'

A tall man was striding across the shingle towards us. He had sparse hair, blowing back in the wind. His balding crown shone. The light glanced off his spectacles, hiding his eyes in a flash of brilliance. He was wearing a cream suit, crumpled and loose-fitting. He had a child by the hand. She slipped beside him, long brown plaits swinging behind her shoulders.

'Where's his wife?' Isolte asked suspiciously.

'Ssshh.' Mummy frowned, struggling to her feet, smoothing her skirt down with her hands. 'I told you. He's a widower.' She waved to the approaching pair. 'Jump up, girls, say hello,' she hissed, moving forward to greet them with a loud party voice. 'Hi! You're here! Wonderful!'

She turned to us with a beseeching smile. 'Girls, this is Frank and Polly.' She touched her windswept hair briefly. 'And these are my daughters, Isolte and Viola.' Frank smiled, and gave us a knowing look, an expression of mock-concern making his eyes wide. 'Goodness! Alike as two peas. So what's the secret?' He pushed his glasses further up his nose. 'How do we tell them apart?' He smiled broadly, pleased with his joke.

I waited for him to point out that I was fatter. His eyes lingered on me and I knew he was thinking it. Mummy's laugh was sharp and forced. 'Oh, you'll see how different they are once you get to know them.'

We glared at father and daughter. Frank's boneless face made me think of badly made plasticine models. I rubbed the back of

152

my calf with one sandalled foot. The child Polly stared up at us with interest. She had a well-fed look about her and pinchable rounded arms. 'I'm seven,' she announced. We scowled.

Mummy laughed again. 'The twins are tongue-tied, Polly. Don't mind them.'

Polly squinted slightly as she gazed at one of us, and then the other.

'You have freckles,' she said at last. 'Like me.'

We did not acknowledge the similarity, though she was generously speckled. Small brown spots patterned her face, gathering in density across the bridge of her nose. Unlike us, her eyes were olive. Almost black, so that pupils and iris bled into the same darkness. Under the freckles, her skin was thin and blue-veined.

'Food!' Mummy sang loudly. 'Let's eat.'

We sat in a semi-circle on the rug, munching sandwiches, snapping sticks of carrot. Mummy poured out glasses of wine for her and Frank. He took neat, restrained sips, maiden aunt lips puckering at the rim. Shadows flickered across us, cast by fast-moving clouds and seabirds. Taking a bite of egg sandwich I crunched on something sharp inside glutinous mush – a bit of shell. It disintegrated like sand between my teeth. I turned to spit it out but was met by Polly's unblinking gaze. Swallowing hastily, I choked and gagged, and fell into a coughing fit, tears blurring.

'Put your hand over your mouth,' Mummy snapped at me. 'Would you like some cake, Polly?' Mummy proffered a plate. It contained slices of Battenberg. Shop-bought, luridly pink and yellow, sticky and delicious.

Polly shook her head. 'No, thank you.'

'Polly doesn't eat almonds,' Frank explained quietly. 'She's allergic to nuts.'

Our electricity had gone off halfway through cooking the Victoria sponge. It had collapsed in a gooey mess, and there was no hope of rescuing it. With no time to start again, Mummy had given in to our pleas for shop-bought. We longed for the taste of the chequered Battenberg and its layer of marzipan. Our mother faltered, glanced at us doubtfully and put the cake back in the container, clicking the lid on it. We opened our mouths to complain but the look that she gave us made us shut them again.

'Your mother says you're twelve?' Frank addressed us as one. His tone was brisk and friendly. He'd dropped a dollop of mayonnaise on his trousers. The grease spread in a small oily stain.

We nodded warily.

'Enjoying school?'

We moved our heads a fraction.

'I think they'd enjoy it more if their friends were in the same class – but the boys are at secondary school, aren't they?' Mummy said quickly, flashing a bright smile at us.

Frank raised his eyebrows. 'Friends with boys, eh?' All jocular surprise.

'Another pair of twins,' Mummy laughed, 'what were the chances?'

'Anyone I'd know?' He rubbed at the stain on his trousers with his thumb, licked it and rubbed again.

'John and Michael Catchpole,' Issy mumbled grudgingly.

'The Catchpoles? Really?' He cleared his throat. 'I know the family. You could say they're ... famous around here.' He shifted on the blanket and leaned closer to Mummy, muttering into her ear. We watched his mouth move, sly and fast, his eyes darting towards us. Mummy nodded and pursed her mouth.

'Well,' he turned back to us, 'so you're running with a rough crowd, eh? You should be careful of those boys. But it can't be easy staying down a year. Expect you'll be glad to leave primary school behind. Looking forward to starting big school and making new friends?'

'We like the friends we've already got,' I murmured under my breath.

'Jolly good.' Frank pressed on as if he hadn't heard, his pale eyes earnest. 'And what about sport?'

He was trying so hard that we were embarrassed for him. The pebbles had made tiny indentations in the white flesh of his ankles.

'In any teams? Hockey or netball?'

We stared at him, nonplussed.

'Music?' A note of doubt had crept into his voice.

'I'm a music scholar,' Polly said. 'I play piano and violin.'

'How lovely,' said Mummy. 'You must play for us one day.'

'I'm going for a swim,' Issy announced, beginning to shrug off her jeans. A picnic at the beach meant we'd put our swimsuits on under our clothes. But looking at the sea, I shivered. Then sighed and stood up. 'Me too.'

As I inched into the water, it was as if a frozen hand grabbed at my ankles and gripped tight. I held my breath, shuffling carefully across the knobbly bottom. Thick waves swirled around my calves. Isolte was doggy-paddling grimly backwards and forwards a few feet from the shore. The beach sloped down almost vertically, so that you lost your footing within moments of wading in. The tide was fierce. There was a sign up warning swimmers.

Polly came down to the edge and watched us. 'I don't swim in the sea,' she offered.

Isolte ignored her. My sister's lips had lost their colour, becoming blanched as a corpse. She was ploughing through the waves, slit-eyed and determined, her mouth gasping for air between strokes. I turned, hissed so that Mummy wouldn't hear, 'You're only a proper swimmer if you swim in the sea. Swimming pools are for sissies.'

'I'm not a sissy,' she said reasonably, 'but Daddy says I might get drownded in the sea.'

I dropped down into deep water and lost all bodily feeling. My numb limbs thrashed about, hoping to keep afloat. I could hear Polly's voice droning on, but I refused to understand her words. Isolte and I swam for what seemed an eternity. When we turned for the shore, blue-skinned, our teeth chattering so much we couldn't speak, Polly had gone back to sit with the grown-ups.

The three of them – backlit on the rug, clothes fluttering – might have been arranged by a painter; my mother's graceful shape bending towards the other two, offering plates of food, refilling plastic cups. Polly had kicked off her sandals and said something that made the grown-ups laugh. Mummy put out a hand and touched her arm. We limped towards them over the pebbles, furious as wet wolves slinking around the edges of a camp fire.

'Hope we never have to see *them* again,' Issy said that night when we were in bed.

'What a brat,' I agreed.

'And him so . . . ' Isolte struggled to find the word.

'Boring?' I offered.

'Yes.' She lay sprawled against my side, familiar as one of my own limbs, beginning to giggle. 'Dull. All he can think about is school.'

'And wood,' I added.

'Hammers and nails, if he's being daring . . . ' We laughed.

'What a waste,' I murmured, 'when we could have been with the boys.'

'The rough crowd!' Issy mimicked Frank's voice.

I let the day drift away. Polly and Frank melting into something already forgotten: the mistake of a picnic we once had long ago. There were more important things to think about. Downstairs, we could hear Mummy humming, talking to the cat, opening and closing cupboards. Darkness pressed in at the bedroom window, bringing the sounds of the forest: the mellow hooting of an owl, a sharp animal noise, startling but far off. I edged further into the warmth of our combined body heat. The core of me was still cold from my swim, blood chattering through my veins like seawater.

18

'Shame I can't come with you,' Ben mutters into her hair, rolling away, hot and sticky, his hand trailing across her breasts. 'If you just waited for me to do this job, then I could take a couple of days off . . . '

'Better that I go on my own,' Isolte says, meaning it. 'But I will miss you.'

'Spoilsport! I'd like to see where you grew up,' he complains, kissing her shoulder. 'It might tell me something about you. Fill in some of those gaps you like to leave blank.'

She pushes him gently. 'Don't be silly,' she says, kissing him lightly. 'I'll be back before you know it.'

He's asleep within moments; Isolte lies awake listening to the rumble of traffic, a distant growl of an underground train, the throb of a taxi outside, sirens wailing, voices and footsteps in the street below. How will she sleep without this crowded city comfort? Without Ben? His dreaming shape pressed up against her, snoring gently, relaxed as a child. She strokes his impervious shoulder, wonders at her untrustworthy heart, her unravelling feelings spooling away from the empty centre.

*

She takes the train from Liverpool Street, the novel on her lap open but unread as she gazes out of the grimy window at the changing landscape. Watches the edges of the city, the washing flapping on the balconies of council blocks, the graffitied walls and dank canals sliding past. And then the countryside laid out in squares. Different shades of green. Fences. Crossings. The placid faces of tan cows turning towards her. She changes trains at Ipswich, getting a smaller connecting train, hearing the Suffolk accent around her again. A woman with a box of rabbits sits opposite, chewing gum, staring into space. Isolte glimpses the river between buildings, a brown strip of water.

At Woodbridge there is a light shower. People run from the sudden rain, scattering towards the shelter of cars and houses. Isolte stands alone on the platform with her back to the railway line, looking out across mudflats and boats, listening to trembling masts and the sound of rain on leaves and grass.

The B & B cottage is a white bungalow, close to the sea, with only a picket fence between it and the shingle. The taxi drops her off at the road, the driver unwilling to risk his suspension on the bumpy, pitted track that leads to the beach. She opens a door set into a wall and finds herself in a yard. She is met by the stare of a stone woman. The yard is full of sculptures, female nudes, many of them life-size. Isolte walks among them, gazing up at an arm reaching with languorous grace behind a head. She meets a frozen yawn, lips drawn back over small teeth. She touches the smooth hollows and curves, a cool, fine grain running beneath her fingers.

The back door leads into a conservatory. She knocks and a voice bellows for her to come in. Light floods through the glass, setting the rugs aflame with Turkish oranges and reds. There are

159

ornaments and bits of driftwood, a pile of books tottering on a rough wood table. She can smell coffee.

Dot Tyler is short and round and she wears a pair of men's corduroy trousers held up with binder twine. Her black hair, cut short, shows a feathery stripe of grey along the parting. She strides forward and clasps Isolte's hand in a firm grip, speaking through thick vermilion lipstick. 'Travelling light, I see? My kind of girl.'

An asthmatic wheezing makes Isolte glance down. A grinning pug looks up at her, eyes bulging.

'Don't mind dogs, I hope?' Dot bends with a grunt, sweeping the creature into her arms. 'I'll show you to your room. Let you get on with it. Just brewed some coffee. Shout if you'd like a cup.'

The room is small; three of the walls are sloping, tucked under the eaves, with brand new Velux windows letting in weak sunshine. As she'd suspected, the sash window looks straight over the beach out to sea. She looks at the sluggish water. There is one ship on the horizon, probably an oil tanker. Isolte tries the single bed. The mattress gives too easily, the bed sinking under her weight. Her fingers explore the damson velvet cover, discovering a cigarette burn near the fringed hem.

Isolte finds it hard to be alone. She likes to spend her nights with Ben. She is used to hearing him breathing. Used to the animal warmth of his body beside her. She looks down at the bed. Narrow as a coffin.

'I'm going out,' she calls to Dot.

'Do you need a map, directions?' Dot emerges from the kitchen, cigarette in hand, pug at her feet.

'No, thanks.' Isolte pauses, continues cautiously, 'I lived here for a while, when I was a child.'

'Marvellous. See you later then.'

Dot is not an asker of questions. Isolte is grateful. She was afraid that she'd have to fend off some nosy landlady. Isolte shuts the door of the yard behind her. She wonders if she will remember how to find her way. The idea of looking at a map is ridiculous somehow, not just unnecessary. Her feet will remember, she tells herself.

There are sheep in the field opposite, and a panicked rabbit sprints through the long grass, ears back. The sheep graze on, unconcerned. Isolte glances at the sky. The rain clouds have gone, and the early evening light is pink and hopeful. She looks at her watch. There is plenty of time to get there and back before dark. She sets off determinedly down the old Roman road; 'a bit of straight,' the boys called it.

Three horses wait by a gate with heads hanging low. She holds out her hand towards velvet muzzles, feeling a rush of awe. She'd forgotten how huge they are, how solid their bones, the depth and breadth of their chests. One of them stretches out its neck, pushing its nose into her hand. There's the prickle of whiskers, the leathery curl of lip. She wonders if Viola remembers the day they found the stallion in the forest. She hadn't said when she looked at the photograph.

Isolte glances at the distant farm buildings and stable blocks, sees two young men in blue shirts hanging bales of hay from a far gate. She gives the horse one last pat on its muscled neck and sets off in the direction of the village, walking away from the sea and the marshes.

Not much has changed in the village. Some new houses, all orange brickwork and plastic window frames, stand in a neat cul-de-sac on the outskirts. She can hear a radio playing a pop song and a child's miserable wailing. The village shop looks exactly the same; even the cartons of Daz and dusty packets of biscuits in the window don't seem to have changed. The pub has been recently done up; there's a blackboard propped outside advertising fish and chips and cottage pie; several tables have been arranged on the tarmac with red umbrellas leaning drunkenly on white poles.

Out of the village, she follows the narrow road between hawthorn hedges and steeply sloping banks, tangled with hogweed and nettles. Tractors have left clumps of earth and a scattering of straw, the tarmac worn into ridges by heavy wheels. She flinches at dead rabbits, turns away from the hulking mess of a badger. At the cottages, she sees at once that things are not the same. Gnomes and vegetable patches have disappeared from some of the gardens, replaced by gravel drives and rose beds. There is a new Saab parked in front of the end cottage and someone has put a plastic swing in the garden. Two brothers used to own the cottage. 'Bert and Reg.' Michael liked to tap his forehead slowly. 'Not right in the head.' Whispering behind his hand, 'Their mum and dad were cousins.'

The brothers' garden had been a profusion of perfect produce: neat lines of leeks, frothy carrot tops, and canes tied together bearing luxuriant curling bean shoots. Silver bottle tops fluttered in the wind. They'd put an old table at the end of the path by the gate and it was always covered in seasonal offerings, including eggs from fat brown hens. When anyone dropped pennies into the jar and took a box of eggs, the two men stayed indoors or kept their backs turned, bending towards the soil with such intent that they looked as though they'd lost some precious jewel.

Once Bert shuffled down the path towards Isolte, his brown trousers patched at the knees, white shirt with frayed cuffs. In his hands, two eggs, fresh from the hen. He'd placed them tenderly inside her palms. They lay on her skin, warm and smooth. Bert's hands, touching hers, were big and ingrained with earth: black soil silting up the webbing of cracks and lines. She'd held her breath against the stink of unwashed clothes and old body. His mouth hung open, moist and gaping, white spittle sticking to his lips. She'd fled without saying thank you, the eggs curled too tightly in her hands. One of them had cracked, and a trickle of slime leaked into her palm, the viscous liquid looping through her fingers.

She rubs her fingers together now, remembering the stickiness, and how she'd scrubbed her hands at the boys' kitchen sink. She frowns, unable for a moment to remember which number John and Michael lived at; there are none of the clues she expected to find: no rusting tractor or heaps of empty cans; no chopper bikes thrown down in the dust and no cage of ferrets. The cottage looks neat and anonymous. There are some children's toys in the garden, and a black cat sits on the front step in a patch of sunlight. The Catchpoles have gone. They've moved, she thinks. Of course they have. It's been years. The foolishness of presuming that they would still be here brings a flush to her face, but her disappointment is quickly replaced by a sense of guilty relief.

She's already turning away when a thin woman marches around the side of the house, a child clamped to her hip. The woman has a frizz of white hair. She bends to pick up a plastic rocking horse and disappears round the corner again, the child's feet banging against her hips.

Isolte smells nail polish and cheap hairspray, remembers that awful disco, and the rash of love bites on Judy's neck.

Isolte puts her hand on the gate, hesitating. Her heart has begun to beat too fast, banging against her ribs like something

163

trapped. She feels Viola close, her arm brushing against her, Viola's mouth at her ear, whispering. The urgency in her sister's voice has stayed with her. She hears it now inside the whisper. Go on. Viola's words are simple, insisting. Go on. Isolte pushes at the gate, walks up the path and knocks.

The door is opened just enough for the woman to peer out. The woman coughs. 'Yes?' Her voice is unfriendly. She has dark smudges under her eyes; her expression is guarded. She pushes a spray of snowy frizz out of her face. Nobody else has hair like that.

Isolte glimpses the sitting room. It looks different. The walls are covered with a purple-flowered paper, its sprawling petals unfurling oppressively into the small space; she's certain that there are fewer knick-knacks: no porcelain dancers or china cherubs. A giant TV is blazing silent flickering images from the corner it used to stand in, although of course it can't be the same set.

Isolte takes a deep breath and smiles. 'Hello.'

The woman frowns. She doesn't show a glimmer of recognition.

'Um, this may seem odd.' Isolte clears her throat, unsettled by the woman's blank stare.

The woman shakes her head slightly, frowns again. Her shoulders are squared with impatience.

'I don't know if you remember me. I'm Isolte. My sister and I used to play here . . .'

The woman does not blink. She scratches her arm and Isolte sees red marks dragged through skin weeping and raw with eczema.

'It's just that I think I know your twin brothers.' It comes out in a rush. 'John and Michael, I . . .'

The child crawls to the woman. Clutching her knees, it buries its face in her skirt: a thin, awkward creature with flailing arms. A boy. He turns and looks at Isolte with vacant eyes. Snot crusts his nose, seeps in a slow, dark slime into his mouth. He begins to whine, making a low animal noise.

'Don't know what you mean. You've made a mistake.' The woman pulls the child to her protectively. 'Don't have twin brothers.'

She stoops to pick the boy up. Every part of her looks weary. Isolte sees in one lucid moment that the child is much too old to be carried, but that he must be held, because he can't walk, can't control his splayed limbs.

'Sorry.' Isolte backs away from the door, afraid that her pity shows in her eyes. Knows that the woman doesn't want it.

'Sorry,' she says again in a small voice. The door already closed.

At the road, she turns. There is a face at the window. The face moves, ducking out of sight. Isolte walks slowly in the direction of the sea and Dot's cottage. She puzzles over it. She can't be mistaken; Judy's face, aged by time and exhaustion, has not changed that much. Isolte remembers the narrow nose, papery cheeks and jutting chin Judy had as a teenager. And that extraordinary hair.

She'd somehow thought that life here would have remained the same. There's always been some small, naive part of her that expected to find the boys tinkering with the broken tractor, sitting down to eat chip sandwiches in their kitchen.

Viola's accusation from her hospital bed comes back to her: 'We deserted them, Iss.' At the time she'd bitten down on a reply, wanting to argue with the word 'deserted'. Surely it was too strong?

They'd been parted by circumstances greater than themselves. They were children; they weren't in control of their destinies.

Isolte stops off at the pub on the way back. The bar is busy. Heads turn towards her. There is a brief pause, an almost imperceptible hush, before conversation resumes. An old man sitting in the corner is staring at her, with no attempt to conceal his interest. He hunches over his beer, a cigarette stuck to his lip, watery eyes fixed. Three teenage boys lounging against the bar nudge each other, nodding in her direction. She shifts uncomfortably, pulling her hair from behind her ears, raising her shoulders against the room. None of these people can possibly know who she is, she reassures herself.

Most of the drinkers appear to have lost interest, turning away, back to their talk or their meals. She still feels uncomfortable and out of place; she gets up to leave, but it occurs to her that John and Michael could wander in at any moment and order a pint. She looks at the door expectantly. One of the teenagers leers at her, and gives her a wink.

She is hungry, and won't be driven away by an awkward atmosphere and her own paranoia. She orders fish and chips. When the food arrives at her table, she keeps her head down, concentrating on eating. She doesn't see Dot until the pug is panting at her feet; startled, she looks up. Dot is carrying a whisky. She nods at the empty chair next to Isolte – 'Mind if I perch? You can tell me to bugger off if you want to be all Garboesque.'

'No, no.' Isolte smiles, relieved to see a friendly face. 'Sorry, I was miles away. Of course, sit down.'

Dot grips the chair with one hand and lowers herself heavily. 'Bad back,' she explains. She looks at Isolte's plate. 'I do dinners for a little extra. It's not cordon bleu. But I can cook.'

'That sounds good.' Isolte swallows a mouthful of fish, crunching batter. 'I don't have any plans for eating tomorrow.'

She looks at Dot warily. She doesn't want to ask her too many questions in case it invites them in return. The sculptures seem a safe subject.

'Went to the Slade originally.' Dot spreads her warped and weathered fingers as if they are some kind of proof of her profession. 'The ones in the yard are from an earlier period. They're all the same model. Milly Brown. Love of my life.'

'And is she ... '

'God, no. She buggered off with a dancer from the Opera House. Broke my heart.'

'Oh.' Isolte finds that the pug is sitting on her foot. 'I'm sorry.'

'The thing is there was only the one, you see. Only one love. Happens like that, doesn't it? For some people.'

'Yes. I suppose so.' She thinks of Ben. She wishes she could know with that kind of certainty that he is her one love.

'What are you working on now?' Isolte tries to extricate her toes. The dog is an immovable lump. A foul odour reaches her nostrils, drifting from the floor. The dog blinks.

'I've just finished a commission for someone in London.' Dot takes a gulp of her drink, roots around in her bag for a packet of cigarettes and lights one. 'Looking for new inspiration at the moment.'

'I'm surprised you want to take in paying guests,' Isolte says, trying to speak without breathing. 'Don't they disturb you when you're working?'

'Not really. I like the company, to be honest. Gets lonely on my own.' Dot knocks back her whisky in one last swig. 'Most of my guests are birdwatchers or other artists, single people. I don't

167

do families. Haven't the room – or the patience.' She turns suddenly, exhaling a stream of smoke. 'Where did you live – as a girl? Was it in this area?'

'Yes.' Isolte, taken aback, gestures vaguely through the ashy cloud. 'A cottage in the forest.'

'Really? Impossible to rent those places now. They only go to Forestry Commission workers.'

On the train down, Isolte had worried about whether to visit their old cottage or not. She knew that seeing it would unleash a powerful blend of bittersweet memories. Hearing that it's inhabited by Forestry Commission staff convinces her that she shouldn't go. It would be upsetting and strange to see the remnants of their old life, and even worse to see what time and strangers had done to the place.

Dot seems to sense Isolte's reluctance to engage in further talk. She pats the seat next to her, encouraging the dog to scrabble on to her lap by slapping her thighs loudly with both hands, the cigarette jammed in the corner of her mouth.

'Well,' she says, talking to Isolte but looking into the pug's snuffling face, as it balances, panting, on her knees, 'weren't you lucky? What a place to spend your childhood. Like a fairy tale.'

19

'But why do we have to go?' I wailed.

'They're not even relatives,' Issy added.

Mummy had been unfazed. 'Don't be spoilsports. It'll be lovely. Inspiring. We need more music in our lives,' she said. 'And anyway, Frank got the tickets. It's all arranged now.'

We were forced into dresses and suffered the torture of the stale flannel again. I scrunched up my eyes, the soggy cloth scrubbing at my cheeks, filling my mouth, while Mummy's fingers dug into my scalp. She was unmoved by complaints, not letting us go until she'd forced a comb through our tangles. All for a boring concert. Polly, with her music scholarship, was playing violin in her school junior orchestra. We sat scowling in the front row. I was next to Mummy, and Frank sat on her other side. It turned out that he was a maths teacher at Polly's school. He taught woodwork to adults in an evening class because, he'd explained, it was his hobby and he liked to share his passion with others.

The stuffy school hall was filled with expectant parents and siblings and grandparents. The room was much grander than our school hall: it had a lofty ceiling and dark wood panelling; there were plaques inscribed in silver with the names of sporting heroes. Gilt-framed portraits filled another wall. I stared at the painted faces, all serious grey-haired women; there were dates under each one and I realised that they must be ex-headmistresses. Some of them looked as though they belonged to the Victorian era. When we'd been told that it was a private girls' school with a boarding house, we'd hoped for something entertaining, like St Trinian's.

Glancing sideways, I noticed that Mummy looked odd. Her hair fell loose over her shoulders instead of twisted into plaits. There were no jangling Indian bracelets around her wrists. She'd even put on a new pair of Clarks sandals instead of her usual flip-flops. She twitched her toes, as if they felt confined in the leather straps. Her hands – nails scrubbed of garden soil – were linked in her lap.

Isolte sat on the other side of me, hunched and glowering, staring at the floor and kicking her chair legs in a mutinous drumming. Mummy leaned across to shush her. Isolte stopped for a few moments and started to jiggle her feet instead. She was wearing clogs and the wooden soles made a loud clacking on the floor. A woman further along the row craned her head and frowned. Mummy stretched out her hand and managed to give Issy's knee a sharp slap. The tapping stopped. Isolte's body became stiff as the soles of her shoes. The portraits looked on disapprovingly.

Up on stage, Polly stood at the front, her face a mask of concentration as she worked her bow across the violin. Her body bent and straightened as if the tiny instrument was too heavy for her shoulder. Wailing filled the room as the other stringed instruments took up the melody, classical and dull. I let it float through me, carrying me away from the hard chair and crowded room.

I had a memory folded inside my mind. I took it out and smoothed the edges. I wanted to consider every last detail of what had happened when I'd been left on my own at home for the afternoon. Mummy and Issy had gone to the dentist in Ipswich for Issy to have a filling. I'd complained about the bumpy egg, and the waiting room where Mummy knew the smell made me sick. 'If I can stay at home I'll do my homework,' I'd pleaded, struck by a moment of inspiration. 'If I go, I'll throw up. I know I will.'

It was a warm day, the sky full of light wisps of cloud, the air alive with butterflies and wasps. I had the whole house to myself. Outside, the garden and the fringes of the forest were all made strange by my isolated state. Everything was brighter and more definite. The atmosphere changed, became electric and tight, carving out a hollow sensation in the pit of my stomach. I had the feeling of being watched. I knew it was silly and I tried to ignore it. But the conviction that someone was there hiding in the trees became intense, until the desperation of it made me blurt out loud, 'I'm going to sit in the garden for a while!' as if calling to a relative.

'Oh fine, yes, you both stay inside if you're more comfortable there,' I continued, my imagination peopling our cottage with friendly faces. It occurred to me that a pretend father would cast a stronger protection and so I shouted, 'I'm fine out here, Daddy. I can see you in the kitchen.' It felt odd saying the word Daddy, but it was comforting to think of a father watching over me. I felt better after that.

I lay in the garden with *Tarka the Otter*, rolling on to my tummy on the picnic rug, inhaling traces of spilt apple juice and old cheese. The cat settled next to me, leg in the air, intent on a good wash. I'd made myself a jam sandwich and a glass of milk. Despite the tingle of fear, I was relishing the feeling of being completely alone. I didn't miss Mummy or Isolte. I felt wickedly excited, as if I'd stolen something precious and got away with it. The sun was bright on the pages of the book, making me squint, the print blurring and wavering. Every now and then I shouted at the house: 'You should come out!' or 'It's lovely and warm!'

I didn't hear him until he was standing over me. And then I jumped and spilt my milk. The cat shook herself and stalked off. His lone shadow slipped over me, cool and dark, like a sheet falling across my skin. I stared up, my heart beating too fast.

'You gave me a shock!' I told him.

His lip was cut, showing a deeper red inside the pink. There was dried blood on his chin, dirt crusted his knees and a blue scrape tore across his shin.

John looked over my head, his toe digging at the grass. 'Who're you shouting at?'

I went crimson. 'No one. I wasn't. They're out.'

'What, even Issy?'

'At the dentist.' I sat up. 'What are you doing?'

'Nothing.' He shrugged. 'Michael's an idiot.'

The chopper was abandoned at the side of the track.

'Do you want a drink?' I asked. 'Milk or ... something.' He looked hot. I tugged at my shorts, aware of my bare legs, the jam on my mouth. I felt naked without the others.

In the gloom of the kitchen I looked into the empty fridge. There was only a drop of milk left. But he wanted water anyway. He drank two glasses thirstily, straight down, the liquid making hard gulping sounds in his throat. I breathed in, tasting his mushroomy smell.

'Do you get sick of it sometimes?' he asked, wiping the blood off his chin. 'Having a twin. Them getting in your hair, bossing you, nicking your stuff?'

I nodded, feeling relief at the admission. I glanced behind me guiltily as though Issy was there in the corner watching my betrayal. There was a sharp twinge in my jaw. At that moment the dentist would be looking into her mouth, the howling drill in his hand, metal biting into her tooth. I knew how her fingers would clutch at the seat.

'Issy can be a pain sometimes,' I said, my heart doing little skips in my chest.

'Is she the oldest?' John leaned against the sink. 'Michael's older by five minutes. Acts like it's five years.'

'Yes!' I nearly shouted. 'Iss is older as well! Mum can't remember by how long though.'

We grinned at each other foolishly.

'What d'you want to do?' he asked. His voice was casual but I saw the twitch of his mouth, his eyes blinking as he looked away.

We ended up getting the crayons and drawing paper out of the cupboard in the sitting room and taking them outside. We sat on the rug and drew maps of treasure islands with detailed landscapes full of crocodile-infested rivers and pirate ships anchored offshore and jungles full of snakes and cannibals. His pirates had real expressions on their faces, and his crocodiles snarled convincingly. When I admired them, he flushed. 'You should see Michael draw. Don't take much to see he's really good.'

Our fingers, inked with blues and greens, brushed against each other as we picked up crayons and stubs of chalk and put them down. We talked about our plan for rescuing the animal sacrifice, how we'd take our bikes to make a quick getaway, whether we should find something to wear to protect us from bad luck and curses. 'Garlic?' I suggested, thinking about the things I'd been told about vampires.

He shook his head. 'Rabbit feet are the thing. Hang 'em round our necks.'

'I'm glad,' he said suddenly, 'that Issy in't here. I like spending time with you. I watch you sometimes, I see you thinking things and I want to know what they are. Yer sister – she's too busy makin' sure everyone is looking at her.'

Oh, but Issy is cleverer than me, funnier than me, I open my mouth to say. I close my lips over the words. John likes me. He thinks I'm the interesting one. I've never thought of myself as interesting before. When he got up to go he gave me one of his looks, steady and intent. 'Don't tell them 'bout this afternoon.'

'No,' I whispered, suddenly breathless.

He smiled. A conspiratorial smile. Then he touched my arm.

After he'd wheeled the bike round and pedalled off down the track, disappearing between the shadows of trees, I could still feel his fingers. Though he'd touched me briefly as a falling leaf, it seemed that I had his imprint on me: particles of skin left behind and the shape and texture of each finger, the patterning of his fingertip whorls.

The music had stopped and there was a roar of clapping. Polly was bowing, her face flushed and grinning. I touched my arm in the place where John had touched it. Isolte jabbed me in the ribs.

'What a show-off,' she growled. But I didn't reply because I'd just noticed that Frank had stolen one of Mummy's hands and was squeezing it in his. Neither of them turned to look at each other and that somehow made it worse – like a secret. My mother's eyes were bright and she was gazing at the stage, straight at Polly. I looked again. They were both clapping. I must have been mistaken. I decided it hadn't happened. I hadn't seen it.

I pulled at Mummy's arm petulantly. 'Can we go home now?'

1975

John,

Maybe one of these days I'll pluck up the courage to actually post one of these letters. But how could I let you see these things I write? I hate myself. I feel so ugly, so filled with the ugliness of what I did. I keep trying to make myself smaller so that people won't see what I've done and who I am. I wouldn't feel like that with you. You always accepted me for who I was and anyway, you know everything. I wish I could talk to you. I can't talk to Issy – she's changed – there's a distance between us that I can't cross. It leaves me lonely.

John – it seems like hundreds of years since we saw each other. I don't even have any photos of you – of how we were. I should be nicer to Hettie. She's been so kind. You'd like her. But I'm angry all the time. Only nobody understands that the person I'm angry with is me. Everything I say comes out wrong. It's better not to say anything. Listen to me! You can see now why it's better that I RIP THIS UP . . .

I'm glad that you and Michael are together – you two never needed words. You belong together just like you belong in the forest. I wish I could be there with you.

Viola

20

By the time they get back from the pub, it's too late to call the hospital. Isolte has nothing to report anyway, only Judy's puzzling refusal to acknowledge her or John and Michael. She'll call Viola in the morning. She sits at the hall table and dials Ben's number. There's a green glass jar on the table for coins. But she doesn't need to put many in, because the phone rings for a few moments and then goes to the machine. She listens to Ben's voice enticing her to leave her name, number and message, and puts the receiver down quietly.

She wonders where he is. It was stupid of her to imagine that he'd be home waiting by the phone. She climbs the short, winding stairs to her room and gets ready for bed. The sound of the waves against the shingle makes a slow call and response: a rattle of stones and the sigh of the sea. She closes her eyes, and conjures up the energy of a London night. He'll be with a group of friends in some bar or club, music thumping, lights low. She knows how the others will gather round, their bodies inclined towards him as if drawn in by an invisible magnet. She can't blame them. She hadn't been immune. From the moment they met, Ben has made her feel unique and witty and engaging, so that when it's just the two of them, their intimacy, with all its in-jokes and tenderness and sex, fools her into believing that with her he's different. Seeing him with other people is a shock. He belongs to everyone, she thinks with a dull understanding. Here in Suffolk, she can't connect with him, has no sense of him.

She feels the tethered connection between her and Viola even when she doesn't want to. It's a physical sensation, jerking and tugging, as it unwinds across the space between them – over marshes, across fields and towns and motorways, above city roofs.

People always used to ask them if they could tell what the other one was thinking, or if they knew what the other twin was doing at that moment.

'Yes,' they answered, straight-faced, 'of course.'

They got so sick of being asked that they began to make up answers, inventing silly stories. It turned into a kind of competition, to see which one could come up with the maddest tale of thought transference or incredible coincidence, and get somebody to believe it. But although she can make a good guess, Isolte doesn't always know what Viola is thinking. In fact, there have been times in their lives when it felt almost as if her sister was a stranger.

Isolte looks out at the dark mass of water through her bedroom window, where a shimmer of moonlight catches the rise of rolling breakers.

John and Michael had raged at each other as if they'd wanted to rip apart their bond and destroy the mirror image that stared back at them. Isolte knows that hurting your twin is worse than hurting yourself. She remembers the boys' father – the look on Linda's face when she heard the lorry pulling up, the menace of him in that tiny cottage, the fear of his violence polluting every-thing. Abuse spawns abuse and the boys had punished each other with punches and kicks and thumps. It was more effective than the self-harm that single children might inflict with knives or scissors or drugs.

This is dangerous, she tells herself. What does she know? It was a long time ago. They were children. She can't remember any-thing with certainty. She frowns at herself in the mirror above the dresser. She's been around magazine articles too much. She, of all people, should know not to simplify things.

It's strange to be alone, and even stranger to be in Suffolk after an absence that stretches like another lifetime. It makes her feel disoriented. Things are the same and not the same. She walked past this cottage when she was a child, rode past it, that day on the horse. Anyone standing at this back-bedroom window has an open view of the beach. Years ago, someone standing just here would have been able to look down and watch her and Viola and Rose meeting Frank and Polly for the picnic. She turns away from the window, pulling the blind. Downstairs there is a brief, sharp bark and Dot's muffled voice. Isolte wonders if she will be able to sleep. She climbs into the narrow bed, tugs the velvet bedspread up to her chin, smelling mints, recognising the whiff of turpen-tine and mothballs.

Shingle shifts and crunches beneath her feet. It is dark. The wind whips her hair into her eyes and she shivers, pushing strands away, straining to see in the blackness. Clouds stream back from the moon and Isolte watches as the sea lights up in silvered ridges.

The moonlight catches a figure at the edge of the shore. Rose.

Her thin arms are thrown out to the side to steady herself against the swell of waves as she wades into the water. Isolte sees the white nightdress puff and ripple around her mother, a pool of brightness. She watches it sink, consumed by dark water.

Isolte is inside the sea, splashing up to her knees in icy water. The cold shock explodes inside her bones, crushing her. Her mother is just ahead, water lapping around her waist, around her shoulders. Isolte cries out, but no words emerge. Her lungs struggle, lips and tongue flail; ragged sounds puncture the air, are torn away by the wind. She is sobbing in frustration and pain. Her limbs are numb; the waves shove and push her.

She staggers. 'Mummy!' she manages.

But Rose has gone. The water has taken her and Isolte didn't even see the moment that she went. Isolte's hands sweep through the grainy chill of the water, hopelessly searching for the feel of a sodden nightdress, a handful of hair, a hand to grasp.

This time she's not waking in bed with Ben leaning over her: 'It's that nightmare again, sweetheart.' His hands on her shoulder, sleepy voice, yawning, 'Issy – wake up.'

She is wet. She is shivering.

She opens her eyes into night sky, stars and flicker of moonlight on black water. She gasps and stumbles on stones, goes under, and there is real seawater in her mouth, a salty rush up her nose, stinging behind her eyes, shocking her brain. She's choking and snorting, flapping her arms, as she struggles to her feet. The waves drag at her. She tries to resist the pull and tug of them, but the force of the sea swells and breaks across her, digging the ground from beneath her feet.

Hands hold her firmly: human fingers gripping, pinching her skin. She turns, eyes stretched wide, and there is Dot, knee-deep in the water, her face open with shock, her mouth a grimace. They clutch each other and stagger up from the steep shingle slope and clawing waves. Wet fabric clings to Isolte's legs; she's wearing her pyjamas. She feels sick. She blinks through sea-water, pushes a snarl of hair from her face.

'What happened . . .?' Her voice trails away, losing energy. She can't stop her teeth from chattering. Her body is stiff and stuttering with convulsions that grip her limbs, heart, lungs, so that she can hardly move or breathe or talk.

'Don't talk,' Dot says. 'Let's get you inside.'

Dot has her arm around Isolte's shoulder. 'You're freezing. Come on. Got to get you into the warm.' They burst through the front door. The pug yaps and bounces at their feet, bangs into her shins. Warm breath on her ankles.

'Get out of those wet things. You'll get hypothermia in those. I'll run you a hot bath.' Dot pauses for a moment. 'Would you like a bath?'

Isolte nods. She can't think for herself. Her mind is empty.

Later, warmed and wrapped in Dot's old dressing gown, Isolte curls up in an armchair with a cup of sweet tea. She feels limp and exhausted, her body hollowed out.

'Sure you don't want me to put a slug of whisky in that?' Dot asks.

Isolte shakes her head. 'Alcohol doesn't agree with me.'

There is a pause.

'I suppose I was sleepwalking . . .' Isolte says. 'Odd. I've never done it before.'

Dot, looking relieved, nods. She leans forward to open the

180

door of the stove. The coals inside glow red. 'So this is the first time?'

Isolte nods.

'Must be the jolt of being somewhere different.' Dot looks at her sideways. 'Places have a big impact on us, don't they?'

Isolte sips the tea. It is thick with sugar.

The room is lit by one lamp, a fringed, amber shade shielding a low-wattage bulb. Isolte is glad of the gloom. She knows that Dot is looking at her intently; the questions forming on her tongue are already pressing into the space between them. Isolte squints into folds of light and dark. There is a bronze head of a boy. The shadows catch the slope of his cheeks, turning his smile into a grimace. Curling postcards and bits of driftwood clutter the mantelpiece. She looks at it all, pulling the reality of the room to her, pushing the nightmare away. The pug is snoring on a colourful Moroccan rug. She puts her toes on to his coarse fur, presses against the warm rolls of his fat. She waits for Dot to speak.

'You know,' Dot says quietly, 'when I first saw you out there in the water ... well, I thought maybe you were ... you were going to drown yourself.'

'No. God, no!' Isolte is shocked.

'To be honest, I've been rather worried since you arrived,' Dot goes on. 'You seemed so distracted. And when I saw you in the pub I had a feeling that you were ... frightened of something.'

'Suffolk has some bad memories.' Isolte's heart is beating fast. 'My mother,' she says shortly, 'she drowned at this beach.'

'Oh!' Dot puts her hand to her mouth.

'It was a long time ago. She ...' Isolte's face twists, 'she was drunk.'

Why is she reducing her mother's death? She couldn't tell

Ben the truth and now she's doing it again. It was her fault: hers and Viola's. They'd ruined their mother's happiness, stolen her chance of a future. Isolte feels her silence like a betrayal. But she can't force any more words out, they are stuck inside her, clogging her throat.

'What a tragedy,' Dot leans forward, 'and you were just a child?' Her voice trembles slightly.

There is silence, only the sound of waves, muted behind glass. At their feet comes the stutter and wheeze of the dog and his sudden sleeping yap, paws twitching the carpet.

'It was lucky I saw you,' Dot says quietly. 'I'd gone to bed. It was the phone ringing that got me up again. Then I saw the back door wide open.'

Isolte can't think about what would have happened if Dot hadn't seen her. The cold sea swirls closer and she hears the suck of the tide. She breathes deeply, leaning into the curve of the armrest, her fingers tight around the circle of the cup.

'Well, I think it's time we both got some sleep . . .' Dot stands up, bent over awkwardly, hands on the small of her spine. She groans. 'Wretched back. Stiff as a board.'

Dot hobbles over to the phone. 'But first,' she says, 'perhaps I should see who it was . . .' She leans down, wincing, and presses the blinking answerphone button, muttering that it might be urgent. 'It was awfully late.'

Ben's voice enters the room, loud, confident and familiar. 'Hello? I'm trying to reach Isolte.' There's a hesitation and then, 'Not sure who will get this message. But can you tell her Ben called? Tell her he sends his love. All of it.'

'Sorry,' Isolte says, not sorry at all, but glad. 'He has no idea about time.'

'Don't apologise,' Dot says gravely. 'I think he probably saved your life.'

Isolte sips her tea and looks at the machine. She wants to reach out and press the replay button. She wants to hear his voice again. Those words.

21

The four of us sat in our garden on the patchy lawn, exactly where John and I had lazed on the rug, drawing pirates and snakes. Sunlight misted the edges of gorse bushes and pine trees. I sat away from John, plucking daisies from the grass, pulling them to bits, one petal at a time, crushing yellow hearts between my fingers. John hovered at the edges of my vision, staring at the ground. I caught him in fleeting glances, watched him worrying the raw skin around his bitten nails, tearing at it with wolfish teeth. When he looked up, I was unable to meet his eyes. He was quiet too. And I was afraid that he was embarrassed by our afternoon, that he regretted keeping it secret from Michael.

The time I'd spent with him pressed into the air like a parallel universe. I thought that Issy and Michael must be able to see it too – it hung so clearly before us: the colours of our drawings, the tickle of the grass against my bare legs, his hand on my arm. How could the others not see it? I'd never concealed anything from Isolte before and it caught like a pain inside me.

'Let's go to the tower,' Michael suggested.

'We could have a swim,' Issy said, getting to her feet. 'I'll get some towels.'

I heard a sudden clatter of pans from the kitchen. Frank and Polly were coming to supper. Mummy was chopping and mixing already. 'Be back by five,' she'd said, slicing skin from a chicken viciously, 'or else.'

'We can't go to the tower. There isn't time,' I said blankly, staring hard at my arm as if examining the glinting hairs. I felt I was coming down with flu. And we had to get through an evening with Frank and Polly. I groaned faintly.

Meals that Mummy prepared for Frank and Polly acquired the importance of Christmas dinner. This time Mummy had made elderflower water ice for pudding. The sugary smell remained in the kitchen, a sweet thickness in the air. I'd helped her pick the elderflowers days ago, delicate stems holding sprays of tiny flowers. We'd stuffed them into cheesecloth bundles to steep in sugar water. Dead insects floated on the bubbling scum.

'Well, what shall we do then?' Isolte scuffed her heels, looking impatient.

'Let's find a dead rabbit,' John suggested. 'Make good luck charms. We can wear them in the oak woods.'

'What's lucky about a dead rabbit?' Issy asked.

I blushed and looked down at my dirty toes sticking out of the holes in my plimsolls.

'It's their feet that are lucky,' John explained. 'Gypsies use them.'

We set off down the sandy track. The pines stood straight and tall, trapping shadows inside a thicket of trunks. I could smell the seep of sticky resin and fermented cuckoo spit. I batted a mosquito away from my neck. Michael had picked a piece of bracken

185

and was tearing away the fronds, his hands stained with green. He whipped the naked stalk around his head.

'What's going on with this Frank bloke, anyway?' Michael said. 'He's always round at your place.'

'Yeah,' Issy sighed, 'he's annoying. Mum will get sick of him.'

'You dossy woop!' Michael shoved her. 'He's her boyfriend!'

'Is not!' Issy snapped, pushing him back, hard enough to make him stagger.

The two of them sprinted ahead, yelling at each other as they ran up the track. A pheasant flew up with a sudden fan of wings, squawking. John and I followed on slowly, our silence closing in on us like a tight and impenetrable trap.

Michael was laughing over his shoulder: 'Boyfriend! Boyfriend!' Issy lunged for him and he dodged her, laughing still, teeth bared. 'She's got a lovey-dovey boyfriend!'

The riotous noise of the other two had become our private embarrassment. I struggled to think of something to say to John. Anything.

He cleared his throat. 'Viola,' he said quietly, 'I made this for you.'

He pressed a shape into my hands. It was a stone: a grey pebble worn flat and smooth. On one side he had carved my name in spiky letters.

I examined it carefully, tracing my finger over the shape of the letters, and then curled the stone inside my palm. We walked on side by side, not looking at each other. My chest felt big with happiness. The feeling swelled and crashed inside me, thunderous in my ears. I didn't realise that my heart could radiate such joy. I sneaked glimpses of John's profile from under my hair. His face was quiet, indecipherable, but then I saw a smile twitch his lips, heard him humming tunelessly under his breath. He felt it too.

As we got nearer to Issy and Michael, I slipped the pebble into my pocket; it sat among the biscuit crumbs and bits of tissue and a broken pencil stub. I kept touching it to make sure it was still there.

'Over here!' Michael was beckoning to us.

A dead rabbit lay on the sandy track, stretched out as if it had died in mid-run. We gathered round the carcass in a circle. John prodded it with his foot. The brittle skeleton stood up through parchment skin.

'Shot,' announced Michael, and he bent to touch the rabbit's back. 'Been dead a while.' Squatting, he gripped a back leg and twisted hard, pulling until the skin tore. He stood up, holding the foot high like victory spoils.

There was movement inside the dusty fur. Ants. I grimaced, grabbing the left front foot with one hand, and the top of the leg with the other. And then it was a kind of tug of war with the fabric of sinew, bone and hair, all parts of it clinging together as if they'd been glued, until with a sickening snap I felt the bone break. Removed from the body it became a talisman: sun-warm, patched with fur, the curved claws packed with dirt.

'Now what?' Issy asked, flushed and clutching her rabbit foot.

'Tie it on some string,' Michael said, 'and hang it round your neck.'

At dinner, pushing my fork through bits of chicken and gravy, I felt the rabbit foot pressing against my skin. I put up my hand and touched the lump it made under my top. It hung low on the string, itching the space between my breasts. I scratched, wondering if it had fleas.

Noticing Polly looking, I took my hand away quickly. Put a mouthful of chicken to my lips. I could hardly taste it. I'd lost my appetite, filled instead with thoughts of John: his secret look as he'd explained about rabbit feet being lucky, the memory of our afternoon shared without the others knowing.

There were roses in a vase on the table: red velvet mouths on long, thorny stalks. Frank had arrived with them wrapped in cellophane. Mummy made a fuss, smelling them and admiring the fleshy petals. Whenever we picked wild flowers she said she didn't like to see them in vases; it made her sad to watch them dying.

Frank was leaning over his food, eating with concentration. He stopped for a moment to take off his glasses and wipe them on his napkin. Mummy had gone to the trouble of folding napkins at each place. Even so, I saw that there was an oily dribble of red juice on his shirt.

'How nice,' Frank said, swallowing and smiling. 'This is what I call a proper meal. It's delicious, Rose,' he proclaimed. 'Isn't it, girls?' He looked at the three of us, nodding encouragingly.

Polly beamed. 'Yummy.'

Issy and I remained silent. We refused to be lumped into a threesome.

'I like brain fungus more,' Issy said.

My mother gave her a hard smile.

'Odd name,' Mummy explained quickly to Frank. 'But it tastes wonderful, actually.' She waved her hands, making a frilly shape in the air. 'Prettier than a real brain. It's sort of lacy.'

'A fungus?' Frank frowned. 'Do be careful, Rose. It's hard to distinguish between deadly and edible sometimes.'

'Oh.' Mummy flushed. 'Well, if you saw it . . . it's unique. We've eaten it lots of times.'

He cleared his throat. 'Don't take this the wrong way, but I do worry about the weeds and leaves you cook. Food poisoning is a nasty thing.'

Issy and I raised our eyebrows at each other.

After supper Mummy suggested that 'we three girls' get a puzzle out to do together. Isolte and I bridled at her words, and it wasn't as if we ever did puzzles. We rooted about in the untidy games cupboard and pulled out one called The Whispering Island, from an Enid Blyton book of the same name. It was a very easy puzzle. It had been a present from Aunt Hettie. She got confused about our ages, and often sent us things for much younger children.

I knelt on the floor, running my hand across the scattered bits of puzzle. I longed to dip my hand in my pocket to check that the pebble was still there. I had a need to push my thumb over the scratches and trace my name. But Issy would know something was up if I touched it. *What's the matter with you?* she'd demand, her eyes narrowing. *You've gone all weird.*

'Do you read Enid Blyton books?' Polly asked, fitting a piece of turret into the castle.

'Sometimes.' Issy was guarded. 'They're a bit babyish now.'

'I like them.' Polly grinned. 'I like the one where they go on holiday and there are wild ponies on the moor and then they discover the gypsies are stealing them. I can ride. I have lessons. Do you have riding lessons?'

'No,' Issy muttered.

Delighted to find us on the floor, the cat came over and walked backwards and forwards over the puzzle, purring and dislodging pieces, her tail flicking against our faces.

Frank was sitting comfortably on our sofa, his face shiny and smug, like an overfed and overgrown baby, with his smooth pink cheeks and fat lips. Mummy had kicked off her flip-flops and curled next to him, tucking her feet under her. The way she kept fiddling with her hair – twisting it and making little half-finished plaits – I could tell she was dying for a rollie. Frank disapproved of smoking. Mummy said it was about time she gave up anyway.

I looked at her warily: the mother I knew was changing. Mummy thought discipline and rules inhibited the natural development of the child. She'd read all Rudolf Steiner's philosophies, underlining bits in firm pencil. I'd heard her quote him to add weight to her own ideas. Routines and clean socks weren't important; fathers were not necessary. Love was the thing, she said. Give a person love and they'd be all right.

'I don't think you ever told me why this part of the world tempted you?' Frank asked, sipping from his mug of tea.

'Oh, you know, Suffolk is so beautifully out of the way, isn't it?' She angled her head, glancing at him briefly. 'Proper country. I can't breathe in cities.' She shuddered. 'And suburbs are so . . . deadening. And then,' she continued, 'I used to spend time here when I was a child. So I wasn't a stranger.'

I was half listening. We'd already heard the story about how her uncle and aunt ran a small tearoom in Aldeburgh, how she and Hettie had spent holidays there, helping put cream on scones and serving old ladies tea in green china cups. When Uncle Horace died he'd left her a small amount. A surprise windfall. Unhappy with the Welsh commune, she'd thought that she should use the money to settle in Suffolk, find a place where just the three of us could live.

But Frank was caught up in the death thing, not listening to the important part about the three of us together, alone. He was mumbling condolences.

190

'Oh, don't be sorry. Poor Horace was in a terrible state,' Mummy interrupted him. 'I needed the money, and Horace . . . well, at eighteen stone and missing a leg, he wasn't enjoying life. Blood poisoning.' She raised her eyebrows. 'They couldn't find a coffin to fit him. When the undertakers rang to explain the problem, Aunt Sarah suggested cutting off another limb.'

'Good heavens!' Frank jolted upright, his tea slopping out of his mug, wetting his trousers. 'What an . . . enterprising woman.'

'Mmm.' Mummy tucked her hair behind her ear and arched her spine like a cat. 'You could say that. So much so that she's already remarried and gone to run a pub in Norfolk.'

Frank rubbed at the tea stains with his cuff.

'I'll pour you some more,' Mummy suggested, putting her hand on his leg. She tipped the pot. Gleaming liquid fell in an uneven trickle, splattering from the chipped spout.

'In the end,' she said, 'they stuck the coffin together and everyone kept their fingers crossed that it would hold during the service. Which it did,' she went on quickly. 'I've often thought,' she murmured, 'that when I go, I'd like a pyre at sea. Like a Hindu. Or King Arthur.'

'Rose, you are an incorrigible romantic. What am I to do with you?' He seemed to forget about the tea stains and gazed at her as if he'd just noticed that she was made of chocolate. Her hand returned to his knee. Her long fingers wrinkling the linen of his trousers.

'Finished!' I yelled. 'We've finished the puzzle.'

I wanted to sweep Frank and Polly up, push them out of our house and slam the door. My head ached, bringing deep, deadening tiredness. I wished the three of us could be alone in the kitchen with the radio on and Mummy making pancakes. I wanted to be in bed, with no secrets, no muddle, Issy warm beside me, and Mummy's long hair drifting over my face, her smell and her low laughter.

*

'Where did we live before the commune?' I'm polishing a round table in the back of Hettie's antiques shop in Lots Road, the friendly smell of beeswax on my fingers. 'Me and Issy and Mummy. I don't remember anything.'

Both Issy and I enjoy poking about in the shop. Among the dark wood tables and chairs are Victorian dolls, embroidered silks and butterflies in glass cases. Now that I've turned fifteen, Hettie pays me pocket money to work for her on a Saturday. Isolte has a Saturday job in Biba. She says I'm welcome to the antiques.

There are no customers and Hettie sits on one of the new spindly chairs. 'Well, Rose lived here, in London,' Hettie says. 'She came back from California pregnant with you. That really put the cat among the pigeons!' She has a bunch of white price tickets in her hands, freshly inscribed. She attaches one to her chair. I read '£150' written in neat figures.

'Daddy was apoplectic, insisting that she have you adopted. Rose refused, even though he threatened to throw her out. She was absolutely determined to keep you both.' Hettie shifts, getting comfortable, and the chair creaks under her weight. 'Then he had a heart attack, and we inherited the house.' She purses thin lips, remembering. 'I was divorced at the time, so your mother and I lived together for a while. You were tiny babies. You won't remember me changing your nappies.'

My mouth opens at this piece of information: Hettie holding me. Hettie burping me against her shoulder. I think I remember the shape of a window, someone humming, the sound passing

192

through them into my soft bones, into my uncurling fingers. No strength in my neck. The world at an angle. But that can't be right. My memory can't stretch that far back.

I rub at the table again and my blurred reflection wavers inside the burnished depths of the wood.

'I loved having you both in the house. Didn't mind the wailing and the nappies over the bath.' Hettie smiles. 'I couldn't have children, you see. And having you two to cuddle and feed, it felt like a blessing. I worried about you when Rose took you off to live in Wales. But it wasn't up to me to interfere.'

'Bet you didn't think you'd be looking after us again!' I try to keep my voice bright and steady.

Hettie sighs. 'I won't lie to you, Viola. It was a shock. Rose dying and then having two grief-stricken little girls to take care of . . . ' She shakes her head. 'I'd got very used to my own company. Didn't know a thing about children.'

'But you were wonderful,' I interrupt. 'You still are.'

Hettie flushes and picks at her sleeve. 'I did my best. I think we've all rubbed along pretty well. I know it can't be easy for you girls. And I worry about you, Viola, dear.' She looks at me intently. 'You don't eat enough; you're skin and bone.'

'Oh,' I say quickly, blushing, 'I'm fine. I eat loads. Think I have a fast metabolism.'

'Like your mother. Rose was always slim as a whippet.' Hettie nods. 'She floated about the place in long skirts, with beads and feathers round her neck. No one would know she'd just had twins. I felt very stuffy next to her. I never envied her though, she was one of those people who surround themselves with drama and chaos – just watching her was exhausting. Anyway, next she got involved with a little fabric company off the King's Road. Batik and tie-dye.' Hettie waggles her fingers at me. 'Came home with stained hands. It didn't last.' She sighs.

It's odd to think we were babies in the city. That we were wheeled up and down the King's Road by Mummy in her floating skirts.

'There was another man then,' Hettie remembers, 'a musician. The truth is, your mother wasn't good at seeing things through. Daddy said she was like a magpie. Picking things up and dropping them. But one thing she did stick at was being a mother. She was very proud of you. She loved you, Viola. You and your sister. Never doubt it.'

I blink away sudden tears and notice that Hettie's eyes are damp too. We both clear our throats noisily and I concentrate on rubbing the table again.

'It was then,' Hettie continues in a huskier voice, 'that Rose announced out of the blue that she was sick of London. Said she wanted to bring her girls up somewhere they'd learn healthy values. That was when she told me about moving to Wales.

'We'd sold Daddy's house by then.' Hettie stands up, fixing a price tag on to a standard lamp. 'Turned out there was a mortgage on it, so we didn't become rich overnight. But I was able to open this place. My ex-husband had been in the trade so I had some contacts. Of course Rose lost a bit of money in the design venture. Gave some away too, probably. Money didn't stick to Rose. But she had enough to get you to Wales with her latest boyfriend, an artist – maybe you remember him? Tim, I think … But that relationship broke down after a couple of years. Then she wrote to tell me that you three had moved to a commune nearby. She was very excited about it. Said that at last she'd found the perfect way to live and bring up her children.'

The bell jangles at the front door and Hettie runs her palms over her tweed skirt, putting on her shop face.

There is the stir of air from the street, a man's voice. The dust motes at the back of the shop dance around me. Do I remember Tim? I think I remember a smiling person with paint on their shoes. But mostly I recall the similarity of the men passing through the commune, how they blurred into one: baggy jumpers, dirty feet and guitars. They smelt of nicotine and unwashed hair. With their loud male voices and languid gestures, they had stood between our mother and us.

22

Mummy suggested that we have Polly over for tea when Frank was teaching his woodwork class. Mummy said she didn't need to learn about woodwork any more. The letterbox stood at an angle at the end of the drive. Sometimes we lifted the heavy lid to peer inside, but we didn't often find letters, just woodlice and mould blooming in damp corners.

Polly sat opposite us at the table; she grinned, showing the gaps in her front teeth. 'I like coming here,' she confided. 'Your mummy is funny.'

The late afternoon sun slanted through grubby windows, warming our skin and glinting on knives and forks. The kitchen was full of the smell of bubbling cheddar cheese and frying bacon.

'What a gorgeous evening,' Mummy said, dropping spoonfuls of macaroni cheese on our plates. 'I'll let you off clearing up if you take Polly and find a game to play outside.'

The cat had jumped up to settle on the table next to my plate, her tail curled neatly around her paws. She blinked slowly.

I gave her my cheesy finger, and she licked it clean with her careful tongue.

Polly's eyes grew round as marbles. 'Won't you get germs? Isn't your cat's bottom dirty?'

'Oh, we all need a bit of dirt.' Mummy laughed. 'It's good for you, helps to make you stronger.'

Polly chewed thoughtfully. She put out a hesitant hand and touched the cat's tabby fur.

Polly was seeker. Isolte and I split up, dashing in opposite directions while Polly counted out loud laboriously, hands clasped over her eyes. I got down on my knees and wriggled under the shed. There was a gap where piles of bricks held it off the ground. I shuffled inside weeds and dank grasses, lying flat in the cobwebby shadows; I was invisible to anyone standing up. I guessed that Isolte was crouched in the bracken at the edge of the garden. Or she might have climbed a tree and hidden herself in the leaves.

'Coming!' Polly sang out and I watched her as she walked, peering behind trees, craning her neck to look up as if we might be hanging in the air above her head. As she failed to find us, she got more and more anxious. She panted slightly, cheeks flushed, jogging from one end of the garden to the other. 'Where are you? Coo-ee,' she called out, her voice straining for hope; and I had to bury my face in my hands to stop myself laughing aloud. She stood for a moment on the brink of the forest. I craned my head to see her. She dithered and I saw her bend down to scratch her calf. I knew she wouldn't venture out of the garden on her own.

When she began to cry, I thought at first she must be pretending. Nobody cries because they can't find people in a game. But there she was, rubbing her eyes and making gulping noises. I frowned and glanced around the garden for Issy. Perhaps we should come out. I had cramp in my arms. I'd just begun to squirm from under the shed, when I saw Mummy's legs come striding into the garden. Raising my head too quickly, I hit it against the low planks.

Mummy seemed angry and I wondered what Polly had done. But then Mummy was squatting next to Polly, talking to her in a low voice; I couldn't hear any words, but her tone was unmistakably soft and soothing. Polly was nodding and shaking her head, shoulders shuddering. Mummy slipped her arms around her, and pulled her in for one of her bear hugs. They hugged for a long time. I stared, mouth open, a sticky cobweb catching on my tongue.

'Never mind,' Mummy was saying, leading Polly into the house. 'You come and play with me.'

Isolte dropped out of the apple tree, wiping green stains on her jeans.

'I can't believe it,' she said, eyes blazing.

I nodded. We looked at the closed door of the kitchen. We waited for a while in the garden until the air got cold, and the ground damp.

'She's our mother,' Issy said angrily. 'It's hard enough having to split her up between *us*.'

'But at least we have equal rights to her,' I agreed.

'Blood rights,' Issy said darkly.

When we went in, Polly glanced up briefly, her face smeary and pink. She had a drink of hot chocolate by her elbow and was placing a Queen of Hearts on the table. 'Sevens!' she shouted excitedly.

'You've beaten me!' Mummy told her, smiling and throwing down her hand of cards.

She'd put a tape in the cassette machine Frank had given her, and the air was full of Jim Morrison's voice, the smell of burnt milk and cigarette smoke. Mummy didn't even look at us.

'I expected so much more of you,' she told us after Frank had come and taken Polly home. 'That child needs us to love her.'

At bedtime, Mummy still wore her disappointed face and, lighting a rollie, she left us alone in the dark, the bedroom door banging shut behind her.

23

The nightmare remains, washing around inside Isolte, darkly wet, insidious and accusing. She walks up the track to the stud. Her feet raise small clouds of dust, whitening her shoes. Rose didn't get her flaming pyre out at sea. She was cremated in the local cemetery, a dreary, red-brick bungalow. There'll be a small plot somewhere there, a plaque with Rose's name on it.

Tomorrow evening, Isolte thinks with relief, she'll be in London. Ben said he'd pick her up from the station. She'd phoned him early, before Dot put a huge cooked breakfast on the table. She didn't tell him about her sleepwalking. He'd been in a rush. There'd been a cab coming to take him to a studio in Primrose Hill. As he spoke to her, he'd spluttered and cursed, burning his mouth on his coffee.

'I'll be home tomorrow,' she'd said.

His 'Good!' was emphatic, but she could tell he wasn't really concentrating. He was excited about being taken on by a new agent and already immersed in that day's work. About the love thing, she'd wanted to ask, did you mean it? But he answered his doorbell while he was talking to her. She heard his 'Be down in a minute, mate,' placating-the-taxi-driver voice. He was distracted, anxious to get on. 'See you at Liverpool Street,' he promised before hanging up.

The stable yard is full of the smell of horse and manure. Flies drone in clouds above a heap of droppings. She waits near the gate, sunlight in her eyes, the heat like a hand on her back. She'd thought someone would be here to meet her. She'd imagined some sort of ceremony, like cutting a ribbon or breaking a bottle of champagne. But there's no bunting and everyone ignores her. A man in a blue shirt is busy hosing down a horse's hooves. And another man, also in blue, is trundling a wheelbarrow piled with straw and dung across the yard. She looks at an older man in tan cords and a checked shirt. He's harnessing two Suffolk Punches to a brightly painted cart. He looks as though he's in charge.

'Yes,' he introduces himself when she approaches him, 'it's me you're looking for: I'm Bill. Stud manager.' He runs a finger around his collar. She sees sweat prickling his forehead.

'Meet Nettles.' Bill strokes the head of one of the horses, caramel hair speckled with white. 'He's big for a Punch. He stands over seventeen hands.' The horse chews at Bill's hand thoughtfully. 'We have to put him in harness with another one big as him, see. Else they can't work as a team.'

Isolte inhales the smell of warm horse. She's twelve again. John is blowing into a stallion's nostrils. The huge animal settles under his touch. Michael is turning to her, asking, 'Want to get up?' She's putting her foot in his palm, his fingers grazing her ankle.

Bill is still talking. Isolte makes an effort to concentrate, nodding and asking questions as he takes her on a tour, pointing out the new block that her donation helped to finance. He tells her that the horses are an endangered species – only one hundred and fifty left in the country.

'All the Suffolks can be traced back to a single stallion,' he's saying, 'Crisp's horse of Ufford.'

Isolte finds that she's enjoying the experience. The atmosphere of the place is unhurried. The horses move with ponderous grace under the bright midday light. And she likes Bill. He's kind. He reminds her of an animal, but she can't think what. He's a neatly built man with a narrow chest. His close-cropped beard barely conceals a pointed chin. He looks at her steadily. He doesn't miss much, she thinks.

'We keep two stallions here,' he tells her, 'and twenty-one mares and foals.'

'And the men in blue shirts?' she asks, raising an eyebrow.

He laughs. 'They're all from the local prison,' he says. 'It's an open prison. Certain inmates who volunteer and are up for parole or release, they get work here as a kind of privilege.'

'I didn't know.' She glances behind her as one of the men empties a bucket on to the grass. He doesn't look up.

'They used to send gentlemen here, prepare them for life as farmers in the Colonies. Times have changed.' He rubs his nose. 'I think it's good for the inmates. Working with horses is calming. Helps them feel the rhythm of things.'

He takes her to see the new foal. It staggers around its mother, long legs splayed. It snorts and ducks away from her hand when she reaches out to stroke it. The mother looks on placidly, chewing hay.

'Little one's still nervous.' Bill leans on the stable door. 'We're going to name her Isolte, if that's all right with you.'

A ferret. Bill is like a kind ferret, Isolte realises. It's been a long time since she's seen one, in the twins' kitchen, standing on its back legs. And weeks later, in the boys' yard, the new ferret taken out of the cage, writhing in John's arms. Daring to touch the pale fur, feeling it soften under her hand.

It's on her way back through the stable yard that she notices a man with his back to her. He's sweeping energetically with his head down, watching the movement of bristles, the dirt and straw that he collects before him. Patches of damp darken his blue shirt. His hair, a deep red like the rust on old metal, is cut short, sweat-soaked around his neck and ears. As he moves, his shoulders strain under his shirt. Even at a distance she feels the simmering energy of him. She stands watching, waiting for him to turn.

When he does, she understands how the boy's features have grown into this adult face, with lean bones, and a short nose over a long, lopsided mouth.

'John?' The name comes to her as instinct.

He stands with the broom in his hand, shading his eyes. A slight tremor runs through his body when he sees her. But he says nothing. For a moment she thinks that he's going to ignore her. Then he comes forward slowly, without speaking. There is such intent in his walk that she swallows nervously, takes an involuntary step backwards.

He comes close enough for her to see the individual hairs on his face, the grime streaked across his cheek. She'd forgotten how blue his eyes are. Flecks of violet surround the pupil. The boys shared a precise and unnerving gaze, as if life was something to be examined intently. John looks at her with that same un-disguised scrutiny. She reddens beneath it. Unexpectedly, he touches her face. She starts at the shock of his fingers, unnerved by his nails trailing the surface of her skin. It's an act of will not to move away. He's like a man reading Braille. His eyes are half closed, his hands calloused, rough-skinned. She feels his fingers on her lip.

'Isolte,' he says.

She nods. She swallows, speaking slowly, her words catching in her throat. 'I can't believe it ...' Her hands rise and fall away. 'How strange to find you here ... such a coincidence.'

She blushes again. She's saying the wrong things. Other words hang unspoken between them. *What have you done?* He smells of horse, and the musky, feral smell the twins had – the mix of bark and earth and sweat. She feels nervous and dizzy with the past rushing up to meet her as if she's falling from a height.

'Viola?' He looks over her shoulder as if he expected to see her sister standing there.

'She's ...' Isolte pauses, 'she's not here. She's not well at the moment. She's in London.'

'Not well?' He looks anxious.

'It's all right. Nothing serious,' she lies.

Shouldn't she hug him? Shouldn't she be filled with joy? Instead, she is awkward, uncertain of how to behave. She's embarrassed. She can't quite accept the reality of this adult John. His prison clothes make her feel uncomfortable. He does nothing to make her less nervous. He hasn't smiled once. She stares at him. He is familiar and strange. He's not as tall as she imagined he'd be, only a bit taller than her. But his broad shoulders are thickened with muscle. He stands with a straight back, limbs tensed as if for sudden flight. Sunlight catches burnished cheekbones, skin like an outdoor worker's, coarse and tanned by days of sun and wind. He shuffles restlessly and looks behind him. 'Well then. I should get back to work.'

Isolte clears her throat. 'Where's Michael?'

But John is already walking away. He doesn't answer her. She knows that he must have heard.

By the time Isolte gets to the row of cottages she is hot and thirsty. Her sandalled feet are coated with dust, making her toes itch. She hooks her hair behind her ears, licks dry lips. Inside the neat garden, the white-haired woman is hanging washing on a rotary line. She reaches up to peg a pair of jeans to it. At her feet there's a basket of damp clothes.

'Judy,' Isolte calls.

The woman starts and twists, lets the jeans drop. She begins to turn, as if to walk away. But then she changes her mind and swings round to Isolte, chin up, her expression closed.

'What do you want?'

'To talk to you for a moment.' Isolte opens the gate. 'Please?'

Judy inclines her head in a curt nod and walks off. Isolte follows her into the kitchen. Judy stoops and picks the child up out of a playpen. She holds him close to her chest as if he's a shield, and looks at Isolte.

'Well? I don't have long.' She glances towards the garden. 'You can see I'm busy.'

The child's head falls back loosely on his neck. He smiles vaguely, his features twitch and tremble. His fingers clutch at his mother's shirt, pulling it open so that Isolte sees the thin curve of her collarbones, the white expanse of chest.

'I won't keep you long.' Isolte crosses her arms, and then uncrosses them. 'I've just seen John.'

Judy looks down at her child, smoothing his hair away from his damp forehead with gentle fingers.

'Judy, what happened? Why is John . . . What did he do?'

'What's it to you?' Judy looks up, holds the child tighter. 'You weren't here.'

Isolte takes a deep breath. 'We had to go,' she says briefly, 'after Mum died.'

Judy shakes her head, glances away with rolling eyes.

'They used to talk about you all the time. Issy this and Viola that.' She laughs, a short, humourless sound. 'Dad told them they were daft to think you were their friends. Said you were too posh for them.'

Isolte blinks. Judy has lied to her; she feels indignation tightening her chest. 'You told me you didn't have twin brothers.'

'Well, I don't, do I?' Judy bends to put the child down in the pen again. His legs crumple beneath him and he begins to cry. A thin, strangled wailing. 'Not any more. Michael's dead.'

Isolte grips the back of a chair tight. 'What?' She's not sure if the word makes any sound.

Judy looks at her hard. 'John.' She pronounces his name as if it doesn't fit in her mouth.

'I don't . . . I don't know what you mean.'

'Of course they were both wasted. Pissed.'

Judy comes close, and Isolte sees clumps of mascara clinging to her pale eyelashes, notices dry flakes peeling like dandruff from her chin. The flesh across her cheeks is mask-like.

'He won't say what it was about,' she says, her voice low and dull. 'Can you believe it? The fight. The knifing. The argument. John says he can't remember any of it.' She looks at Isolte. 'But he stabbed Michael. Killed his own brother.'

It's like being punched in the stomach. The loss of breath. The room tipping and spinning. Isolte swallows, lowers her eyes, mumbles words of regret, hardly knowing what she's saying.

The only thing that she can focus on is getting out of that room, away from Judy's blank face, from the memory of John and Michael as boys standing there, proud of their catch, cloudy fish dead in their hands.

24

'Come on, Vi,' John says quietly. 'Help me feed the ferrets.'

Isolte and Michael don't look up from the table – they are sticking matches into a cribbage board. 'Cats are better,' Issy is arguing. 'They have souls ... not like dogs just following people around.'

Their voices trail us out into the still air. I hear Issy's laugh.

The ferrets' noses push up to the wire, small eyes glinting. I shove a carrot through mesh; feel the tug as the animal takes it in his sharp teeth. John stands close, his arm brushing against mine.

'Vi,' he says in a funny, gruff voice. 'Do you want to be my girlfriend?'

His words hover in the air. I quiver with pleasure and anxiety. What should I say? I don't know the proper response, only that I want to be with him so much that it hurts.

I nod eagerly, my smile spreading wide.

He takes my hand in his grubby one and presses our fingers together. His are warm and rough around mine.

Later, I repeat the word to myself – girlfriend. It is unfamiliar and thrillingly adult. All my feelings find a place inside it. Issy and

Michael don't know. We don't want them to, they will only make fun of us, tease us and set traps. 'This is just about me an' you,' John says. 'Let's leave them two out of it.'

I have a boyfriend. John is my boyfriend. He calls me Vi, which sounds soft and warm, like a sigh. The excitement keeps me awake at night, pleasure welling up when I think of him.

Isolte and Michael are bobbing in the water, the waves catching them like driftwood, throwing them up and down. They are shrieking and splashing. Isolte keeps screaming and grabbing hold of Michael's head, half drowning him. There are no boats today, just the vast expanse of water, the rush of sea and air and the gulls swooping overhead.

John is covering me with pebbles, sometimes placing sunwarmed stones carefully on my skin; sometimes digging down to heap big handfuls, cool and gritty, over my arms and legs.

'Your sister has a pair of lungs on her,' he says, putting a pebble on my chest. 'No chance of her being swept out to sea without the whole county knowing it.'

As I breathe the pebble moves up and down, slides into the slight scoop between my small breasts. His fingers trail my skin as he repositions it and I have goosebumps.

'I'd rescue her, if she was,' I say. 'If she was drowning, I mean.' Trying to keep my voice level.

He nods. 'We made a pact last year, me and Michael,' he tells me. 'We agreed that if either of us ever gets crippled – you know, in a motorbike accident or something – then the other one will put him out of his misery. Clean kill.' He makes the motion of a knife across a throat. 'Like a rabbit.'

I shudder. The pebbles are heavy on my legs and I have a sudden desire to move them. 'That's awful,' I say.

'No.' His voice is surprised. 'That's what you'd do fer someone you love.' He looks at me, but the sun is in my eyes and I can't see his expression. 'Before I met you, Michael was the only person in the world I'd do that fer,' he goes on quietly. 'But now, I'd do it for you, Vi. It's like you're a part of me. Like Michael is, but different.'

My heart starts to beat so loudly that I think he'll hear it echoing through the stones. Does that mean he loves me?

He says it a few days later. Aloud. And he takes me by surprise as he always does.

'I love you, Viola,' he says, scratching his fingers at the stone of the tower.

I'm not sure if I've heard him properly. The other two are already inside. I'm standing by the dangling rope with John. My heart beats faster and I blush, uncertain and embarrassed by the possibility of getting it wrong. But he says it again, louder, and this time he looks at me. 'Do yer love me too?'

I nod and put my finger on a faded green stain below his eye. His skin is surprisingly soft, it yields to the slightest pressure.

'Does it hurt?' I whisper.

He shakes his head. 'Takes more'n that.'

*

My fingers are shaking as I hold the needle inside the small flame. Silver blackens, and there is a smell of hot metal. The Sex Pistols on the turntable. Black vinyl spins and crackles under a needle, spitting angry words into the room. The noise helps to mask the mutter of voices from downstairs. Isolte has brought three friends back from school. They shriek and call out to each other. All fourteen-year-olds sound the same. Except me. I know exactly how Isolte will be tossing her hair, what voice she'll be using. I've shoved a chair under the handle of the door, just in case.

The ice cube has melted against my skin. Water drips into my hair, smudging cheap dye in grey streaks. I squeeze my earlobe to check that it is numb. Carefully, I place the hot metal point of the needle against the fat part of my lobe. But the skin doesn't break when I press. There's a trick with an apple a girl at school told me about. Only it's hard to balance an apple behind an ear. The round, waxy contours are too slippery. Holding my breath, concentrating, I can hunch my shoulder to wedge the apple in place.

Pain wells and bursts. Streams of fire run across my face, shooting deep into my brain. I touch my throbbing earlobe. Fingers come away bloody, sweetened with apple juice. Breathe slowly. Don't faint. The room spins, tilts beneath me.

Trembling, I stare at myself in the mirror. I fix my gaze there until the room settles. My face is white. My eyes are black holes. I feel sick. Carefully, wincing, I'm guiding a thin silver hoop into stinging flesh.

25

After Frank's comments about mushrooms, Mummy discarded the wild food manual in favour of a recipe book by Elizabeth David. It was her new cookery bible. This kind of cooking required cream, butter and exotic ingredients like avocado and aubergine. We lived off bread and porridge all week so that we could feast at the weekends. Every Saturday and Sunday Mummy laboured over crab soufflé, *polpette* of mutton or duck with cherries, serving them at meals where Frank told bad jokes with forced jollity, and they tried to trap me and Issy into conversation. We answered in monosyllables and went to bed with aching stomachs.

Frank liked to entertain us at his house as well, perhaps to prove that being a widower had taught him domestic skills. On these occasions, Mummy was nervous, fiddling with her hair and putting on blue eye shadow and pink lipstick that made her look more ordinary, more properly grown-up. She squashed her feet into shoes and chewed parsley to disguise the tobacco on her breath. She couldn't give up completely, compromising with pin-thin rollies, smoked outside the kitchen door when Frank wasn't there; 'hardly a cigarette at all really,' she'd say, picking a stray fragment of tobacco from her lip.

She stroked our arms before she rang the doorbell. 'Be good, girls,' she pleaded. 'And for my sake, smile.'

So we endured sitting in the neat living room, which smelt of polish and stale air. We sank into the squashy sofa, our knees pressed against horrible green and yellow flowers, feeling resentful.

Trooping around the house after Frank, while he pointed out the furniture he'd made, we set our jaws, staring with stony eyes. Mummy gave her breathless laugh. 'How ingenious,' she said, pretending to admire the headboard on Polly's bed; she ran her fingers over a bookcase, and gasped when he pointed to a window frame. 'Goodness! How on earth did you make that?' Frank knocked his knuckles on the kitchen table. 'Believe it or not, this is actually an old barn door,' he told us. 'See this? Can't get wood like this any more. It's so thick I broke two saws on it.'

Polly's music certificates were framed on the wall of the dining room and the clock on the mantelpiece ticked loudly. Lunch was on the dot of one o'clock; it was always roast lamb, potatoes, carrots and peas. We pushed the bloody bits of meat around in greasy pools of gravy and longed to be outside in the forest or down by the sea with the boys. And I missed John silently; that pain separating me from Issy.

One hot Sunday there was a long, slow trip to Southwold in Frank's Morris Minor to have a picnic. We sat crammed in the back with Polly in the middle, insisting we play cat's cradle with her.

'First one to see the sea!' Frank shouted cheerfully.

'Gosh, I can't wait to feel sand between my toes!' Mummy

wound down the window and her hair flew out like silver ribbons.

We rolled our eyes at each other over Polly's head. Why did we have to suffer an hour's car journey when there was a perfectly good beach ten minutes away from our front door?

And then Mummy began leaving Polly with us. 'Just let her tag along with you for a while,' she'd tell us. 'Frank and I need to pop into town.'

The Vespa sat unused on the garden path. Frank liked to drive Mummy in his car. He opened the passenger door for her, waited with his head on one side for her to slide into the seat. Then he shut the door with elaborate care, as if she didn't have the wits or the ability to do it for herself, as if she was an old, old lady, or the Queen. We hated it. Watching them drive away, it felt as though she'd never come back.

Isolte complained. 'But Mummy, why do you like him? He's boring!'

'I don't want to hear you talking like that.' Mummy looked at her sternly. 'He's not boring,' she said. 'He's actually very clever. But even more important, he's kind. And reliable. And practical. God, you have no idea what a relief it is to be with a man who can change a fuse, make a chair, for heaven's sake!' She tossed her head. 'You have no idea ... I'm sick of men who lie around contemplating their navel fluff, bloody sick of them.'

Polly wanted to do things with us. She followed us everywhere.

My frustration grew. It was hard enough to snatch time alone with John when Issy and Michael were always watching us. But with Polly around too, it was impossible. I longed to tell her, 'Because of you I can't see my boyfriend!'

214

She was determined not to let us out of her sight, staring with hungry eyes, tipping her round face at us; she seemed babyish and pathetic to me. *She doesn't know anything!* I thought furiously, she has no right to interfere with our life, with our summer. 'Look,' I snapped, 'stop hanging around all the time.'

She cried then, big tears welling up, sliding across her cheeks, wetness creeping around her nose and chin. To my surprise, she didn't run off and tell tales – she stayed with me, trailing after me with slumped shoulders, dejected as a scolded dog. I moved my hands uncomfortably, my fingers working out a way to touch her. Perhaps, I thought, I should slip my arm around her shoulder. But before I could, she recovered and began her incessant chatter again, and none of our stony silences or sarcastic remarks could shut her up.

'But why don't you have a toilet in the house?' she asked for the hundredth time. So we explained through tight mouths that not all houses had indoor bathrooms and that Mummy liked the outdoor privy because it was 'authentic'.

'It's scary,' Polly whispered. 'I don't like the dark. Or the spiders.'

'Well, don't go then,' Issy said. 'Cross your legs.'

'Or wee behind a bush,' I added.

The privy was a hut across the yard. It was wooden and there was no light inside. Large spiders crouched in corners. It had an earth floor. In wet weather, rivulets of water flooded under the door and turned it to mud. We didn't like the outdoor privy much either.

One wet afternoon when we'd been left alone with Polly again, we got out the drawing things. Summer rain battered at the windows, the cat came in shaking her damp fur. Isolte hunted through the boxes of broken pencils and dried-out felt-tips, handed out paper torn from an old exercise book. At the back of the cupboard I found a scrap of paper with John's pirates and crocodiles on it. I smoothed the paper with my fingers and tucked it in the back pocket of my jeans. I hadn't seen him for days. Missing him felt like homesickness.

Polly sat on the floor, a curl of tongue protruding in concentration. Her first picture was supposed to be a house. But really it was just a black square with tiny windows. 'You've forgotten to put in a door,' Issy pointed out. Polly looked at her drawing and began to scribble over it like a baby until her pen cut through the paper. We ignored her and began to draw princesses. This time Polly managed to make a decent effort. Sniffing, she leaned over the paper, taking care not to colour over the lines. Her princess had long brown hair and felt-tip tears fell from her eyes.

'Why is your princess crying?' I asked.

'It's my mummy.' Polly's moon face stared up at me. 'She's a princess in heaven. She's sad because she can't see me any more.'

I swallowed, embarrassed. Mummy had said that we should love Polly. We knew that Polly's mother was dead, and that was a very sad thing; but nobody had told us what she'd died of or when. I opened my mouth and closed it again. It was impossible to love someone as irritating as Polly.

'Rain's stopped,' Issy said. 'Let's build a den.'

The boys were unimpressed when we turned up at their place with Polly trailing behind. 'We can't do anything with *her* around,' they complained. That day the boys ignored us and spent the afternoon with Ed, trying to mend the old motorbike that squatted in the front drive. Judy, who was slumped in front

216

of the TV painting her toenails, uncurled herself from the sofa when she saw Polly.

'Sweet,' she proclaimed, picking up one of Polly's plaits and flicking it. 'She's like Dorothy in *The Wizard of Oz*.'

Judy and Kevin Kerry were an item by then, and Judy wore a ring of dark bruises on her neck. She never tried to cover them up. They were love bites. We wondered how badly it hurt and if Kevin liked the taste of blood. John had never done it to me – I touched my neck briefly and hoped he wouldn't. We hadn't kissed on the mouth yet either. But I wanted to do that. I practised on the back of my hand, squashing my lips against the freckled skin when Issy wasn't looking.

Judy invited us into the sanctity of her bedroom where Issy and I sorted her huge collection of lipsticks and nail polishes into colour categories, lining up the little bottles and pots. Judy pulled Polly on to her lap as if she was a baby, undid her plaits and brushed her hair. Polly slumped against her, compliant and sleepy. After a while she put her thumb in her mouth. 'You're too old to do that,' I told her sternly. Polly took no notice of me, and Judy hugged her tighter. 'Leave her.' She frowned. 'She's only little.'

I felt wounded by the reprimand. Judy was our friend first. Polly spoilt everything. I continued to sort polishes, wondering if John was thinking of me. Every now and then I heard the clank of metal against metal and the muffled rise of boys' voices. As a reward for all our work, Judy painted Polly's nails in sparkly blue polish and plucked our eyebrows.

Polly flashed her nails before her and talked all the way home. We strode ahead, ignoring her. The skin where my eyebrows had once been felt naked, my forehead smarting in the fresh air.

Polly was breathless with the excitement of the day, and she ran to keep up, her questions coming one after the other without waiting for answers: how come Judy's hair was so white? Why was their garden so messy? Why did they have the TV on all the time, even when nobody was watching it? Why did those twins smell funny?

'Shut up,' Issy snapped. 'They don't smell. And because of you we've wasted our whole afternoon. The boys don't like you.'

'I don't like them either,' Polly said, her voice small.

26

It was halfway into the holidays before a day came when we were free of Polly and could meet the others at the tower. It was hot, but humid and sullen, so that even first thing in the morning the air felt heavy. Issy and I ate breakfast in the garden, celebrating our freedom by dipping stale fairy cakes into glasses of undiluted Ribena. We tipped our heads back, draining the sweet remains, swallowing soggy cake crumbs, mouths stained red.

Mummy had the sewing machine out, sitting in the kitchen with a pile of pink and yellow floral fabric heaped on the table. She was puzzling over a new dress pattern that seemed more complicated than usual, swearing and frowning, leaning into the sewing machine, pins in her mouth. She had the radio on. We could hear the music from the garden. A song ended and someone began to read the news.

We stepped into the gloom to say goodbye, dropping our cups in the sink, not listening to the droning man's voice. But Mummy heard something that made her mouth twist. 'Oh,' she gasped, 'my God.' She shook her head, looking up from her sewing at us with wide eyes.

And we listened while the voice on the radio reported that a man had shot people, a mother and her children, strangers in the street. Mummy put out her hand to turn the voice off. She wiped her eyes and her face crumpled, her lips pursing and opening as if she wanted to speak but couldn't.

I frowned, thinking of a soldier in combat gear, a rifle to his shoulder. 'Where?' I asked, my mouth suddenly dry, imagining the boys shot down in the dusty lane.

'Oh, darling!' She grimaced. 'No. Not here. It happened far away. In another place.'

She forced her face into a half-smile. 'I wish we hadn't heard.' She stared at us. 'Where are you going?'

'Out,' we said. She never asked us that.

'With the boys?'

We nodded warily.

She sighed. 'Be careful; you know they come from . . . a different kind of family. It's not their fault, poor kids, but they won't have the same boundaries as other people. You just need to remember that.' She stared at us. 'Perhaps, perhaps you should stay here with me. You can do some sewing . . .'

We frowned and looked at her, examining her face for signs of a suppressed joke; surely it couldn't be a further lapse into her newly found attempts at discipline, one of the unpleasant side-effects of Frank – would she really make us stay at home? I felt panic, a sense of injustice rising into my throat. She'd ruined days and days by making us look after Polly.

'No. Sorry. Go on then.' Mummy shook her head again, tried to smile. 'It's all right. I'm being a nitwit. Everything is fine. That man . . . just forget him.'

We turned, relieved.

'You know,' she said, raising her voice as if she was speaking to a whole crowd of people, not just us, 'the way we live is our choice and our right – nothing should make us afraid of being free. Not ever.'

We forced polite smiles, waiting at the door. Whatever had happened in a town called Hungerford had nothing to do with us. It was just voices on the radio. The day fell open, hot and full of promise and belonging to us.

We took our bikes. The forest was hushed, flattened by heat. Limp trees hung motionless over us. The tarmac road was melting, our tyres sticky on the surface. Grass prickled against burnt ground, and sheep and cows drooped in patches of shade. But as soon as we turned on to the sea wall, a sharp, salty wind blew our hair into our eyes, buffeting us, making it harder to cycle. The coolness was a relief. We opened our mouths to swallow it.

There were two cars, a brown Rover and blue Cortina, parked at the end of the track. A couple of holidaymakers were lugging picnic baskets and blankets over the shingle. The woman held her fat son by the hand, and the man was carrying a squalling baby. They staggered against the wind.

We were relieved that there was nobody else on the sea wall. Twice when we were with the boys we'd met a man on the edge of the marshes. He'd smelt of earth and woodsmoke, a battered coat wrapped round him even when it was sunny. He'd stared at us with narrowed eyes and hissed like a goose through stumpy teeth. As we passed him he sucked in and spat a long gob of yellow. We'd heard the soft splatter at our heels.

'Poacher,' John said.

'We'd fight him if we had to,' Michael added.

'Yeah, we can take anybody on,' John said. 'Nobody gets the better of us fighting together.'

I thought about their dad then, but I didn't say anything. I believed the boys. I wouldn't want to be the person they ganged up against. It was bad enough watching them go for each other.

Glancing behind to make sure that nobody was watching, we dragged the bikes under the usual bush. The boys' choppers were already there, hidden under leaves. I touched John's bike, my hand trailing the cold spokes of a wheel. I would see him soon. Excitement fluttered inside me. The family on the beach seemed unaware of us. The father was helping his son unfurl a kite. The wind caught it immediately and the red and yellow triangle flew straight up into the sky. I could hear the flap of plastic as the kite strained against the air, seagulls wheeling around it.

The shadows inside the tower blinded me; I followed Issy carefully, picking my way over broken floorboards, feathers rustling under my feet; the boys were already at the steps, turning impatiently. I caught a glimpse of John's profile, and my mouth went dry.

Out on the roof, in the distance I saw the fat child walking backwards, attached to his kite by a long, straining leash of invisible string. The parents were half hidden behind a striped windshield. They were the only ones on the beach, apart from two fishermen further up – anonymous silhouettes crouched by the water's edge.

'Maybe if I jumped off, I'd fly,' I said, leaning over the wall so that my hair fell forwards, 'like that kite. Just take off into the wind.'

'Don't be daft,' Michael said. 'You'd break your neck.'

'Look, a tanker.' John stood close behind me. My skin prickled with the nearness of him. I imagined I could hear his heart beating. Before us hung far-flung mists of space, an endless clear sweep of air and beach, sea and sky. The lone tanker crawled like a small beetle along the track of horizon. But I wasn't really looking. I was alert to the strands of feeling between us, the soft pull of them tugging at my insides. My stomach contracted with queasy, floating pleasure.

'It'll be a full moon next couple of days,' Michael said. 'We need a plan.'

I put a hand in my pocket, touched the stone. It hadn't been hard to keep this secret from Issy, because sharing it would dilute the pleasure, and I knew that she would be jealous, giving me sideways looks, working out how to take it from me. I kept the pebble safe in my pocket, transferring it to the bottom of our unused doll's house when I had to. *Viola*. My fingers traced the letters, following scratches on a smooth surface.

Issy trod on something as she jumped down from the wall, swearing as her foot twisted and slid away. A tin can rattled across the roof and I stooped to pick it up. It was an empty tin of pilchards. John took it from me, his fingers grazing mine. He winked at me and I clamped my lips together to suppress a giggle. He held up the tin and sniffed at it. There was a slick of tomato left, a fragment of fish spine. We puzzled over how it could have got there. Michael looked up at the swooping seagulls, shrugging. 'One of them greedy buggers must have dropped it.'

Sitting cross-legged in a circle among the sprouting weeds, we discussed our plan. We had the date now and we arranged to meet at half past eleven at the crossroads between the forest and the oak woods. We'd need to bring torches and some string. It would have to be done without anyone finding out. We'd pretend to be asleep, stuff our beds with pillows.

'I'll bring my knife,' Michael said. The knife was always on his belt. A long hunting knife sheathed in a leather case. Ed had given it to him as payment for a favour. John was envious of that knife. He looked away whenever Michael took it out to dig up pignuts or slice through string.

'Anyone swimming?' Issy asked. 'I'm boiling.'

'Last one in's a monkey's uncle,' Michael called, already making for the stairs.

Racing each other over the sea wall, sea grass tearing at our ankles, we ran straight down the slope of shingle into grey waves. The cold was a shock. Even though the sun was out the waves were freezing. The family further up the beach were huddled behind their wind shelter eating their picnic. The boy had abandoned kite-flying to have his lunch. We could hear the baby, the wail of its crying. We plunged recklessly into the water, diving under the waves. I bruised my knees on the pebbly bottom, swallowed a mouthful of North Sea and surfaced spluttering.

Issy and I came out first. Hobbling over the shingle, we grabbed at our clothes, teeth chattering in the wind, and dragged them on over damp skin. I scowled at Issy. She'd got to my T-shirt before me. I looked at the jar of cars on the front of her chest, the faded words *Traffic Jam* printed underneath.

'You didn't ask.'

She shrugged. 'You can wear mine.'

I sighed deeply. 'You know that's my favourite.'

She turned away, pleased with herself. I couldn't raise the energy to argue. I scowled, buttoning up her shirt.

We crouched in a dip, hugging ourselves to keep warm, our skin a rash of goosebumps. I picked up a cuttlefish bone, admiring its solid whiteness in my palm. A hawk was hovering over the long grass by the sea wall. We watched it drop, saw it swerve up and away with something inside its talons.

There was a flash of brilliance from the sea wall: light bouncing off glass. The birdwatcher. I nudged Issy.

'Pervert,' she muttered. 'I'm sure he spends his time watching us. The birds are just an excuse to get his binoculars out.'

John and Michael were showing off in the water. They were strong swimmers, going too far out, risking the currents. A yacht came by, hugging the bank; it passed close to us, carving its way through the deep channel of water so that it could tack into the mouth of the river. We heard the snap of canvas and rope. A woman sitting by the tiller waved at us. The boys in the water shouted up at her. She stood suddenly, startled by their voices, and motioned to them urgently, waving her hands, indicating that they should go in closer to the shore. One of the boys, I'm not sure which, threw up an arm and pretended to drown. She looked agitated, standing at the helm looking back at their bobbing heads, their laughter blowing away.

'Don't!' I shouted. 'It's bad luck to pretend to drown . . .' My throat constricted with anxiety, words choked into silence.

'Come in,' Issy enticed them. 'We've got bread. And apples.'

After we'd eaten, we lay spreadeagled, face down with our arms as pillows. Lying flat to the ground we could avoid the wind and bask like cats in the warmth. My drying skin tightened, and I rubbed away the thin crust of salt on my fingers. John was lying next to me. I longed to find his hand and hold it. At that moment he yawned and sighed and his leg fell across mine, as if accidentally. I trembled a little, feeling his hot skin, the thin bone of his shin pressing into the softness of my calf.

A butterfly skimmed past – a brief tilt of yellow. I wondered what it was; I'd memorised some from the *Ladybird Book of Butterflies*: Clouded Yellow, Common Blue, Flash of Brimstone. Naming things brought them closer. *John*, I whispered inside my head, imagining the letters of his name, looping them together behind my eyelids.

We dozed, listening to the cry of the seabirds – Black-Headed Gulls, Herring Gulls – and the wash of waves against stones.

'I'm going to have a boat like that,' Michael said, 'when I'm older. I'll sail round the world.'

'What about John?' Issy asked.

'Oh, he'll come too.'

'Maybe I will. Maybe I won't,' said John and he rolled away from me. The missing weight of his leg was an absence that hurt.

There was a silence; I knew they could never live apart, do different things, let a boat carry one of them away from the other.

'Nah,' Issy teased them. 'You'll end up like Bert and Reg; a bit odd in the head, planting vegetables together.'

Michael tossed pebbles at her half-heartedly. None of us could really imagine being ancient, like the brothers. This was our life: the beach, sun on our faces, sea salt itching our skin.

Back in the tower, Issy stumbled and nearly fell through a gap in the rotten boards. I caught her arm, swinging her back.

'Let's play 40-40,' John suggested. 'Home is the roof. The left side.'

'Bagsy I'm catcher,' Michael shouted. 'Starting now!'

We scattered apart as Michael marched up the stone steps, counting out loud. I squeezed into a space behind a dank partition. It was airless behind the board, and cobwebs dragged soft strands across my face. My plan was to make a dash up the stairs

226

when Michael was chasing one of the others. I didn't know where everyone else was. I heard my stomach gurgle in the silence.

Michael came into the room, looking around. I could tell from the way he swung his arms that he was fed up with not being able to find anybody. I held my breath, pressing myself back, squeezing my eyes. I listened hard, thinking I could hear him going up the staircase. Daring to peer around the board, I made out the blur of a crawling figure coming from the direction of the entrance, blonde hair shimmering. Issy, on all fours, looked warily from side to side, crouching inside the big chamber, knees and fingers in sooty dust. I was about to hiss at her to come over and hide with me when there was the clatter of descending feet.

It was John, not Michael, who came into the room. He stopped when he saw Issy crouched there. With sudden intent, he crossed the space towards her, his hands carving a path through thickened air. I came out of my hiding place, opening my mouth to call. But John caught hold of Issy's shoulders and pulled her to him. She stood up into his arms. And he put his mouth on hers.

Their lips moved, stuck together but twisting. He had his arms around her, and she'd tipped her head up. He stood with his feet planted, and Issy seemed to fall against him, her knees sagging. He moved one of his hands, cupping her face. Gloom gathered around them, except for a beam of light that fell across John's shoulder like a sword.

It was all wrong. My body recoiled as if I'd been hit. I didn't know what to do. I wanted to tell them to stop. I wanted to disappear. Another scuffle of footsteps on the stairs and Michael sprang into the room. 'Seen you!' he shouted. He faltered, suddenly uncertain, straining to look at the shape they made, pale faces pressed together.

Isolte and John broke apart. John turned on his heels. He started when he saw me, stumbling in my direction as if he wanted to reach me, and then he stopped, pushing his hand through his hair.

'John?' Michael asked. John turned to his brother. Issy had her hand over her mouth, her eyes wide. There was a moment – perhaps it was only a second – when the four of us were held motionless. Then a rook burst in through one of the windows on outspread wings. Frightened by us, it scrabbled to leave. There was a panicked beating. The swing of its body brushed close to me, wings beating down and snapping up. I flinched, crying out as feathers skimmed my cheek; and I saw the slide of a dark eye, trailing claws hooked close. Dust stirred, swirling like smoke around us. And there was confusion, the game half continuing.

I walked past John and Issy. No hole opened in the rotten boards for me to fall into. Michael called half-heartedly, 'Seen you, Viola!'

Suffocating, I tasted dust in my mouth, between my teeth like grit. My cheek held the feel of feathers, the sense of them slapping my skin. I ignored Michael. I needed air. I needed to breathe.

'Where are you going?' Issy called after me.

I stood in the entrance, looking out at the huge sky, at birds wheeling above and small scraps of cloud floating high up. Up there it was open and free and full of light. I felt weightless, boneless, as if part of me had fallen away. And I knew then that I could fly.

'Watch me,' I whispered, opening my arms. And I jumped.

27

Isolte sits on the purple sofa, a cup of tea in her hand.

'This is Carl,' Judy says, turning to give the child a broad smile. 'He's got cerebral palsy. The cord got caught round his neck.'

'I'm sorry.'

'Yeah, well.' She shrugs. 'Life doesn't work out like we think it will, does it?'

'And your parents?'

'Mum got into one of the almshouses. She's such a help with Carl.' Judy bends down to wipe Carl's nose. 'Dad died of a heart attack a few years ago. Bastard never changed his ways. We were glad to see him go.' She sniffs, smiles. 'Ed's done all right. Works at the garage at Martlesham. Got two kids. Both healthy.'

'What happened to the twins?' Isolte asks her.

'After you left?' She shakes her head. 'They were wild. Ran off all the time. Hardly went to school. Always in trouble with the police. Dad nearly beat them to death, but it didn't stop them.'

She puts Carl on her lap. He pushes at her clothes fretfully, thin fingers pulling at the fabric of her shirt. She undoes her buttons and he nuzzles into her breast.

'I know he's too old.' Judy looks down at the child's head. 'But it's the only thing that settles him.'

Isolte looks away. She sees herself in the reflection of the blank television screen, perched awkwardly on the edge of the frilly sofa. There is no noise, except the ticking of a clock and the wet sounds that Carl is making. Isolte remembers the kiss in the tower. Her first kiss. The shock of his lips. It made her stomach lurch, the push of his tongue in her mouth.

Isolte clears her throat. 'And then . . .'

'When they were about fifteen or sixteen, they left home. They moved into an old caravan in the forest. They got themselves a lurcher, took up poaching. Lamping nearly every night. Fishing in the lakes. They managed to feed themselves. I went to see them sometimes, took them something to eat.' She shakes her head. 'It stank in that place. You wouldn't believe. Dead rabbits, skinned things everywhere. Dirty plates piled up. Funny thing was, you wouldn't expect it, but the walls were covered with paintings and drawings.'

'Really?' Isolte leans forward.

'Yes.' Judy smiles. 'Michael. He kept on with his painting and drawing. That was good, wasn't it?'

'Oh, but I didn't know that . . .' Isolte falters, 'about his painting.' She nods. 'But what . . . what went wrong?'

Judy snorts. 'What went right? They used to drink. Homemade scrumpy mostly. It knocked them out for days. And when they were drunk the fights got worse. Living with our dad, yer would have thought they'd had enough violence.'

Carl is asleep. Judy moves his mouth from her nipple. He falls away, slack mouth dribbling milk.

'It was manslaughter in the end, thank God. Not murder. And

he was still a kid at the time. John will be getting out soon – October or November, I think. Though what he'll do I don't know.'

She frowns, looking down at her child. 'I miss them. Both of them. It wasn't right that Michael died. It broke Mum's heart. Mine too. I can't see John. Not yet. So don't ask me to. I just can't be near him – I can't breathe, can't hardly stand up when I think about it.'

Isolte swallows, starts to speak. 'I don't want to interfere, but if there's anything I can do . . .'

Judy, her face hardening, interrupts her. 'We don't need your help. Don't want it. You can't do any good. It's too late. You got what you came for – had a look at what you left behind. I'm sure you'll be glad to get back to yer nice life in London, eh? I've seen yer name in the magazines.'

Isolte shakes her head. 'It's not like that, Judy. I just thought . . .'

'Look, don't take this the wrong way, but Kev is due home for his tea soon, and he won't like having someone here.'

Isolte stands up. How can she argue with Judy's resentment? The plain facts of her life are too stark, too dignified and terrible to try and soften or change with words. The past is not nego-tiable. She looks down at the clean nylon carpet and nods briefly.

Isolte puts her half-finished cup of tea in the kitchen. The place is shiny. Everything put away and the surfaces wiped. Under the tang of disinfectant, she can smell something meaty cooking in the oven. The fishing rods and guns that used to clutter the place are gone; and there are no muddy boots or wellingtons piled up by the door.

Judy has left Carl asleep on the sofa, his arms thrown above his head. At the front door she says, 'I liked having you and Viola around. Seeing yer with each other made me a bit green. Always wanted a sister.'

Isolte walks back to Dot's through the whispering lanes. Dusk is falling. A dog barks somewhere on the hill, the sound echoing in the stillness. She thinks of the boys in their caravan, imagines a dilapidated carcass, rotten wheels embedded in pine needles, sunk into crumbling earth. Their life in the forest must have been a struggle for survival: fishing, shooting and trapping creatures, lurking always on the fringes of things. She remembers the bleak secondary school. There would have been no exam results, no bits of paper giving them permission to progress into a new life.

She sees them crouching in long wet grass, darkness pressing in, dead rabbits hanging from their hands with heads lolling back, rodent teeth grinning. She senses dripping blood, the burnt smell of shot, the dog beside them trembling with excitement, his warm flank pressed against their legs. She smells dank weeds, the harsh scent of tobacco smoke, rotting metal and rubber, unwashed clothes, the fusty, rank odour of feral boys becoming men.

Michael was rougher, tougher, harder than his brother. He'd been her sparring partner, tormentor and friend. He never talked about art, never said he'd been drawing or showed her anything he'd done. It had been a jolt, hearing about it; she'd lacked the understanding to see it in him.

He'd found her behind the privy at home, days after the kiss, after Viola's fall. 'Liked it, did you?' he'd asked, leaning against the wall, watching her with his long, blue gaze. 'Liked snogging my brother?'

She'd shaken her head, embarrassed, disconcerted by the

challenge of his body turned towards her, his arms angled against the wall, trapping her. She felt the menace in him, sensed it as both predatory and playful. Turned away to hide the flush of heat in her face, her confusion.

'Piss off, Michael.'

'How about a snog with me then? I'm his elder and better.' He stepped closer, so that she saw the chapped skin on his lip, the fading bruise under an eye. 'Dare you.'

She'd pushed past him, her heart hammering. His hand grasped her arm for a moment and then fell away. She could hear his laugher, the mocking ring of it. She'd felt the need to tuck her shirt in, smooth her hair with her hands.

Boys she met in London later seemed tame in comparison. She couldn't stop holding them up to Michael in her mind. It took a long time to stop doing that. She's ashamed now, but thinking of him had excited her. She'd had fantasies about him alone in her room, pressing her hips into the mattress, her breath coming faster, his name on her lips.

'Supper will be ready soon,' Dot calls out.

The pug comes snuffling at Isolte's ankles. There's a smell of basil and fried butter coming from the kitchen, reminding Isolte that she's hungry.

'Just need to use the phone,' Isolte calls back, searching in her bag for change. She sits at the hall table, looking out through the circle of glass in the back door towards the restless sea.

She rings Ben first. By some miracle, he picks up the phone, and she tells him that she's going to stay on for another night.

'But why? I've arranged it so I could get you from the station. I've booked a table at Edmund's. Thought we could eat before the party. You said you couldn't wait to get back,' he complains. 'And you know this is my first time meeting everyone from the new agency.' She hears the petulant note in his voice. He hates it when his plans are changed.

'There are a couple of things I need to sort out before I come home.' She is vague. She can't begin to explain to Ben. It's too complicated. She's not sure what she can achieve by staying on. John hadn't suggested meeting again. But she owes it to Viola to try one more time. When she considers the chain of events that took her to the stud, the way in which she found John when it would have been so easy to miss him, it seems to promise a pattern, a meaning. She doesn't know how to make sense of any of it. She's tired, exhausted by the shock of Michael's death. She doesn't want to see John again; she would prefer to get the first train home.

'Well,' Ben says, 'it seems a bit odd. Do you want to tell me?'

Isolte holds the receiver tightly; if only she could, she thinks. She doesn't know where to start. There are too many things he doesn't know. She feels suddenly guilty and furtive; the past is bigger here, what she hasn't told him looms over her.

'I hope it's important, these mystery things you suddenly need to sort out, because I would have really liked you to come . . . ' His voice takes on a wounded tone.

He doesn't need me, she thinks, irritated. He just wants to have things his own way.

'I'm sorry.' She is brisk. She feels the force of his will in the silence. She clears her throat. 'I know that you'll end up talking business and I'll be stuck in a corner with some boring person.'

She pushes the guilt away, thinks of him at Jonathan's party, engrossed in lengthy conversation and recreational drugs with the most beautiful woman there.

She waits for a moment before calling the hospital, chewing her lip and thinking. Viola is waiting. What can she say? One thing will lead to another. If she reveals any news at all – meeting Judy or finding John – then Michael's death will come out. She can't tell Viola. Certainly not over the phone.

She can hear the muffled noises of the hospital ward, knows that one of the nurses will be wheeling the phone trolley towards Viola's bed.

'Yes, thanks, I'm feeling much better.' Viola's voice is impatient. 'Tell me what's happened.'

Thank God she can't see me, Isolte thinks, as she takes a deep breath and begins to ramble about Dot and the pug, about the stud and the foal. She talks about the forest and the changes that have been made, the new houses on the edge of the village and the extra cars clogging up the roads.

'But what about the boys – any news?' Viola interrupts. 'Have you found them?'

'No,' Isolte says quickly. 'Not yet. I'll stay on for a day or two. Ask some more questions.'

'Really?' Viola's voice is dull. 'I'd thought—'

'No,' Isolte cuts her off. 'I'm sorry, Viola. Nothing yet.'

'Do sit down – supper's ready,' Dot calls.

Dot has laid the table in the conservatory. There is a candle burning on the table. Canvases are stacked against the walls; others have been hung in groups. Suffolk landscapes, in soft greens, burnished browns and grey-blues. Isolte recognises the marshes, the shingle beach, and a field with horses grazing. She stands in front of them, hands in her pockets, looking at each one in turn. Michael is there somewhere, skulking through those landscapes:

that vital boy she knew, his sinewed body camouflaged inside brushstrokes of thrift and foxglove. She comes to a small water-colour of the Martello tower: a stark block of stone against a bleeding sky. She lied to Viola. Shame makes her cheeks flush. She turns away quickly.

Dot is there in the doorway with plates of food in her hands. 'Do you know it?'

Isolte nods and sits at the table, pouring out a glass of water.

'I painted that one years ago. It's been turned into a house now – a London architect did it. George Hobbs. Do you know him? It has a spectacular glass roof – they had to find a way to get light into the place. It's listed, of course, so they couldn't change the windows.'

'How interesting.' Isolte takes a mouthful of fish. She can't taste it. 'This is delicious,' she says, hoping to distract Dot. All she can think about is Viola, the disappointment in her voice, the doubt. She chews and swallows, forcing her mouthful down.

Dot beams. She tells Isolte exactly how she cooked it and talks about the wonderful fishermen in Aldeburgh. She's delighted when Isolte tells her that she'd like to stay on for a couple more nights.

'Do you know, I was hoping that you might let me sketch you.' She bends down to drop a piece of fish into the dog's mouth. 'Would that be too much of a bore? I'd only need you for about an hour.'

Isolte thinks of the evening stretching ahead of her. 'No prob-lem. I'd be happy to sit for you. If I can keep my clothes on.'

Dot throws back her head in a short, deep laugh. 'My dear, I wouldn't dream of making you take off a thing – you can sit exactly as you are.'

28

The little girl is leaning over me, shaking my shoulder. She's saying something. The words pull at me.

'Come back.'

I can feel her breath on my face, sweet as honey. I can hardly focus. Her features are a blur.

'You've been away too long.'

She kisses me. At least, I think she kisses me. I can feel something touch my cheek: it feels like wing tips or the brush of dry lips. I struggle to the surface and emerge into the ward gasping, drawing oxygen into my lungs as if I've been submerged in water. The air is tainted with the stink of boiled potatoes and disinfectant. It must be lunchtime. The child has disappeared. Perhaps she's not real. Perhaps I dreamed her too.

I suck in more breaths, pushing and hauling myself into a semi-reclining position.

'Ah, glad to see you're awake,' a nurse says, coming over in her sensible shoes. The plump one. I like her. 'The doctor wants to talk to you after lunch.' She nods towards the heart monitor. 'You can do without this now. The antibiotics have done their job.'

'Has anyone phoned?' I ask. 'My sister?'

She shakes her head. 'Not that I know of.'

'Who does that little girl belong to?' I ask her as she begins to turn away. 'You know, the one with long brown hair.'

The nurse looks puzzled. 'I don't know, love.' She smiles at me brightly. 'We get so many people coming and going. Can't keep track of them all.'

*

I didn't fly. I fell straight down, landing heavily on the uneven ground, the breath knocked out of my body. I lay among nettles and thistles; dark clumps of butterbur and ragwort hanging over me. I heard the trickle of the stream, saw birds wheeling like white paper aeroplanes in an empty sky. There was blood on my lip. I could taste it. My ribs were a vice squeezing my insides tight.

The others scrambled to land beside me.

'You're bleeding!' Issy cried, her arms around me. 'What have you done?'

I was stiff in her arms, like a piece of driftwood. I saw a smear of dirty red on her chest, my blood staining my T-shirt. I knew that I would never wear it again. I clamped my knees together, my bowels dissolving into a watery rushing. The kiss throbbed through my head. Their lips stuck together and twisting, twisting. I wanted to push Issy away, but my grazed hands stung and I had no strength. There was something wrong with my nose. My skin screamed, hot and flaming with itchy pain, as if I'd fallen face first into a bucket of wasps.

Michael leaned down and wiped at me with his bunched-up shirt. I cringed with the shock of his touch. 'You've cut your face open,' he said.

John stood behind him. 'Shall I fetch someone?' His voice was empty.

'No.' I moved my head cautiously. 'I'll be all right. I can cycle home.'

'What shall we tell Mum?'

I shrugged. My brain was pounding. 'Anything. I fell off a wall. It doesn't matter.'

I sat up slowly, putting a testing finger to the warm, wet opening in my face.

*

Justine is awake, propped up in bed. She looks frail. Her nose juts out of her emaciated face. I put my hand up to my own face, and under my fingers the rim of my thin scar traces a line through my nose into my lip.

She makes an effort to give me a smile. She hasn't got her teeth in and I glimpse dark, empty gums. When we were children we would have thought Justine was a witch. In those days country people hung horseshoes against witches; they curled the skeletons of dead cats inside the walls of their houses.

Justine somehow remains dignified in her flimsy nightdress, thin grey hair sticking up over a speckled scalp. I raise my hand in greeting. She nods. The last time we had a conversation she showed me photos of her grandchildren. She'd remembered that the baby was called Hector. 'Family,' she'd said, rubbing a gnarled finger over the picture of a chubby baby. 'In the end, all that matters are the people we've loved and who've loved us. Nothing else counts, does it? I'm lucky to have had time with my grandchildren, lucky I've held them as babies and seen them begin to grow up.'

The life of the hospital continues around us: patients shuffling by, the efficient movements of doctors and nurses, orderlies performing tasks with blunt good humour, the same routines, same jokes, same tragedies.

What am I doing here? I curl my fingers into fists. Why am I wasting my life?

A nurse stops at the bottom of my bed, and I see she's wheeled over the ward phone.

'It's for you, Viola.' She pulls the phone next to me. She talks in a sotto whisper, pointing. 'Your sister.'

The nurse helps me to sit up against my pillows. I press the phone tight against my ear and my heart is thumping under my pyjama top.

'Isolte,' I smooth the sheet over my lap, breathing deeply, 'have you found them?'

She doesn't answer me. She begins to talk about Suffolk. She tells me about the woman she's staying with, about a pug dog. I don't care about the new housing estate. I don't care about the Suffolk Punches. She has something important to tell me. I can hear it in her voice.

'No,' she tells me. 'No news yet.'

I smell pine resin and moss. I can feel the imprint of his fingers on my arm. The air curdles around me, thick with dust and feathers.

And I know that she is lying.

*

'Do you remember that time when John . . .' I start to say and she glares at me.

'Why do you keep going on about them?' Isolte looks exasperated. She turns away to study herself in the mirror. 'It isn't

240

healthy. Dragging it all up. We're sixteen, for heaven's sake! We would have outgrown them anyway.'

I open my mouth to protest, but she's concentrating on shading her eyelids with blue shadow; and I can tell from her expression that she's refusing to listen.

She has a boyfriend: a grammar-school boy she met at a joint-school dance. He arrives at Hettie's door with a bunch of flowers, blond hair cut above his collar; it's me who opens the door and he blushes, glancing away from me as if he's seen something embarrassing.

'You're not really twins, are you?' I hear him say as they shut the door, stepping out into the summer evening.

I watch Isolte and the boy from our window. She tips up her chin, laughing into the peach-coloured light, muggy with traffic fumes. He looks at her admiringly, reaches out a hand to touch hers. They pause on the pavement before crossing the road. A bus comes and I can't see them any more.

> My heart
> is dark and ripe
> as a bruise.
> An ache
> hollowing me out.
> Missing you
> has no purpose, no point.
> But still I do.

*

I understand now that she needed to be different from me. Perhaps she'd always resented me holding her back, stopping her from belonging. When we came to London, she didn't want to be considered weird any more. The signs were there when she admired herself in the school uniform that Hettie bought us. 'We'll look like everyone else,' she said with satisfaction, tying the green and white tie carefully in front of the art deco mirror in the hall.

On our first day at the new school, we walked into the classroom together, my heart thumping, and she moved slightly apart from me, smiling at girls who milled around us asking our names.

We both knew that she was the popular twin. She was thinner than me, cleverer than me. She always knew how to talk to people. But John liked me best.

I can't outgrow John, because he is woven into my veins and bones, stitched into my heart. The moments we spent together in the forest and on the beach live inside me; more than memories, they are the things that remind me who I really am, where I really belong.

1977

John,

> *At night, as I fall asleep – listening to motorbikes roaring outside my window, and snatches of strangers' conversations – I imagine you and Michael inside the hush of the forest; I pray hard that your father is away in his lorry, that he will never hit you again. And I see you happy – you must be happy, John, for me, it's the only thing that lets me make sense of things. When I'm walking down school corridors filled with giggling girls, or tramping along the dusty Fulham Road, deafened by traffic, I am really walking our forest paths with you beside*

me. Then I wake up to the real world, knowing you are miles away. I wonder if you do the things we used to do together – trespassing on the Malletts' farm, fishing in the lake, climbing into the tower . . . but writing that makes me feel sick. The thought of the place. Do you still go there?

Viola

29

The stable yard gives off the familiar smell of dung and ammonia, and the scent of horse. A beaten-up old radio sitting on a windowsill plays Rick Astley's 'Never Gonna Give You Up'. Two young men in blue shirts, one of them whistling along to the tune, are tacking up two horses. They place harnesses on mighty shoulders, bending down to do up straps, moving lightly around the dozing animals that stand quietly with heads lowered. The radio fills the air with bouncy sound and the whistling comes in breathy, staccato bursts. 'Give it up, Tom,' one of them says. 'You're killing me.'

Isolte is looking for Bill. She thinks about asking the men, but they are so intent on their task, it puts her off. She stands watching. The horses have blinkers on; their manes and tails are neatly plaited with black ribbon; hooves shine with oil. All around her, empty stables stand open. She supposes that the other horses must be out grazing. The whistling man steps back, slapping the flank of the horse nearest to him. Isolte sees that they've finished the job. The horses are harnessed to a painted cart.

Bill appears round the corner; he's holding a driving crop.

He looks surprised to see her, but tips his hat. 'Can't stay away, eh?'

She smiles. 'It turns out that I know one of the ... prisoners. He's a childhood friend. I wondered, if he's about, could I have a quick word with him?'

Bill scratches his head. 'Well, it's not strictly proper, but, well ... just this once. Who are you looking for?'

She tells him. Bill nods. 'He's over in the back paddock.'

He motions towards the horses and the cart. 'We've got a local funeral to do today. So I've got to be off. Can you make it quick? If you want to see Catchpole again you'd better go through the proper channels.'

John is alone in the field. He grips a shovel. He's stooping, shovelling and throwing dung into a wheelbarrow. His shirt clings wet across his back. He pauses for a moment to wipe his forehead with his sleeve.

She leans on the gate, uncertain of whether to go into the field or call him from there. But at that moment he looks up. He leans the shovel against the wheelbarrow and comes over.

'Knew you'd be back.' His face is slick with sweat.

'Did you?' She holds the top bar of the gate. It's rough beneath her fingers.

'From before, I mean. Michael and I, we knew we'd see you again. Thought it would be Viola who came though.' He looks behind her again, as if checking for her sister.

'I only have a moment. I don't want to get Bill into trouble.'

'Bill's all right.'

'Yes. He is.'

He blinks at her. The sun is in his eyes. She sees the reflection of trees and her own dark shadow floating across the blue of his iris. 'I came to Suffolk to find you,' she says. 'I went to your old house – I saw Judy.'

'Haven't seen her since I've been inside,' he says. 'She won't see me. Don't blame her.'

'She told me about . . .'

His face is a mask. She can smell salt on his skin, the ripe stink of horse manure. A fly brushes against his face and he waves it away.

'I'm sorry.' She looks away. 'About Michael.'

He looks past her into the middle distance. His mouth tightens.

Isolte remembers Michael's knife: the long blade in its leather sheath. He'd fingered the razored edge, sharp enough to cut a dangling thread with a single swipe. It was a man's knife. A tool. A weapon. She wonders if John used it in his moment of lost temper when the muddled world went red and dark.

She glances at his hands, trying not to think of it, and notices that they are flecked with colour. She looks closer. There are smears of oil paint on his fingers. She sees green and ochre and blue flaking off between the golden hairs on the back of his tanned, freckled hands.

'You've been painting?'

Her words fall into a silence and she's struck by embarrassment, by the fear that he's not going to answer her. He is mute and inscrutable. She shifts uncomfortably and looks at the top bar of the gate, the wood weathered with age and splattered with bird shit.

'Art therapy, they call it,' he says quietly. 'I like to paint. But it's not me that had the talent.'

'I heard about Michael's work.' She looks up, relieved. 'But it's good that you're painting too. What do you paint?'

'Faces,' he says, chewing the inside of his lip. 'I paint faces.'

'Perhaps,' she is hesitant, 'perhaps I can see them some time.'

She wants to use words that will have meaning and significance. She wishes she had the courage to ask him about Michael and what happened and how he feels. But she can't. The years between have stripped away familiarity. Absence and guilt have made them strangers.

'Well . . .' She clears her throat, searching for something else to say, for a link, a connection to make. 'Strange how things work out. All the time, while you were here, I kept a picture of a Suffolk Punch on my wall at work. A stallion, like the one we found in the forest. Just above my desk.'

He looks at his feet. 'In London?'

'Yes.' She is eager. 'In London. I worked for a magazine.'

His face is expressionless. It was a mistake to talk of the city, of her work, to bring up a world that is so remote from this one.

He frowns. Somewhere behind them in the stable block there is the sound of laughter and a bell ringing. In a distant field, a horse neighs. Isolte feels the sun on her scalp, the prickle of sweat at her neck.

He's looking at her intently. 'We never blamed you.'

'Blamed us . . .' she repeats, watching his mouth.

He swallows. 'We would have run away too. But you can't ever get away, can you?'

'No.' She can hardly speak. Her heart is thumping in her chest.

'It was good for a while, in the caravan.' He looks away again, squinting at the horizon. 'Felt like real freedom. Felt like we were cowboys or something. But it was the nights, see.' A minute twitch flickers over his right eyelid. 'There was nothing – just black. Only she was there too, see. In shadows behind trees, tapping at the door.'

Isolte shakes her head, appalled.

His voice is flat. 'Drink was the only thing that stopped it.'

She doesn't know what to say. 'I'm sorry.'

'Sorry,' he repeats, dragging it out as if he can't find the next syllable. He looks at her, scratches his head. Isolte hears his nails against his scalp. 'What's done is done. No help for it now.'

Everything he's said is true, she thinks. She has nothing to add. She feels helpless, her body limp and heavy in the heat. She's aware that her guts are churning, rising nausea floods her mouth with saliva, and she frowns, worried that she's actually going to throw up. She steps away from the gate. 'I'd better go.'

'Wait.' He puts his hand over her arm. His grip is strong and his skin is hot and damp. She catches her breath, startled.

'I'm not going to hurt you,' he says impatiently. 'I want to show you something.'

He puts his hand in his pocket and pulls out a pebble. He holds it out.

'It belongs to Viola. Will you tell her I've kept it safe for her?'

Puzzled, Isolte looks at the pebble. It's an ordinary stone, like the millions that are heaped on the shingle beach. An ancient flint licked smooth by the sea.

'Viola?'

'Promise,' he says fiercely. As if they were children again.

She says hesitantly, 'But John, it's just a stone.'

He holds the stone carefully between blunt, earthy fingers as if it's made of something precious, and turns it to show her. She sees that something is scratched on to the surface. Looking closer, she makes out Viola's name in spidery lines. What is Viola's name doing on the pebble? She frowns.

'She lost it,' he says, 'in the woods. I've kept it for her.'

She reaches out to take it. But he shakes his head, closing his fingers around it possessively. He slips the stone back into his pocket. 'Best I keep it. But tell her I've got it. You will tell her, won't you?'

'Oh.' Isolte feels confused. Her head hurts. 'I'll tell her,' she says, longing to get away.

His mouth twists. 'And will you tell Viola about me? About Michael?'

'Do you want me to?'

He nods. 'She's all right, isn't she?' He looks at her sharply. 'I was worried. After you told me she wasn't well. She needs looking after.'

'It's OK, John. I'm her sister. I love her.' She tries to stop an edge creeping into her voice. 'I am looking after her.'

'But it's the people we love most that we end up hurting. Isn't that right, Issy?'

It's strange to hear him call her by her childhood name. 'I'm not going to hurt Viola,' she says firmly. She should reach out and put her arms around him, tell him he's not alone. But that would be a lie.

'No.' He rubs his hand over his eyes. He speaks quietly, shaking his head. 'No. You wouldn't do that.'

She watches him walk away. He walks like an old man, head bowed over stooped shoulders, big feet dragging through the scrubby grass. Trying to merge him with the child of her memories gives her the disconnected tilt of a hallucination.

She feels exhausted. She bends over, squats for a moment. She spits experimentally into the grass, gobs of saliva sticking to dry grasses, but she doesn't vomit, and she stands again, wiping her mouth with the back of her hand. John is back at work, the automatic movement of stooping and shovelling. He doesn't look up.

Isolte is overtaken by a series of cars on her way down to the sea wall. She watches them pass, piled high with picnics, brightly coloured rubber rings and baskets of towels. When they were children they hardly saw any vehicles, only tractors and locals. There is a small car park by the sea wall and it is full. A sign warns people from swimming beyond the flag.

The tide is high and waves send foamy fingers towards the families that have set up their picnic rugs on the small strip of white sand beyond the banks of pebbles.

Isolte clambers up the path on to the sea wall. She sets out away from the car park, with the beach to her right and the marshes to her left. There's a man crouched in the long grasses with a pair of binoculars trained on a flock of geese in the field; the geese peck at the ground, complaining in harsh babbling voices. She remembers the birdwatcher they saw as kids – how he used to appear on a wobbly bike, anorak zipped up whatever the weather. Sometimes a sudden flash of sunlight on glass would alert them, remind them that they needed to be careful he didn't discover their hiding place. She'd wondered about him later. But none of them knew his name or where he was from. She couldn't even remember what he looked like – his features always hidden under a woollen cap and behind those black binoculars.

Spiky grass and sea lavender brush her ankles. The wind is strong out of the shelter of the bank, and she's grateful for it. She needs the coolness and the sense of being blown clean. She feels better. The sickness has gone. Above, a skylark swoops and calls. She sees the tower rearing up out of the flat landscape.

The heavy, round mass dominates the skyline. A domed glass roof sparkles and flashes in the sun. There's a fence around the tower and someone has planted trees and flowers to make a garden out of the rough ground. Close up, the tower has other alterations. There is a new blue door in the wall, creating an ordinary entrance at the top of a flight of steps, instead of the opening high up in the brickwork that they had scrambled up to with the help of the rope.

A blonde woman is lying in a deckchair, a magazine slipping from her lap. A navy pram with big silver wheels is parked in the shade of the tower. Gauzy netting hangs over the hood, offering protection against flying insects. Isolte stands and stares. The woman has dark glasses on. She's dressed all in white and she's pulled her top down over her shoulders to avoid strap lines. Isolte is seized with a sudden desire to shout, throw an insult like a rock into the settled, affluent peace. The tower belonged to them. It is filled with private memories. How dare this woman – a stranger – lie in a deckchair flaunting her complacent ignorance?

Isolte looks up at the tall bulk of stone. The windows are glazed. She wonders if gulls and rooks batter against the glass, trying to find their way inside, and if the stink of their shit remains. The Martello tower has become a weekend retreat; it'll be an acquisition to impress friends with over the dinner table. The woman probably lives in Chelsea. Her husband will have made his money in advertising. As if she can hear Isolte's thoughts, she sits up and looks over her glasses.

Isolte steps back hurriedly, turning away. She is embarrassed. Any minute the woman, or her unseen husband, will come over to ask her what she wants. She scrambles over the sea wall down on to the beach. Her legs are trembling so that they no longer hold her weight; she sinks on to pliant shingle. She hugs her knees, facing the sea. She doesn't know how long she sits there, but the movement of the waves is hypnotising, soothing. Inside their wash and grate she can hear children's voices.

Isolte thinks about the pebble in John's hand. The scratch marks were old, had been made with the point of a knife. She supposes that John put them there himself. But if he'd given Viola the stone all those years ago, then why hadn't Viola told her?

Isolte remembers the feel of John's lips: the yielding flesh, the edge of his teeth on her tongue. She'd let him, not really understanding the feelings. She didn't know why he kissed her. Although even then she knew that boys liked her. Boys at school said things, and Michael was always looking at her in a certain way. But now it seems that John and Viola had shared a secret. She tries to make sense of this new knowledge even as it begins to scrape away at her memories.

30

Mummy was in the kitchen. She leapt up, mouth open to say something. But she closed it into a tight line when she saw me limp in behind Issy, my hand across the gash. Mummy shook her head as she sat me on a stool in the kitchen and draped a towel around my shoulders. 'Honestly, Viola. Your timing is dreadful.' She put the kettle on to boil. 'What have you done?'

She looked pretty and clean, her hair all shiny and lips pinked like rose petals. She was wearing a flowery dress that I hadn't seen before. Tying on an apron, Mummy poured boiling water and salt into a bowl, and set about dipping a flannel, wringing it out to pat against my face.

'Hold still,' she directed.

I longed for her to put her arms around me. I yearned to hide in her warmth and familiar smells. But she was hard-edged and angry. I hunched up, miserable and round-shouldered against her rejection, pulling my tears inwards. The scalding flannel pressed. Pain prickled and stabbed. My mouth strained with the effort of silence. I tried to move away.

'Don't!' she ordered. 'I need to see what you've done.'

The water swirled pink. She frowned. 'Bloody hell, this is going to need stitches. We'll have to go to A & E. I'll call Frank and tell him.'

Why did Frank need to know? But I forgot about him as I climbed into the sidecar, holding a handful of loo roll. My head was thundering, and the torn flesh throbbed. Mummy drove fast, Issy clamped around her waist like a limpet. The egg took off over bumps and skidded around corners. I lurched from one side to the other, bracing myself against the floor. Summer verges passed in an emerald blur, nettles and branches slapping against the scratched windscreen.

It occurred to me that I would be ugly and nobody would ever want to kiss me. Isolte had stolen my kiss. I might never get the chance to know what it felt like to be held like that. To have John hold me. He loved her instead. I dribbled slime and blood into the disintegrating tissue. I hated John. I hated Issy. I put my hand in my pocket, jamming my fingers into the grubby corners. The pebble had gone. It must have fallen out when I jumped. I shivered. The sidecar lurched over a pothole, making my stomach heave. I gagged, sourness stinging my throat. Vomit spurted through my fingers: a rancid curdling liquid spilling into my lap.

We didn't have to wait long at the hospital. They motioned Mummy and me into a cubicle and drew a curtain around us. A doctor in a white coat threaded a large needle and asked about tetanus shots. He leaned towards me so that I could see the fringes of his eyelashes and the pores on his nose. 'I'm afraid this will hurt a bit,' he said. His mouth opened and closed like a fish. I saw his crooked front teeth, smelt his thick breath.

I closed my eyes and gripped Mummy's hand. 'Hold tight,' she murmured, and her voice trembled.

Pain burst through my head. Sharp glass stabbed at my mouth, burrowed into my nose; and I was falling again, a lump of flesh, a sack of fat and bone falling through the air. I felt the weight of myself inside the fine mesh of light and wind. Nothing held me up. The ground came for me, fast and hard and angry.

'Oh, Viola,' Mummy whispered. 'My brave girl.'

I let out a tight sob, and I was crying at last.

We came out of the cubicle into the waiting room. My eyes were swollen into slits, my face sewn together with black thread. Antiseptic powder stung the back of my throat. Under the bright lights of the waiting room, Frank and Polly were sitting on plastic chairs next to Issy.

'Why are they here?' I leaned against Mummy, still feeling dizzy.

She let go of me to kiss Frank on his blubbery cheek. His hairless arm slid around her, and she leaned into his creased shirt as if she liked being that close, didn't mind his armpit hooked over her shoulder. I realised the dress she was wearing was made of the same fabric she'd been labouring over that morning. She'd never made a dress so fast from start to finish.

'Viola.' Frank shook his head, keeping his arm clamped around Mummy's waist. He fixed me with washed-out eyes. 'What's this I hear about falling off walls? I think you girls are spending too much time with those boys. I was afraid that something like this would happen – I told your mother they were a bad lot.' He frowned. 'The apple doesn't fall far from the tree.'

Mummy shrugged and glanced at us. 'Maybe they are too wild.' Her voice was low, apologetic.

Issy and I looked at each other. Wild was good. Mummy had always told us that wild was wonderful. It was rare and beautiful and exciting. We'd lived by the code of wild all our lives. Now she'd turned against it.

'Well.' Mummy took Frank's hand. She cleared her throat and looked at us. 'This isn't how I'd imagined the evening would turn out, but ... we planned to tell you tonight. So—'

'What your mother is trying to say,' Frank interrupted, smiling at her patiently, 'is that I have asked her to marry me, and she has done me the honour of saying yes.'

Polly yelled, letting out a trill of joy, and clapping her hands together loudly.

Mummy looked embarrassed but pleased. She laughed and bent down to give her a kiss. Polly threw her arms around our mother's neck with unnecessary force and hugged her. Mummy hugged her back, and Polly pressed her lips into Mummy's neck.

I could feel Issy closing down. Felt her run deep inside herself. She said nothing. Stared ahead. She didn't look at me. I put my hands up to my face; it felt as though I needed to hold myself together. I concentrated on pressing my cheeks, feeling the tired pain chase itself through the threads of my stitches.

The waiting room was packed. Those sitting close by looked up, keen for more entertainment. A man cradling his hand inside a plastic bag winked at me. Out of the corner of my eye, I noticed a woman sway in our direction. She was drunk, with a gash on her forehead, a drooping nightdress exposing her long breasts. The entire waiting room had been trying to avoid eye contact with her. And now she was staggering in our direction, belching. 'I'm gettin' married in the morning ...' she sang in a broken, slurred, hiccuping voice.

'Can I be a bridesmaid?' Polly was asking breathlessly.

The woman, losing the words of the song, muttered to herself, leaning into our little group, grinning and breathing fumes on us. 'Wish one of you is the lucky woman?'

'You can all be bridesmaids,' Mummy said quickly, moving towards the door, beckoning for us to follow. 'Won't that be lovely?' she threw over her shoulder.

'I think I'm going to be sick,' I said.

The wedding, planned for the end of September, would be a quiet affair at the local register office. Mummy told us that afterwards we would move in with Frank and Polly. 'They have more room than us,' she said. 'It'll be easier for you to catch the bus to your new school.'

We were sullen. 'We don't want you to marry him,' Issy said. 'We don't want to move.'

'We'll have a proper indoor bathroom,' Mummy said enticingly. 'And central heating in the winter.'

'You said you liked the privy. You said it was authentic.'

'We couldn't stay anyway,' Mummy said in a flat, quiet voice. 'The money's run out. I'm not qualified to do anything. I asked at the supermarket. It was humiliating. And nobody bought the dolls.' Her face hardened. 'I'm useless.'

'But you said,' I went on, not looking at her, 'you said it would be just the three of us.'

'Well, I was wrong,' Mummy snapped. 'I got it wrong. I thought I could manage. But I couldn't.' Her voice wavered. 'It's lonely, you know, doing it all by yourself.'

We looked at her uncomprehendingly. She had us.

'Frank is a kind man, a good man. Give him a chance. You're both so bloody stubborn.' She blew her nose on a scrappy tissue fished from her pocket. 'It'll be all right. You have to trust me.'

'We won't ever trust you again,' Issy told her. 'Not ever.'

'You'll have Polly as your new sister . . . '

We stared at her, our eyes bright with resentment.

'Well, I love him and I'm going to marry him.' Mummy raised her chin, her face closed. 'You're only children. You can't understand. You'll just have to get used to it.'

I was brushing my teeth gingerly. It hurt if I opened my mouth wide. I spat into the kitchen sink. There was a fleck of blood in the white froth.

'Maybe it's not too late,' I said quietly. 'I've been thinking that we could ask the witches to put a curse on Frank. Curse the wedding. Make it go away.'

'Instead of rescuing the sacrifice?' Isolte asked.

'Well, we don't know that they killed the dog,' I said. 'But we do know they go to the woods at full moon. We know they have powers.'

'Yes.' She looked up, eyes widening. 'You're right. Mummy doesn't love him.' She put her toothbrush in her mouth and took it out. 'She'll thank us for it later.'

Nothing should make us afraid of being free, that was what Mummy said. But she was afraid. We felt it in her nervous smile and the way she pretended things when she was with him; she was always laughing at things that weren't funny; she didn't pick food from the hedgerows any more; she crammed her long feet into shoes. He made her different. Was he forcing her to marry him?

'Maybe we should bring the witches something,' I suggested. 'Like an offering.'

*

It was difficult at first, seeing the boys. John and Issy circled each other warily, not making eye contact. Michael was moody, quick to lash out at John, sullen around Issy. John said nothing at all, but I caught him staring at my wound. I was humiliated by the criss-cross of black stitching. I felt ugly and stupid. Issy hadn't talked about the kiss. I couldn't bring myself to ask her what it had felt like. She thought I was upset about my face, and she tried to be careful and considerate with me. I hated her for it, and I punished her by hugging my misery close, staying pinched and quiet.

But the news of the wedding swept away tangled jealousies. It was a safe subject for discussion and it folded us into the problem equally. The boys seized on the idea of finding an offering. 'Leave it to us,' Michael said. 'They're culling deer up at the farm.'

We thought about what life would be like in that red-brick house in town – the horrible furniture and Polly's framed certificates on the walls, meals spent sitting in silence around their ugly table, and Frank persuading our mother that we were too wild, that we shouldn't see the boys, should instead spend our time in music lessons and doing our homework.

Michael and John were waiting for us in the churchyard. Sprawled on a grave, they looked sweaty and hot, and pleased with themselves. They had a bag with them. We crouched next to them among the tombstones, and Michael opened it. Inside was something pink and raw, a naked creature folded up like a secret in the bottom of the bag. I smelt the ripe sweetness of flesh.

'It's a foetus,' John said. 'A deer foetus. It was in a bucket. The men up at the farm cut it out of the mother's stomach.'

They took it out to show us. It was small as a hand. The tiny feet were creamy and delicate as sickle moons; its eyes webbed shut inside bulbs of violet. There were tracings of veins under the translucent skin. Dead rivers.

Issy put out her hand. 'It's beautiful,' she said, and her voice trembled. 'Weird. Like an alien or something.'

I made myself touch it. The hairless skin was stiff but warm, tacky on my fingers. I thought about Tess's kid and a shiver ran through me.

'Someone walked over yer grave? Maybe it's here,' Michael said, pressing his foot against a raised mound.

I ignored him and John pushed his shoulder. 'Shut yer mouth, boi.'

'Tomorrer night,' Michael said. 'We'll meet you at the crossroads.'

John put the dead foetus in the bag and looked at me. 'You al'right?' he asked quietly.

I nodded, pulling the curtain of my hair across my face. I'd seen myself in the mirror in Mummy's bedroom. I knew the way the thread bit into my skin, pulling it tight. Small lumps of sore flesh were raised around each stitch. The severed line that ran down my nose and through my lip had turned dark red. It itched. The stitches were due to be cut out in a couple of days, but there would be a scar.

1980

John,

  It's me again. I had to go into hospital for a while but I'm out now and I'm feeling stronger.

  We're not living at Hettie's any more. She's sold up and gone to Ireland. It's been her dream to live there and rescue stray dogs. Issy and I convinced her that we'd be fine without her. Hettie insisted on putting some money into an account to go towards our rent. Issy and I live in separate places now. There was a time when I could never have imagined that. She's moved in with friends and I'm in a squat in Brixton. I like the people here – mostly artists. It's the first place that feels a bit like home.

I wonder what you're doing? Have you found a job? Do you and Michael still live together? Perhaps you've even settled down – got married. I can't let myself think that. Sorry. I just can't.

I'm not sure what you'd think of me if you could see me now. I look different. Remember how Michael sometimes teased me for being plump? I'm thin now. Ugly thin. Issy hates it. In a strange way I almost like making her angry with me. I suppose I'm angry with her too – for being happy, or pretending to be happy, when I know that underneath she isn't.

I have a nose ring. Everyone has them here. Got it done in Camden Market. When I was younger I tried to pierce my own ears. Made a mess of it. You would have called me a dossy woop. I miss you so much. Even after all this time. You'd hate London. But I often pretend that you are here, walking beside me.

Viola

31

As Isolte comes into the conservatory, she hears Dot's short, gruff laugh and a male voice responding. Damn. She's not in the mood for small talk with strangers. She'll slip up to her room. But the pug rushes into the hall to greet her, his stout body barrelling against her legs, tongue protruding from his panting mouth. She bends down to pat him. 'Sneak, you've given me away,' she murmurs, as he presses a dry nose into her hand.

'Isolte?' Dot calls.

She hears the other voice. 'I see she's made a friend of the dog.'

Funny, she thinks. That sounds exactly like Ben.

And then she's standing on the threshold of the living room, and Dot is smiling up at her from the old velvet sofa, and Ben is unfolding his long body out of a chair and coming towards her.

'What on earth are you doing here?'

'Surprise,' he says, pulling her into his embrace. She smells his peppery aftershave and traces of London. She presses herself into the comfort of it. But she can feel something in the deep fibres of his body, some tension or urgency.

'Seriously,' she says, stepping back, 'what's wrong? It's not Viola?'

'Everything is fine,' he says quickly. 'I just thought I'd come and keep you company.'

'But I thought . . . what about the new agency party?'

'It's only a party, Issy.' He glances down. 'There'll be plenty more.'

'I showed him the sketch I made of you the other night,' Dot tells her.

'I like it.' He smiles at Dot. 'She's agreed to part with it for hard cash.' He puts his hand on Isolte's arm. 'And then I'm taking you back to London with me. No argument.'

'But not before you have some supper,' says Dot. 'I'll leave you two to get reacquainted while I go and see what I can rustle up.'

They sit on the sofa, listening to Dot rattle around the kitchen, cupboards opening and closing. The pug waddles off to join her, its claws scrabbling across the wooden floor. Isolte puts her hand on Ben's knee.

'You haven't driven over a hundred miles just because you couldn't spend one more hour apart from me.' She looks at him. 'Something's up. Tell me. You're frightening me.'

'Shit.' His face collapses. 'I don't know how.'

He drops his head into his hands, hair flopping through his fingers; and a long shudder runs through him. Her chest tightens.

'What?' Her voice is sharper than she'd meant it to be.

He raises his head and looks at her, his eyes dark and miserable. 'It's Stevie.'

'Stevie?' Isolte is confused.

Ben is staring down at his fingernails. 'He's got AIDS. He rang me this morning. I didn't know what to say. I felt so useless. But what are you supposed to say, for fuck's sake?'

'Oh, God!' She reaches for him, automatically rubbing at the welt of muscle across his shoulders. 'Poor Stevie.'

An inappropriate burst of relief bubbles and dies in her throat. She'd thought Ben was going to break up with her. And now this. She reels, emotions skidding and colliding. Poor Stevie. Vain, witty, sly Stevie. She's never really liked him. But this is horrible. She sucks in air. Tries to steady herself. She knows that Ben thinks of Stevie as a real friend, sees something in him that she doesn't.

'I heard on the radio that one person a day is dying from it in Britain.' He's shaking his head, gives a short humourless laugh. 'Seems like they're all from the bloody fashion business.'

She's seen pictures of AIDS patients splashed across newspapers. Like starvation victims. Edwina Currie said that good Christians wouldn't get it. One of the make-up artists that Isolte worked with is already dead.

'Isolte,' he grabs her hand, pulls her to her feet, 'I need some fresh air after that drive. Come on. Show me the beach.'

They stand on the shoreline. Waves curl and swill at their feet. He slips his arm around her and pulls her close.

'Thing is,' he says, 'this news about Stevie, it's made me realise how easy it is to take things for granted. Take life for granted. You know the first thing I wanted to do when I heard?'

She shakes her head.

'It was to find you. Hold you.'

She bites her lip, pleasure filling her.

He turns to her urgently, grabbing her wrists so that they face each other. 'Let me in, Isolte.' She is startled by his fierce voice. His fingers dig into her skin. 'You have to trust me.'

The wind whips her hair across her eyes. She pulls her hand away from his and pushes strands away. She hesitates. 'I want to.'

'Then let's start with why you're here. All this secrecy!' He waves his arms around and a seagull veers away screaming. 'It's driving me mad. Why did you need to rush down here? What could be so important?'

He looks at her expectantly.

'Viola wanted me to come.' She licks her lips. 'I came to find two boys who were our best friends. We haven't seen them since we were kids. I've tracked one of them down.' She speaks breath-lessly. 'It was an accident, really. I saw him when I was being shown around the stud. He's in prison.'

'What?' He looks at her with his head on one side, heavy eye-brows arching. 'Prison? Good God, Isolte. What's he in prison for?'

'He killed his twin brother.'

'Jesus!'

'I know it sounds bad,' she says quickly, 'but it was an accident. He was drunk. It's damaged him – he's like a broken man.'

'I'm not surprised. That would finish most people off.' Ben takes her hand in his and squeezes it. 'Should you be mixing with murderers?'

'He's not dangerous in the criminal sense. He's not wicked or a psychopath. He and his brother were like wild creatures; I remember my mother telling us they had different boundaries from other people, and I suppose in the end they were a danger to each other. Anyway – I can't exactly abandon him now, can I?

265

I want to try and help. I'd like to see his sister before I go, say goodbye and get her number. She lives in the village.'

She grips his fingers hard, feeling the flicker of a tiny pulse.

'Can we call in and see the sister on the way home tomorrow?' he asks.

She nods.

'You don't have to do this on your own.' He pulls her close. His chin rests on top of her head. 'Give me a chance, Issy. You never know, I might be able to help.'

Her body softens at his words; she slumps into him, her nose pressed into his chest, prickly wool in her mouth.

Entering the cottage, they hear the sound of Keith Jarrett's piano playing and sniff at the homely smell of frying onions.

'By the way, I haven't told Viola any of this yet,' Isolte says, her voice casual and light. 'I think it will upset her too much.'

Dot unfolds the sofa bed in the sitting room for them, shakes out clean sheets and fetches a double duvet. They sleep with the curtains open. Moonlight filters through broken clouds. The waves hiss and sigh against the shingle. Isolte has got used to the sound of the sea. They don't make love. It doesn't seem right, not here in Dot's cramped house, where they can hear the whistle of her breathing, and the wheezing dog. And anyway, they are tired.

Ben holds her. Pressing the length of his body against her, he spoons her from behind. She fits him, her curves tucked inside his. She raises her hips, folds her knees, so that she sits, weightless, on his lap. It seems that they float, welded together, in the dark.

Isolte stays awake, her mind sweeping restlessly through everything that's happened in the last couple of days, darting back in time, racing ahead to think about Viola. She smells the tang of air that comes through the open window, bringing fishy brine and damp grass and the distant breath of sleeping horses. Somewhere, John lies in his single bed, under his regulation blanket, behind a locked door. She can't imagine what thoughts he has, alone at night.

The boys were more than just human; they'd always seemed part earth, part animal, and always inextricably bound into each other. Seeing John had made her realise how far she's come from this place, from their childhood. It is hard to understand that Michael is dead because for her he will always be a boy wandering the paths of the forest, with his chipped tooth and dirty face, watching for forestry workers. She squeezes her eyes shut, feels the pull of loss, but sorrow slides across disbelief like oil across water.

She wonders what Michael's paintings are like and if they have been kept safe somewhere. John said he painted faces. Perhaps he paints the four of them as they were before everything changed, unformed, unfinished, wearing their innocence like skin.

Ben is heavy behind her, weighted with sleep. She turns and looks at him, closed and twitching in his dreams. His lashes cast shadows across his cheeks. She likes his need of her. She craves it. She's used to the symbiosis of being a twin, used to the bond she shares with Viola, roped by blood, even when they are miles apart. She thinks about what Ben said on the beach. She wants to open up to him; it would be such a relief if she could just tell him everything. She is beginning to understand a different side to him – someone stoical and steady. She doesn't deserve someone like that, someone who would love her despite everything. He says he wants her to trust him. Only how much can she really expect him to take? The thought of what she's holding back terrifies her.

The waves are bringing things to the shore. Yesterday she found the body of a small shark, partly eaten and decomposing. Tomorrow morning there will be tin cans, driftwood, coils of wire, odd shoes: a clutter of lost things littering the shingle. The sea swallows things, she thinks, and the sea returns them.

32

'I'm going out with Frank tonight, to meet up with his best man and some other friends,' Mummy told us at breakfast. 'So Polly will stay here with you. She's looking forward to it.'

'She can't,' Issy said quickly. 'She can't come. Not tonight.'

'What?' Mummy frowned, looking over her cup of coffee.

'Nothing,' I said, kicking Issy under the table.

We went into the garden. We'd lost our appetite for toast and honey. I followed Issy as she climbed on to the shed roof. It was our favourite thinking place. The cat found us there and sat against my knees, dribbling and purring, squinting her eyes at wasps zig-zagging past. The sun was already hot. I put my hand on the cat's fur and she arched her spine, pressing her warm back into my palm.

'What shall we do?' I asked miserably.

'I don't know.' Issy slumped her chin on her hands, letting her feet dangle off the edge of the slate roof. 'Polly!' She spat the name. 'She always has to spoil everything.'

We watched Mummy scraping breadcrumbs on to the lawn. She hummed as she went back into the kitchen; the breadboard clamped beneath one arm, a tea towel swinging from the other.

There had been a herd of deer in the garden overnight. They'd left the damp earth pitted with impressions of their feet. The two-horned toes made shapes that resembled narrow hearts. From our vantage point I could see that the feet traced a pattern across the garden leading from the edges of the trees up to our front door.

'The boys will know what to do,' I said.

'Right.' Issy looked at me scornfully. 'They'll be really pleased to see Polly tagging along, won't they?'

We continued to squabble for the rest of the day. The weather was thundery and humid and the air clung to us in heavy, damp swathes. The trees seemed to draw together in a dark mass around the garden, nothing stirred inside the shadowy depths. The deer were nowhere to be seen. Not even a rabbit broke cover. Halfway through the afternoon the cat came limping in with her front paw swollen up like a club foot.

'Poor puss.' Mummy picked her up and examined the paw. 'She's been stung by something.' She looked up at the shed. 'Wonder if there's a wasps' nest under the roof? I'll ask Frank to take a look.'

When we heard Frank's car pull into the drive, our instinct was to run – escape into the forest, throw ourselves under bracken and hide. Instead, we drew together, shoulders touching, and met Frank and Polly with smiles on our faces. We had to be normal, we told each other. Mummy looked relieved as we stood politely, offering to carry bags and help with supper.

We sat on the bed and watched Polly unpack her floral overnight bag, pulling out her pink teddy-patterned nightie, folding it carefully on a mattress placed on the floor in our room. Next she unpacked a pair of fluffy slippers, a hairbrush, clean knickers and a toothbrush. She arranged them neatly in a row. Lastly, she took out a worn Sasha doll with a chipped nose. She placed the doll on her pillow and looked up with flushed cheeks.

'What time do you go to bed?' she asked. 'Can I stay up as late as you?'

'Maybe,' Issy said. 'Maybe not.'

We were uncertain as to whether we should take her with us or leave her behind. We'd been discussing the possibilities all day. Our preference was to leave her sleeping; but we had a strong suspicion that she wouldn't oblige us by falling asleep if we were up. 'We'll have to pretend,' Issy said.

After tea we cleared the table while Mummy went upstairs to change into a clean skirt and put on her lipstick. The three of us waved goodbye at the kitchen door, Polly standing between us. The car bumped down the track, dust rising behind; Mummy fluttered her fingers out of the window. Frank's domed head looked straight ahead. He was a careful driver. Somewhere an owl hooted.

Mummy had left us a packet of Bourbon biscuits and a carton of orange juice. Bribes for good behaviour. We sat around the kitchen table, munching, dropping chocolatey crumbs into our laps. Filling time, we played Snap and Sevens, flipping our cards without any care, glancing at the kitchen clock. Polly won, and we hardly noticed, not listening either to her chatter about bridesmaid dresses. At about nine o'clock we started to yawn extravagantly and rub our eyes.

'Bedtime,' Issy said.

A hazy mist lay over the garden. Trees floated upright in a calm, white lake. We drew the bedroom curtains and lay down, holding our breath, listening for Polly's breathing to change. She fidgeted and asked questions, and we ignored her, staring up at the bluish light.

'I need to go to the toilet. I can't go on my own.' She peered at me.

I sighed and rolled my eyes, getting up and going with her over the damp lawn, pale mist lapping at our ankles. I opened the door of the privy and stood waiting, arms folded like a jailer or a butler, while her anxious voice came from behind the door. 'Still there?'

Back in bed, she began one of her pointless questions again, but Issy roared, 'Shut up and go to sleep!'

The cat nudged the door ajar, came in limping and chirping, her tail lashing. Her paw had gone down quite a lot. She walked over Polly's head, stepping on her hair.

'I don't want the cat,' Polly whined. 'She might bite me.'

When, at last, Polly was breathing deeply through her mouth, we lay still, listening, and waiting for darkness to swallow the last dim shreds of light dancing on the walls.

Polly muttered in her sleep and turned over. We slid carefully out of bed, each jounce of the old springs pulling nervy gasps into our mouths. The rabbit foot dangled at my neck, claws against my skin. We shrugged on jeans and plimsolls. It took ages to get down the winding stairs, feeling our way over creaking boards and squeaking joists. Outside a turbid sea breeze washed against us, pulling us into its cool flow. The relief of escape made us giggle as we lugged our bikes from the shed, stumbling in the darkness, banging shins and elbows. Just as we stood on the drive, hands on handlebars, ready to go, the bedroom window opened and a shape leaned out into the night. 'Where are you going?' Polly's voice wavered. 'Wait for me!'

We had to take her. There was nothing else we could do. We were stern. 'We have to do something important,' I told her.

'Yeah, and if you come, you have to cross your heart and hope to die you'll never tell,' Issy said.

Polly agreed to everything, nodding furiously, her eyes wide with expectation. She was good after that, pulling a jumper on over her nightie and putting on her shoes. She sat pillion on Issy's bike. We cycled through dark paths towards the crossroads; Issy had to stand on her pedals, struggling with the extra weight through the sand. Polly squealed as the bike lurched and tipped and we hissed at her to be quiet.

A stag stepped out of the undergrowth. It was a big, heavyset creature with a muscled neck holding up the weight of its antlers. It stood in the middle of the track, moonlight silvering its back, waiting. We kept motionless under its scrutiny. I couldn't stop myself from thinking of the foetus in the bag. Remembered the earth and blood smell of it.

We continued to the crossroads without speaking. The boys were waiting for us.

'*She* can't come,' they said fiercely. 'No way.'

We huddled in a circle, while Polly hung about by a tree, yawning and trying to look as though she wasn't listening.

'If we take her home, she'll only try and follow us again,' I said.

'The tower,' Michael suggested in a low voice. 'It's not far out of our way. She can wait there. She won't be able to follow us.'

Cycling through the violet night, Polly on the back of John's bike, forest noises snapped and called around us. I was glad to be with the others, outlines of trees blurring into a deeper darkness. The temperature had dropped and I shivered. The landscape was lighter by the sea; the moon on the water cast an eerie glow. The shingle was gauzy with silver as if frost had come early. In front of us, the tower rose up like a giant thumb smudge.

'What are we doing?' Polly asked breathlessly. She was subdued by our resolute looks but excited by the adventure.

'We're going to show you a secret,' Issy told her. 'It's our hiding place.'

It took a lot of pushing and pulling to get her into the tower. Her legs and arms were like jelly. She stood up in the passage and banged her head.

'I don't like it. It smells,' she said doubtfully.

'This is a special place.' I was severe. 'We have to do something now. We'll come back for you.'

Realising the trick, Polly let out a long wail and clutched my hand. 'I don't want to. I don't like it.' Her nails dug into me. I tried to shake her off, but she was persistent; fear seemed to give her superhuman strength. Plump fingers gripped in steely bands around my wrist, while her body hung limp as a sack.

I pulled away, yanking hard, feeling a wrench at my shoulder as she resisted. I shook again and tried to unpeel her, to prise away the lock of her fingers with my own thumbs and fingers, scrabbling skin, the scrape of nails. She wouldn't let go. She gripped and clung. I smelt her breath, felt the hammering of her heart. She wasn't supposed to be here. 'You should have stayed asleep,' I panted in frustration, 'shouldn't you?'

She began to scream like an animal in a trap. It made me want to clamp my hand over her, close up the gaping hole of her wet mouth to shut off the squealing. Her face looked weird, pulled apart, as if it was melting. Even though I struggled and wrestled, she wouldn't let go. Her nails bit deeper. We swung across the narrow passage together; I cracked my forehead against knobbled

274

stone. Darkness and moonlight flickered so that bits of Polly flashed in and out of nothingness: wild eyes; a push of shoulder, wet protruding tongue. Panic made me desperate, and I pushed blindly, roughly. She gasped, fell back against the wall, defeated.

As I reached the ground, trembling, the rope swinging through my fingers, she was squatting near the entrance, so that I could just make out the shine of nose, a twist of hair hanging down.

She was moaning, her voice weary and lacking belief, but still running out of her mouth, unable to give up her protest. 'Don't go!'

I was frightened by what we were doing. 'Will she be all right?' I asked in a shaky voice.

'Course she will.' Michael had removed the rope, rolled it up and tucked it behind a clump of thistles. 'Be quiet,' he told Polly in a hard whisper. 'If you don't shut up Black Shuck will get you. Nothing will happen if you keep quiet.'

Polly's hysteria had subsided into a shuddering weeping. We could hardly see her in the dark.

'You'll be fine,' I called up to her. My hands were shaking. 'Don't be a crybaby. We'll come back soon. Here.' I took off my jumper and threw it up to her. 'Put this on.'

Her hiccuping sobs were audible in the hushed air. But as the tower fell away behind us, we could hear nothing except the waves, the swish of tyres moving over the track and our own breathing.

*

The shapes of the ward rise up, clear and ordinary, closing around me: walls, beds, drooping curtains and the figures of two nurses in the half-light.

'Did you call?' A night nurse pauses, looking in my direction, and comes over. She leans over me. She looks tired and irritated. 'Do you want something?'

Another patient has begun to cough in the bed next door: a choking cough. A woman calls out, 'Nurse. Water.' The cough starts again, like a car engine trying to start. The nurse straightens and frowns. She tuts sternly and walks across to the other bed in her squeaky shoes.

*

The oak woods were steeped in night blacks. The sky was overcast. Occasionally the wind moved clouds away from the moon and light struck parts of the trees, showing branches reaching up, twigs snatching at stars. We stumbled along the path, blind and uncertain. I thought eyes were watching us from behind leaves. Black Shuck. I walked so close to Issy that I trod on her heels.

We got scratched and torn, branches hitting our faces, tendrils grabbing at our legs. Nobody spoke. We stumbled around for what seemed like ages before we found ourselves in an open glade. Issy said it was the one with the tree with the dog's head. I wasn't certain, but Michael examined the trees around us, feeling his way with outstretched hands. 'Yes, this is the place,' he said. 'Here's the holly.'

Our eyes became used to the lack of light and we could make out shapes, see our own darker silhouettes. The head must still be in the hollow tree; a stench of rot remained, staining the air. I thought about it decaying inside the bed of leaves, the bones showing through. There would be the knotted squirm of maggots, a caving-in of flesh.

We drew a circle on the ground. Circles were magic shapes. The ground was soft and mossy and the stick sank in deep and

276

turned the earth as we dragged it around us. 'Shouldn't we say something?' I asked.

'Better not,' John muttered. 'We don't know the right things.'

The boys took the foetus from their bag and laid it in the middle of the circle. The flesh glowed faintly in the dark. We knelt around it. Issy sneezed. Nobody came.

'We could make our own spell,' Issy suggested. But none of us did. Not aloud anyway. We listened instead, pulling sounds out of the night. Every creak and groan and whisper magnified.

'Is anyone there?' Issy suddenly shouted.

A bird flew up with a squawk. I jumped and had to bite my tongue to stop myself from screaming.

'What did you do that for?' John hissed.

And then we heard something: a thin, shrieking wail, like a child in pain. My heart was aching and thundering, and I was stupid with fear, for a moment frozen and unable to move or speak. Another sound. Closer. The noise of feet, of someone or something, moving through the undergrowth in our direction.

The trees and the night snatched and tore as I broke through them, John beside me, Michael in front, Issy catching hold of my shirt behind, a sob in her throat. We were running like deer.

And then the terror was falling behind and we were on our bikes and pedalling as fast as we could down the lane. There was fire in my legs and my mouth was dry. A car passed us, a blue Cortina, its headlights sweeping over our flickering forms. It slowed and then speeded up. I thought I saw the driver's eyes in the mirror, watching me. The ribbon of tarmac took us further from the woods and the dead foetus. We slowed down, caught our breaths. I was trembling, my fingers weak around the handlebars, my legs loose and floppy. Michael began to laugh.

'Jesus!' he said. 'I nearly wet myself!'

By the time we'd got to the sea path we all had different versions of what happened, weaving them into a new account. We got off the bikes and pushed them along the narrow, uneven path, talking loudly. I touched my mouth and felt sticky dampness on my fingers; I must have torn some of my stitches. I didn't care. The relief of being out of the woods, away from the sounds and that noise, made me dizzy. I was tired. I could hardly move one foot in front of the other. We wanted the night to be funny now, and so we retold it to ourselves, drawing strength from our retelling and from each other and our forced laughter.

The tower stood before us. We were gathered below the doorway, exhausted and yawning.

'Polly,' I called, 'you can come out now.'

The sea crept in, crawled back. The grass whispered. We called again.

'She must have fallen asleep,' Michael said.

The dark mouth of the entrance gaped.

33

Judy answers the door, head slanted, in the middle of fiddling with an earring; her eyelashes are stiff with black and she's wearing a fuchsia dress, tight across the bust and waist. Isolte remembers the Judy she used to know, that glamorous teenager in her white flares.

'Oh, it's you. I'm expecting the minibus. They come and collect Carl today, take him to the day centre. I'll be off into town when they do.' She looks at her watch. 'They'll be here soon.'

'I've only come to say goodbye,' Isolte says quickly to reassure her. 'I'm going to leave you my number. And I'd like yours, if that's OK. I think we should stay in touch, about John.'

Her face closes. 'Why?'

'I'd like to help. When he comes out. I've asked the woman I've been staying with to visit him. Dot is an artist – she says she'll take a look at his paintings. He's been doing art therapy.'

'Messing about with paint?' Judy frowns. 'He's supposed to be in prison. It must be like a holiday camp for him with all those horses.'

'He is in prison,' Isolte says quietly.

Judy shrugs. She searches through the mess on the coffee table and picks up an old newspaper, rips off a corner. She scribbles some figures and holds it out. 'Don't call unless you have to. Kevin won't like it.'

Isolte puts it in her bag. Puts a piece of paper into Judy's hand. 'I've written down my home number. And my address, in case you need it.'

'Do you think about her?' Judy looks at Isolte. 'That little girl.'

'Polly.'

'Yes. Do you think about her?'

'Every day.'

'They never questioned Bert or Reg.' Judy folds her arms and looks out of the window. 'Maybe I should have said something. Bert tried to touch me up, when I was little. All the kids knew about them. Knew they were weird. They'd undo their trousers, let their cocks hang out.'

'I didn't know.'

'No reason you should. You weren't local, were you?' She lets her lip twist, a sneer slipping into her tone. 'Just passing through really, like those weekenders.'

'I'm sure they were questioned. Everyone was.'

'Well, they're dead now. In hell, I hope.'

There is the sound of a horn outside. Three polite beeps. Judy starts. 'Oh, they're here. I've got to get Carl ready. He's still having a nap.'

'I'll let you get on.'

Judy has already opened the door; stretching up, she gives a theatrical wave to a yellow minibus parked outside the gate and hurries back into the house, heading towards the stairs. The two women brush against each other. Isolte feels the sharp jab of

Judy's hip. The jolt of her body up close. The sugary, bitter smell of her.

'I know you think it's our fault.' Isolte hears the pleading in her voice. 'But we were children. We didn't mean it.'

'Yeah, well, that doesn't make anything go away, does it?'

'But I'm sorry,' Isolte says. 'For what it's worth.'

'Words are cheap.' Judy pauses by the door. Her face softens. 'I know you never meant it. Of course not. But it's like we've been cursed. And I don't know how to stop it.'

Isolte is grateful that Ben is waiting in the car. She slides into the passenger seat. The car smells of leather and London. Ben leans across and squeezes her leg. 'You look like you've seen a ghost.'

'I have. Lots of them.' She puts her head in her hands. 'God. I want to go home.'

He starts the engine, puts the car into gear and they move away from the cottages. The car accelerates through narrow lanes; the hedges are a green blur beside them. She can see the horizon above a sloping field of yellow stubble; and although it isn't visible from here, she knows the sea moves there, at the junction between earth and sky.

Another stubble field is burning and the acrid smell drifts into the car. She sees black smoke circling into the sky, drifting and smudging like paint in water. Ben turns on to the A12 and Isolte sits back in her seat and closes her eyes. Dot said she would be happy to visit John. 'If they have art therapy there, maybe it's something I could get involved in?' she'd said, looking interested. 'It would be good to do something in the community.'

Isolte thinks about the pebble in John's pocket. Why did Viola keep it secret? Perhaps she was embarrassed about showing the

281

stone, after the kiss. She tries to remember how Viola and John were with each other; all she can recall is that they were quiet together sometimes, walking apart from her and Michael. But then they were quieter types of people, both of them prone to dreamy or sullen silences.

Isolte frowns. She has made a promise. But she's not sure how to tell Viola about the stone without revealing what's happened. Viola is already anxious about the boys. She seems to have attached such importance to finding them – both of them.

Isolte is confused: why would John kiss her if he liked Viola? It's so long ago. They were kids. It shouldn't matter. But it does. It was after he kissed her that everything went wrong. Viola's fall from the tower, their mother's engagement, and the disastrous night in the woods. Everything came tumbling down. Everything was broken. And Polly, left alone in the dark, in that stinking, empty tower. Had it been empty? That was what the police had asked – one of many questions. They'd all remembered the pilchard can then, understood its significance.

They'd thought Polly must have been hiding in some small corner. They'd peered through cracks in floorboards, shouting her name, imagining that she'd fallen through and was lying with a broken leg. They'd tramped around the perimeter of the tower, afraid that they would find her there, dead from the long drop, her head smashed in. But there was no sign of her, not in the tower or around it, or on the desolate sweep of beach. There was just Viola's red jumper left in a limp pile inside the entrance. They had had to go home and tell the adults, and the nightmare of hysteria and blame began. Hope running out, day by day, like sand in an hourglass.

'I have to talk to Stevie today,' Ben says, his eyes on the road.

'Just be normal,' Isolte tells him. 'I think he'll want you to go on treating him exactly as before. Same jokes. Same banter. It will let him know you're there for him.'

Ben nods.

'He'll open up to you if he wants to, if he needs it.'

She isn't as confident of this as she makes herself sound. She can't imagine Stevie indulging in any emotional honesty, but perhaps she has misjudged him. Perhaps the disease will change him – the thought of his own death. She glances at Ben's face, his jaw muscles working, eyes set and tense. He's cut himself trying to shave in Dot's inaccessible bathroom mirror, and there's a ridge of dried blood near his mouth.

'So when will you tell your sister the news?' he asks.

Isolte is silent. Eventually she says, 'I don't know if I can tell her.'

'But you have to!' he exclaims, taking his eyes off the windscreen for a moment. 'Wouldn't you want to know,' he asks, 'if it was you?'

'But she's ill,' Isolte protests. 'I don't know how she'll react.'

'I don't understand. You're twins!' Ben almost shouts. 'Surely she'll know that you're not telling her the truth?'

Isolte sets her face and looks out of the passenger window. 'It's complicated, Ben.'

34

'Viola, you can come in now.' A policewoman looks over her glasses at me.

'Remember,' Issy hisses.

The plump lady with lank hair beckons to me. She is a social worker, and she's called Ruth.

'Sit down, Viola.' The policewoman takes her glasses off and puts them on the table. There is a man next to her in a brown suit. He doesn't smile. Ruth sits near me and fiddles with her pen, sniffing, pushing a boiled sweet around her mouth. I smell pear drops and sweat.

I am frightened. We've made Polly disappear. There are blanks in my memory, as if pieces of a jigsaw are missing. I look at the marks Polly's nails have left on my wrists, rubbing the edge of my thumb across the red half-moons, as if they will open little mouths in my flesh and talk to me, tell me where she is.

'Can you tell me why you left Polly in the tower?' the lady is asking. The man in the brown suit is staring at me; his finger rests on a tape machine. I can hear it whirring.

'Don't say anything,' Issy's voice whispers in my ear. 'They think we've killed her. They want to put us in prison.'

'We didn't mean it.' My words stumble. 'You'll find her, won't you?' I ask, wiping my nose on the back of my hand.

There has already been a search with hundreds of locals and the police. They spread out, marching over the farmland, marshes and beach. Dogs barked and men poked with sticks into streams and clumps of brambles. Pictures of Polly's face are pasted on to trees and pinned up behind the counters of shops.

'Take your time, Viola.' The policewoman pushes a plastic cup towards me. 'Would you like a drink of water?'

I twist the fabric of my shirt, rolling the edges up tight. I haven't seen John for days. They are keeping us separate. Mummy said the boys are being questioned too, but at a different time from us.

'I gave her my jumper.'

'Can you speak up?' the man in the suit says. He combs his hand through thin strands of hair. The bald patch on top of his head is smooth and shiny. I think of Frank. The last time I saw Frank he was crying.

The room has one window high up. I can see patches of cloud torn by the wind. A bird swoops from the sky, disappearing from view.

Ruth's pen scratches at her notepad. She sucks at her sweet noisily. The black tape recorder whirs. I feel unbalanced without Issy, as if I might fall off my chair. The air gapes at my side, cold and lonely. I look up, my fingers twisted into my shirt. I need my sister to speak for me.

The investigation is over, the conclusion 'misadventure'; case left open because of the lack of a body. But when I stare in the mirror, all I see is the scar tearing through the centre of my face. And I know that it is the mark of the devil. I am evil. Cursed. The spell went wrong, somehow we'd called up something awful and dark, and it had taken Polly away, sucked her into nothingness. Anybody who sees the mark will know what I have done.

*

All the part-time jobs – barmaid and waitress – that I took after dropping out of college were undemanding. I liked the kind of work that let me daydream my way through it: pouring beer, washing up glasses, hands raw in soapy water, taking orders with a smile fixed on my face.

In chilly studios, students looked at me with their heads on one side; charcoal and lead scratching against paper, and they cleared their throats, stepping back from their work, one eye closed to consider me. There are hours at a time where nobody speaks to an artist's model. Nobody expects anything of you, except your naked skin and your ability to hold a pose. I turned myself inwards. I learned the art of stillness, of non-being. I spent the hours selecting eight-year-old memories, looking at them, rewinding, replaying. I had my favourites: lying on a beach while John piled pebbles over me; John by the ferret hut, the rub of his sleeve against my bare arm, the stink of ferret fur and dirty straw. I stretched time like elastic, the anticipation never failing me. He was going to ask me in a moment. I turned towards him, milky air at my mouth, remembering how the sun over the shed caught my eye, blinding me.

'Viola.' The tutor's voice sliced through the dazzle. John falling away from me, mouthing words soundlessly.

'Could we do some five-minute standing poses now?'

I stared up into a row of faces: a jumble of eyes and noses and mouths. I was surrounded by easels, suffocated by a smell of chalk and dust. The students were focused on me, pencils poised, foreheads frowning. A small fan heater near my feet singed my skin, roasting my ankles, while the rest of me shivered.

I shrank away, covering my breasts with my hands. They were all gazing at me; looking expectant and blank at the same time; with a prickling fear I knew that they saw who I really was; the centre of me exposed. There was a restless shifting of feet around me, a low muttering. I doubled up, clutching the sheet to me. I couldn't do it any more. I needed to be invisible.

Behind me there was a sudden burst of voices as the door swung shut, consternation clattering and the tutor calling me back. I felt sick. Wrapped in my coat, I hurried away down the corridor, making for the street, my fingers feeling for the scar that ran the length of my nose into my lip.

35

Isolte sits on the edge of Viola's visitor's chair. She folds her hands in her lap to stop herself fidgeting. But it hasn't worked; Viola is looking at her suspiciously with her head on one side.

'Viola.' She clears her throat now, leaning close. 'I have something to tell you ... I didn't want to tell you over the phone.'

The ward clatters and hums around them. Viola looks at her sharply and frowns. 'I had a feeling that you were keeping something from me.'

'I met Judy while I was in Suffolk,' Isolte says quickly.

'Judy?' Viola sits up straighter. 'How is she?'

'She's OK. She's married with a son. I found her living in the old Catchpole cottage. The awful father is dead. Linda is in the almshouses, apparently. It was odd being there again.'

Isolte clears her throat. She needs to stop procrastinating. There's no easy way to tell Viola about the boys.

'I met John too.'

'John?' Viola's eyes open wide.

Isolte takes a deep breath. 'I sort of bumped into him when I was being shown around the stud.'

'What was he doing there?' Viola leans forward eagerly. 'Is he working with the horses?'

'Yes, he is. But not in the way you're thinking . . . ' Isolte swallows. 'He's there as part of a prison sentence.'

'Prison?' The colour has drained from Viola's face. 'What's happened?' She grips the sheet with tight fingers. 'Tell me.' Her voice is a harsh whisper.

'I'm sorry. There's no easy way to say this,' Isolte says slowly, reaching to take Viola's hand. 'Michael is dead.'

Isolte sees shock bloom and catch on Viola's face. She adds quickly, 'There was a fight. This time John got hold of a knife. It was a mistake. He was drunk. They both were.'

'No.' Viola pulls her hand away, puts both hands over her ears. 'No. I don't believe you.' She has begun to rock her head from side to side, and a low keening comes from her. Isolte looks around the ward quickly. Nobody seems to have noticed. She takes Viola's bloodless fingers, unpeeling them gently.

'Listen,' she says urgently. 'Listen to me.' Viola's hands are like dead things. 'I've seen him, and he's doing OK. He's nearly finished his sentence.'

At first Isolte thinks Viola didn't hear, or doesn't understand. She looks unfocused, her eyes distant, staring.

Then she struggles up, her hair a mess around her accusing face. 'You should have told me before.' Spit collects at the corners of her lips. 'You should have told me.'

'It didn't feel right,' Isolte says loudly, holding to the conviction of truth, 'not over the phone. Not when I was far away from you.'

Isolte is telling me things about Judy and a child. It's as if I'm floating far away. I hear her thin voice brushing against me, snatches of what she's saying hooking into my thoughts.

'So strange to find him there,' she's saying. 'Like fate or something.'

She goes on. I manage to hold words. Sentences. John has been painting in prison. A woman has been to see him and says that he has talent. Dot. He might go to art school when he gets out. I'm trying to focus. Images of John's drawings of pirates, ships and whales flash up behind my eyes; and that afternoon in the heat, on the lawn, the stillness of trees surrounding us. He'd shrugged, embarrassed. What had he said? Michael was the better artist.

He puts his hand on my arm; his touch is on my skin.

There is bile in my throat. Bitter tasting. I keep seeing him stagger away from Michael's body, blood on his hands, on his clothes. I can feel him knowing, through the fug of alcohol, that this one act of violence is irreparable, endless. He's staring down, and he's seen animals die, he understands how it happens. How it's happening now in front of him. And the animal is Michael. He's cut into his brother, thrust cold steel inside a lung or through the dark curl of liver. There is haemorrhaging, a black-red flooding.

I don't understand how it didn't create a shock wave in my own body, how I didn't hear it, not even an echo. All this time I've been thinking only of myself, seeing the rise of my solitary needs, my bones, my pain.

John.

That he could exist without Michael is impossible. I'm frightened for him; I don't see how he can survive, how he can go on without his brother.

And I know that I have to go to him. He needs me.

36

The chair is empty. Isolte must have gone home. I can't remember her leaving. I look around the ward, feeling useless. This has to stop. I have to get better.

I feel a purpose for the first time. There is a sense of something else more important, bigger, than my own pain, my own problems. I hang on to the feeling – I will use it to get better, to eat, to get out of here.

Justine's bed is empty. I watch as an orderly comes with clean sheets and begins to make it up, unfolding sheets, smoothing corners.

A nurse passes my bed.

'Where is Justine?' I interrupt, my voice abnormally loud and abrupt.

'Justine? You mean Miss Mortimer?' She frowns. 'I thought you knew, love.' She pauses, lowers her voice. 'She passed away. Died. Yesterday.'

'Oh,' I say, 'I didn't know . . .'

'Happened in the middle of the night.' The nurse looks at me kindly. 'It wasn't my shift.'

I remember Justine's toothless smile.

'Does her son know?' I look at the empty bed, the stretch of clean sheets.

The nurse looks puzzled, shakes her head. 'I don't know what you mean,' she says.

'But all her grandchildren . . .'

The nurse is looking at me oddly; she gives her head a little shake again. 'Never had a visitor, poor soul.'

There's a flash of movement behind the nurse. It's the little girl. I lean forward. She's hurrying through the ward, passing beds without turning her head, running too fast as usual; her hair is tied into plaits today. They fly behind her. If she's not Justine's grandchild, then who is she? I open my mouth to ask the nurse but she's already moved away to the other side of the room, talking to a doctor.

The little girl is bouncing on her toes in the way that children do, loose-limbed, defying gravity. She stops as if she knows I'm thinking about her. Turning, she moves towards me. She's looking at me with olive eyes, and they are steady, unwavering, dark inside that pale, freckled face.

I think I always knew.

For a moment I feel fingers gripping my wrists. The nails dig into me, sharp in my flesh, making me wince. She leans close so that I feel her breath, soft on my skin. I can smell the sea.

'You,' I whisper.

I want to touch her, hold her. But I am frightened. So frightened that I sit exactly as I am, silent and still under the sheet, with my mouth open and my hands clasped tightly. My skin is like ice, cold and lifeless. I can't breathe.

She turns, with a flick of two brown pigtails. Sun flash. A billowing of air, a rush of feathers. And she is gone.

The ward bleeds in: the clatter of the lunch trolley, the mutter of patients and the chink of cutlery and trays. Complaints. Mouths opening and closing and chewing. The stink of boiled cabbage and potatoes. Words of refusal and protest.

I think I can hear her laugh.

I'm straining to hear the echo, to catch it and examine it for meaning. Hospital noises fill the space so that there is no room for anything else. The urge to scream, to shout at them all to be quiet is almost unbearable. I press my lips together and close my eyes, searching for another sound from her. When I open my eyes, Vera, the lunch assistant, is hovering by my bed. She is despondent, droopy and spotty in her blue overall. Her name badge is on upside down.

She looks at me. 'Soup?'

I stare down at my hands, thinking, with a shock, that Polly's nails have left red marks again. But when I lift them closer, there is nothing to see, except my wrist bones, sticking up like little boats sailing under my skin.

'I'm sorry,' I whisper. 'Polly. I'm sorry.'

*

'How can she just disappear?' Mummy asked, over and over, into her wine glass, into the wind. 'I don't understand.'

At first there was an expectation, a hope that she would turn up – everyone kept saying that she'd come back. Then days stretched into weeks, and expectations changed. It was a body they were looking for. They didn't find that either.

Children do disappear. I know that now. It happens more often than you'd think. Children are taken from front gardens and

293

doorsteps. They vanish from car parks and shops. It only takes a moment. There are files full of the missing. Photographs taken on family outings, gap-toothed smiles and bright eyes staring out.

Polly Hollis. Aged seven and a half. Four foot, two inches. Brown hair and dark-brown eyes. Freckles. Missing. 27 August 1972.

I've often thought about what happens when a name, once innocent and private, becomes public property in that way, how it becomes synonymous with grief and speculation, the shape of it marred by grubby fingers turning a newspaper. People mouth it with superstition. It becomes charged with fear. The meaning of it changed for ever, emptied of the person who once owned it.

37

It's been three weeks since I heard about John. And I'm eating. Every day I put food into my mouth, chew and swallow. They've taken the tube away. My consultant, Mr Groff, is pleased. He taps his pen on his knee and smiles. 'If you can keep this up, we'll soon have you home.' And he looks at me, instead of just above my head. 'Excellent progress, Viola.' I find that I like this praise; I absorb it like sunshine. 'Well done.'

When I'm lying in my narrow bed, instead of disinfectant and overcooked food, I smell the forest: the underneath of things, damp and fungus, the milky fibrous flesh of mushrooms sprouting. There is the resin tang of fallen pine needles. Breath of horses and fox hair and mist rising from grass surrounds me. I smell river water, the density of muddy banks packed with samphire and sea peas, rushing streams opening into the sea. Wash of brine, foam and sun-warmed pebbles.

He tried to give it back to me. I wouldn't let him. There, in woods, inside the darkness, our hearts beating fast, listening for witches, John came close, leaned against me. 'Viola, I'm sorry,' he whispered.

'For what?'

'You know.'

'I don't care.'

'It was the T-shirt. It confused me.'

'I don't care.'

'I've got the pebble. Take it.'

He fumbled for my fingers, trying to press the stone into my hand. And I refused him, threw it from me. I thought I heard it land, a muted thud on moss. Lost for ever inside that place. My name etched into the woods, into the magic and the evil.

Thinking of that moment spurs me on. I have to get better so that I can tell him that I'm sorry for rejecting him. I wish I'd taken the pebble from him. I wish I had it now. I've long forgiven him for kissing Isolte. I know that he was telling the truth – kissing her had been a mistake. I think despairingly of the letters I wrote him at Hettie's and the squat – all those teenage outpourings. If only I'd had the courage to send them. It hurts to think that he has spent so many years not knowing how I really feel about him, not knowing that I've been thinking about him daily – wondering and worrying and longing for him.

Since beginning to eat, I've had the strength to practise walking around the ward. It's getting easier to swing my legs out of bed. My forgotten stomach muscles quiver, my hands clutch at the edges of the bed, and I find that I can haul myself into a sitting position. Pushing back sheets that grip like bandages, I slip my skinny legs out and lower them one by one on to the floor.

It's time for my walk around the beds now. The floor is cool beneath my feet, smooth, slightly gritty. My weight falls, the surprise of it, shock bearing down into my knees, my ankles and my toes. It still feels too much – a hammering inside joints and cartilage, crushing muscle fibre. But I am upright and balancing and taking a step at a time. I calculate how many steps before I'll reach the entrance to the ward – twenty perhaps? And then there will be corridors and lifts and roads to navigate. One step at a time, I tell myself.

Shuffling carefully from bed to bed, arms out to help me balance, I remember that inside the darkness of that night, despite my panic and fear, what I really wanted was to forget Mummy and Frank and their stupid wedding, forget Issy and Michael and their quarrels, forget the witches. I wanted to take John's hand in mine and go with him through the undergrowth to somewhere safe and quiet where he could hold me in the way he held Issy, and we could fit our lips together and make the shape that lovers do in films: the half-moon curve of two people pressed together, all of them touching, closing off the air between them.

I'd forgotten Polly, waiting in the tower. I think we all had. The woods were full of everything except her. I was overcome by the nearness of John, sore from the ripe bruise of my aching heart, and beyond that, there was the crouching darkness and the way that every sound exploded inside my consciousness like a bomb.

'Viola!' A nurse takes hold of my arm. 'You're up again! Without your slippers . . . you naughty girl. Let me help you.'

She has her large, capable arm under my elbow and we shuffle together, her fingers tight against me. I lean into her, resting on her, and I feel the firm bulk of her stomach pressing into my hip. She's turning me away from the door, away from the rest of my twenty steps.

'Let us know next time you want to get out of bed,' she says.

'No,' I protest. 'I have to go . . .'

She's guiding me back towards the bed; and she pauses, puzzled. 'Did you want the toilet, love?'

I shake my head. 'I have to go home.'

'That's the spirit.' She grins at me. 'You're doing ever so well. Your weight is up. You just need a little longer.'

'Now.'

But I think I whispered it, because she doesn't acknowledge me. She's sitting me back on the bed as if I'm a doll, tucking me in and straightening the sheet and talking, talking.

Why would John have wanted to kiss me? I was ugly. My face a closed wound. I was like Frankenstein's monster. Stitched together. I thought I heard pity in his voice. I didn't want that. I didn't want his pity. I wanted him to love me.

I've started to keep a food diary. I write down everything I've eaten and the calories: little numbers in the margins that add up every day. I've worked out that in about another three weeks I should be nudging my target weight. I need all the strength that food can give me if I am to be strong enough to look after John. It doesn't matter what I look like or how I feel. It only matters that I can do something good and useful, that I can see him again.

Dr Feaver visits me and she is pleased with me too. I've told her that I no longer see food as an enemy. It can help me to be a better person, help me to get back into the world; instinctively, I use words that will reassure her. The cunning that I've used for years to hide the truth and starve myself is coming in useful for different reasons; I'm convincing her to write positive things in her notes, so that when the doctors confer about me they will agree that it is time I was discharged.

38

Isolte moves down the supermarket aisle slowly, pulling things off shelves, checking packets for ingredients. Viola needs healthy food, high in calories. Her stomach is still delicate and her appetite small. She likes simple things: white rice, vegetable stews, toast and Marmite. There has been a pattern of Viola getting slightly better, only to relapse again. She is easily triggered. So Isolte is wary. But this time Viola appears anxious to get well. And Isolte has begun to hope that her sister has beaten the disease.

Isolte frowns at the meat section, glancing at sausages and packets of mince. She also has to feed Ben – he's coming over for supper later – and he'll want something more substantial, proper food with meat. She pauses and looks at the cuts of chicken in their plastic containers, pale slabs with opaque, dead skin curling. She reaches down and drops a packet of thighs and drumsticks in the trolley. She'll get some fresh tarragon and parsley too.

Viola has been staying with Isolte since she got out of hospital. It's not an ideal situation, because Isolte doesn't have a spare room and Viola has to sleep on the sofa bed in the living room. For days now, they've put the bed back every morning together, sliding the mattress inside the frame, folding the sheets and bundling the duvet into a cupboard. Isolte offered her own bed, but Viola only accepted the invitation to stay on the condition that she'd be sleeping on the pullout; she was firm, 'I won't be more of a nuisance.'

It's obvious to Isolte that Viola should live with her properly, permanently. She's done the maths. If she sells the flat, she'll have enough to buy a two-bedroom place in a slightly less desirable area. She hasn't told Viola or Ben her plans yet; she wants to get a valuation from an estate agent first.

Viola seems so much better, but any more shocks could cause a relapse, so Isolte keeps her message about John and the stone to herself. She'll tell her soon. There's no hurry.

Outside on the street, Isolte smells smoky, autumnal dampness. Leaves are turning on the trees, yellowing and dying. Gusts of wind send them fluttering down. There are some brown and orange ones in the gutter, heaped up with bits of newspaper and cigarette butts. Isolte walks briskly. The supermarket bags swing against her legs. She feels the pointed edge of a packet jabbing her calf.

A bus goes past. It has an advert on the side. A rapturous bride looks down on the passing traffic. Her wedding dress swirls in a lacy circle, confetti scattering around her like pink snowflakes.

*

'Frank, please . . .' Mummy is following him into the cottage, pulling at his arm. 'Listen.'

Polly's bag is ready for him on the kitchen table with her clothes and her toothbrush packed inside. He hesitates for a moment before picking it up; the pink-flowered fabric looks odd inside his broad, male grasp.

'Is this everything?' he asks, hardly moving his lips.

Isolte remembers then and runs upstairs to get the Sasha doll; she comes back, nearly tripping on the hole in the carpet, and thrusts it out to him. He takes it without looking at her. His mouth trembles inside dark stubble. He is hollow-cheeked and stooping as an old man.

'Don't go. Don't just leave without ...' Mummy hovers behind him, her fingers trawl the air, opening and closing. Her eyes are swollen from crying. She stumbles and bangs her knee against a table.

'There is nothing to say.' He turns, the doll clutched to him. Its head lolls to one side. Yellow hair sticks up in tufts.

'Please stop, Rose.' His voice is blank. He pushes past her. 'It's over,' he says very quietly. 'I can't marry you.'

He's gone. The door shuts behind him, but Mummy wrenches it open to shout after him, 'I loved her too.' Her voice breaks. 'I loved her too.'

The words hang inside the stillness of the forest. There is no answer from Frank. The girls sit on the stairs and listen to Frank's car starting. It rumbles away over the track, bumping up the hill towards the turn in the road. If he looks in the wing mirror now, Isolte thinks, he won't be able to see the cottage any more.

Mummy is crying again. From the kitchen they can hear the clink of glass against glass and her choked sobbing. The girls don't move from their place on the bottom step of the stairs. Outside, the sun slides behind the trees, the sky spread out like silvered fish scales. Shadows fall, long and black across the garden.

Isolte remembers Polly hugging Mummy in the hospital, the way she'd clasped Mummy around the neck, her shining face.

*

Viola is standing on her head. She is balancing in the centre of the room, supported by her linked hands and planted elbows. All the blood has rushed downwards, so that her face is puce and her floating feet look bloodless.

Isolte ignores her, going through into the kitchen, dumping the bags on the surface. She knows better than to talk to someone in a headstand. She unpacks the ingredients for supper, leans down to pull out a saucepan.

Viola appears at the door, flushed and breathing heavily. Isolte notices her collarbones protruding, ribs visible under the thin fabric of her T-shirt. It'll take a while for her to put on enough weight to stop looking gaunt.

'You've started to do yoga again?'

Isolte wants to grab her sister around the waist and hug her. There seem to be improvements every day. Recently she's acquired a better complexion and her eyes seem brighter.

Unpacking the shopping, Isolte inhales the lemony bite of tarragon, the peppery scent of parsley. 'Mmm, smell this.'

Viola sticks her nose inside the spray of green, breathing in obediently, holding the bunch of herbs like a wedding bouquet. 'Lovely,' she says.

'So how does it feel to get back to headstands?'

'It's such a relief to be able to use my body again. A miracle really.'

Isolte has begun to chop an onion and some carrots. She puts a chunk of raw carrot in her mouth and crunches.

'Talking of miracles,' Viola says slowly, 'something weird happened when I was in hospital.' She straightens and looks directly at her sister. 'I saw Polly's ghost.'

Isolte stops in mid-chop, her mouth falling open. The half-eaten carrot catches in her throat and she coughs violently.

'What?' The knife trembles in her hand.

'I know it sounds strange, but it really happened. I saw her quite clearly, exactly as I remember her . . .'

Isolte is shaking her head. 'You must have been dreaming.'

'No.' Viola is pale, stubborn. 'I did see her.'

Isolte shivers. There is a gathering tightness in her belly. Viola has always been over-sensitive, over-imaginative.

'Even if it was Polly,' she's struggling, throat dry, her voice rasping as if she hasn't spoken for weeks, 'why would she come to you?'

'I don't know. She didn't say anything.' Viola frowns. 'But can't you see what this means?' She leans forward and Isolte sees a vein jumping under the skin on her neck. 'If she's a ghost then she's dead. She must have died when she disappeared. The child I saw was the same age as the child we knew.'

'But of course you'd see her like that,' Isolte argues. 'It's how you remember her. You must have invented her yourself . . . like a waking dream or something.'

'Do you think I'm making this up? Come on . . .' Viola sighs, rubs her hands across her forehead. 'Issy, you used to believe in things.'

'What, like witches and Black Shuck!' Isolte clears her throat. She puts the knife down and turns to face her sister. They mustn't have a row. She must remember how ill Viola has been. Still is.

'Look, it's a lot to take in. Give me some time to think about it.' Isolte pauses, speaks earnestly, her hands curled into fists. 'Her body was never found. Children reappear years and years after they went missing – you know they do. Look at Suzy Lamplugh's mother, still campaigning, refusing to give up hope. Polly could be alive.'

Viola is shaking her head. 'Suzy Lamplugh has only been missing for what, a year? Polly has been gone for fifteen. And she was a little girl. She's dead. That's why I saw her – so that we could stop hoping she'll turn up one day, stop torturing ourselves.'

Isolte takes a deep breath, ignoring the throbbing in her head. She makes her voice calm. 'I can't do this now. We should talk about it later. Ben will be here any moment.'

Viola turns away, her shoulders hunched.

'He doesn't know, does he? About Polly?'

Isolte continues to slice and chop. Small orange rounds spin across the board.

'He doesn't need to know.'

She understands, rationally, that as twelve- and thirteen-year-olds, they hadn't done anything wicked – thoughtless, stupid, but not wicked. Polly's disappearance was someone else's doing, someone who's never been caught. She used to dream about Polly. She used to have nightmares about a faceless person crouching in the shadows of the tower, fish on their breath, nicotine fingers inching through dust. Yet she's come to realise that there is no proof that person existed, or had been there that night. She can't stop herself from going cold if there's a news item about a missing girl, or worse, when some victim's remains have been dug up. But if her body hasn't been found then Polly could be alive. The habit of looking for her is ingrained. She sees the older Polly in laughing, brown-haired young women, or sitting on cardboard, huddled among the homeless, scars on her arms. She never passes a vagrant girl without looking into her face, pressing money into grubby hands. Polly could even be happy and well, having been brought up by some other family that had, for whatever reason, wanted a daughter of their own.

Isolte knows how to bend, to smudge the lines of things, make compromises. She knows that about herself. Just as she knows that these are the skills that allow her to survive. Viola doesn't have those same abilities. There is something rigid about her sister. Ironically, Viola's fragility comes from her unbending character, her unrealistic code of honour.

Ben enters the kitchen, his collar turned up, bringing cold air and traffic fumes with him. His face looks heavy, his mobile mouth droops, as if under the weight of itself. If his face isn't animated, it flattens under his big features, settling easily into sullen despair.

'Chilly out there. Weather's changed,' he says, pulling a bottle of beer out of his pocket. 'Autumn's here, though I don't see any mellow fruitfulness, just rotten leaves.'

'That's London for you.' Isolte leans across the kitchen counter to receive his kiss. He nods in the direction of Viola, who's slumped on the sofa watching TV, and raises his eyebrows in a silent question.

'I'll tell you later,' Isolte says quietly, shaking her head. 'How was Stevie?' she asks, passing him a glass.

'He kept cracking terrible jokes. He looks bloody awful. They all do in that ward. It's so depressing.' He pours the liquid into the glass too quickly and it foams, spilling over the sides. 'Shit!'

'Here, I'll do it.' Isolte takes the glass, wipes the surface, and turns round to adjust the heat under the chicken casserole.

Viola is quiet over supper. She won't eat the chicken. She has a helping of potatoes and carrots, kept scrupulously separate on her plate, and she chews each mouthful for ages. Isolte tries not to watch her. Ben is talking about an empty cottage he's found in

305

Islington. He's attempting to make conversation, trying to smooth things over.

'It'll make a great location. All the original features are in place – mantelpieces, butler sink, shutters . . . the lot.' He's got an idea for a shoot there. His eyes, seal brown, blaze with small flecks of gold. His features lift into expressiveness. 'Maybe you could style a shoot for me? We need to get in there quick before someone tarts it up.'

Isolte scrunches up her face, pretending to consider. 'Can you afford me?'

'Funny. Start thinking of ideas – it needs to be dramatic, maybe couture or something eccentric,' he says, chewing and talking at the same time.

She spoons extra food on to his plate. It's an effort to remain cheerful, to keep up a pretence of normality. Viola does nothing to contribute. She nibbles her food, staring down at her plate silently. She has the hurt look of one who is wronged. Isolte watches Ben rise above his own unhappiness, leaning across the table to speak kindly to Viola, trying to please her. How can she expect him to cope with more of this?

Isolte looks at Viola pushing her food around her plate. Since getting out of hospital, Viola has seemed too animated, too cheerful. It's such an abrupt change in her behaviour. And she hasn't stopped talking about John, about going back to Suffolk. It's like an obsession. Isolte doesn't want her to go back into that world – to be faced with all those memories, to see John again, knowing that Michael is dead because of him. Watching Viola's miserable face now, remembering all her talk of ghosts, it's clear that Viola isn't better yet.

Isolte has lost her appetite. She feels a deadening sense of responsibility and disappointment. She has a sudden memory of when Viola pierced her own ear, the mess she made of it and the infection that set in, needing antibiotics.

39

The Piccadilly pub is crowded. Even in the middle of the day it's steeped in a gloomy half-light. There is the warmth of too many bodies, the smell of sweat, damp wool, eager breath and spilt beer. The place has a seedy feel, an intimate anonymity. Isolte thinks how much she prefers this to the scrutiny of country pubs. She searches for Dot among the packed bodies, and spots her waving from a corner table. Isolte waves back, making her way through the crowd.

'How are you?' Dot clasps her tightly, and Isolte smells dog hairs on her clothes, the hint of sea under cigarette smoke. They order ploughman's lunches and more drinks. A lager for Dot. A glass of orange juice for Isolte.

'Just been to see the Picasso exhibition at the Royal Academy,' Dot is saying, as she lights another Tip Woodbine. 'Marvellous to see his early work again – the pink and blue periods. One forgets the man's versatility and sheer prodigious output. What an appetite!'

'Mmm. For women as well as art.' Isolte lifts the glass to her lips, wrinkles her nose. It is too sweet, too warm. The unfocused swell of conversation washes around her, presses her closer to Dot, so that she leans through the smoke to hear what she's saying.

'I've been seeing quite a bit of your friend.'

Isolte moves to the edge of her seat and looks up expectantly. Dot makes a face signifying approval – eyebrows shooting up, lips pursed, head nodding.

'He's certainly got talent, but he needs an art school training . . . He needs time to develop. I can help him get a portfolio together, if that's what he wants.'

Isolte is more pleased than she'd expected to be by this news. If John has talent, then there's hope. It creates a future for him. It's good news.

'Oh, don't thank me.' Dot rolls her heavy shoulders. 'It's been fascinating, discovering raw talent. And listening to him talk about his brother, about you and your sister.'

Isolte feels a jolt. 'He's been talking about that?' She thinks of his closed face. The way he'd walked away from her, defeated and silent into the hot afternoon.

'Maybe it's easier to talk to a stranger.' Dot takes a bite of cheese, chews and swallows.

'What's he told you?'

'Oh, anecdotes about the four of you: something about a horse in the forest, the hunt for Black Shuck.' She stubs out her cigarette and looks up. 'I think he was in love with your sister. Maybe he still is.'

Isolte shakes her head. 'We were too young to fall in love. A bit of experimenting in the kissing department. That's all. We were friends. Just kids messing about.'

Dot says nothing, takes another bite of her bread.

Isolte frowns. 'I can't imagine him telling you that. He never was much of a talker.'

'It's all in his head.' Dot taps her own forehead. 'Been locked up there for years. He's been reliving it. He says it helps to say the words out loud.'

Isolte glances at Dot quickly. How much does she know?

'He told me about Polly.' Dot must be able to read minds. 'I imagine it's taken a lot to carry on after a thing like that . . .' She sighs. 'And there was I telling you that you had a fairy tale childhood.'

'Oh, I don't know. Fairy tales are full of darkness, aren't they?' Isolte says, disguising her shock, forcing a smile, chin up. 'Witches and cannibalism and lost children.'

'But this wasn't a story, was it?'

'No.' Isolte looks at her. 'No. It was real.'

They finish their lunch, Dot talking about a forthcoming exhibition and the shocking prices in London, and how different it was in the sixties when she was an art student, living in digs on the Gloucester Road.

They embrace and turn to walk in opposite directions. Isolte heads towards Piccadilly tube station. It's good, she supposes, that John has begun to talk; but Dot was right, better he talks to a stranger. Isolte doesn't want to see him again – it was too awkward; the way he looked at her made her uncomfortable. She and Viola hadn't understood it when they were children, but Frank had been right, as uneducated boys from a violent background, John and Michael had always had the potential to be dangerous. It was Michael who'd suggested leaving Polly in the tower. Of course Viola wouldn't listen when Isolte had pointed that out. Viola was unfailingly loyal to the boys, to the memory of that shared childhood.

Weaving past the lunchtime crowds, she thinks of what Dot said about Viola and John. She has a brief flashback to John holding out the stone. She frowns, blinking the memory away. Even if they did have a childhood crush on each other, what relevance could it possibly have now? If only Viola could find a partner to love her and look after her, Isolte is sure her sister would bloom again, get stronger and confident – the last thing she needs is someone like John, a troubled soul, a man with a criminal record. The death of his brother will haunt him for ever. It's bound to make him unstable; it could easily drive him to drink again.

40

I've been holding my breath, waiting for Isolte and Ben to leave. Isolte had hovered at the front door. 'Sure you'll be fine on your own for the night?' I'd nodded and rolled my eyes. 'I'm a big girl now. You two go – enjoy yourselves.'

They need to spend time on their own, and I can't think properly when they're here. They watch me too closely, their eyes anxious and their smiles hollow. Something is wrong. Isolte is hiding something. It reminds me of when we were teenagers at Hettie's, the way Isolte closed down when I tried to talk about anything to do with the past. 'God, Viola,' she'd say, turning away from me. 'Just shut up, will you.'

But this isn't about the past. This is the future. I wake up every day with a sense of hope, a feeling that there are possibilities left in the world. And it's because of John. I have to make changes; I have to get better.

Mr Groff has advised me to eat six small meals every day and I imagine the energy of those meals as life-giving flames in my gut. I won't let myself think of cold slabs of fat. I curl my hands into fists to prevent myself feeling the extra padding of skin on my arms or poking folds around my waist. I remember my yoga teacher's prayers, the sutras that explain how to use yoga practice to overcome the afflictions of the mind. Issy is careful to keep her wardrobe doors closed so that the full-length mirror fixed on the other side isn't revealed. I know that she thinks something is going to trigger me again. But I am resolute.

When I told Issy about Polly's ghost, she got the same look that she does when I ask her when we can go back: guarded and alert and empty all at the same time. And so I keep my plan secret – to catch a train, get a cab and retrace the journey she took in the summer when she went to see the horses. I'll visit the woman she stayed with. I found her name and address in Isolte's Filofax. I'll find John myself without Issy's help.

I turn on the taps, water gushing into the bath, and pour in a large dollop of pink. Bubbles grow out of the swirling heat, crackling and shining. The smell of rose is overpowering. Lowering myself slowly, I lie with my head against the cold rim. I like the lightness that water lends my body; this buoyancy could trick me into thinking I am weightless. I enjoy the gentle push of water, my limbs moving languidly as seaweed through the warmth.

The dresser in Issy's bedroom is crowded; running my fingers over her pots of shadow and stubs of lipstick, I can't imagine why she needs so many creams and lotions, so many colours to paint her skin; and I experiment with a smudge of pink on my lips, patting silver on to my lids. It reminds me of Judy's vast collection. We'd been overwhelmed by her confusion of jewelled lip glosses and nail varnishes, the tangled clumps of cheap necklaces and gaudy earrings, all those knotted teenage splendours.

I've got almost no clothes with me: a tracksuit, old jeans and jumpers. We used to dress up to speak to the gods. I remember a grubby nightdress that belonged to Mummy. I loved the whisper of its transparent fabric against my bare legs, the ruffles on the hem swinging at my heels.

I pull open Issy's wardrobe. A long slice of glass holds my reflection lightly, offering myself back to me. Mesmerised, I drop the towel. There I am. Or am I? I am looking at something that pretends to be Truth. I blink. I know better. My reflection has lied to me for years. It has presented cunning angles of bone. It has warped and moulded my hips into hillocks of fat, swelling my breasts and distorting my ankles. I should turn away. But I am compelled to gawp at the thing that my mind wishes me to see. One small, removed part of my brain is curious to know who the rest of me determines I am.

A girl with protruding ribs and sharp hipbones looks back at me warily. She is damp, her skin glistening with moisture. I swallow and stare harder, realising that the door is at a slight angle so that the reflection is skewed and slanting away. I reach out to straighten the door, but the naked girl has gone, and standing in her place is a child, a sturdy blonde with freckles and grey eyes. She has a vicious mark running down her nose into her lip, her face sewn together with black thread.

Squeezing my eyes shut against the image, I shove my hand into the wardrobe, grabbing at fabrics; different textures graze my fingers: knobbly, smooth, rough and hairy. Feeling across the wooden edges of clothes hangers, I grasp something slippery: a sheath of beige silk. I slide it over my head and Issy's dress fans around me, tucking soft, intimate folds between my legs. I smell her perfume. Sounds from the street seep in: a car door slamming, the roar of an engine and a woman's voice. An aeroplane passes overhead with a deadening roar. The silk dress lies across my skin like a limp, meek animal. I wonder what John would think of me now. I remember Judy's disco, how she dressed us up in her clothes. I'd wanted John to see me looking pretty and grown-up.

Isolte has grown more beautiful with age, while I have shrivelled away. After Polly disappeared, I stopped wanting to look pretty. It felt right to be ugly. But now I wonder if I could ever look like my sister again. I imagine how she must look in this dress. I glance into the mirror, hoping; but of course I am ridiculous inside folds of fabric. My breasts have shrunk and the dress gapes across my collarbones, hanging loose around my arms. Shivering, I can hear John's voice in my head. I feel the heat of him, the brush of his soft worn jeans and shiny jumper. I have thought about him kissing me so much that it has taken on the quality of memory. I have put myself inside my sister's body – flown out of my skin to inhabit hers – to be the one he held, the one he kissed in the darkness, inside the tower. I imagine that I remember the feel of his lips, the rub of his tongue, the slide of his teeth under saliva. It seems so real.

He never kissed me. He kissed my sister.

'John.' I say his name aloud.

The thought of him makes me dizzy. I have spent years imagining him fishing by a river staring into the sun, swinging sticks through bracken, or laughing with his brother while they mended some old car, oil on their hands. But he stuck a knife into his brother; he watched him die. He's spent years in an institution. And I didn't know.

When people die, you lose the way they loved you. You lose the way they saw you. Nobody can replace that. Nobody will love me as my mother loved me. I cannot be a daughter to anybody else. Nobody will see me as John saw me. Loving me, he'd understood the truth of me: how I existed in layers, like a painting. He could see the separate me, distinctly and delicately alone, transparent as a watercolour sketch. But he knew that that girl was conditioned by the magnetic pull of the picture underneath, the bold and vivid brushstrokes of Viola-and-Issy. He understood, because, like me, he was hooked into the implacable equation of being two.

Wrapping my arms around myself, slippery silk against the hard curve of my ribs, I sink to the floor, folding myself up; and I allow myself to feel the ache I have inside: the terrible ache for him.

41

'Morning.' Ben nuzzles into the back of her neck and she catches a whiff of the Chinese meal they'd shared last night, a faint trace of his aftershave and stale morning breath. She sniffs, wanting the other smell lingering underneath, the one she loves. The smell of him.

Their familiarity thrills her. She can read Ben's mannerisms, like his habit of pulling his left earlobe when he's concentrating. Inside his trainers she knows that he has bony, battered feet with fallen arches and under his floppy hair an obstinate whirl grows in a spiral at the nape of his neck.

The jolt she gets from his sheer physicality, his broad bones and twisting thigh muscles has never left her. He confronts her with his unapologetic, absolute male need. 'Let me see you,' he'd said, the first time, pulling the sheet away from her. She'd been insecure, resentful, until she realised that he really liked the slight droop of her breasts, the spongy texture on the back of her thighs, the spidery stretchmarks on her hips. The imperfections she hid from men are impossible to keep from Ben. 'I want all of you,' he told her.

'So,' he says now, sliding his hands between her thighs, 'I'm not working till this afternoon . . . How does a nice long lie-in sound?'

Isolte squints at the clock on the bedside table, propping herself up on her elbows regretfully. 'Think I should get home, I don't want to leave Viola for too long.'

Ben sighs and pulls her to him for a quick hug. 'Oh well, another time.'

'I'll have a shower and breakfast at home.'

'I'll drive you.'

'No, don't be silly, it's your morning off. I'll get a bus or something.'

But Ben has already thrown the covers back and hauled himself out of bed; he's pulling on a jumper, pushing his bony feet into trainers.

'I'll have a shower when I get back – we can be filthy together.' He sniffs at his arm. 'Hmmm, nice . . . you're on my skin.'

After last night, Isolte can smell a salty hum on herself. She likes to have the sticky residue of Ben on her, tightening like glue on her skin. Her body is alive, tingling with nerves. She pulls on her clothes, tugs a brush through her hair; the perm has dropped out, leaving a few last curls.

'So, not even a cup of tea?' He's picked up the car keys. 'Last chance?'

She shakes her head, noticing some estate agent's details on the hall table. She picks it up. 'What's this?'

'Oh, that's the place I was telling you about.' He plucks an apple from the fruit bowl and bites into it. 'It's on the market so we'll have to get in fast if we want to shoot there.'

Isolte glances down at a photograph of a Georgian cottage with a neat front garden and picket fence.

'Isn't it a bit small for a location?' she says.

'It doesn't have many rooms but it has the dimensions of a much larger house. Big doorways and windows – it's got a kind of quirky, *Alice in Wonderland* feel.'

She reads, *plaster cornices and coving, picture rails and skirting boards, south facing*. 'Sounds lovely.' She accepts a bite of his apple. The sour-sweet flesh fills her mouth. She crunches and swallows. 'Let's go see it later this week; I'll get some ideas together, call in some clothes.'

In the street, she leans against Ben, his arm over her shoulder. There is a light wind teasing leaves off the trees, sending them turning, flickering through the air.

'Did you know,' she says, 'that catching a falling leaf gives you luck for the year?'

Ben springs into a run. Dashing towards a leaf he makes a snatch and misses. Spinning on his heels he lunges for another one. The leaves twist and turn, changing direction and speed. A woman walking on the other side of the road turns to stare as he flails, nearly falls, and springs again recklessly for the leaves. Isolte puts her hands over her mouth, laughing, as he hops and swears, staring up into the sky. A large maple leaf floats close and he stretches out his fingers to it, clutching it inside his fist. 'There.' He presents it to her, breathless. 'Luck for a year.'

She takes the leaf, yellowed and splashed with age spots, and laughs. 'Who knew you believed?'

'Load of old bollocks,' he says. 'But I like a challenge.'

In the car, Ben slaps his hand on his forehead. 'Nearly forgot to tell you. It's my parents' wedding anniversary soon.'

The car idles across Chelsea Bridge, inching through rush-hour traffic. Isolte looks out at the wide stretch of river. Low tide.

Brown water laps against mud banks. Albert Bridge shines in the distance.

'They're having a dinner party. It'll be a formal affair – all the best silver out. It's one we can't get out of, I'm afraid.'

'When?' She feels guilty. Ben will have to negotiate this grid-lock to get home again.

'Fifteenth of October,' Ben says, turning into her street and pulling the car over. Parking outside Isolte's flat, he adds, 'We won't stay the night – I know you'll want to get back. I'll stay sober to pay the penalty for my appalling parents.'

42

As Isolte enters her flat, she falters. The matter of Polly's ghost remains here like a palpable presence, waiting for her attention. She doesn't want to talk about it. But they must. She feels resentment, a twinge of irritation. Why is Viola so dramatic, so difficult?

The flat is dim, the blinds drawn against the bright morning. At first she thinks that Viola must still be in bed. But the sofa bed isn't out and she sees the back of Viola's head. She's sitting in the living room, motionless. Isolte calls her name quietly. Viola rises from her seat, fumbling towards the sound of her name like a blind person.

'What are you doing, sitting in the dark? It's beautiful outside.' Isolte goes to the window and pulls the blind. She turns to her sister, but they don't touch. They stand apart.

Viola looks tired and shaky. She blinks in the sudden daylight. Her eyes are smudged with grey make-up and for some reason she is wearing one of Isolte's evening dresses, a column of silk that gapes and sags on her tiny frame, making her look like a child dressing up in her mother's clothes. The fabric is creased as if it's been slept in.

'What's the matter?' Isolte bites her lip, feeling the pleasure in her body draining away.

'Nothing.' Viola sways slightly. 'I didn't get much sleep last night.'

'Didn't you go to bed at all?' Isolte moves towards her. 'You must be exhausted. Come and lie down.' Isolte gestures towards her room. 'Use my bed.'

Viola is obedient. She curls up like a foetus, her face pressed into the pillow.

'Are you in pain?' Isolte sits on the bed and strokes the cold skin of her shoulder between the silky straps.

Viola shakes her head. 'I just keep thinking about things. You know – about John and Michael. About what's happened to them.'

Isolte catches a sudden hint of Ben on her own musty skin. The smell of life. She wants Viola to have this warmth, this joy.

'Look at me,' she whispers.

Viola turns on the pillow and stares up. Isolte sees a wariness, a watchful passivity in her face. Feeling love and frustration, Isolte places her hands either side of Viola's face, leans forward to press her lips briefly against her sister's. She feels the give of Viola's chapped skin, the softness of flesh. The bottom lip is fatter, a deeper cushion. She tastes her breath.

'You have to get better, Viola.' She looks down at her and the urgency of her words brings tears to her eyes. 'You must.'

Viola lies back on the pillow for a moment, touching her lips. She looks dazed. And then she gives a faint smile. 'Do you remember,' she says, 'how Mum kissed us goodnight sometimes?'

322

'Yes.' Isolte sits up, opening her mouth to laugh. 'Pretending we were people in films. Lovers. Her hair used to fall into my face.'

'She smelt of cherries.'

'She'd want you to get well, Viola,' Isolte says. 'She'd want you to be happy.'

'She was happy with Frank, wasn't she?' Viola rubs her eyes. 'He was good for her. I don't know why we had to spoil that. We ruined it all. She went back to drinking because of us. She killed herself because of us . . .'

'Stop.' Isolte grabs her hand, holds it tight. 'We didn't know. We were just children. We can't bring her back. All we can do now is live lives that she would wish for us.'

'To seize life with both hands,' Viola answers immediately. She smiles. 'To be joyful. To be curious.'

'Yes. Can't you just hear her? She wasn't always right about things. But she did love us.'

Viola nods in recognition.

Isolte says in a serious voice, 'You know she wouldn't want you to be like this.'

Viola nods again, tilts her face to look at her sister. 'And she thought we had each other, didn't she? When she died. She didn't know that we were going to drift apart.'

There is silence. Isolte grimaces. 'I'm sorry. I know I was selfish. It was the only way I could cope. I needed to fit in. You were so determined not to. I didn't know how to help you. But,' she touches Viola's hand, 'here we are, we've survived somehow. We still have each other, don't we? We can make things better. We mustn't screw it up this time – I mustn't.'

'And now there's John too . . .'

323

'Listen,' Isolte says quickly, 'Dot is going to help John get into art school. He has a chance to start over again. It's not up to us any more.'

'No.' Viola shakes her head in disagreement. 'I want to see him, help him.'

'He's not the boy you knew, Viola,' Isolte persists. 'John has changed. We've changed. Life moves on. You have to let go of the past. Think about the future.'

Viola has opened her mouth to argue again.

Isolte changes tack. 'What do you think Polly's ghost was trying to tell you?' she asks.

Viola looks surprised. 'You said you didn't believe in that.'

'The point is,' Isolte struggles to find the words, 'you saw her. That's what counts. She came with forgiveness. That's it, isn't it? You needed to see her. You needed her to let you go.' She frowns. 'I've been thinking about it. Viola – you are right about Polly. She is dead.' Isolte blinks. 'However much we wish it was different, there's nothing you or I can do – don't you think you could try and forgive yourself? You're talented and bright. There's so much you could do with your life if you gave yourself a chance.'

Viola sits up. 'It's hard to let go, Issy. It's just so hard. I'm not as strong as you.' She looks at her sister. 'Just tell me one thing – I need to know. Did John talk about me? Did he ask about me?'

Isolte pauses for a moment and then shakes her head. She clears her throat. 'Well, of course he asked how you were. But I could see he didn't want to get lost in the past. To be honest, he didn't seem particularly pleased to see me.' She looks down at the floor. 'He needs a fresh start. The best thing you can do is let him have that.'

'So you don't think he's thinking about us, about me . . .'

Isolte sighs. 'Why should he? We've been out of his life for years.'

Isolte has got off the bed. The mattress dips and moves under her weight. She's standing, pushing her hair behind her ears. 'Are you hungry?' she asks. 'I could make scrambled eggs.'

There's something about Isolte's brisk, practical manner that reminds me of the nurses. Although actually being a carer is not natural to my sister, just as it wasn't to our mother. She is impatient with illness, with anything that demands a continuous sacrifice from her. Her energy brims at the skin's edge, childlike, eager. But she has honed her temperament for me, to take care of me. I can feel the effort it requires. What I see in my sister is her strength, her courage. Isolte isn't like me. She could exist alone.

I think about the adult John. A man with muscled shoulders and a steady gaze. Of course, what Isolte said is true. Whatever childish, romantic ideas I've hung on to, the truth is that I don't know him any more. Part of me thought that he might have asked Isolte to pass a message on – even just to say hello. Stupid. Of course, he has more important things on his mind. I am just a reminder of everything he wants to forget.

As Isolte stands in her kitchen cracking eggs into a bowl, I get up and move slowly through the small spaces of the flat, looking at my sister's things: her camel-bone boxes, African tribal figures, her bowls filled with coloured beads, and postcards leaning against the mirror and stuck on the fridge, notes from her friends, people I've never met; and I realise that she has made a home. She has been able to do something that I haven't managed. She has lived a life.

Pleasure was the word that Dr Feaver had been looking for – the answer she'd wanted me to give. But pleasure has not been something I have deserved.

Through John I felt that I would reach Polly too. Through him I thought that I could fall through time into my childhood, into the forest, winding everything back to a fresh beginning when we could all be new and whole again. None of us can have that. Polly has gone and that will never change. There is no way around it.

43

Issy and Ben procrastinate, finding things to delay their departure to the Hadley supper. Even after they leave, Isolte dashes back in, breathless and noisy, to take a forgotten bottle of champagne out of the fridge, Ben sounding the horn impatiently outside.

She clatters down the stairs again, shouting her goodbye. 'Back tonight!'

The air molecules swirl around the remains of sound. I watch the car accelerate away to the end of the street, brake lights flashing at the crossroads. The atmosphere settles, a calm descending. It's a relief to have the flat to myself again, to wander from room to room, to be alone with my thoughts.

It's windy outside. The trees in the square are lashing their branches. The sky flares violet across the rooftops. There are no birds. No black rooks hopping across the grass in the square or flapping heavily across the skyline.

I won't see John again. Isolte is right. I am nothing to him now. I should leave him in peace to begin his new life. I catch sight of myself in the hall mirror, turning away from the sharp lines of my jaw and cheeks, and the ridge of nose. He wouldn't even recognise me, I think. My body feels numb, lifeless. I wonder how I am going to get through the evening, and then the rest of my life. There is no point in cooking a meal and going through the charade of eating it, no point in trying to distract myself with a book or a TV programme. I stand in the darkening flat staring out at the windy square for a stretch of unmeasurable time, until I rub my eyes and force myself to turn back into the room.

There's a mess of unopened letters piled up on the hall table. For something to do, I pick them up and begin to arrange them into piles, putting private letters on one side and bills on the other. A small brown envelope has my name on it. I hold it closer, looking at it in surprise. I don't know the handwriting, but my heart has begun to beat faster as I rip it open, tearing through Sellotape and brown paper.

I pull out a small painting of two children's faces and immediately recognise John and myself. We look out of the painting, exactly as we were all those years ago. He's painted me without my scar and we are both smiling. With shaking fingers I turn it over to see if there is a message. There are no words. On the other side is a painting of John as a grown-up, as he must be now. His eyes stare steadily into mine.

Frustrated by the lack of words, I examine the envelope and discover a lump tucked into a corner. Slipping my fingers inside, I touch something cool and hard, and feel the crackle of paper. With a shake, I dislodge the lump and it falls into my hand: a pebble wrapped in a folded letter.

Vi – I've kept this safe. It's the only thing I have that's part of you so it's hard to give it up. But I made it for you. I know we were just kids – but it doesn't matter to me. I've never felt the same for anybody. The thought of you has kept me going. I

*was planning to hitch to London to try and find you. Michael
said I was a fool. He said that even if I found you, you
wouldn't want me. We got into one of our fights. Only it got
out of hand. I picked up a knife. By now you'll know the rest.
It scares me to think that you might be disgusted by me. I don't
need to explain to you how much I regret what I did and how
much I miss him.*

*Your sister said you were ill and I've been worrying about it
ever since. I want to take care of you, Viola. Will you let me?
We never used to need words, and it's taken me a long time to
think of how to say all this. If I could see you now, I'd hold
you in my arms, and we wouldn't need to speak.*

*I don't deserve you, Vi, I know that. But I had to send you
this – to see if you still care about me. Whatever you decide,
I'll respect it. I wish only the best for you, only good things.
Killing Michael and being locked up have changed me. I know
what's important in life. I know what I want. I want to be
with you. If you think you could see me, even just to talk, I'm
here waiting. I love you, Vi. Always have.*

John

Turning the pebble slowly I find faint, etched lines. But I can
hardly make out the letters of my name for the blurring of my
tears, which are falling, wet and salty, on to my hands and on to
the pebble, darkening it. I've lost the power to stand up, my legs
buckle and I slump into a chair. Sitting in the darkening room, I
clutch the pebble and letter to me and sob.

He walked beside me in the forest on a summer afternoon, kicking his feet, not looking at me. I walked beside him, holding the

pebble. My fingers rubbed the fresh marks he'd put there. *Viola.*
We were made mute by our embarrassment. But that was the
moment that feelings leapt into my throat, into my heart, into my
body, leaving me breathless. Those same feelings flood through
me now.

> *Your purity of being*
> *Distilled like nectar*
> *Sweet on my tongue*
> *As the word I had been*
> *Looking for.*

Isolte is wrong. All my life I've thought that she is the one who
knows best, who gets things right, who knows what to say. I sit up
straighter, wiping away my tears, pushing a tangle of damp hair
out of my face. My legs are still trembling, but I can't sit here,
wasting time. He wants to see me. He's waiting for me. The words
dance in my head as I stumble around the flat, banging my shin
on an armchair, searching for my bag. With shaking fingers I
check that my purse is in it. My sense of purpose is back and I
stride over to the hall table and, with a twist of my wrist, rip the
address of the stud out of Isolte's Filofax and the page with Dot's
telephone number.

The crash of the wind against the window is like applause. The
colours in the rug and the curtains seem to gather fresh depth and
brilliance. I was right. Everything I felt was true, I think, pushing
my arms into my coat, closing the door of the flat behind me.

44

Ben turns into his parents' drive. The wind that buffeted them on the motorway is here among the trees in the long expanse of front garden, setting branches twisting and bending. The big chestnut tree next to the house creaks. Naked roses in the flowerbeds swing backwards and forwards.

Clutching a bottle of champagne, Ben and Isolte hurry out of the car over to the porch. Dead leaves spin, blowing over the gravel and piling up around the pillars. A pair of heels clicks rapidly across the hall floor.

'Here you are! At last.' Anita holds the door open. 'Thought I heard the car. Goodness, isn't it windy? Was the traffic terrible? Come and join everyone. We're in the living room. There's a couple of people you don't know – otherwise it's the usual. Uncle Robin and Aunt Penny, the Goodfellows. Oh, and their daughter.' She turns and whispers loudly, 'Poor girl hasn't got her mother's looks.'

Isolte makes a face at Ben and he shrugs, opening his broad palms to her.

A crowd of people are gathered under the chandelier. The men are in suits and ties, the women in Laura Ashley. Isolte, in black trousers and transparent chiffon shirt, suddenly feels provocative and outlandish. She hovers at Ben's elbow as she's introduced to smiling strangers.

'Call me Peter,' Mr Goodfellow is telling Isolte, staring through chiffon to her black bra.

'Still working as a photographer?' He turns to Ben, shifting his weight on to his heels. 'Much money in it, is there? Would have thought you'd be thinking of a steady job at your age. City not appeal?'

Isolte doesn't hear Ben's reply, her attention caught by a sudden snap and rattle of window glass. The wind is getting stronger. She wonders if Viola is all right; she'd seemed depressed when they left. Isolte glances surreptitiously at her watch, calculating what time they might be able to leave. But there is a four-course dinner to be got through.

To her dismay, she finds Peter Goodfellow is seated on her right. His daughter, Charlotte, is across the table from her. A plump, nervous girl with wide eyes and carroty hair, she wants to work in fashion.

'Mother doesn't think I'm thin enough,' she says in a whisper. She glances up the table to a woman with hair scraped back from a still beautiful face. Hands circle the air, rings glittering. Isolte notices Uncle Robin staring. He adjusts the cuffs of his tweed jacket, swallowing.

It happens quickly, beginning with a hollow ripping sound, a tearing that seems to come from the bowels of the earth, stopping conversation. A hush, and then a deafening crash and the shattering of glass. Women scream, wine glasses spill, there are shouts and exclamations and a hurried pushing back of chairs. A sudden howl of wind whistles into the room. Cold air on skin.

Branches protrude through the velvet curtains. The fabric flaps open, revealing the jagged remains of glass in the window frame, clawing fingers of wood pushed through. The chestnut tree has come down, crashing its top branches through the dining-room window. Bits of wood and leaf scatter across the carpet among fragments of china and shards of glittering glass.

Only Penny has been injured. A trickle of blood runs towards her elbow and she stares at it, uncomprehending. She is led trembling from the room by Anita. The men gather at the window, scratching their heads. Someone opens the front door and they troop outside to inspect the extent of the damage.

Isolte follows them into the wild, wailing night, leaning into the buffeting wind. The rest of the trees in the garden are thrashing back and forth. She hears the straining of wood and stretch of tree ligament. The chestnut is a felled giant – its tangled roots have ripped open the ground. She can smell dank earth. The tree has fallen across two of the parked cars, including Ben's.

'Look at this! Think if it had fallen further into the room,' George shouts, the wind whipping his words away. 'God knows what would have happened.'

She shivers by Ben's side, arms crossed, bent over, hair tangling around her face. He runs his fingers over the buckled metal of the roof. 'Jesus, crushed like a tin can.' He takes Isolte's arm, staring at the sky. 'Come inside. Another one could come down any moment.'

In the sitting room, Anita is flushed. She is issuing orders, making plans. Her arms pump up and down with military zeal.

'You must all stay the night,' she's saying. 'I'm afraid the drive is impassable.'

The radio is on. People tell each other to hush, listening in. A report says that winds of 70 knots are sweeping the south of England.

'But Michael Fish said very breezy on the six o'clock news,' Anita says disapprovingly. 'No mention of a storm.'

Robin is nodding. 'Extraordinary that it slipped under the radar, so to speak.' He laughs briefly at his own joke. Rubs his hands together, the confidence of his subject transporting him back to his classroom. 'But then weather can surprise even the experts. Did you feel the air outside? Quite warm. That's the front that's being pushed in from the sea.'

At that moment the light bulbs flicker and die. The room is cast into darkness, apart from the glow from the fire. There are cries of dismay and complaint and a call for candles. Anita and Charlotte find nightlights in the kitchen and bear them back to the sitting room. The room takes on a soft, dusky glow. Ben pours brandy into tumblers and passes them around.

Isolte tries to phone Viola, but the line is down. 'She's alone,' she tells Ben. 'I don't like it.'

'She'll be fine,' he reassures her. 'It's probably not so bad in London. She'll sleep through without knowing about it.'

Isolte sips the fiery liquid tentatively. It burns her throat. Everyone has gathered in the sitting room, listening to the shuddering windows and the wind ripping tiles off the roof. There are abrupt bangs and crashes, and a constant low howling roar; it sounds like the sea, Isolte thinks. The energy of the unexpected enters everyone differently – some are softer in their bodies, as if drugged; others, like Anita, seem excited and alert. The magnitude of natural forces has brought them together, erasing constraints and social niceties. Mrs Goodfellow and Penny huddle by the fire.

'Listen, I've been meaning to tell you something. Well, to ask you, really.' Ben shoves his hands in and out of his pockets.

She looks at him expectantly.

'I've put an offer in on that Georgian cottage. The one in Islington.' She sees a muscle twitch at his temple. 'Thought it was too good to let go. If you fancy shacking up with me? Viola too, it's big enough. What do you think?'

She puts her hands over her mouth. 'You've bought it?'

Her heart is racing with happiness. But she can't accept without telling him. She turns away, scrunching up her face. This is it, she thinks. She has no choice.

'Ben,' she says, turning back to him. 'Before I say yes, I have something to tell you. Something you should know.'

'You're not pregnant, are you?' Then he sees her face. 'Sorry. What is it? Whatever it is, you can tell me.'

'But this is something terrible.' She shakes her head. 'I'm afraid, Ben ... afraid of telling you.'

'Here.' He guides her over to a sofa in the darkest corner. 'Let's sit down. Take a deep breath. I'm listening.'

She sits on the edge of the sofa and begins, haltingly, in a strained voice, to tell him about Polly and what happened that night. She stops, bites her lip, nipping hard enough to feel a welling pain. She gives him all the facts, clearly and in order. No excuses. Ben says nothing. She can feel the tension in his body. She stares straight ahead while she explains that Polly has never been found. She finishes in a rush, needing to get it over with.

'You mean, never?'

Isolte shakes her head. '1972. It was in the papers. For years there were sightings. But they never came to anything.'

He rubs his hand over his eyes, blowing out through his lips, making a faint whistling sound. His face is closed and shut off from her. She sees that he looks older like this, his features overblown and heavy. She waits. Her fingers tremble and slip against her knees. She looks away, not able to meet Ben's eyes.

'So,' he asks slowly, 'is that why Viola . . . '

Isolte nods. She swallows and looks up at him. He's frowning, pulling his eyebrows together across his nose. He remains next to her. Their legs are touching. She wants to collapse, rest her head in his lap, close her eyes. She sits rigidly, staring straight ahead. In the line of her vision Anita is bending over to pick up a glass. Isolte hardly sees her; her senses are focused on Ben, alert to any tightening of atmosphere or the rise of a wall of disgust sealing him off from her.

'I see.' He takes her hand in his. Squeezes tight. 'I'm glad,' he says, 'that you told me.'

'Really?' Her fingers are limp inside his. 'Aren't you . . . put off?'

A gust of wind rattles the window. Candles waver, flickering in the draught.

'I told you before, you can tell me anything. I love you.' Ben shakes his head. 'It's the bit that was missing from the puzzle. It makes sense, knowing you and Viola, how you are together.' He leans forward. 'I think I understand Viola's illness now. And your mother . . . '

Isolte can't hold his gaze. Her mouth is trembling and her face contorts. She looks down, her eyes filling with tears.

'Yes,' she says, when she can catch her breath. 'It's there, always. It's behind everything.'

All the feelings that she's kept locked up for so long are tearing through her in big shuddering sobs. The relief makes her dizzy.

'Come here.' He's pulled her into his arms. 'Thank you for

trusting me,' he says quietly. She nods, unable to speak. Under his shirt, she can hear the beat of his heart.

There is a sudden rasping noise and a slither of soot comes down the chimney. A tumble of debris and black smoke surges into the room. Penny screams, jumping to her feet, coughing. Ben gets up to comfort her, leading her to the other side of the room. Penny pats her cheek, gazing up at him, her mouth quivering. He looks over Penny's head to find Isolte, and they exchange a look that makes her stomach contract.

But there is something scratching at the underneath of things. She stops, suddenly alert, listening. She hears the scrape of nails on glass. Viola is close. Fingers holding fingers, the papery brush of Viola's skin. Isolte stretches out her hand and closes on air. A void gapes at her side. She didn't tell Viola about the stone. She goes cold. She bites her lip, her heart beating fast. She has to go home.

The main lights flicker into life, flooding the room with blazing electric light. Everyone is blinking at each other in surprise.

'Got the bloody generator going,' George is shouting from across the room.

Lights flashing: red, green, yellow. John's arm around Viola, holding her safe on the whirling fairground ride; 'I think he was in love with her,' Dot's voice says; John and Viola whispering in corners, out by the ferret hut, alone; Viola's fall from the tower after John kissed the wrong twin. The wrong twin.

It's been there all along. She just couldn't see it. Didn't want to see it.

But it's the one thing that can be rescued from the past, the one good thing to come out of it: Viola and John.

Isolte leaps to her feet, wiping her face. She must get back to Viola. Pulling back the curtain, she stares out of the window.

Through the pale reflection of herself she can see the bent huddle of Ben's car. Three other cars are untouched, but hemmed in by the massive bulk of the fallen chestnut. A moon swings wildly inside the broken sky. Leaves swirl in tornados; plastic bags and scraps of paper catch and spin.

Ben is behind her, his arms slipping around her waist.

'No help for it,' he says. 'We'll have to camp here with everyone else. We'll find a way to get home tomorrow.'

Her frustration makes her breathless. 'But I forgot to tell Viola something.' Her voice is small and flat. She squeezes her hands into fists.

'What?'

She shakes her head. 'That John has something that belongs to her. A stone.'

'Well, it doesn't sound too important,' Ben mutters, puzzled, his breath warm on the back of her neck. 'You'll see her tomorrow. It won't be too late, will it?'

'I promised him I'd tell her.' She turns and looks at him with a level gaze. 'I broke my promise, Ben.'

I have a whole train carriage to myself. Empty seats face each other under strip lighting. Outside, clouds race, streaming across a low-slung moon. It looks as though the wind is getting even stronger. There are plastic bags and scraps of rubbish flying through the air; bushes are flattened; washing lines in back gardens snap and flap; I see a section of fence falling as if a giant has pushed it.

I lean my head against the smeary window, feel my body jolting with the movement of wheels on tracks, the steady pulse of forward motion. Inside me there's a pull like a physical ache and tug.

It's as if I'm the only person left in the world. My breath, caught against the glass, comes back to me, trapped and warm. I see my reflection wavering, lost in the dark. I am separate from Isolte, removed and pasted into the wilderness like an outcast. I miss her. My fingers slide down the glass and feel it tremble. Ghost fingers touch my own, my reflection coming back to meet me. She didn't mean to hurt me. She is my twin. I can never stop loving her.

Beyond the simulacrum of myself, between wild trees, branches bowed by the wind, I glimpse the countryside rushing past. Inside shadowy shapes I imagine landmarks of my childhood flickering into life: the cottage, the tower, a row of desolate houses.

The pebble is in my pocket, a small weight against my hip. I slip my hand inside to find it, fitting the shape into my palm, holding it close.

Scenery is rushing past, history falling away; lost things and mistakes caught in the wind behind me. I am impatient to get there, to see his face. And I say his name out loud into the empty carriage. *John.*

I am coming home.

AUTHOR'S NOTE

The setting for *The Twins* is inspired by the place where I grew up. Anyone who is familiar with this area of Suffolk – Tangham Forest, the oak woods at Butley, and the wild stretch of shingle beaches along this coastline – will recognise the Martello towers, the Suffolk Punches in the fields and the colours and textures of the countryside. However, I have used artistic licence to re-imagine this territory to suit the fiction of *The Twins*; so distances have altered, new cottages have sprung up and lanes have been invented. But when describing and naming the flowers and plants of the area I have tried my best to be accurate; I hope if I've made any errors, they will be forgiven.

ACKNOWLEDGEMENTS

First, I would like to thank my editor, the brilliant Emma Beswetherick, for believing in this book; her dedication and skill made it possible. Many thanks also to Lucy Icke and the wonderful team at Piatkus and Little, Brown. I am indebted to Eve White, my agent, for her enthusiasm and tenacity, and thanks to Jack Ram and Abi Fenton. My gratitude goes to friends and relatives who have read and responded to the manuscript at different stages: to Alex Marengo who has given me love and support throughout; Sara Sarre for her generous spirit and editing insight; my sister, Ana Sarginson, for her belief in me and for reading everything I've ever written; Karen Jones, for her positivity and for all our discussions about the drafts she read. Thanks to the talented writing group from the MA at Royal Holloway who were involved in workshopping early sections: Mary Chamberlain, Viv Graveson, Laura McClelland, Lauren Trimble, Cecilia Ekback and Diriye Osman. I'm grateful to Andrew Motion, Susanna Jones and Jo Shapcott at Royal Holloway for their encouragement, and to Dr Rathmell at Cambridge University. Thanks also to my brother, Alex Sarginson, for his support and for being the only person who can take a picture of me! And last but not least, many thanks and much love to my wonderful children: Hannah and Olivia (who, over twenty-one years, provided the ultimate research into the complications of being identical twins!) and their brothers, Sam and Gabriel. All of them put up with a mother who is often stuck in another world at her computer.

the · twins

Reading Guide

READING GROUP
DISCUSSION POINTS

>4

READING GROUP DISCUSSION POINTS

* Do you think that being a twin is a comfort or a constraint for Viola and Isolte – as children and then, later, as adults?

* Viola's self-punishment as an adult is obvious – but in what ways does the adult Isolte also inflict punishment on herself?

* In what way do you think Viola's obsession with flight links into her eating problem?

* Why doesn't Isolte tell her sister the truth about John and pass on his message about the stone?

* Who changes the most throughout the story and why?

* What is the central theme of the book and how did it resonate with you?

* What could the Martello tower stand for, symbolically and metaphorically, in the novel?

* Fairy tales are referenced several times in the novel – do you think that this book could be read like a modern fairy tale?

* Compare and contrast the settings of rural Suffolk and

London and how these environments impact on both Viola and Isolte.

* Why do you think the author doesn't reveal what happened to Polly – and how does this unanswered question affect the book?

AUTHOR Q&A

What inspired you to write *The Twins*?

Having identical twin girls gave me the opportunity to study the fascinating relationship they have with each other: the struggle for power and identity, the competition between them, but also the unspoken loyalty and the extraordinary bond they share. I knew that I wanted to write a story with identical twins at its centre. But I also wanted to test the limits of the relationship inside the story.

I chose to set it in Suffolk because I grew up there and find the area inspiring to write about; with its dense pine forests and bleakly beautiful shingle beaches, it's rich in atmosphere, myth and history.

Why did you choose 1972 and 1987 as your main dates?

I wanted to set it in a time before technology took over, with no mobiles or CCTV – it meant that Polly's disappearance could have happened more easily and left no traces. In 1972 there was little TV and no computer games and at that time Suffolk was off the beaten track and unspoilt – the perfect place for Rose to run to, and for the girls to run wild. Thatcher's Britain in 1987 was an interesting period and one that I remember well – it was a good contrast to Rose's hippy ideals. Those dates also have key events in them that I wanted to weave into the novel. I love retro novels – particularly ones in a time that is full of personal nostalgia for me and, I hope, many readers.

What do you think happens to Isolte/Ben and Viola/John in the end?

Although I left the ending a little open, I always intended that there would be a feeling of hope. There is no such thing as 'happy ever after', but I wish good things for all of them when they walk off that last page.

Why do you never reveal what happens to Polly?

I think that revealing what happened to Polly would have nudged the book into the genre of crime fiction. Also, leaving something unsaid is often more powerful than stating it, and I wanted her unexplained loss to stand for the loss we all experience as humans.

What comes first for you – plot or characters, and how do they evolve?

Characters always come first; and with them a feel for what I want to say in the book, the central themes and ideas. As the characters develop they seem as real as my own family and I begin to fall in love with them. The plot stays flexible; you can't be rigid about what is going to happen or how it happens. That is one of the most exciting things about writing – never knowing exactly what is going to happen next!

Have you always written?

Since childhood I've written short stories and poems. My working life has been spent as a journalist, copywriter, ghostwriter and script-reader. But it was only in my forties that I had the confidence to sit down and attempt to write a novel. I was used to writing short stories, but I soon discovered that the longer length was a format that I loved.

Did doing an English degree as a mature student influence your decision to write a novel?
Definitely. Doing an English Literature degree at Cambridge with three small children to care for was challenging, but it was also liberating, exciting and inspiring. I received a lot of encouragement in my creative writing from some of the tutors. It really did change my life. Afterwards, I began to take writing fiction seriously.

What advice would you give to others who also want to start writing fiction?
It's never too late to begin. But you have to want it with a passion that borders on obsession, because it requires hard work, total commitment and the ability to pick yourself up each time you have been felled by rejection, criticism or disappointment and somehow maintain faith in yourself.

What does it feel like to have your debut novel in print?
Extraordinary. When I finally allowed myself to believe that it was really happening, my overriding feeling was one of immense relief and a sense of being very lucky. My anticipation about how it'll be received out there in the world is tinged with nerves – it's odd to have something so intimate and close to you put into the public domain.

What are you working on next?

I'm working on another retro novel (60s through to early 80s) also set in Suffolk – but this time the story plays out against the backdrop of marshes, mudflats, the river and a forbidden island. It's about Eva, a teenager who is thought to have drowned, and what actually happened to her. Meanwhile, despite being the only one who thinks she's alive, her younger sister is determined to bring Eva back. It is also the story of Eva's parents and the lie they told about Eva's history that triggered the tragedy in the first place.

Read on for the prologue
to Saskia Sarginson's
incredible new novel,
Without You

PROLOGUE

It was April when I drowned, a month after my seventeenth birthday. We were out at sea when the sky darkened to black and a storm blew up out of nowhere. We worked fast to get the sails down and start the engine. At the tiller, Dad tried to hold the boat steady. The engine strained against huge waves, as we wallowed and rolled. There was a creak of fibreglass, and water washing over the deck. We'd never been out in anything as big. I should have been afraid. Except I didn't believe that I was going to die. It wasn't just that I had faith in Dad's sailing; I was angry with him, and my rage made me feel superhuman.

When the wave hit sideways I saw it from the corner of my eye: a wall of water towering over us. As it crashed down, the boom must have swung around and caught the back of my head, because I felt a blow against my skull, and I was falling, slipping across the tilting deck and over the side. I saw Dad reaching out, his hand opening in slow motion. Water closed over my head and there was nothing except darkness and cold.

It's odd, because I have no memory of waking, just of existing at a distance, hovering far above the ground. Moonlight spun around me. The universe was rich in stars, a great sweep of planets, and I floated with them. Below me I could see the white spume of breakers rolling onto a shore, a helicopter circling out at sea, and the lights of the village shining through the dark. I noticed a form lying on the pebbly beach: something thrown up by the waves. I couldn't make out what it was: a coiled wet rug perhaps, or a large fish. Looking again, I made out the curve of a hip, an arm thrown back, hair spread like seaweed. A girl curled on her side, motionless.

An upright figure toiled into view: a solid shadow moving towards the dead girl, his feet rolling and crunching over the uneven camber. He jerked to a stop when he saw her, then lurched into a run, dropping to crouch beside her. I watched all this without any real interest. I felt detached and calm with a lovely floaty sensation in my stomach, like the flicker of butterfly wings.

The man moved the girl's head and her neck fell back limply so that I saw her face and I was staring into my own features, darkened and smudged by the night, but definitely belonging to me. A distant voice in my head wondered at how strange it was to be up here and yet at the same time able to observe the details of my gaping mouth, teeth showing between slack lips, and my wet pointed eyelashes. I had a bruise on my cheek. I thought I looked peaceful. Empty.

I watched as the man hunkered over my body. He threw his head back and shouted something into the sky. He looked ridiculous, desperate. Then he put his hand on my chin, tilting it up and his fingers slipped into my mouth, stretching it wider. I wanted to leave the two humans there: the dead one and the live one. But it was as if I'd become heavier. I'd dropped down through layers of night sky, closer to the man. I noticed the curly depths of his greasy hair, an unravelling elbow in the wool of his jumper. Underneath the man's bent shoulders, I saw the girl's chest shudder, the rise and fall of her ribcage. My ribcage. He pulled me back with his breath. It hurt. With a shock I became aware of the clumsy alignment of bone and cartilage under my skin, the density of flesh. I was disappearing out of lightness, sucked back into myself, squashed into the crushing weight of my body.

I woke with him above me, his mouth covering my own. Rough, hot lips. My lungs burning inside my chest. His heat inside me. I struggled to gasp fresh air, raising myself onto my elbow; then I was retching and gagging. He sat back to let me be sick on the pebbles, salt in my throat, as an ocean flooded out of me. I was so cold. His hands were on my shoulders, fingers clenched tight against my wet jumper. He leant close, and I smelt musty clothes, unwashed skin. He whispered in my ear, 'Thank God I found you.' I struggled to understand. I was shivering so much I could hardly hear for the chattering of my teeth, but I thought he said, 'She sent you. You're mine.'